D1349946

DEATH AND BRIGHT WATER

Callan wants out – out of the Section, out of the whole dirty business – but his reputation as a ruthless, ice-cold professional killer precedes him. He seems the ideal man to rescue the daughter of a radical Greek politician from her kidnappers, or so say both his former employers in the Section and his long-time enemies in the KGB. With his only trustworthy ally, the timid and often pungent Lonely, Callan sets off for Crete knowing that failure or refusing to do the job could result in his own name on one of the Section's deadly Red Files.

DEATH AND BRIGHT WATER

DEATH AND BRIGHT WATER

by

James Mitchell

Magna Large Print Books
Long Preston, North Yorkshire,
BD23 4ND, England.

British Library Cataloguing in Publication Data.

Mitchell, James
    Death and bright water.

    A catalogue record of this book is
    available from the British Library

    ISBN   978-0-7505-4135-0

First published in Great Britain in 1974
Ostara Publishing Edition 2014

Copyright © James Mitchell 1974

Cover illustration by arrangement with Ostara Publishing

The moral right of the author has been asserted

Published in Large Print 2015 by arrangement with
Ostara Publishing

Magna Large Print is an imprint of Library Magna Books Ltd.

Printed and bound in Great Britain by
T.J. (International) Ltd., Cornwall, PL28 8RW

For Derek Horne

EDITOR'S NOTE: At the time of the writing of *Death and Bright Water*, Greece was governed by military dictatorship following the coup by a junta of anti-communist Army Colonels in 1967. Until democracy was restored when the junta collapsed, the period 1967–1974 was known as 'Greece under the Colonels'.

1

She was far too early. That was a sign of nervousness, and she admitted it to herself, admitted too, that she did not want to sit and wait until the time for her appointment. Instead she went into the big department store on the other side of the street. Detsky Mir, she read. One of the annoyances of coming to Moscow was that she could just about read the alphabet, but had no idea what the words meant. She wandered about from section to section, and stopped at last before a huge display of dolls, the cunningly made peasant dolls that fitted one inside the other, and picked up the most intricate of the lot. It was foolish, and she knew it to be foolish. Her daughter was a grown woman. Yet she bought it even so. Perhaps there was something symbolic in the purchase. She looked at her watch; it was time to keep her appointment, more than time. She left the store and crossed the street, not hurrying, but not dawdling either, heading towards a huge stone building that dominated the block: Number Two, Dzerzhinsky Street, the headquarters of the K.G.B....

'She's late,' Karsky said.

'She'll be here,' said Benin. 'To arrive a little late will remind us of her independence – and also of the fact that she is a woman.'

'Do you wish me to be with you when you see

her, comrade?' Karsky asked.

'Of course,' said Benin. 'You have such a frank, open face, such ingenuous blue eyes. Who could believe that you would lie to a helpless widow?'

'And will I?'

'Almost certainly. She wants our help in choosing a man for an operation – rather a tricky one.'

'One of our wet job squad?'

'No,' said Benin. 'I can't risk one of ours. The job is too risky. I said I would find her a mercenary... Here. See for yourself.'

He handed Karsky the file, and he leafed through it.

'But she's not even a member of the Party,' Karsky said.

'Don't be such a snob, Karsky,' said Benin. 'Her party has worked with us in the past.'

Karsky read further: good anti-Fascist record with the partisans in Crete during the war, more of the same later, then it tailed off to nothing but leaflets and speeches and eventual exile. Lived mostly in Paris: subsidised by a millionaire cousin.

'With respect, comrade, I shouldn't think she's worth it,' said Karsky.

'She's not.'

'Then why help her?'

'She wants her daughter back,' said Benin. 'Her daughter is held as a hostage for her good conduct in Crete. To lift her would involve a very tricky operation that will almost certainly fail. After its failure she will be discredited – and superseded.'

'Is she doing this without the authority of her party?' Karsky asked. He sounded shocked.

Benin chuckled. 'No, no. The party has authorised her visit.'

'But if they wish to replace her–'

'Not all of them, do,' Benin said. 'But they will
– once this has failed.'

'And who will replace her?' Karsky riffled the
file. 'This sleeper they mention?'

'He is the even money favourite,' Benin said.
'My money is on a 33 to 1 shot.'

Karsky looked in the file again.

'He is too much of an outsider even to be
listed,' said Benin. 'He's a dentist. He is also a
drunkard and a homosexual.'

This time Karsky managed to look both shocked
and baffled. Like everybody else in the building he
had been superlatively trained, but it was impossible to teach a man to acquire a sense of humour,
Benin thought. Even in Dzerzhinsky Street.

The buzzer sounded. Benin flicked it on.

'The lady is here, Comrade Benin,' the receptionist said.

'Show her in,' Benin said, then turned to
Karsky. 'A little refreshment,' he said, 'then we'll
take her to the computer.'

'But you've got the answer already,' Karsky
said, 'and I must say it is a very good answer,
comrade.'

'Thank you, comrade,' said Benin. 'I also like to
settle old scores.'

'Then why take her to the computer?'

Really, thought Benin, I am plagued by this
young man's literal mind.

'Because,' he said, 'it is an opportunity to display yet another triumph of Soviet technology,

13

and besides – the Greeks have always been addicted to oracles.'

She was shown in then, and offered vodka, which she refused, and tea, which she accepted. Benin made a short and graceful speech in almost unaccented English, in which he complimented her party on its struggle against oppression and she listened restlessly, thanked him and asked at once if they thought the operation would succeed. Karsky gazed at her with his frank, blue eyes, and assured her that it would, then they took her to the computer, past set after set of guards, every one of whom checked their passes.

The computer was housed in one vast room, dust-free; air conditioned. All that was visible was a series of steel cabinets. The woman found it disappointing. A white-coated man programmed it, and it delivered the answer so swiftly that she felt cheated, but she had come a very long way. Patiently she waited until the answer was transcribed, and the white-coated man handed her a slip of paper. On it were two words: David Callan.

2

Callan looked down from the overpass. Below him the road gleamed in the sun, the cars, tiny as toys, whispered by. But beyond the road was beauty: moorland now gold, now green, flecked with white dots that were grazing sheep, and beyond that, when you were lucky enough to get clear days like

14

this one, you could see the sea: green, then blue, then purple; calm, immense, and somehow, infinitely soothing to contemplate...

The ganger yelled at him, and he bent once more to shovel cement, but not in too much of a hurry. Even after weeks of roadwork, his back still ached at the end of a long day, his throat was dry with the stuff, flakes of it fell on him, clinging like grey snow, and hard work only made it worse. Not that hard work hadn't helped him, he thought. It had purged his body of too much whisky, purged his mind of too many nightmares, and earned him a bit of money too; the only trouble was it was boring: monotonous, repetitive, predictable. He could feel his hands sweating inside the work gloves, so much that the insides of the gloves were wet, but for all that, he thought, his hands were clean. It was a good thought, and he went on shovelling till the ganger yelled that the shift was ended.

The road gang dropped their shovels and straightened their backs: it was like seeing slaves liberated. One by one they moved off, then coalesced into groups: the micks, the West Indians, the Geordies, the student from Cambridge who preached Maoist Communism even in the pub, and as they walked their pace quickened. They were walking towards freedom after all, thought Callan. And so am I. I'm hurrying too. He slogged on past the dumper-trucks and cement mixers – a panzer division trying to make itself useful for a change – and pulled off the work gloves as he walked, looked down at his hands: hard enough when it came to Saturday night punch-ups, but supple still, and fast, their skill

15

unimpeded by callouses. Maybe he should have let them go – he had the same thought at the end of every working day, and every working day he came up with an answer: he still had some pride left, the birds liked his hands the way they were, supposing he decided to take an office job? And every time he knew he lied. He wanted his hands to stay the way they were because of the things those hands had done, could do again... He moved on to the temporary path that led down to the roadway, and the cluster of mobile huts that were his home from home: a bunk, and a chemical toilet and a one tenth share in a shower – and a chance of a lift to a caff and a pub: egg and chips and beans, and perhaps a pint, or more likely half a gallon. Not exactly a high protein diet, but in this job you sweated it off even faster than you put it on – and it was restful. After what he'd been used to even the Saturday night punch-ups were restful...

He reached the road at last, and was about to hurry on to the group ahead of him when he saw the man on the motorbike: except that the motor-bike was the thing he saw first; all five hundred c.c.s. of it, the chassis and seats as red as squashed tomatoes, the wheel-spokes glittering silver and the rider apparently no more than an extension of the bike itself: leather gear studded with steel rivets, white scarf round the mouth, crash-helmet of the same tomato-red. As Callan drew closer the rider pushed back his goggles with one black-gauntleted hand. Usually they hunt in packs, thought Callan, rev up and ride and wait for you to show you're scared. But that would be in Acton,

16

or Notting Hill, or maybe Brighton if they fancied a day by the sea. What's this one doing so far from home – and all by himself? He hurried on to the group ahead of him: four Geordies homesick for Geordie beer. Callan walked with them and joined the lament: it was good beer.

The cement dust trickled in runnels down his body, even with the shower on full, but he was clean at last, freshened with the hard jet of the water, first hot, then cold, the muscles soothed by the towel's friction. Three months ago, he thought, a day's work like this would have killed him. Now all he felt was thirsty. He combed his hair, put on a clean shirt, his one good suit that wasn't all that good any more, the old, expensive shoes. Outside the Geordies were waiting in the beaten up old Jaguar they had bought collectively for fifty pounds. It moved off before Callan had shut the door. On the way to the caff they were still lamenting: this time it was the absence of Association Football in the month of July. As they roared down the road Callan took one casual look over his shoulder. Sure enough the motor-bike was there, but it stayed well clear of the Jaguar's exhaust.

The caff was crowded, and they had to queue. Callan noted, without surprise, that the bloke in the leather gear queued right behind them. It was eggs, sausages, peas and chips that night; stewed apple and custard to follow. The Geordies scoffed it as if eating was on piecework, but the food was terrible anyway; what they wanted was beer. Callan took his time, and promised to join them later, then went back to the counter for coffee.

The bike-rider was sharing a table for two with Spencer Percival Fitzmaurice, a gigantic and very black Barbadian who had joined the road gang the week before. Callan walked up to their table, and the Barbadian glared at him.

'White trash,' said Spencer Percival Fitzmaurice.

'Nigger bastard,' said Callan. Carefully he put down his coffee cup, and the negro moved into a fighting crouch.

'I'm going to kill you, white boy,' he said.

'You couldn't kill time,' said Callan. The negro sidled forward, reconsidering the matter.

'Yes sir. That's what I'm going to do. First I'm going to hurt you, then I'm going to kill you – for the glory of the coloured people.'

From the table there came an old, familiar smell. The thing had gone on long enough.

'Get lost you black layabout before I put you over my knee and spank you,' said Callan.

Spencer Percival Fitzmaurice dissolved into laughter, then looked around the room. Apart from the bike-rider, who was trapped behind him, there was nobody within twenty feet of them.

'Man, we get better every time we do it,' he said, and slapped Callan on the back. 'See you in the pub, Dave.'

'If you haven't drunk all the beer before I get there,' said Callan. The negro left, still chuckling, and Callan sat down at the table.

'What the hell are you doing in that get-up?' he said. 'And for God's sake control yourself. You're stinking the place out.'

'I thought you and the spade was going to have a punch-up,' said Lonely.

18

Callan said, 'He likes doing it. It's a joke, that's all.'

'A joke?' Lonely was rigid with indignation. 'It didn't seem funny to me.'

'It would have done if you could have seen your face,' said Callan.

He looked again at the little man in the leather gear five sizes too big for him. Lonely. His mate. His mucker. The geezer he'd done bird with: the only friend who'd stuck by him at the time he'd desperately needed friends: a coward with a hygiene problem that defied the resources of science, a liar, a loser, a cunning if unsuccessful thief: his only friend.

'What the hell are you doing in that get-up?' he asked again. 'Don't tell me you've joined the Hell's Angels.'

'Of course not.' Lonely had found another source of indignation. 'You know I don't approve of violence, Mr Callan.'

A flaming red motor-bike, thought Callan: a flaming red crash helmet, and the leather so studded with rivets he could have used it for chain mail – and he doesn't approve of violence. Patiently he tried again.

'Then why the gear?' he said.

'It's my Cousin Alfred's,' said Lonely.

No one in the world had more relations than Lonely, and every single one of them was bent.

'He's a Hell's Angel is he?' said Callan.

'Used to be,' said Lonely. 'He had to resign. The other Angels made him.'

Callan looked at the little man with something approaching awe: to be related, however dis-

tantly, to someone who had committed a nastiness too appalling for even his fellow Angels, this
was distinction indeed.

'He must have done something pretty awful,' he
said.

Lonely considered. 'I wouldn't say that, Mr
Callan,' he said at last. 'It was more like a sort of
– well a bit of bad luck as you might say. Could
happen to us all. As a matter of fact, come to
think of it – it does happen to us all.'

'Would it be too much to ask what the hell you
think you're talking about?'

'He got too old,' said Lonely. 'Mind you he
always did look young for his age, but even so–'

Let it go, thought Callan. I mean what's the
point for God's sake? But Lonely's relatives had
always had a sort of horrific fascination for him.
He couldn't let it go.

'How old was he?' Callan asked.

'When he had to resign?' Lonely counted on his
fingers. 'Thirty-seven,' he said at last. 'The other
Angels said it made them look silly. People just
stood around and laughed.'

'So he gave you his gear and joined the Boy
Scouts instead?'

'No he never,' said Lonely, his indignation
switching once more. 'I've read about them Scoutmasters in the papers. Cousin Alfred isn't like that.
He's got a wife and four kids.'

'So why are you wearing it?' said Callan.

'I came to see you,' said Lonely.

'Do you know,' Callan said, 'I rather thought
you had? You travel two hundred miles out of
London and wait for me coming off shift and let

20

me see it's you and then follow me to this caff – and I thought to myself, hello, I thought, Lonely hasn't just run into me by accident, I thought, he's come to see me. But there's another question, isn't there?'

'Is there?' said Lonely.

'Yes there is,' said Callan. 'We know *how* you've come to see me – on your Cousin Alfred's bike. Right?'

'Right,' said Lonely.

'But what we don't know – I'm not going too fast for you am I?'

'Not so far,' said Lonely.

Not for the first time Callan wondered if perhaps the little man was capable of an irony far more subtle than his own.

'What we don't know,' said Callan, 'is *why* you've come to see me. Now are you going to tell me? Because if you're not you seem to have wasted your journey.'

'Course I'm going to tell you, if you'll let me get a word in edgeways,' said Lonely. 'This geezer asked me to.'

'Which geezer?' said Callan.

'Feller called Blythe,' said Lonely. 'Dr Randolph Blythe. Didn't look to me like no doctor. More like a poof if you ask me.'

'I am asking you, you great nit,' said Callan.

'Now he'd be more like them Scoutmasters you read about,' said Lonely. 'Very la-di-da he was.'

'Where did you see him?' said Callan.

'Your place,' said Lonely.

'You took him there?'

The words were soft, but Lonely knew that

voice: the smell came again.

'Course I didn't, Mr Callan,' he said. 'You know I wouldn't dream– I go in once a week. I mean you did give me a key–'

'I know I did,' said Callan. 'But why bother? You know I'm not there.'

'Well I like to keep an eye on things – and I give the place a bit of a clean-up.'

Silently Callan cursed himself. This was a mate all right, smell or no smell.

'And I thought there might be letters for you,' Lonely said.

'Were there?'

'No,' said Lonely. 'You and me we never seem to get no letters, Mr Callan. Not even bills... Well I went over yesterday and I was dusting and that when the door-bell rang and I thought it must be the gas man or the electric or something, so I answered the door and it was this Dr Blythe geezer. And guess what?'

'What?' said Callan.

'He looks at me, and he says, Mr Callan I'd like a word with you. To me, Mr Callan. I'd like a word with you he says.'

'So you said you were the butler and told him to get lost?'

'I told him I was an old acquaintance of yours,' said Lonely, very dignified, 'and I said you'd been called to the country on business and would not be back for some time.'

'He probably thought you meant I was doing a stretch,' said Callan.

'Him?' said Lonely. 'He wouldn't even know the language. Never go inside in his life – unless

22

it might be for the Scoutmastering lark... He says he has to see you urgent and can he have your address and I say no – I did do right, Mr Callan?'

'You did,' said Callan.

'So he says can I get a message to you and I say give me a good reason. And he did, Mr Callan.'

'What was it?' Callan asked.

'Twenty quid and expenses,' said Lonely.

'Where to?' said Callan.

'Not here,' Lonely said. 'I told him I'd have to take a train to St. Ives – and a taxi from there. Seventeen quid return I told him. He paid out straight off.'

Lonely contemplated the phenomenon of such largesse.

'Berk,' he said.

'You sure he believed you?' Callan asked.

'Positive,' said Lonely.

'He didn't have you followed?'

Lonely looked pained.

'Mr Callan,' he said, 'if I didn't want to be followed, could you follow me?' Callan shook his head. 'Well then, what makes you think a poofy doctor could do it?'

'He might have friends,' said Callan.

Lonely was indulgent.

'So he might,' he said. 'They might even know what they're doing. That's why I went to see Cousin Alfred. He works in a garage, see? Keeps his bike in a shed round the back. So all I do is walk in the front, put the gear on – and off I toddle.' He looked down in disgust at his leather-clad chest. 'I won't half be glad to get out of it an' all,' he said.

'Did this Blythe geezer say what he wanted to see me about?' Callan asked.

Lonely concentrated. His face had the innocent intensity of a child's about to recite a poem.

'Tell him it'll be like old times,' said Lonely, 'except for the money. The money will be far in excess of his usual emolument.' The intense look faded. 'That's all,' he said.

Callan had no doubt that Lonely had quoted the doctor word for word.

'He didn't mention a contract?' he asked. Lonely shook his head. 'Or a gun?'

This time Lonely's face showed nothing but fear.

'For God's sake don't start stinking the place out,' said Callan. 'I only asked.'

'Just old times,' said Lonely. 'Honest. Cross my heart and hope to die. You – you wouldn't kill anybody, would you, Mr Callan? Not any more?'

Callan remembered Lonely's Aunty Gertie, caught in a plastic bomb outrage because Callan needed her help; remembered too how Lonely had been conned into a nightmare chase through an office-block, live-bait leading the prey to Callan the hunter, crouching in safety with a .22 rifle.

'The only one I'm likely to kill is me,' he said. 'And that'll be just through hard work. They tell you it never killed anybody. Don't you believe it, old son.'

The little man relaxed then, and swigged cold tea.

'Let's go and get a drink,' said Callan.

The pub he chose was one the road gang didn't use, but even so he kept Lonely in the shadows, and bought the drinks himself, twenty quid or no twenty quid. Lonely couldn't be more note-worthy if he'd wandered in stark naked.

'Did this Blythe tell you how to get in touch with him?'

'Phone number,' said Lonely. '937-7162.'

That put him in Kensington.

'Did you write it down?' said Callan.

'Think I'm barmy?' Lonely sucked at his pint. 'This beer's terrible,' he said, and added the time-honoured phrase: 'I'll be glad when I've had enough.'

'You just have,' said Callan. 'You're going back to London.'

'Tonight?' said Lonely. 'I was going to kip here. The poofy feller's paid for it.'

'Kip on the road back somewhere,' said Callan. 'I don't want you here where people might re-member you and me. You're not exactly invisible, old son. Get yourself a room en suite. You can afford it.'

'Maybe the beer'll be better an' all,' said Lonely. 'It couldn't be worse. You want me to call this Blythe geezer? He said I could reach him any time.'

'No. I'll do that,' said Callan. 'When I'm ready.'

Lonely finished his beer.

'I better be off then,' he said.

'So long old son,' said Callan. 'Drive carefully.'

'You know me, Mr Callan,' said Lonely.

'My God I ought to,' Callan said.

Lonely adjusted his impossible helmet, and turned to the door, then checked. 'Mr Callan – what does en suite mean?' he asked.

25

'It means you get a bath all to yourself,' said Callan.

'I'd sooner share it with a bird,' Lonely said. This time he left.

3

Callan sat over his half of bitter. Dr Randolph Blythe meant nothing to him, not a bloody thing. The only queer doctor he'd ever known was a geezer called the Groper, a bloke he'd done bird with in Wormwood Scrubs. And the Groper didn't want to know about Callan, and Callan didn't blame him, not after what had happened to his boyfriend. Just like old times, this Blythe geezer had said. Well, he could remember the old times all right. The hard, smooth feel of a .357 magnum revolver with a target sight, the whipcrack of the bullet that missed you, the look of surprise on your enemy's face when your own bullet hit. Old times. Violent times. Dangerous times. The need for excitement, even for fear, eating into his resolution every time: the hardest of hard drugs... Until he'd watched a girl try to kill him, then kill herself – and he thought he'd kicked the habit at last, switched to whisky until the stuff disgusted him, and turned to work instead, falling into bed exhausted at the end of each exhausting day. But now his body had recovered: he was as hard and fit as he had ever been, the work beginning to bore him, his mind crying out for use – and again, it seemed, he needed this one special drug, and this Blythe geezer was going to be the pusher. Unless he just let it go – but he knew that was impossible. Blythe knew him, his address, his reputation, and even if Callan did nothing else, he had to find out how he knew.

He left his beer unfinished, and walked to the road gang pub; jukebox blaring, one-armed bandits clanking like goods-trains, and every geezer in the place shouting his head off. They make even more noise drinking than they do working he thought, and one of the Geordies put a pint in his hand.

'Get it down quick, kidder,' he said. 'You've got a long way to catch up.' But Callan was determined to make this one last. If old times were coming back, he'd need his brain and reflexes unimpaired, and when the job was over he'd drink whisky... Spencer Percival Fitzmaurice loomed over him, black and menacing.

'Hey, whitey,' he said. 'What you done with your bodyguard?'

'Bodyguard?' said Callan.

'The cowboy,' the negro said. 'It won't do you no good, man. If I coming to get you, it no good hiding behind no Hell's Angels.'

'That poor geezer?' said Callan. 'You frightened the life out of him. I had to stay behind and apologise... But he scarpered anyway...'

'You whiteys going to do a lot of apologising when the black people take over,' Spencer Percival Fitzmaurice said. 'But it won't help you none.'

'If they're all as thick as you they'll never take over,' said Callan.

'White trash,' said Spencer Percival.
'Black trash,' said Callan.
'Capitalist reactionary.'
'Dirty commy.'
'Fascist running dog.'
So he's been talking to the Cambridge student again, thought Callan, and sought for the coup-de-grace.
'Male chauvinist pig,' he said.

Spencer Percival roared with laughter. 'For once you tell the truth, man,' he said. 'Black Power's one thing but Woman Power I just ain't joining. Let me buy you a rum.'

To refuse would start another argument; would be, besides, a memorable eccentricity. Callan took it, and got rid of most of it in a Geordie's beer. The Geordie didn't even notice – but he let Callan drive the Jaguar back, and Callan enjoyed the thrust of power still surviving even in that clapped-out wreck. More old times, he thought, and coaxed it up to eighty and held it there. The Geordies didn't even notice. They were trying to remember when last Newcastle had won the F.A. cup.

He woke before the others, hurried his breakfast and was the first of them on the site, then went to the site-foreman's hut. A big feller, a bastard, eyes in the back of his head, and hating Callan because he was trying to get through his paperwork, and sums made his head ache.

'Well?' he said.
'I want my cards,' said Callan.
'When?' said the foreman.
'Tonight,' said Callan.

'All right. Sod off.'

Hardly a valediction, Callan thought, but at least there hadn't been any witnesses. He'd wait behind that night till the others had gone, change into his suit and old, expensive shoes and leave the rest of his gear for whoever it happened to fit, then hitch a lift to the station and take the first London train. He would miss the Geordies for a day or two, and Spencer Percival Fitzmaurice, and maybe they would miss him... A line of men moved slowly, reluctantly on to the site, and Callan bent to pick up a shovel. At least he wouldn't have to handle one of those things again.

Lonely hadn't spared the elbow grease: the place was glittering clean. He went from hall to kitchen to living-room to bathroom, and everywhere it was the same: windows washed, carpets swept, woodwork polished. He went to the chest that held his model soldiers, and only there did he find dust. Lonely knew very well that Callan didn't like anybody else but himself to handle them. That Stein woman didn't know the half of it, he thought. A mate is a mate is a mate... But even mates aren't infallible. He *had* got a letter: just one.

'You will have learned by now how anxious I am to see you,' he read, 'to talk about old times. With this end in view I shall call upon you each evening between seven and eight, in the fond hope that what Hamlet somewhat ambiguously designates as country matters will not detain you much longer.' No signature, and probably no fingerprints either, thought Callan, except his

29

own. And even if there were and he went out and bought an insufflator and started messing around with powder, where would it get him? There were no archives for him to go to: not any more... He looked at his watch. It was two in the morning – a bad time to make a telephone call he wasn't sure he wanted to make anyway. Better to have a kip and relax, and look forward to a day without a shovel in sight.

He woke late, and dialled 937-7162. A voice said, 'Parnassos Restaurant', and Callan hung up, looked in the yellow pages, then went out to buy eggs, milk, bacon and bread, came home and cooked the best meal he'd had in weeks. For dessert he set up the big table and laid out the Battle of Chancellorsville, another of those cross-roads in the middle of nowhere that the American Civil War alone made memorable. The Federal general, Joe Hooker, was on his way to Richmond to end the war, but Lee and Stonewall Jackson hadn't read his script... Carefully Callan laid out their dispositions, the dark blue of the North, the grey and butternut of the South, in the landscape he had so skillfully and painstakingly made: the dense woods of the wilderness, the Wilderness Church, Dowdall's Tavern and the Catherine Furnace... More than a hundred years ago the two armies had fought there, and a lot of them had died. But the blood had long since dried, the pain receded, and all that was left were heroism, glory, legend. Callan laid out the battle and fought it blow for blow, taking now Hooker's part, now Lee's, and saw that it had its own terrible logic that there was no escaping. Given that Hooker and Lee were the men they were, the North had no hope of winning the battle: given that their armies were composed of the men they were, the South had no hope of winning the war: not even if Jackson had survived. Maybe if Lee hadn't decided to divide his forces... He laid out the troops again...

The doorbell rang, and Callan left the Virginia woodlands of 1863 and looked warily at the present. Nothing else for it: he'd finished with country matters. It was time to open the door.

He was so plump and smooth he might have been polished on a buffer: glowing skin, gleaming teeth, hair that shone like copper. Even his clothes, Callan thought, Mao boiler suit to show he was one of the righteous, but hand-sewn, and made of silk.

'Mr Callan?' he asked. Smooth voice too: it flowed like treacle.

'Who wants him?' Callan said.

'I do,' said the smooth man. 'Dr Blythe. Let me in, man. We can't talk here.' He pushed at the door, and Callan made no move to stop him: the chain did that.

'Urgent, is it?' said Callan.

'Old times,' Blythe said. 'I told you. Twice.'

'Put your hands behind your head,' said Callan.

'This is ridiculous–'

'Or get lost.'

Resignedly, a man humouring a child, Blythe did as he was told. Callan silently lifted the door-chain from the hook, and suddenly he moved very fast indeed. It seemed to Blythe as if Callan reached out for him, lifted him into the flat, shut the door and searched him for a gun, all in one

31

flowing, continuous movement.

'Well,' Callan said at last, 'you're clean, anyway. Sit down.'

Blythe remained standing, straightening out the rumpled Mao suit. He was containedly angry, like a cat with wet fur.

'There was absolutely no need for that,' he said.

'When you start believing that, you're dead,' Callan said. 'What do you want with Callan?'

'Please drop this pretence,' said Blythe. 'I know you're Callan.' He walked to the table and looked at the battle. 'Ah, the toy soldiers. Who's winning?'

'Models,' said Callan. 'Lee's winning, Hooker's losing and Jackson's going to die. What makes you so sure I'm Callan?'

'Your face,' said Blythe. 'And your manners.'

'You've seen my picture?'

'I have indeed.'

'Who showed it to you?'

'All in good time,' Blythe said.

Callan stood up then, and faced him. His eyes were without expression.

'It could be you don't have any time at all,' he said.

'You're being ridiculous,' said Blythe.

Callan said, 'You don't believe that. Look, Mister Blythe—'

'Doctor, please.' He'd got guts anyway.

'All right, *doctor*. I don't like people who know who I am and where to find me and come here to talk about old times. Now you ask me why?'

'Very well. Why?'

'Because nobody else knows. Nobody. Not a soul. I set it up that way... So tell how you know.'

'Your flat isn't very big, is it?' said Blythe. 'Do you have a bathroom?'

'Yeah,' said Callan. 'I've got a bathroom.'

'I should like to see it please.'

Callan thought: Well at least somebody's taught you something.

He led the way, and Blythe drew the shower curtain.

'It's not a bad bathroom,' he said but the surprise in his voice made even that an insult. Callan waited as Blythe turned on the bath taps, the wash-basin taps, and last of all the shower.

'You're wrong, you know,' Blythe said. 'You arrogant types so often are.'

'Coming from you that's bitter,' said Callan. 'How am I wrong?'

'Somebody obviously knows where you are, as you pointed out. I do. So what possible logic can there be in your statement that nobody knows?'

'All right,' said Callan. 'Who told you?'

'A man from Moscow,' said Blythe.

'You can do better than that.'

'I think not.'

Callan took two handfuls of the Mao jacket, close to Blythe's neck, and twisted his fists inwards.

'You may be strong on logic, but I'm the one with the muscle,' he said, and continued to twist. Blythe's face turned an unpleasant scarlet, and Callan eased the pressure.

'Try to do better than that,' said Callan, 'just to please me.'

'He gave an address in Dzerzhinsky Street,' said Blythe at last.

'That's better,' said Callan. 'Did he also give a name?'

'He did. But it has no relevance.'

'I'll be the judge of that,' said Callan. Blythe sighed.

Very well, He was introduced to me as Gospodin Niemand. Niemand, as you may or may not know, is the German word for nobody: Gospodin is the Russian word for Mister. Mister Nobody told me about you, Callan.'

'Mr Nobody from Dzerzhinsky Street,' said Callan. 'Are you asking me to work for the K.G.B.?'

Once again Blythe fussed and fiddled with his Mao jacket.

'Certainly not,' he said. 'I dislike them intensely.'

'But a mate of yours put you on to them?'

'A colleague – yes.'

'What kind of colleague? D'you work in a hospital?' Blythe was silent. 'Don't make me mess up your suit again,' said Callan.

'I should like to get out of here,' said Blythe.

'I bet you would.'

'I should like both of us to go to a more congenial atmosphere. All this running water is depressing.'

'Tell me about your colleague and we'll see.'

'I am not a doctor of medicine,' said Blythe. 'My degree is that of doctor of literature. I hold a readership at the London School of Archaeology. The colleague I referred to is a fellow academic. I would prefer not to give his name.'

'You don't work for the Ivans?' Blythe looked bewildered. 'The Russians?'

'Certainly not.' Blythe was genuinely indignant.

34

'Who then?'

'If you come with me, I will explain.'

'Come where?'

'A little restaurant I know. I presume you haven't yet dined?'

'That's right,' said Callan. 'I haven't. You taking me out to dinner?'

'Yes,' said Blythe. 'It's a little place I know well. I promise you we won't be overheard.'

'And then you'll tell me about the job?' Blythe nodded. 'Suppose I turn it down?'

'I don't think you will. But if you do I pay you fifty pounds for your trouble.'

'O.K.,' said Callan. 'How do we get there?'

'I have a car,' Blythe said.

'Parked right outside?'

'Indeed not,' said Blythe. 'I was instructed to leave it some distance away.'

'You're new to this business, aren't you?'

'I've never done anything like this in my life.'

Again the indignation sounded genuine.

'All right,' said Callan. 'Let's go and eat. But we'll take a taxi.'

In fact they walked a while first, and Blythe complained that his shoes were pinching, and complained even more when Callan let three empty taxis go by. But they flagged one down at last, and Callan learned without surprise that he'd be eating Greek food. The address Blythe gave was the Parnassos Restaurant. Callan looked back a couple of times. There was no sign that they were being followed.

The Parnassos was a long, low cavern that spilled out in a litter of chairs and tables on to the street, but Blythe ignored these and marched straight inside: the place was as Greek as an evzone's kilt – pictures of Delphi, pictures of the Acropolis, sheepskins and woven wool and worry beads and wineskins. And noise, more noise than a hard rock concert, and from what Callan had been told that was very Greek too. Amplifiers bawled out bouzoki music, customers yelled, waiters clashed cutlery on to marble-topped tables. The place was secure all right. The only problem would be to exchange any information at all.

A young waiter, whom Blythe addressed as Nicky, scurried up, left them two menus, and disappeared.

'What would you like?' Blythe asked.

Callan looked at the list: fetta, souvlaki, seftalies, tara-masalata, giouvetsi. 'I don't know,' he said. 'You choose for me.'

'You've never been to Greece?' Callan shook his head. 'Their cuisine is Levantine, of course, and the Turkish influence is very pronounced. Traditionally, the Greeks detested the Turks, but one must assume that propinquity determined that they should adopt their food ... propinquity and a common source of raw materials. Lamb, for example, and fish, and vegetables of course.' The voice droned on, and Callan found no difficulty in believing that Blythe was a teacher. When the waiter returned he broke off and ordered in Greek, or so Callan supposed it to be. Almost at once Nicky came back with two bottles of wine: one white, one red.

'The white is resinated,' said Blythe. 'It's called

36

retsina. You won't like it.'

Callan believed him, and stuck to the red as Blythe continued his lecture on Greek food between gulps of retsina. Nicky brought a pile of dishes, and Blythe switched his lecture to them: their origin, preparation and precise name in Demotic Greek. Callan ate kebab and salad: Blythe ate everything in sight, polished off the bottle of retsina, and shouted to Nicky for another. His Mao suit was still finically neat, unmarked by food, but his face was flushed and he was beginning to sweat. It didn't make him more endearing.

Callan looked around the room. The diners were almost all English, homesick for Greek holidays: couples for the most part, with here and there a family party. The waiters were all male: dark, harassed, frantically busy. Callan ate the last of his salad.

'Tell me about the job,' he said.

'In a moment, my dear fellow,' said Blythe. 'I hate to talk business while I'm eating.' His eyes looked beyond Callan as he spoke, then he concentrated once more on the plates in front of him.

'Not in a hurry are you, old chap?' he asked.

Callan observed that wine at least made Blythe more agreeable.

'I can wait,' he said.

There was an ear-splitting crash from behind him. He looked round, and saw that a waiter had dropped a pile of plates. As he bent to pick them up the woman at the cash desk began to curse him in Greek. Even above the noise of bouzouki her voice could be clearly heard. It was a formidable voice, and she, Callan thought, was a formidable woman: hard, elegant, perhaps even beautiful, if beauty without sex could exist in a woman. She went back to her desk at last, and punched the till as if it had been the waiter's face.

'About the job,' said Blythe, and Callan returned to reality. 'It's possible that it could be dangerous–'

'I somehow thought it might.'

'–though that is by no means inevitable, old chap. By no means. That would depend on how you handled it.'

'Is it legal?'

Blythe considered. 'Dear fellow, I could best answer that if you could tell me what you meant by legality.'

Their waiter came then to clear the table, and Blythe gave more orders in Greek as he left, then listened as Callan bawled out his ethical beliefs against the opposition of a folk singer of in-exhaustible lung-power.

'I don't steal,' said Callan, 'and I don't commit murder for hire.'

'What do you do – in the way of naughtiness I mean?'

Callan found that he could no longer go on yelling to this drunk: not about that. 'Oh no,' he said. 'You tell me what you want, then I'll tell you if I'll do it.'

But that was just talk, he thought. No one takes a job where a lush is controller.

'Ah,' said Blythe. 'The empirical approach. You know what empirical means?'

'Yeah,' said Callan.

'You surprise me,' said Blythe. The words were

38

entirely without offence. 'What I am asking you to do is ethical – absolutely ethical but it is also illegal – if one accepts the enactments of de facto governments as constituting legality. Do you follow me?'

'No,' said Callan. 'But I don't think I have to. Get on with it.'

But the waiter came back then with two cups of coffee – black and sticky-sweet. Callan poured a little more red wine, and waited.

'We – I want you to rescue a political prisoner,' said Blythe.

'From prison?'

'House arrest. Are you in favour of the idea?'

'Depends,' said Callan. 'Who? Where?'

'Not till I know if you'll do it.'

'What's he in prison for?'

'The wrong beliefs,' said Blythe.

'And that's all you want me to do? Just lift him?'

'That's all, dear boy. It will not – I need hardly add – be easy.'

'You don't want me to kill anybody?'

'No,' said Blythe. 'There are quite a few people we'd like to see dead – but we don't want you to do it.'

'This geezer under house-arrest – has he done any killing?'

'No,' said Blythe. 'Never.' For what it was worth, he sounded honest. Callan waited as he took brandy, gulped at it, and said, 'I was given to understand that it might be your sort of thing.'

'How much are you offering?' said Callan.

'Ten thousand pounds,' Blythe said, 'or its equivalent in any currency you care to nominate.'

'You're carrying that kind of money?'

'Of course not,' said Blythe, 'but if you'll accept a ten per cent advance, I can get it to you by tomorrow. Well?'

'I'd like to think about it,' said Callan.

'Good gracious – and I was told you have nerve.'

'I've seen a lot of corpses in my time,' said Callan. 'They all had nerve. What they didn't have was one of two things – luck or brains – I'll let you know tomorrow.'

'Very well, sweetie,' said Blythe. 'You can reach me here.'

Callan stood up.

'I'll do that,' he said. 'Only don't try to drive your car home yourself. You might get nicked – and then I couldn't call you. And we don't want that, do we, sweetie?'

He took a tube home, and when he got to his door he was sure no one was following him. Getting into the flat was a ritual; Callan had made the locks himself, and a novice couldn't even open them with a key: even Lonely had to concentrate. The locks told him that while he'd been out someone had tried a break-in; they also told him that someone had failed. He went inside, picked up the directories from the telephone table, and learned without surprise that no Dr Randolph Blythe was listed. Neither was there a London School of Archaelogy.

4

It was time, thought Callan, to find out a little more about Dr Randolph Blythe: such an enterprising light shouldn't be allowed to stay under a bushel for ever... He would have to ask questions, discreet questions, but that had been part of his trade for longer than he cared to remember. He picked up the telephone...

'The Groper?' said Lonely. 'He's still got that posh house in Notting Hill. There mustn't half be some money in abortions, Mr Callan.' There was a pause. 'You sure he'll see you?' he asked at last.

'He will if he has to,' said Callan.

'You're saying he'll have to?'

'That's right.'

Lonely suddenly felt very happy that Mr Callan had decided to talk to him by telephone. It was never easy to make your excuses sound convincing when his eyes bored into yours. 'You won't want me to go with you, will you?' he said. 'I've got a lot of jobs piling up–'

'I've got other plans for you,' said Callan.

'I really am very busy, Mr Callan.'

'Don't get nervous,' Callan said. 'All I want you to do is go out and eat lunch – on me – and see me in your local afterwards.' He talked for a while, and at last Lonely agreed. It sounded barmy, but then a lot of the things Mr Callan made you do sounded barmy: but at least it didn't

41

sound dangerous. And anyway, he was hungry.

'Just as you say then, Mr Callan,' he said. 'And don't give my love to the Groper. I had enough of that in The Scrubs...'

The house was as immaculate as he remembered, the brass knocker gleaming, the pretty paintwork unscarred, net curtains white as icing sugar. Callan pressed the bell-push, then stepped back quickly. On the ground floor a curtain twitched. He pressed again, and nothing happened. Callan put his thumb on the bell-push and kept it there, and got to work on the knocker with his other hand. One thing about roadwork, he thought, it did wonders for your arm muscles. The Groper stood it for a minute and a half, but after that he gave in, the door opened, and they looked at each other.

'Hello, Groper,' said Callan. The Groper sighed.

'You always were an impatient boy,' he said. 'I didn't know you could be malicious as well.' He stood aside. 'You'd better come in.'

They went into the drawing-room, painted white this year, the furniture all of a dark and glowing red. Everything beautiful, everything neat, and somehow, everything expressing the Groper's loneliness, that was as sharp as pain. And I've come to bring him more pain, thought Callan. Ah well, better get on with it.

'I've come to ask a favour,' he said.

'You did that once before,' said Groper. 'As a result my friend got his face carved.'

'It wasn't my fault,' said Callan. The Groper shrugged. 'How is your friend?'

'At rest,' said the Groper. 'At least that's what it

42

says on his tombstone. Terry killed himself. You see he couldn't stand not being pretty.'

'Oh my God, I'm sorry,' said Callan.

'Sorry?' The Groper spoke the words as if it had no meaning. 'I never took up with anybody else, you know. I thought I would, but somehow I found I couldn't. I just sit here and run my Ladies' Aid… It's very boring – but I'm not the suicidal type.'

'The geezer who carved your friend,' said Callan. 'I killed him.'

'It's very kind of you to come here and tell lies just to cheer up an old queen,' the Groper said.

'I'm not lying,' said Callan. The Groper looked into his eyes.

'No,' he said at last, 'you're not. But you didn't kill him for me – or Terry.'

'Not even for myself,' said Callan. 'I killed him because he was trying to kill me.'

'I think we might treat ourselves to a modest drinkette,' said the Groper.

He went out and Callan went to the drawing-room window. Nobody was watching the house. By the time the Groper came back with the ice-bucket, Callan was examining a pair of bronze figures: two naked youths wrestling.

'Pretty,' he said.

'They're *said* to be Graeco-Roman,' said the Groper. 'My God I hope they are. They cost me even more than the live ones.'

'Abortion's still paying, then?'

'The membership of the Pudding Club,' said the Groper, 'is unlimited.' He handed Callan a scotch and water, took one himself. They drank

43

in silence.

'Terry's wake,' the Groper said at last, 'I never thought you'd be at it.' He drank again. 'I never wanted to see anybody hurt, you know. Not even when you and I were in the nick together and those rough men teased me so. But the man who did that to Terry – I couldn't bear that he should go unpunished.'

'He didn't,' said Callan.

'Thank you, dear.' The Groper refilled Callan's glass. 'And what can Aunty Groper do in return?'

'Help me find a feller,' said Callan. 'A feller who calls himself Blythe. Randolph Blythe. Claims to be a doctor of literature who specialises in archaeology. My guess is the name's made up–'

'What makes you think so?'

'Randolph Blythe,' said Callan. 'Randy to his friends. And blithe means gay, doesn't it? Come off it, Groper. It has to be a made-up name.'

The Groper giggled. 'That's what all our crowd thought too,' he said. 'But oddly enough it isn't.'

'You mean you know him?'

'Not intimately,' said the Groper, 'no matter how you may choose to interpret that word. But I have met him a couple of times at parties. Naturally he *hoped* people would call him Randy, but you know what bitches we all are. We called him Gladys.'

'What's he look like?' said Callan, and the Groper told him. The description was as accurate as it was malicious.

'And where can I reach him?' Callan asked.

'I don't know,' said the Groper, 'but if it's all that important I could find out.'

'It's all that important,' said Callan. He finished his drink.

'Give me your telephone number,' the Groper said. 'I'll call you as soon as I've got any news.'

'No,' said Callan. 'I'll call you if you don't mind.'

'You always were a cautious boy,' the Groper said.

'I still am,' said Callan. 'When you ask around, I want you to be cautious too.'

'Me, dear? I'm never anything else,' the Groper said. 'How could I be? I'm an abortionist...'

Lonely hadn't enjoyed his lunch, and said so, but when it came to food Lonely was a chauvinist to whom even tomato sauce on fish and chips was suspect.

'Nothing fit to eat,' he said. 'I couldn't even get a proper glass of beer.'

Callan signalled the barmaid and ordered the little man another pint.

'They gave me wine,' Lonely said.

'How was it?'

'Full of turpentine.'

Callan bought him a pork pie and a packet of crisps.

'Thanks very much, Mr Callan,' said Lonely. 'I'm famished.'

'So what happened?' said Callan.

Lonely spread mustard on his pie.

'Nothing,' he said. 'Not a bleeding thing. The Blythe geezer wasn't there, and no more was that bird.'

'You sure you didn't miss her?'

'How could I miss a bird like that?' said Lonely.

'Nobody could. Not the way you described her.'

'Who was on the cash desk?'

'Feller,' said Lonely. 'Fat. Getting on a bit. Slipped me an Irish 10p. They're all alike, them foreigners.'

'What did you make of the place?' Callan asked.

'They were straight, I suppose,' said Lonely, 'apart from that git on the cash-desk, but it didn't feel right.'

'How?' said Callan, and waited patiently as Lonely struggled to fit words together. Rational speech was always a problem for Lonely, but his instincts for crime were unbeatable.

'Not like a proper caff,' he said at last.

'You're not trying,' said Callan. 'Just because you didn't like the food—'

'I didn't mean that, Mr Callan. It was the waiters.'

'What about them?'

'Two or three of them was hard geezers. Not proper waiters at all.'

'I thought you said the place was straight?'

'Well, so it is,' said Lonely. 'So what do they want hard geezers for?'

Because you can be as hard as hell, and still not be a criminal, thought Callan. On the contrary, if you do your job and get back to the people that sent you, you're a hero. Aloud he said, 'It's a facer, isn't it?'

'If I was you I'd forget it, Mr Callan,' said Lonely. 'And that Blythe geezer. You go running after poofs and people'll start talking.'

Callan left him to his crisps and went to a library, worked his way through the university

46

directories. It was a long, boring and ultimately useless job. None of them owned a Dr Randolph Blythe. He'd have to ignore Lonely's advice and run after a poof: or at least phone one.

The Square was an estate-agent's dream: neat, Georgian houses all the way round, except for the church that took up all of one side, and that was Early English, and perfectly preserved. Brass gleamed, windows sparkled: the whole place smelled of money. Even the sunshine is golden, Callan thought, and threaded his way past the Bentleys and Jensens and Mercedes that filled the square. Twenty minutes from Waterloo, frequent trains, the best kind of woodland all about you. To live here all you needed to be was rich... Number twenty-three the Groper had said, and there it was: dark door, white-framed sash-windows, and a worn plate of polished brass: Randolph Blythe, D.D.S. At least he hadn't lied about being a doctor.

The receptionist said, 'Dr Blythe can't possibly see you today.'

'I think he can,' said Callan. 'Just take my name in, will you? It's Callan. David Callan... Tell him it's urgent.'

She looked again at the old, worn suit: the shoes that were beginning to crack. Once they'd cost a lot of money, but that day was a long time ago. On the other hand some of Dr Blythe's clients were so rich that they didn't even care if their clothes were old; didn't even think about it. Reluctantly she went into the surgery, and Callan looked at the magazines, aligned like guardsmen, on the mahogany table: *The Connoisseur, Vogue, Field, Country Life, Réalités.* And all up to date. Whatever else Blythe was doing he was making it big.

He was only kept waiting ten minutes, then Blythe came bustling out of the surgery. The delight in his face could not have been more obvious.

'My dear Mr Callan,' he said. 'How very nice to see you. Come in. Come in.'

And the geezer means it, Callan thought. He really means it. What the hell's going on?

He moved to the door, with Blythe smiling and beckoning as if there were a seven course banquet inside. Behind him the receptionist said frostily: 'We have Lady Bromwich at three-thirty.'

'For once in her life Lady Bromwich will have to wait. Give her something to read – if she *can* read.'

Callan turned and looked back at her. From her face it seemed as if Blythe was full of surprises for her, too. He went into the surgery, and Blythe shut the door.

'Welcome to my humble abode,' he said.

But there he was about as wrong as he could be. The last possible word for that room was humble. Everything about it, from the chair and drills and sterilising equipment to the collection of ancient vases on the wall, spelt money: money spent in such enormous quantities that you were quite sure you would feel no pain, not even when you sat in the chair: not even when you signed the cheque.

'Do I seem surprised to see you?' Blythe asked.

'No,' said Callan, and Blythe laughed the laugh of a man whose every prediction is coming true.

'We knew you'd track me down after all those naughty lies I told,' said Blythe, and watched as Callan walked over to the collection of ancient vases: slender and elegant, their terracotta and black surfaces embellished with figures of a perfect simplicity.

'Not that they were all lies,' said Blythe. 'I do quite a bit of archaeology – in an amateur sort of way. In fact I dug those up myself – in Sicily. Fourth century B.C.' Callan looked at him. He had his collector's face on; pride and complacency nicely blended.

'They're not really all that common,' said Blythe.

'I thought knocking off antiques was illegal,' said Callan.

'Well of course it is,' said Blythe, 'if you're caught. But then so many things are.'

Score one for Blythe, thought Callan.

'Do you still want this job done?' he asked.

'Even more so.'

'And what's that supposed to mean?' Callan asked.

'You tracked me down – found me. All by yourself. That proves you're still good.'

It proves I know another poof, thought Callan.

'How did you do it?' Blythe asked.

'I asked for you at the Parnassos.'

Blythe chuckled, delighted again. 'You're lying,' he said. 'But we thought you would. I don't blame you. Like Holmes you have your methods and why should you share them with us?'

'How do you know I'm lying?' Callan asked.

'If you'd been to the Parnassos I'd have been

told. If *anybody* had asked for me there, I'd have been told.'

Callan thought: why didn't anybody tell you about Lonely? Or maybe somebody had.

Aloud he said: 'You keep talking about "we", "us". Who else is in on this?'

'Does it matter?'

Patiently Callan said, 'Of course it matters. The more people who know about this job, the more chance there is of a leak. Who's we?'

'I think,' said Blythe, 'we'd better take a little trip to Paris.' Callan waited. 'That is if you really want to know who we are.'

'All right,' said Callan.

'Just that?' said Blythe. 'No more questions?'

'You wouldn't answer them,' said Callan.

This time Blythe laughed aloud. It really was his day.

'You've been to Paris before, I take it?' he said.

'Yeah,' said Callan.

Once. On a day trip. To kill a man called Lebichev, a K.G.B. Major who'd got an Air-Marshal's daughter hooked on hard drugs. But Hunter had found out about it and sent Callan to Paris, where somebody had slipped him a .357 magnum revolver and a silencer, and sent him to a hotel in the Avenue Georges Cinq, a nice hotel, elegant, expensive, and Callan had gone up to Lebichev's room and waited until Lebichev came in then shot him twice; once through the heart, once through the head. Lebichev had never had a chance, but then neither had the Air-Marshal's daughter. She'd died two months later: blood poisoning from a rusty needle.

50

'I've been to Paris,' Callan said.

'Oh good,' said Blythe. 'And don't worry about your passport. We have one for you.'

Well well well, thought Callan. Somebody knows what they're up to.

'What about the photograph?' he said.

'All taken care of,' said Blythe. 'Would you like to see it?'

Either hit him or laugh, thought Callan. One or the other. If you don't he'll drive you off your nut.

Blythe unlocked a filing cabinet and took it out, and Callan felt more frustrated than ever.

'You're sure it was safe in there?' he asked. Blythe looked hurt.

'Of course,' he said. 'My receptionist never looks in the locked drawer. She can't. I've got the key.'

In a minute, Callan thought, I'm going to scream.

Callan looked at the passport. A nice job. Very nice. Cover right and paper right, and the photograph just a photograph. Callan against a blurred background that could have been anything, and was in fact the Parnassos Restaurant. Callan glaring into the camera trying to make sense of Blythe, and looking like a man who's only sitting in the photographer's chair because he must... He looked then at the stamp on the photograph. Somebody had got that right too. Somebody knew his stuff.

'When do we go to Paris?' Callan asked, and looked at the name on the passport. Henry Robertson. That was nice too. Common, but not obvious. Real clever stuff.

'Would tomorrow suit you?' said Blythe.

51

'Fine,' Callan said. 'I'd better hang on to this.'

He put the passport in his pocket and Blythe didn't turn a hair. He even looked pleased.

'Well,' said Callan, 'I'd better be off.'

'Oh no no no,' said Blythe, 'you can't. Not yet. You're forgetting the drill. I haven't even *looked* at your teeth. In the chair please.' Callan hesitated. 'We don't want my receptionist getting suspicious, do we?' said Blythe.

Callan looked at him, and wondered if he'd been outsmarted. Whether he had or not, he knew there was no way in which he could refuse.

He sat in the chair and opened wide, wider, as Blythe loomed over him. For the first time Callan was aware of the width of his shoulders, the power in his wrists.

'Well well,' said Blythe, 'we have been a good boy. Brush our teeth twice a day, do we?'

'Aagh,' said Callan.

'And very wise too. Prevention is always better than cure, don't you think? Hallo.' He reached for a probe, and Callan willed himself not to shrink as he delicately tested. 'No,' said Blythe. 'A little tartar, no more. Still now you're here we may as well have a clean and polish.'

He set to work, deft and efficient and quick, and Callan thought, you may be a terrible spy but you're a bloody marvellous dentist.

'Just rinse out,' said Blythe, and Callan rinsed out, and wondered why anybody who knew his stuff well enough to organise that passport should have picked this clown for a go-between.

'Splendid,' said Blythe. 'We'll notify you of your next appointment when we send you our bill,' and Callan found himself floated out on a tide of brisk professional charm.

'Hold on,' he said, 'what time tomorrow?'

'Good lord,' said Blythe, 'what's happening to my memory? Eleven o'clock at Heathrow by the Air France check-in. I'll have the tickets.'

'See you then,' said Callan, and the professional charm started up again, easing him past the receptionist, and Lady Bromwich, who looked very much like the picture of the Labrador she was looking at, and out into the pretty, sunlit square.

5

Eleven o'clock at Heathrow by the Air France check-in, Blythe had said, but Callan was on the concourse balcony at 10.30. Blythe arrived at five to eleven. He looked very establishment in well-worn tweeds, and carried a slim leather suitcase just – and only just – small enough to qualify as hand luggage. By three minutes to eleven he was already looking at his watch: by five past he was in a panic that didn't match his tweeds at all, but he never once looked up at the balcony. On the other hand, nobody seemed to be watching him. Callan gave it a couple more minutes, just to be sure, then moved quickly, silently, up behind Blythe.

'Hallo,' he said.

Blythe couldn't have turned quicker if Callan had swung him round.

'You're late,' he said. 'You're seven minutes late.'

Callan gave no answer. 'Suppose we missed the plane?'

'We've got fifty-three minutes,' said Callan.

'How can you possibly know? I've got the tickets.'

'I checked,' said Callan, and thought to himself: What am I doing here? This geezer's incredible. But he knew the answer. Somebody was behind Blythe, somebody with a pipeline into Dzerzhinsky Street, and Callan had to know who it was.

Blythe looked down at the tatty air-line bag Callan carried.

'You haven't brought much stuff,' he said.

'I haven't got much stuff,' said Callan.

Blythe sighed and led the way to the check-in.

'I need a drink,' he said.

They were travelling first, which didn't make them any less conspicuous, but at least it was comfortable. Callan let Blythe lead the way through passport control: politeness cost you nothing and the passport he carried was his own, and anyway Blythe was jumpy enough as it was without hurting his feelings after all the trouble he had gone to. The clerk at the desk was alone: no stewards or ground hostesses loitered near, and the glance he gave Callan's passport was as efficient and bored as all the other glances he had given: no more, no less. Callan breathed a little easier as he went through. If they were looking for a man called Robertson it wasn't him. He looked round for Blythe. He was already at the bar, clutching a large brandy as if it were his only hope.

'Get you something?' he said.

'I'll get it myself,' said Callan, and went to

where they sold coffee. This time it was Blythe who looked bewildered.

The flight call was on time, the steward affable, the first class hostesses plastic-pretty. Callan sat next to Blythe and waited for takeoff. Elegant seat, all the leg-room he needed, and if the hired help's charm was synthetic at least there was plenty of it. The take-off was easy, and by the time the 'No Smoking' lights went off Blythe was already looking for a drink. Callan unzipped his flight bag, and took out a copy of Sir Charles Oman's *Wellington's Army*. What had happened in Spain one hundred and sixty years ago wasn't exactly relevant, but it did help to pass the time.

Blythe got his drink, and it was champagne. He drank his share, and most of Callan's too, and on the principle of waste not want not pocketed Callan's issue of free cigarettes. By the time they came to land at Orly, Callan wondered if he would be sober enough to remember where they were going, but apparently Blythe had thought of that too. They walked through passports and customs and nobody cared, then Blythe looked round the Orly concourse, elegant, glittering, and with just the faintest crackle of grit under the feet, then headed straight for the café, and three cups of coffee, bitter, scalding, black.

'Sorry about this,' he said. 'The trouble is I'm nervous, you see.'

The way you go on, you should be, mate. But Callan said nothing.

'The trouble is you're used to this kind of thing, and I'm not,' said Blythe.

'Nobody ever gets used to it,' said Callan.

55

'At least you don't drink,' said Blythe. Again Callan made no answer.

'Why don't you drink?' said Blythe, and his voice held the last residue of drunken grievance.

'I'm too scared,' said Callan.

Blythe swallowed aspirin, swigged down the last of his coffee, and looked at his watch. 'We'd better go,' he said.

They went outside, and Callan thought he knew Blythe well enough to know that he wouldn't need the sign marked 'Autobus'. He didn't, but he didn't need the sign marked 'Taxis' either. Right beside the sign marked 'Arrêt Interdit' was a dove-grey Rolls-Royce Corniche, and beside it a traffic policeman who kept looking away from it as if its presence embarrassed him – as well it might, thought Callan. Blythe gave a grunt of satisfaction, and headed for the car, and a chauffeur in a uniform of the same dove-grey as the coach-work got out and opened the door, then went back to his own seat and drove off without a word. The traffic policeman looked away again, but all the same he'd seen them both.

'You certainly travel in style,' said Callan, but Blythe nudged him and grimaced at the chauffeur. So now he's worried about security, thought Callan. They finished the journey in silence.

The house was tall, narrow, mid-eighteenth-century; the street lined with lilac trees with not a petal, not a leaf on the ground. Around them the frantic uproar of Paris's traffic was muted to no more than the murmur of a distant, tranquil sea. This was where money came to enjoy itself undisturbed, entrenched, secure until the H-bombs fell, or at least till the next student riot. This made Blythe's Regency square look like a slum... A butler in white gloves opened the door, looked at their luggage, snapped his fingers, and a footman appeared out of nowhere and took it away, then the butler preceded them down the hall to a salon, and opened the door.

'Doctor Blythe and Mr Callan,' he said. So much for security.

She rose to greet them, and her movement had the contained gracefulness of a cat's, of all felines. Not one single gesture was wasted, and not one was ugly. She wore a simple sheath of red linen that had cost somebody Blythe's weekly income at least, and the solitaire – the only jewellery she wore – had to be a sapphire. She looked, walked, behaved, as if money had never once in her life been the slightest problem. She was the woman behind the cash-desk at the Parnassos Restaurant.

'I am Sophie Kollonaki,' she said. 'How do you do, Mr Callan?'

'I'm very well,' said Callan, 'thank you. Madame?'

He made the last word a question.

'That is correct,' she said. 'I am a widow. Please sit, won't you? May I offer some refreshment?'

Blythe said at once, 'No thank you.'

Callan looked at the pretty French clock on the mantelshelf. It said twelve-thirty-five, and it would be right.

'A little whisky and water, please,' he said.

'You really mean a little?'

'Yes, please.'

She poured it herself, and gave him exactly what he'd asked for.

'Have you ever heard of me before, Mr Callan?'

'No,' said Callan. 'But I've seen you before.'

'Oh – the Parnassos. You are a very observant man.' Callan bowed. 'Later we will discuss that.' She paused. 'This is not my house. The car that brought you here is not my car. All that–' her hand pushed it away as if it were contemptible – 'belongs to my cousin. I am not rich, Mr Callan. My cousin is. His name is Michael Vardakis. Perhaps you have heard of *him?*'

Getty, Onassis, Niarchos. Vardakis wasn't in that league, but he wasn't far off it – and not an oil-tanker to his name. He'd started off in fruit, then moved on to land, and finally settled for constructional engineering. You name it, Vardakis would build it, and never fail to show a profit. Callan had once bodyguarded him for thirty-six hours, and he was utterly sure that Vardakis didn't even know he existed.

'I've heard of him,' he said.

'Heard what?'

Callan shrugged. 'That he's a very rich man,' he said.

'He is a Cretan,' she said. 'Probably the only rich Cretan in the world.' Again the quick, disdainful gesture.

'Cretans have a strong sense of family feeling,' she continued, 'and therefore he supports me.' She looked at the solitaire ring. 'Supports me in a way to which I am not accustomed – and a way to which I do not wish to be accustomed. But it is his wish, and so I must obey him. I have very

58

good reason to be grateful to my cousin, Mr Callan. I have also very good reason to hate him.'

Callan said, 'We'd better get this clear, Mme. Kollonaki. I've already told Dr Blythe here I don't do killings.'

'Did Dr Blythe ask you to kill anybody?'

Blythe said, 'Of course I didn't. I told him I wanted him to rescue a political prisoner. But I didn't say who – or where?' He had the look of a spaniel who doesn't know whether to expect a kick or a bone. 'Honestly, Sophie.'

'Randolph, darling,' she said, 'you look to me a little tired. Why don't you take a nap before lunch? Your room's all ready.'

It was a kick after all. Blythe left as if he were going to his execution. Sophie Kollonaki looked at Callan's empty glass.

'More whisky, Mr Callan?'

He put the glass down.

'No thanks,' he said. 'All I want for now is information.'

'My cousin, myself,' she said, 'we are both Greek subjects. But that is the only thing we have in common – except for our parentage.' Callan waited for the disdainful gesture, but it didn't come. Instead there was a smile that was all regret.

'My father and his owned a farm,' she said. 'We weren't rich, but we weren't poor. Not the way Cretans are poor...We never starved. Somehow we even managed to get an education – the University of Athens, no less. It was like going to Paradise... When the war came Michael was with the Cretan division. They fought well. First the Italians, then the Germans. To beat the Italians was easy: to beat

59

the Germans was impossible – with the arms and numbers they had. Somehow he escaped and got back to Crete. Don't ask me how. It would take all day. Just believe me when I tell you: Michael is very brave, very strong, very resourceful.'

'I believe you,' said Callan.

'The British and Australians and New Zealanders came to Crete. And then the Germans. This time I fought beside Michael – and again we lost. Michael and I lived in the mountains... Partisans. Often British officers came to visit us, to help us. They fought very well.' She looked at Callan. 'I think you are like them.'

'Madame Kollonaki,' Callan said, 'I've heard of those men. They were educated, they were idealists, and they were gentlemen.'

'They killed Germans very well,' she said.

Callan sighed. 'When you got my name from the K.G.B. – did they give you a dossier?' She nodded. 'What did it tell you?'

'Your whole life,' she said.

'The fact that I had hardly any education? That I never rose to be any higher than a corporal? That I got busted from even that for belting a sergeant? That I've been to prison for stealing?'

'Everything,' she said. 'But those educated, idealistic gentlemen were just as ruthless as you.' Her face was withdrawn for a moment. She was back with her memories. Callan marvelled again at a beauty that held no trace of femininity: the dangerous beauty of a predator: but not feline: that was wrong. She belonged with the eagles planing over the high mountains, breathing the thin air where only fanaticism can survive.

'My husband came with me to the partisans,' she said. 'He was their doctor. He was not a strong man, but he was brave. We were hunted, we escaped, and we killed many Germans. Over and over. We Cretans are superb mountaineers, Mr Callan. If there are no traitors, it is impossible to catch us in our mountains – and we had no traitors.'

Again there came the withdrawn look, and Callan thought, you crazy, magnificent bitch. You enjoyed every minute of it.

At last she said. 'We survived, all three of us. Michael was shot in the shoulder once – but it was nothing. Then the peace came.' She laughed, but the laughter was bitter. 'Peace, Greek fighting Greek, Right against Left, Monarchist against Communist. And even you, the British we had risked our lives for – even you joined in against us.'

All right, lady, Callan thought. So you're a Red. How else could you go shopping in Dzerzhinsky Street?

'My husband was very – political,' she said. 'From the very beginning he was involved. Then in 1946, three things happened. Three very important things. First, my husband was shot dead in the spring, shot by a man he had trusted all through the war: a man who belonged to his own partisan brigade. There was a meeting arranged in Heraklion between the two of them. By now they were on opposite sides but even so – my husband had no thought of treachery. He took no gun – and he died. Six weeks later I gave birth to a daughter, and two months after that, my cousin found the head of a bull – a little stone head

61

carved out of basalt, with crystal eyes and golden horns. He was helping my father to plough and the plough share turned it over and he picked it up... He never even finished the field.'

'Minoan?' asked Callan.

'Minoan,' she said. 'Four and a half thousand years old. Michael took it to Athens and sold it to an American for forty-five thousand dollars – ten dollars a year. That was how he got the capital to start his business career – by stealing our Greek heritage. Even the Colonels say it is illegal.' She walked to the corner of the room that was in shadow, and switched on a light. At once the corner became a shrine.

'Michael bought it back a little while ago. It cost him–' she smiled '–rather more than he got for it the first time. Come and see.'

The little bull was at once an animal and a god; unquestioning courage, arrogant sexuality, and a timeless endurance to which being buried in Cretan soil or hung on a wall in the Faubourg Saint-Germain were equally unimportant to his divinity.

'It's incredible,' said Callan. 'It's hardly even marked.'

'Basalt and quartz are hard to chip,' she said, 'and gold endures for ever – if it is not touched.'

'What happened to the man who killed your husband?' Callan asked.

'Michael killed him,' she said, as if no other answer were possible. 'Later he bought the man's orange groves – at a very good price. His widow had no head for business.'

'But didn't anyone suspect him?' Callan asked.

'Why should they? By that time Michael was a rightist too.' Then almost in the same breath she added, 'The prisoner we want you to rescue is my daughter.'

'I don't speak Greek,' said Callan. 'I've never even been to Crete. Why me?'

'Because the K.G.B. tell me you can do it,' she said.

'The K.G.B. usually prefer to do their own jobs,' Callan said. 'Didn't they want to do this one?'

'No,' she said.

'Why not?'

'Their computer told them the risk was too great.'

'Well at least you're honest,' said Callan.

'Too great for *them*,' she said. 'But you would have a good chance.'

'I suppose the computer told them that, too?'

'It did,' she said.

Lady, lady, thought Callan. You're as bad as Randy Blythe. Of course the K.G.B. said that; they've owed me a grudge long enough.

'Why would it be easier for me?' he said aloud.

'*Because* you've never been to Crete. Or even Greece. Because you're English. You don't need a cover. Thousands of English tourists go to Crete every year. Because you're good at your job – and you hate to lose.'

Which all means just about nothing at all, thought Callan, and asked, 'How does your cousin get on with the Colonels?'

'Very well,' she said. 'He brings a lot of money into the country – why shouldn't they like him? It is because of that my daughter is not in prison.'

63

'Then we're dead before we start,' said Callan. 'Once your cousin finds out I've been here, he's bound to let them know.'

'I see who I like,' she said, 'and I like some very strange people. Michael never interferes. Besides – how could he possibly know what you are?'

'Does he know what Blythe is?'

'A dentist with an interest in archaeology: a fashionable lefty who's never so much as had a drink with a worker in his life: of course he knows.'

'And a controller for an under-cover operation?'

Again the cold, perfect smile. 'My dear Mr Callan, if you did not know it to be true, would you believe it?'

'Who's putting up the money?' said Callan.

'I am,' she said. 'My cousin will have no part of this.'

'You mean you've asked him?'

'I mean that he is the last person in the world I would ask. Now I will ask a question. Why did you not accept the ten per cent Randolph offered you?'

'I wasn't too sure about the job. I'm still not sure.'

She nodded, reserving that for later. 'How did you track down Randolph?'

'I see who I like,' said Callan, 'and I like some very strange people. I persuaded one of them he owed me a favour. After that it was easy.'

'No Greek could ever allow himself to be critical of Randolph's little amusements,' she said. 'Our early history was founded on them. May I offer you lunch?'

'Thank you,' said Callan.

She pressed a bell twice, then picked up a photograph in a silver frame and brought it to Callan. He looked at it by the light of the bull-god's shrine.

'That is my daughter Helena,' she said.

A woman close to thirty, dark and beautiful, but gentler, more feminine than her mother would ever be. If it came to running up and down mountains, the mother would be by far the better bet. But it wouldn't come to that: it couldn't. The whole exercise was ludicrous.

6

Lunch was served in a small room that overlooked a garden: cherry trees, raked gravel, flower-beds and lawn mathematically precise. Lunch was very simple: oysters, coulibiac of salmon and fraises du bois, and to drink a Chateau Carbonnieux 1961. That was for Callan. Madame Kollonaki lunched even more simply: Black olives, cheese and bread, and a single glass of retsina it broke the butler's heart to pour. While he was there she talked of ancient Crete, a civilisation so old that it had traded with the Pharoahs, and so sophisticated that it had invented the bull-fight, the flush toilet and the topless dress. She told him about the Englishman, Sir Arthur Evans, who had excavated the site of the ancient palace of Knossos more than seventy years ago, and turned up not a palace but a whole way of life: painted buildings linked by flagged causeways and in them paintings and objects d'art of a memorable and distinctive beauty: bulls' heads and jewellery and exquisitely worked gold. She talked of the other palaces that had been found, and the objects that farmers still sometimes ploughed up as her cousin Michael had done, and the frantic efforts every Greek government made to try to keep them in Greece, if not in Crete. When the butler left them to their coffee, Callan asked:

'Is Blythe still asleep then?'

'He's lunching in his room,' she said. 'You make him nervous, Callan.'

'It's mutual,' said Callan.

'The man is terrified, and yet he does this for me. Don't you find that admirable?'

'Among other things,' said Callan. 'Why does he do it?'

'Because even trendy Lefties will take risks to help the real thing,' she said.

'And you're the real thing?'

'My husband was murdered. I have been three times in prison. If it were not for my cousin I would be there still. You may say I am real enough.'

'What did your daughter do?'

'Nothing,' she said. 'She is my daughter. So long as she is in Crete I will be silent – and the Colonels know it. She is a hostage: the guarantee of my good behaviour.'

'And if she does get out?'

'Then I shall fight,' she said. 'I shall fight and I shall win. Will you get her out?'

'I'm sorry,' said Callan. 'The answer's no.'

'Ten thousand pounds is the limit,' she said. 'My cousin wouldn't give a penny.'

'It's not the money.'

'What then?'

'Too many people know,' said Callan.

'Blythe and I–'

'And the people in the Parnassos. What about them?'

'Those people are my friends,' she said. 'I could have called them comrades, but you might have misunderstood the word.'

'They know about your daughter. They know you want her out. And they know about me. And the K.G.B. knows about me too.'

'You are afraid?'

Patiently Callan said, 'Of course I am. I'm afraid on every job. But that's not it.'

'What then?'

'If I took off for Crete now, Mme Kollonaki, I'd still be blown. And if I tried to lift your daughter I'd wind up in the nick, and so would she.'

'Nick?'

'Prison,' said Callan. 'Greek prison. Would you want your daughter to go through that?'

'Helena's a damned nuisance,' Sophie Kollonaki said. 'But I wouldn't wish that on her.'

'It would happen,' said Callan, then added, because he couldn't help it, 'How is she a damned nuisance?'

'She has no aptitude for politics. None at all,' she said. 'If she had she would be here and I would be free to act.'

Callan said again, 'I'm sorry. I'd better go.'

'You will want payment,' she said. 'I'll send for Randolph.'

'Just my ticket,' said Callan. 'I did nothing for you.'

'If you should change your mind,' she said, 'please let Randolph know.'

'I won't change my mind.'

'You make too many categorical statements,' she said. 'Surely an agent should be flexible?'

'When I was an agent, I was flexible too,' said Callan. 'Goodbye.'

He held out his hand, and she took it. Her grip was every bit as strong as he had thought it would be.

This time the Rolls-Royce to the airport didn't worry him, nor the stare of the traffic policeman, nor the deference of the steward and hostesses. Randy wasn't there to help him either, so he drank his own champagne and read his book. There was nothing else to do. The woman was a nut, and an obsessive nut at that. The worst, the most dangerous kind. Wanting her daughter back so she could start some kind of uproar in Greece. And not even caring for her daughter. All she cared about was the uproar. The daughter was a damned nuisance... And all the time chattering like a magpie; to him, to a bunch of revolutionary waiters, to a homosexual dentist who couldn't stay off the booze. No Callan, not for ten thousand pounds. Not for ten million. How can you enjoy ten million when you're dead?

Heathrow came so quickly he had to gulp his champagne, then walk the interminable corridors, show his passport, go out through the green door in customs where nobody showed any interest in him or his tatty flight bag. Then off to the bus – no Rolls-Royce for him in London – and the slog back to the Airport Terminal in the Cromwell Road. Plenty of taxis, but no taxis for Callan, because he'd just turned down ten thousand quid so he could go on living, and money was tight. A bus and a nice stroll to walk off the champagne, that was what Callan got – and thank God it wasn't raining.

He turned down the side-street past the pub with the juke-box. It was belting out some pop-group or other, and suddenly Callan was back on the fly-over, choking on cement-dust, longing for a pint. The side street was dark, its one light only hinting at its two blank walls and jumble of parked cars, but Callan had no doubt at all about the man he saw, walking towards him. He really was back on the fly-over.

'Hey,' he said. 'Hey, Spencer.'

Spencer Percival Fitzmaurice moved up to him, neat and contained as ever.

'Well well well,' he said. 'Dave Callan. What are you doing here, white trash?'

'I live round here, black trash,' said Callan. 'What's your excuse?'

Fitzmaurice grinned. 'We coloured people don't need excuses, whitey. We taking over your world, you dirty commy.'

'West Indian bastard.'

'Lousy crypto.'

'Fascist pig.'

Fitzmaurice was still grinning when he aimed

69

the blow, and it was the kind that ends all fights – if it connects. But Callan had seen Fitzmaurice's hands get set for the punch, but not soon enough, and took it on his left shoulder. Pain exploded along the muscle, and all the way down the arm, as Fitzmaurice swung another one and he leaped inside it, throwing a spear-strike with his good arm. The negro appeared to have a stomach made of sheet-iron, and his timing was wrong anyway. All Fitzmaurice did was grunt and keep on coming. Callan warded off a chop to the neck with his good arm, but the counter punch wasn't there: his left arm still wouldn't obey him. From there on Fitzmaurice came in from the left, playing on the bruised shoulder till Callan risked another blow with his right hand: risked it because he had to, and Fitzmaurice knew it, swayed away, elegant as Nureyev, and clipped him across the throat, a blow delivered with an expert's precision, leaving him conscious, but with all his strength gone.

Carefully Fitzmaurice propped him against the wall, then began, methodically, systematically, to hurt him: a skilled, unhurried beating that would leave no visible marks and ache for days. Before the pain took over Callan struggled to ask why as each blow landed, but soon there was nothing but the pain, and Spencer Percival Fitzmaurice's face, frowning in concentration, as he chose the precise spot for the next blow. Then the pain tightened even further and the face became a blur of blackness that was spreading, spreading, and somewhere a voice he knew, a voice he hated, said, 'Thank you, Spencer, I think that will do.' And

70

then there was nothing but blackness. No pain at all...

'Coincidence,' said Callan. 'In our trade there's no such thing as coincidence.'

The man watching him got up and came over to the bed. Eyes still shut, breathing fast and uneven. Talking in his sleep... He'd make more sense when he woke up. The man went back to his chair. There was plenty of time, he thought, but he kept his eyes on Callan even so. Again that quick uneven breathing, the body restless on the bed, maybe the pain was getting back through to Callan? Maybe consciousness was on the way. The man got up again, moved to the bed, then very deliberately tapped Callan on the left shoulder, and Callan groaned, then the taps became punches, and Callan yelled and opened his eyes.

'I make too many categorical statements,' he said. 'An agent should be flexible.'

'Oh, I'm sorry,' the man said. 'Did I wake you?'

Callan looked around the room that he knew ought to be familiar, then up into a face that was familiar at once.

'Meres, you bastard,' he said. 'Did you set me up for this?'

'It was Charlie's orders, old chap,' said Meres. 'Nothing personal.'

Callan said, 'You always were a rotten liar.'

Meres chuckled. 'I'll tell Charlie you're ready for him,' he said. 'You just lie there and be comfortable.' He dropped one hand heavily on Callan's left shoulder, and Callan yelled aloud. Still chuckling, Meres left the room.

The office was large, comfortable, and rich. A

71

Sheraton sofa-table, an Aubusson carpet, and a little Renoir of a ballet-girl tying her slipper. There were besides, television monitors, banks of them, that monitored the whole building, inside and out. Meres knocked, and was told to go in, but the man in the big leather armchair kept his eyes on one TV screen, on Callan hauling himself up in bed, wincing at every movement of his body.

'Well?' said Hunter.

'He appears to be ready, sir,' said Meres.

'Still feeling pain, I take it?'

'Yes, sir,' said Meres.

'You really do like to make him suffer, don't you, Toby?' Meres made no answer. 'How fortunate for you that I let Fitzmaurice immobilise him first.'

Meres said, 'I offered to take him on myself, sir.'

'You would have lost.' The man in the armchair stood up. 'You really must learn to control these sadistic impulses of yours. They make you vulnerable... Did Callan say anything?'

'He said, "There's no such thing as coincidence," said Meres. Then he said, "I make too many categorical statements. An agent should be flexible."'

'Did he indeed? Anything else?'

'Nothing relevant, sir.'

'Let me be the judge of that.'

'He called me a bastard and a liar.'

The other man smiled. 'As you say, nothing relevant. Let's go and talk to him, Toby – and keep your hands in your pockets.'

When they got to Callan's room he was standing up by the sink, coat and shirt off, holding a wet sponge to his shoulder. The bruises on his body were the colour of purple grapes; enormous slabs of darkness on the whiteness of his skin. Callan transferred the sponge to his ribs, and gasped as the coldness of it bit, then soothed.

'Hullo, Hunter,' he said. 'I had a feeling it might be you.'

'Of course you did,' said Hunter. 'Let's have a look at you.' Callan made no move. 'Or would you prefer me to have Meres turn you round?'

Slowly, carefully, Callan turned and faced him.

'Fitzmaurice really is very thorough,' said Hunter.

'Yeah,' said Callan, and turned back to soak the sponge once more. 'He's thorough all right.' He pressed the sponge to a bruise on his stomach, and asked, not looking back, 'Why, Hunter?'

'That was always your favourite question,' Hunter said. 'It cost you your job once.'

Callan said, 'This time I think I'm entitled to know.'

'Very well,' Hunter said. 'Finish what you're doing and I'll tell you.' More water, and more and more and Meres fidgeting behind him, and Hunter immobile, till at last the pain dwindled down to an ache that could just be borne, and Callan shambled to a chair and sat.

'All right,' he said. 'Tell me.'

'You were naughty,' said Hunter. 'You left this country and didn't tell me. Naturally you were punished for it.'

'I'm finished with you,' said Callan. 'Finished with the Section. You know that.'

'Nobody's ever completely finished with me,'

73

said Hunter. 'You know that.'

'I wanted – just to go away,' said Callan. 'A feller asked me and I wanted to go. What's wrong with that? It's normal, isn't it?'

'Indeed it is,' said Hunter. 'And that's what's wrong. None of us is normal, Callan.'

'True enough,' said Callan. 'It slipped my mind. Lucky you had Fitzmaurice handy to remind me.' He shifted in his chair, and the pain in his shoulder warned him that it was not yet time to move without thinking. Hunter watched the grimace and said, 'I'll send somebody to patch you up. We'll talk later.'

He nodded to Meres, and the two men moved to the door.

Callan said, 'Toby!' and Meres turned, wary and quick, but Callan was still in his chair.

'Next time you can be Sleeping Beauty,' Callan said, 'and I'll wake you up.'

Lonely contemplated his capital. One ten pound note, three fivers, seventeen ones, ninety-seven pence in change. At least he didn't have to go out and work that night. Just as well really. He wasn't in the mood for thieving, not with his back playing him up like it was. He looked round the room at the awesome collection of Mickey Mouse clocks, nude ladies holding lamps, Hong Kong toby jugs and elephant book-ends that he called home. Stay in and rest his back, that was the best thing. Save his gelt. Only his telly was busted and the batteries he'd lifted from Woolworth's didn't fit his tranny. Down the boozer then, and fish and chips to round off the evening. Why not? He could afford it. He opened a copy of *How to Achieve a More Positive Personality* at page 86. The next thirty pages were hollowed out in the middle, and he slipped the paper money inside, all but two quid. Shame to cut up a book, but his personality was as positive as it would ever be, he thought, and he didn't trust banks. Never had. Always getting done, banks were, and how could he prove it wasn't his money that was nicked? Write down all the bleeding numbers? He picked up the change, looked at it again, and there it was. Bleeding Irish 10p. Trust the beeding Irish to put a harp on one side and a fish on the other. Foreigners were all alike, he thought. Those gits in the caff were just the same: putting turpentine in the booze and slipping you foreign coins.

Serve 'em right if I was to slip it to them back, he thought, and then at once, No. That's barmy. Go all that way to eat a plate of foreign muck that'll cost an even quid just to get rid of an Irish 10p. And then he remembered. Up by the wall, a cigarette machine. Take two 10p's that would, and he'd get ten ciggies *and* some change, and serve the bastards right. He got up and put on his raincoat and cap, then hesitated. Mr Callan hadn't said he could go back to the caff. He looked again at the book and thought: Come on mate. Surely you've got a more positive personality than that. Even Mr Callan doesn't stop you from buying some snout.

One injection, the doctor had said, one single injection to kill the pain, but Callan had resisted, and the doctor had settled for ice-bags, and some sort of lotion, that turned the bruises from purple to lead colour. It didn't stop them hurting, but it was a pain he could live with. The doctor had good hands, light and cautious, and after the blarney about the injection he didn't say a word till he'd finished, and that suited Callan fine. Funny jokes now were all he needed. Blimey, what hit you? The Flying Scotsman? Does it hurt when you laugh? He could do without that. What had hit was the Flying Barbadian, and it hurt just to be alive and breathing, so please, no jokes.

At last the doctor said, 'That's the best I can do.'

'Thanks,' said Callan.

'Hunter wants to see you,' the doctor said. 'I'll get a wheelchair.'

'No,' said Callan. 'I'll walk.'

'I doubt it,' said the doctor, but Callan walked. It nearly killed him.

The doctor followed him into Hunter's room, and Callan sat down without being asked. Sat down before he fell.

'Have we run out of wheelchairs?' Hunter asked.

'No, sir,' the doctor said. 'He insisted on walking. And he refused to have an injection.'

'You may go,' Hunter said, and when the doctor had done so, turned to Callan. 'More foolishness, Callan?'

'You'll never see me in a wheelchair,' Callan said.

'My dear fellow,' said Hunter, 'there is no stigma attached to wheelchairs.'

'There is when I'm in one and you're watching,' said Callan.

'And why no injection?'

76

'I've seen people get injections here,' Callan said. 'Remember?'

'Do you really think I'd do that to you?'

Callan pulled open the blanket that had been wrapped round his shoulders. 'You did this to me,' he said.

'A lesson,' said Hunter. 'I hope you've learned it. Would you care for something to eat?'

'No,' said Callan.

'Of course not. Forgive me... A drink then?' He poured Chivas Regal without waiting for an answer. Callan sipped and felt better.

'Spencer Percival Fitzmaurice,' he said. 'Does he carry a gun? Because if he doesn't, tell him to get one.'

'You're being absurd,' said Hunter, 'and you know it. He was only doing his job, whether he watched you, or beat you.'

'Maybe it's you who should get the gun.' Callan sipped the whisky again. 'No I really am being absurd. He was bloody good.'

'If he'd been any less good I would have sent another man with him.'

'Flattery will get you nowhere,' said Callan.

Hunter said at once, 'There is no such thing as coincidence.'

'Come again?'

'I merely offer you cliché for cliché,' Hunter said. 'That one also is yours incidentally. You said it as you regained consciousness.'

'Did I?'

'So Meres says. He has no reason to lie. Why did you say it?'

'I must have been thinking about meeting Fitzmaurice. That was the coincidence. Only it wasn't.'

'I accept that,' said Hunter, and added, 'I make too many categorical statements. An agent should learn to be flexible.'

'I'm sorry,' said Callan. 'You've lost me again.'

'You said that, too,' said Hunter.

'Did I?'

'Again it's according to Meres, and again I can see no reason why he should lie. What does it mean?'

Callan said, 'I've no idea.'

Hunter sighed. 'Lies waste so much time,' he said, 'and I have so little time to waste.'

'Time's the only thing I have got,' Callan said. Hunter looked at him again.

'You have been in pain,' he said 'You are still, I think, in shock. The whisky was premature. All the same I shall let you finish it, then rest. We'll talk later.'

7

The Parnassos was closed: 5p on the tube and another 5p back and the bleeding caff was closed. Lonely crossed over to it and looked in the window. Empty as a whore's promise. Nothing but a notice that said 'Closed Thursdays' – and today was bleeding Thursday. He'd have to get rid of the Irish 10p. at the pub. No sense in slogging all the way back here again. As he turned to go the car came, moving slow. No lifts for Lonely he thought, and kept on going.

Glass smashed behind him with a tinkling crunch, and Lonely whirled. The car wasn't moving slow any more: it was going like the clappers. A bald-headed geezer was driving like he was breaking records, with a young feller beside him, laughing his head off, and he had no trouble in seeing them, no trouble at all, because even as they took off there was a soft woomph from inside the window of the caff, and a light that started off an oily red became jagged orange and yellow flames as the car raced past him.

'Oh my Gawd,' Lonely thought. 'Petrol bomb,' and took off even as he thought it, head down, arms pumping, and ran slap into a copper who was pulling out his whistle. The copper grabbed and Lonely wriggled, body slack inside the copper's arms, slid down to the ground and off again before the copper could get a hold, lost his cap and kept on running, round two corners and on to a bus.

'Nearly missed it,' the conductor said. 'In a hurry are you?'

'Not half,' said Lonely.

'Where you going then?'

'Five please,' said Lonely.

He handed 10p. over, and took his ticket and change. Well at least he didn't have to worry about the Irish 10p. any more. All he had to worry about now was the petrol bombers he'd seen and the copper who'd seen him – and what Mr Callan would say when he found out he'd gone back to that caff in the first place. And the last was the most worrying one of all.

Callan lay on the bed and wished he enjoyed smoking. It was supposed to relax you. Not that people ever relaxed when they came to see Charlie C. Hunter Ltd, the sign outside said, 'Dealer In Scrap Metal'. And a yard full of junk to prove it. And behind the yard what was left of a school, sooty brick, flaking paint, and more scrap metal you thought, but you were wrong. This was the Headquarters of Hunter's Section, the branch of S.I.S. that he'd worked for all those years. Executions were what he'd specialised in; killings if you wanted a more honest word. Nine killings. Eight men – and a woman he'd loved. A great place for setting up killings. Hunter's HQ.: gymnasium, armoury, interrogation rooms... He'd vowed he'd finished with all that, and yet here he was, back with Charlie, and Meres, and Spencer Percival Fitzmaurice.

Cautiously he changed his position on the bed. Whatever stuff that doctor had used on him was good. The bruises hardly ached at all now, unless he put weight on them... Or somebody else did. And here we come to the Number One item on the agenda, Callan. Why on earth should you try to cover up for a crazy bird and a drunken dentist? Why should you want to? He couldn't find any answer, and yet he did want to. It was a gut-feeling. Every instinct told him to stay silent, and reason told him it was impossible. O.K. Take a vote on it. Those in favour? Those against? Reason wins, and the motion fails. For Christ's sake it has to fail. You know the sort of thing that goes on in here, Callan. You've seen it. Remember Snell the Section psychiatrist and his nice, sterile little needles that shot you full of hallucinogens till you finally told the truth and your mind blew? Are you going to risk all that because some mother wants her daughter back so she can start a revolution?

There was a sound at the doorway, and there she was, unchanged. She never changed. Deb-elegant, blue-eyed, golden-haired. Hunter's secretary. So beautiful, so cold. The English rose who slept in the deep-freeze. She came up to him, put pyjamas, slippers and dressing-gown on the bed.

'Hunter sent these for you,' she said. Callan looked at the dressing-gown.

'Red,' he said. 'I look terrible in red.'

'At the moment,' she said, 'you'd look terrible in anything.'

Callan pulled the blanket round himself.

'Leave your suit on the bed when you've changed,' she said. 'I'll see it's pressed.'

'My shirt could do with a wash, too.'

'You'll be issued with a new one.'

'If you don't mind I'll keep the tie,' he said. 'It's my regimental tie. The Queen's Own Royal Losers.'

'One day you'll say that and realise you mean it,' she said. 'Now hurry up and change. Mr Hunter's waiting.'

They were nice pyjamas, white silk with a red-piping that matched the dressing-gown, and the slippers were leather and not a bad fit. Callan felt rather better as he walked along the corridor to Hunter's room., This time it did seem more like

81

fifty feet than fifty miles. He knocked at the door, and the precise, establishment voice told him to come in, and when he did so, there with Hunter was the last of the Old Comrades' Association. Mr Test Tube himself.

'Ah Callan,' said Hunter. 'Do sit down. You remember Snell, don't you?'

'Of course,' said Callan. 'How are you, Snell?'

'That's a very odd question to ask a psychiatrist,' Snell said. 'unless you really do *want* a subjective answer.' He was perfectly serious. He always *was* perfectly serious, particularly when he stuck the needle in.

'Must you always be rude?' said Hunter.

'Serious.' said Snell. 'I was being serious. Isn't that what you want me to be?'

'Oh certainly,' said Hunter. 'I may even want you to be serious with Callan, later on. Stand by, will you?'

'Whenever you're ready,' said Snell, and went to the door.

'Nobody's getting serious with me,' said Callan. 'I've retired.'

Snell kept on going: the door closed.

'As a matter of fact,' said Hunter, 'that's rather what I wanted to talk to you about. But first I'd like to know a little more about your trip to Paris.'

'Why?' said Callan.

'I think it might be interesting.'

'Supposing I said it wasn't?'

'Then Snell would be serious with you as I am being now. It's up to you, Callan.'

'All right,' said Callan. 'All right. I was offered a job.'

'Our kind of work?' Callan nodded. 'It never occurred to you that there might be a conflict of interests?– My interests?'

'That's what I went to find out,' said Callan. Then out it all came: Blythe, Sophie Kollonaki, her cousin Michael, the whole lot; even the fact that the chauffeur's uniform was the same grey as his car. He only left one thing out: the passport Blythe had given him, and he never did know why, except that keeping things from Hunter was always a good idea – if you could get away with it. When he'd finished, Hunter said, 'Well well. Poor old Sophie.'

'You know her?' Callan asked.

'We've met,' said Hunter. Crete, thought Callan. I bet it was Crete during the war: but he didn't put the question. If Hunter wanted him to know he'd tell him: if he didn't there was no point in asking.

'I'm a little concerned about the K.G.B. angle,' said Hunter.

'So am I,' said Callan. 'A bit more than a little.'

'Sophie isn't a Communist of the orthodox sort,' said Hunter, 'though her party is very far to the left. No doubt they have their contacts with Russia. But why should the Russians do them a favour?'

'Insurance for the future?' said Callan. 'If Sophie's lot ever knock over the Colonels?'

'Then why didn't they send a K.G.B. executive to do the job? That would have been even better insurance.'

'That's easy,' said Callan. 'They knew it wasn't going to work.'

'You think so?'

'I know so,' Callan said. 'And so would you if you'd ever met these clowns.'

'I told you that I knew Sophie,' said Hunter. 'She didn't strike me as a clown. Rather efficient at her own line of work I would have thought.'

'As a partisan up in the mountains she'd be great, I don't doubt,' said Callan. 'Part of a sealed off unit with no chance of a security leak. But this is different. Like all politicos she's a talker, and one of the people she chats with is Blythe.'

'Ah, Blythe,' said Hunter. 'The prancing parlour pink.' He leaned across to the sofa-table and picked up a yellow-backed file. 'As a matter of fact we have a file on him.'

'Yellow?' said Callan. 'Surveillance only?'

'That's right,' said Hunter, and flicked over its pages. 'He knows an awful lot of people – and I don't care how you interpret that statement. And when he's in the mood he's really very, very gay – and that can still be useful you know, even in this permissive age.'

Callan said, 'He's also a hell of a good dentist. But when he drinks he talks, and he drinks when he's frightened, and he's frightened all the time.'

'Sophie appears to trust him.'

'Who the hell would trust Sophie?'

'Me,' said Hunter. 'With my life.'

And I bet that's a bit more of your auto-biography, thought Callan. You and Sophie up in the mountains, knocking off Germans. I wonder what your name was then?

'I think you ought to take this job,' said Hunter.

Police Constable Kyle had a trying day. In court

till one o'clock (three parking offences, two shop-lifting, one drunk and disorderly) then straight on to the two till ten shift and more parkings, more drunks, and a husband and wife dispute. A butt to solicitors, an object of loathing to all the public he'd dealt with: cowboy, pig, P.C. Plod. And just when he'd been looking forward to knocking off he'd landed a bloody fire, and even got his arms round the bloke who could have done it – and let the bloke get away. Not the sort of thing that earns a commendation from the bench, or even your own inspector come to that. And that hurt, because Kyle was ambitious. He'd already passed the sergeant's exam and was studying for the inspector's. He wanted to get on, not spend his time re-directing traffic round thousands of pound's worth of burning building when he should have been off duty. He got a relief at last, and walked back past squads of grimy firemen drinking tea out of pint mugs, the grey look of total exhaustion on their faces as they watched the smouldering ruin that had once been the Parnassos Restaurant, Greek food, wine and ouzo a speciality.

His inspector was at the tea-van, talking to the fire-chief. He looked at Kyle, the appraising copper's look, and Kyle thought: All right I'm knackered. And so would you be if you'd been working for thirteen hours.

'Get yourself a mug of tea, Kyle,' the inspector said, and turned back to the fire-chief. 'Sorry,' he said, 'you were saying?'

'Arson,' the fire-chief said. 'No doubt about it. Petrol bomb. Professional job, too. None of your

85

milk-bottles and rag wicks. This bastard knew his stuff.'

'I'll get an alert out,' the inspector said.

'I hope you get him,' said the fire-chief, and went back to his men. The inspector turned. 'Well Kyle?' he said.

'I was coming down Stenton Street,' said Kyle. 'I'd just seen the fire. A bloke came round the corner from Moon Street where the restaurant is – was. He ran slap into me, and I grabbed him.'

'Go on.'

'I lost him, sir,' said Kyle. 'He was like a greased eel, that feller. Slipped through my arms and away. The fire was bad by then and I called in and reported. I didn't have any choice, sir.'

'I don't suppose you did,' the inspector said. 'Go on.'

'I went up to the restaurant and saw it was empty and made sure that everybody got out of the buildings nearby.'

'I heard about that,' the inspector said. 'Hustled them a bit, didn't you? Some of them weren't any too pleased.'

'I'm sorry about that, sir.'

'I'm not. You did the right thing. Go on.'

'Then the patrol car came up and the sergeant put me on point duty. And that was it.' Kyle paused, then said again, 'I lost him.'

'Did you know he'd just committed arson?'

'No, sir,' said Kyle, 'and I still don't. But I knew there was a fire and he was running.'

'Any idea who he was?'

'No, sir. Little feller in a raincoat and cap. I got the cap.'

'Drop it off in the C.I.D. room and go home. You're dead beat, Kyle. Well get on to this in the morning.'

Callan said, 'You must be joking.'

'Am I?' said Hunter. 'I thought it was rather your kind of thing.' He reached for the Chivas Regal bottle. 'Do you think you can cope with this stuff now?'

'I think I'm going to have to,' said Callan, and Hunter poured.

'You really would do it rather well,' he said, 'and of course you'd keep whatever Sophie paid you. I think you can get her to do a little better than ten thousand. Do you pay income-tax, by the way?'

'Not until they ask me,' said Callan.

'There you are then. A year's income at least for no more than a few days' work.'

'If I didn't wind up in prison,' said Callan. 'Or dead.'

'There is that, of course,' said Hunter, 'but you're a very resourceful chap.'

'I'd have to be,' said Callan. 'This job's blown before we start. That girl Helena Kollonaki is bait. A poor little lamb staked out while the hunters wait for the tiger. Well this tiger's too old, too clever, and much, much too frightened. No thank you.'

'Don't misunderstand me,' said Hunter. 'I'm not asking you to rejoin our little group.'

'That's good,' said Callan. 'I'd hate to turn you down twice in one night.'

Hunter poured himself a glass of sherry, and

nodded at the whisky-bottle. 'Help yourself whenever you're ready.'

'No thanks,' said Callan and finished his whisky. 'What with one thing and another I've had a pretty rough day. I think it's time I was going home.' He stood up.

'Sit down,' said Hunter, 'and have another drink.'

You'd left him, and he agreed you'd left him, but he still gave the orders, and you still obeyed them. Callan sat, and poured.

'Blythe's in a yellow file,' said Hunter. 'Do you know what colour your file is?'

Warily Callan put down the bottle.

'Yeah,' he said. 'You told me the day I quit. Mine's a yellow one, too. Surveillance.'

'You were once in a red file,' Hunter said.

'That was when I was dangerous,' Callan said.

'You could be dangerous again.'

'Labouring on a motor-way?'

'But you're not labouring on a motor-way,' said Hunter. 'You're contacting foreign agents. You're being recruited by a notorious left-winger because you were recommended by the K.G.B.' He took a very small sip of sherry. 'Everything you've said in this room has been taped,' he said.

'Including the fact that the job hasn't a prayer?'

'That can be edited out,' said Hunter. 'You know that. There's quite enough to put you in a red file, Callan.' He sipped again. 'Do you remember the significance of a red file?'

'For God's sake... Of course I do.'

'Then tell me.'

Wearily, Callan said, 'Red is the danger colour.

88

The colour of blood. You put somebody in a red file and he gets killed... I used to do the killing, Hunter. That's how I remember.'

'This time I could have you killed,' said Hunter. 'I probably will if you don't do this job.'

'You mean that,' said Callan.

'Certainly.'

'You really mean it. You'll have me killed if I don't pull a stupid stunt that'll probably kill me anyway. I don't like your idea of a deal, Hunter. Either way I die.'

'No,' said Hunter. 'If you work for me you'll have my section behind you. That should reduce the odds a little, don't you think?'

The Section's planning, Callan knew, was impeccable, and Hunter hated to lose men almost as much as he hated failure.

'Why?' said Callan at last.

'Always the same question from you, Callan,' Hunter said. 'I don't propose to answer it. You are being offered the chance to earn at least ten thousand pounds and stay out of a red file. Good and sufficient reasons to accept my offer, I should have thought.' Callan made no answer. 'Be sensible, man,' Hunter said. 'You at least considered the job when Blythe approached you – and the only change in the job is that I'll make it easier.'

'There's another change,' said Callan. 'I'll be working for you. A year ago I swore I'd never work for you again: I'd sooner dig roads. And I did.'

Hunter remained impassive.

'As you say, you're tired,' he said. 'And your day has been rather eventful. Why don't you sleep on it?'

'Don't kid me, Hunter. You're not letting me go. Not now.'

'Of course not,' said Hunter. 'You'll sleep here, of course. We'll talk at breakfast.'

Lonely dialled the number again, and let it ring thirty-three times. That had been the number of their cell in the Scrubs – him and Mr Callan and that nutter who'd got religion and prayed all the time, even when the screws came in one night and gave Mr Callan a belting for talking back. Thirty-three was his lucky number. Always had been, ever since that cell. But it wasn't working that night: Mr Callan was out. And he had to talk to him. He really did. He'd seen the two geezers who'd thrown the petrol bomb, and maybe they'd seen him... And the copper bleeding well had seen him, and no maybes about it.

Throwing petrol bombs was arson. Sounded dirty come to think of it, but that was what they called it, and they put you down for years and years. And he'd got form: a lot of form. Spent nearly half his life in prison before he met Mr Callan. Who was going to believe he'd come back there just to give back an Irish 10p.? He'd be guilty as soon as the rozzers saw who it was. 'Hallo Lonely, me old mate, going into the big time are you? Burning down restaurants now instead of thieving the spoons?' And they'd want to know who'd put him up to it and how much he got paid and what he'd done with the money. And when he couldn't tell them they'd think he was being naughty and get physical. Put him up in court next morning and say he got duffed resisting arrest and how he always got violent when he was nicked, and all that lark. And that would be another three years on the sentence.

He rang the number again and begged Mr Callan to answer. But he didn't. Out with some posh bird in some posh restaurant. Bet they didn't put turpentine in the wine where he was eating. Caviar and champagne for Mr Callan, and his mate in dead shtook. He waited for thirty-three and it still didn't work so he opened up *How to Achieve a More Positive Personality,* took out his money and put it in his inside pocket, then closed the pocket with safety pins. Never leave anything to chance, that was his motto. That was why he was off on his travels, come to that. If anybody came calling, rozzers or hard geezers, Lonely was *out* and not likely to be back. The only trouble was where to go. Aunty Glad would help him, but she was doing bird. And Aunty Gertie was dead. He couldn't run crying to her; never no more. It would have to be Cousin Alfred.

8

Kyle was day-off the next day, but he couldn't sleep, even if he was dead-beat. He kept seeing the face of the little man as he slipped out of his hands. Smelling him too. Gawd, he'd sniffed like a sewage farm. He got up early and his mum bawled him out for being out of bed when he could be having a rest which was her way of showing she cared, but it wasn't half hard on the ears. He ate his bacon and drank his tea and didn't bother with the paper. When she asked him where he was going and he said the station she nearly had a fit. The station was peace after that: even the C.I.D. room.

They were mostly out on jobs of course, they usually were, but the one he wanted was there. Detective Sergeant Walters, banging away on the typewriter and coughing on a cigarette. Very near retirement was Walters. He'd felt more collars than Kyle had hot dinners. If anybody knew the geezer, he would. Kyle waited till the sergeant looked up and said, 'Can I have a word, sergeant?'

Walters looked at the civilian suit.

'Put you in plain clothes have they?'

'Day off,' said Kyle.

'And you come in here? Blimey you must he keen.'

'More like fed up,' said Kyle. 'I lost a feller yesterday.'

'We all lose one now and again,' Walters said. 'You'll get used to it.'

'I think I picked a bad one to lose,' said Kyle, and told him about the little man running.

Walters listened, his face expressionless. The kid was keen, no doubt about it, and clever too, and maybe he had the nose for things going wrong that was even more valuable to a good copper than cleverness. At least he was dead right about one thing, he had picked a bad one to lose.

'Little feller in a raincoat,' he said aloud. 'Clean-shaven. That's not much to go on, son.'

'And he smelt something shocking,' said Kyle.

'There's a lot does,' said Walters. 'Specially the drop-outs. What they used to call hippies. Protesting against the acquisitive society, they reckon. So they stink.'

'This one wasn't a hippy,' said Kyle.

'Nervous probably. A lot of them do get nervous when they're doing a job. Takes them all sorts of ways – and all nasty.'

'Nervous? He was scared rigid. But blimey he could run.'

'Adrenalin,' said Walters. 'Why didn't you run too?'

'And leave the fire?'

Walters grunted. 'No,' he said reluctantly. 'You couldn't do that. Pity.'

Kyle picked up a cap from a table. 'This was his,' he said. 'It's clean, but it stinks. Smell it.'

Cautiously Walters inhaled, then pulled a face.

'You picked a worrier, all right,' he said, and turned the cap over in his hands. 'Sorry, I can't help you.'

'What'll I do then, sarge?'

'Records,' Walters said. 'If he's got any form it's the only way you'll find out.'

'But it could take days,' said Kyle.

Walters remembered the big one he'd let slip: a bank robber that had been. Eleven years ago. He was a detective sergeant then: he'd be a detective sergeant when he retired, and that wasn't far off. 'I know it could, son,' he said. 'But if I were you I would do it.'

'I knew you would change your mind,' said Hunter. 'More coffee?'

'Thanks,' said Callan, and waited while Hunter poured. The coffee was good – it always was – and the eggs and bacon had been cooked exactly as he liked them. His suit was pressed, his shoes cleaned, and the new shirt he had been given was much better than the old one. Spencer Percival Fitzmaurice might have been no more than a nightmare if it weren't for the marks on his body.

'There's just one thing that bothers me,' Callan said.

'Just one? How very fortunate I am,' said Hunter.

'How the hell do I go back and tell Sophie Kollonaki I've changed my mind?'

'I've been thinking about that,' Hunter said. 'I don't think you'll find it too much of a problem. But all that can wait. Let's go down to the armoury.'

'Why?' said Callan.

'I want to see you shoot,' said Hunter. 'Don't tell me you've grown tired of shooting after all these years?'

First the stick, thought Callan, then the carrot. He knows I need to handle a gun far more than I need to drink whisky. And what sort of a donkey does that make me?

Hunter pressed the buzzer, and the steel doors slid apart almost at once. Judd, the armourer, knew as well as anybody else how much Hunter hated to be kept waiting. One look at Hunter's face in the monitor, and he jumped.

'Morning, sir,' he said.

No good mornings for Callan, not that he'd expected any. Once the two men had liked each

94

other, but now Callan was outside Judd wanted no part of him.

'We shan't need you,' Hunter said. 'Take a little break.'

Judd's glance moved from Hunter to the neat line of hand-guns laid out on the bench: clean, bright, slightly oiled, the way the manual said they should be – and all the ammo in the world. Hunter chuckled.

'Don't worry, Judd,' he said. 'I'm quite safe.'

Unless I go barmy, thought Callan. If you drive me barmy, mate – you haven't a prayer.

Judd left, and Callan waited for orders. Hunter waved towards the line of hand-guns. 'Help yourself,' he said.

There was no doubt in either man's mind which gun he would choose: a .357 magnum revolver, adjustable rear sight, ramp-type front-sight, grooved trigger, four-inch barrel and the power to put a bullet through steel-plate. Callan picked it up, hefted it, squinted along the sight, then his hands moved with a craftsman's precision, as he broke the gun, loaded it, then reassembled.

'Whenever you're ready,' said Hunter.

Callan went to the barrier and stood, feet apart, the gun by his side. Breathe slow and easy, and wait till you're ready, till the gun is no more than a part of your hand, an accusing finger pointing. He brought the magnum up at last, and his finger rhythmically squeezed, the target fluttered as each bullet went through it. Behind the target, Callan knew, were banks of London telephone directories eight books thick, and each magnum bullet would have pierced half of them at least.

Hunter wound in.

'Two inners, four bulls,' he said.

'The inners were the first two,' said Callan. 'You've got to get used to a new gun.'

'You're probably right,' Hunter said. 'Try again. A little more quickly.'

Callan tried again, and again and again, till the gun flowed up in a pure, inevitable arc, and the bull disappeared every time.

'Splendid,' said Hunter. 'Let's try Prendergast.'

Prendergast was a tailor's dummy with a solid rubber head and a face of simpering prettiness, and Callan lugged him into position then went back to the barrier, then Hunter gave the orders and Callan fired. He shot Prendergast standing, he shot him prone, he shot him under arc-lights and with almost no light at all, from a crouch, from behind a chair, kneeling, squatting, and finally he stood with his back to Prendergast then whirled and shot him again. And each time he fired the pattern the way he had been taught – heart and head. And each time he hit them.

'Ah well,' said Hunter. 'Prendergast needed a new head anyway.' He looked at Callan. 'You haven't lost your touch.'

'All alone?' said Callan. 'The gun could do with a rest.'

'And you?' said Hunter.

Callan shrugged. 'I've enjoyed myself – and you know it,' he said. 'But I've had my fix – till the next time.'

Hunter ignored him. 'In that case we'll have Judd back in,' he said, 'then discuss our little problem in my office.'

Cousin Alfred was all right, and even Myrtle, his missus, was bearable, and anyway she could do you a smashing suet duff; it was the kids he couldn't stand. Telly blaring all the time, and trannies and record-players, and Myrtle saying don't do that Marilyn, don't do that Eva, and Eva and Marilyn not taking a blind bit of notice. No wonder Alfred kept on saying, 'Let's go down the boozer.' But Lonely was too scared to go out; if he hadn't been he wouldn't have come to Alfred.

'Why aren't your kids at school?' he asked at last.

'They're playing truant,' said Alfred.

He said it as if it were an explanation, and Lonely let it pass. Thick Alfred was, except when it came to mending motor-bikes.

'Come to think of it – why aren't you at work?' he said.

'On the sick,' said Alfred.

'Oh,' said Lonely. 'What's wrong?'

'I'm fed up,' said Alfred. 'That's what's wrong. I miss the fellers.'

One of the kids slung an apple at Alfred then. He ducked automatically, and it hit Lonely on the head. It was the best laugh they'd had all day.

'See what I mean?' said Alfred.

Lonely thought: Even dodging coppers can't be worse than this.

'You got a phone?' he asked.

'No,' said Alfred. 'We ain't got no Rolls-Royce neither.'

'Is there one in the pub?' Alfred nodded, and Lonely took a deep breath. 'Come on,' he said. 'I'll buy you a drink.'

But Number thirty-three had still lost its magic. He tried and tried, but Mr Callan still wasn't in.

'You're quite clear then?' said Hunter.

'Yeah,' said Callan.

'You don't sound very happy about it.'

'It makes me look a right idiot,' Callan said.

'That,' said Hunter, 'is part of its charm.'

'It also means Blythe has something on me.'

'It means Blythe thinks he has something on you. That could be very useful.'

'O.K.,' said Callan. 'So I make contact. Then what?'

'You phone Charlie of course.'

'And do what Blythe says?'

'You *appear* to do what Blythe says,' said Hunter, 'but in fact you do what I say.' His face hardened. 'Let there be no mistake about that.'

'And what happens to the girl?'

As Callan asked the question the secretary came in.

'I believe I mentioned that I was not to be disturbed,' Hunter said.

'This came in from Special Branch,' she said. 'I think you'll find it's urgent, sir.'

Hunter read it, slowly and carefully, as he read everything. Petrol bomb in the restaurant, and one small witness who smelled.

'Quite right,' he said. 'I'll deal with it later. Thank you.'

Coming or going, thought Callan, she was a treat to watch.

Hunter said, 'Somebody's put a petrol bomb in the Parnassos.'

'So somebody takes it seriously,' said Callan.

'The restaurant was empty,' said Hunter, 'but there are flats on either side. Somebody might well have been killed, and the bomber knew it. Would you like a gun?'

'Not unless I'm going to meet Spencer Percival Fitzmaurice.'

Hunter said, 'I know nobody of that name.'

After that Callan left, slightly irritated, which was by no means bad for him, and Hunter put in a call to Detective Superintendent Murdoch of Special Branch. 'I'm most grateful for your message,' he said.

'We do our best.'

As always when he talked to Hunter, Murdoch sounded nervous, even defensive. He could never be quite sure what new demands Hunter would make of him.

'I'm most interested in the small, smelly man the policeman lost,' Hunter said.

'Indeed, sir? You think he might have done it?'

'On the contrary,' said Hunter. 'I know he did not. The bomb was thrown from a car, Superintendent.'

'You can prove this?'

'No,' said Hunter. 'But I know it.'

Murdoch sighed. 'That's hardly the sort of thing I can pass on, sir.'

'Of course it isn't. Is a search being made for this small, smelly man?'

'I should imagine so, sir. Would you like me to check?'

'If you please.'

Hunter hung up and pressed his inter-com

buzzer. 'Send Mr Meres to me, please,' he said. As he waited he thought: Lonely. It could hardly have been anyone else. Was Callan watching the Parnassos too – and without telling me? When Meres came in he said, 'They burned down the Parnassos last night.'

'It was a success then, sir?' Meres asked.

'As a piece of arson it was first-rate,' said Hunter. 'The place is a write-off. But it is possible – barely possible – that they were seen.'

'May I ask by whom, sir?'

'Not at the moment. No... Check on it, will you?'

'Of course, sir.' Meres got up to go.

'And, Toby,' said Hunter, 'it *is* urgent.'

Meres left, and Hunter brooded about Callan and Lonely. Left to himself, Callan was ruthlessly efficient, brave in a contained sort of way, but never foolhardy. Lonely changed all that: Lonely made Callan reckless. It would not be too much to say that but for Lonely, Callan would be dead, Hunter thought, and Callan was not the sort of man who would ignore that sort of debt. Decidedly it would be better if Lonely were not involved in this affair. The phone rang again.

The superintendent said, 'Murdoch... The answer's yes. I spoke to a C.I.D. sergeant a man called Walters, and they've got an "All Stations" out. He didn't sound too hopeful.'

'Splendid,' said Hunter. 'Let's hope he's justified. Do you think he is?'

Murdoch wished that once, just once, he could get some idea of what the hell Hunter was getting at.

'Yes,' he said, 'I do. The only hope they've got is P.C. Kyle – the policeman who lost him.'

'Go on.'

'Kyle's young, sir, and I gather he's ambitious. He doesn't like the fact that he lost a petrol-bomber.'

'Very laudable, but he didn't.'

'With respect, sir, Kyle doesn't know that. He feels it'll be a black mark against him, and he may well he right. So he's looking for the man himself – in his spare time. Bit of a wild goose chase if you ask me – unless he's got form.'

'And if he has?'

'It'll take a bit of time – but if he goes to Records and sees the right pictures and recognises it – well it's a chance, sir.'

'How much of a chance?'

'Two to one against.'

'If this young man – Kyle did you say? – looks like bringing it off, I want you to let me know, superintendent. At once. Can you arrange that?'

'Yes, sir.' The superintendent coughed, then said, 'This smelly man, sir. He isn't one of yours by any chance?'

'No, superintendent. He is not.'

'Then may I ask why–?'

'By all means,' said Hunter. 'But we both know I'm not obliged to answer.'

Cousin Alfred said, 'Is that all you ever do? Make phone calls?'

'It's important,' said Lonely.

'Blimey it must be. That's the fourth one since we got here. Why don't you just sit down and drink your beer? You're making me nervous.'

Lonely sat, and tried to relax. After all he couldn't be in all that much danger, not in Cousin Alfred's local. It was miles away from his own gaff, and nobody knew him, so why not enjoy himself? He sucked at his beer.

'I saw the Angels the other night,' said Alfred. 'Three of them had new bikes. I could have tuned them for them smashing. They didn't even ask. Didn't even see me. I'm glad I packed it in.'

And off he went, rabbiting on about the Angels and all Lonely had to do was drink his beer and make out he was listening, and Cousin Alfred was so grateful he went off to buy the next round himself. There was a paper on the next table, and Lonely picked it up to see what was running, but he never got as far as the sports news. There on page one was the headline: Fire Bomb in London Restaurant. Picture too. The place was burned to the ground. Lonely applied himself to the story. Unidentified witness – evaded policeman on patrol – requested to come forward – help the police with their inquiries. When Cousin Alfred got back with the beer Lonely was on his feet.

'Where you off to then?' said Cousin Alfred.

'I got to make a phone call,' said Lonely.

'Oh gorblimey,' Cousin Alfred said.

Once more it went the whole thirty-three, and Lonely was just about to hang up when he heard the click he'd been praying for.

'Yes?' said Callan.

Never no names on the phone if you can help it, Mr Callan said. Never.

102

'It's me,' said Lonely.

'I know you.'

'I been ringing,' said Lonely. 'Ringing and ringing and ringing.'

'I'm sorry, old son. I didn't get home last night.'

Him and his posh birds, Lonely thought.

'Something you wanted?' Callan said.

'I'm – in a bit of trouble,' said Lonely.

'Pulled a job have you?'

'No,' said Lonely, his voice vibrant with outrage. 'I never. That's just it. They're *saying* I pulled a job – but I never.'

'Who's saying it?'

'The papers,' said Lonely. 'All over the front page.'

Callan thought: Poor little basket. The only time you make the front page they've picked the wrong geezer.

Aloud he said, 'Want to come over?'

'I daren't,' said Lonely.

'All right,' Callan said. 'I'll come to you.'

'That's just it,' Lonely said. 'I'm not at home.'

Patiently Callan said, 'All right, old son. Take it easy. Where are you?' And Lonely told him.

'Stay there,' said Callan. 'I'll be with you in half an hour And get rid of Cousin Alfred.'

All very well you giving orders, Lonely thought, but you don't know what Cousin Alfred's like when he gets in a boozer. You need a bomb to get him out. Oh my Gawd why did I have to think of that word?

'Any luck?' said Alfred.

'Yeah,' said Lonely. 'He's coming round.'

'Who is?'

103

'Mate of mine,' said Lonely. 'We was in the Scrubs together. He's got a job for me.'

'Thieving?'

Lonely shrugged. 'Maybe. It's hard to tell with this geezer. He did his bird for Grievous Bodily Harm. Nearly killed the other bloke, I heard tell there's others he *has* killed only they could never prove nothing.' And that's the truth, Lonely thought, even if the GBH isn't.

'Fancy you knowing blokes like that,' said Alfred.

'Only the one,' said Lonely, 'and that's too many.'

'What you want to work for him for then, if you feel like that?'

'Because I daren't turn him down,' said Lonely. 'He'd flaming kill *me*.' He looked earnestly at his cousin. 'Alfred,' he said, 'when he gets here, you won't like annoy him or anything, will you?'

'Of course not,' said Alfred.

'Only once he loses his temper he goes raving mad,' said Lonely, 'and he takes offence at the least little thing.'

Alfred finished his beer.

'If you don't mind, Lonely,' he said, 'I think I better be getting back to Myrtle. She finds the kids a bit of a handful.'

'I reckon you're doing the wise thing,' said Lonely, and Alfred fled. Lonely bought himself another beer, and a whisky for Mr Callan, and settled down to wait. It was barmy, and he knew it, but when Callan came through the door Lonely felt as if his troubles were over. Callan dropped a folded newspaper on the table.

'Well well,' he said. 'You have been busy.'

Lonely passed him the whisky.

'That's just it,' he said. 'I haven't.'

'What were you doing at the Parnassos then?'

Lonely told him about the Irish 10p.

'So what were you doing waltzing with the rozzers?'

'Well I scarpered, didn't I?'

'Couldn't you just have walked?'

'No I couldn't,' said Lonely. 'I saw the geezers who threw the bomb.'

'Good look?' said Callan. Lonely nodded. 'Tell me.'

'Driving a Ford Capri,' said Lonely. 'Grey. Could have done with a wash. The driver would be about fifty, baldy, putting on weight a bit. It was the other feller threw the bomb.'

'Tell me about him.'

'Young geezer, twenty-four or -five, good teeth, sun-tan, blondy-haired. Not bad-looking,' Lonely added reluctantly. 'And laughing fit to bust himself.'

'Why?'

'Because he'd thrown the bomb and the place was burning. He was *enjoying* himself, Mr Callan. That was why I bumped into the rozzer. It made me nervous.'

'It says in the paper you duffed him.'

Lonely treasured the words: Lonely the terrible, the duffer of rozzers.

'That'll be the day.' he said, but the joke didn't last. 'Mr Callan,' he said, 'I really am in trouble, aren't I?'

Gently Callan said, 'Yes, old son. I'm afraid you

105

are,' then added. 'Don't start stinking the place out.'

'You know I can't help it,' Lonely said. 'That rozzer – he saw me. I was right under a street lamp. If he goes to Records–'

'It could take weeks,' said Callan.

'He could still find me.' He looked at Callan as an ancient Greek might have looked at an oracle. 'What am I going to do?'

'Move in with me,' said Callan.

'I daren't go up West,' said Lonely.

'You'll be all right,' said Callan. 'I'll look after you.'

Lonely looked relaxed, then the depression returned.

'But how am I going to get about?' he said.

'You could grow a beard,' said Callan. 'Be a bit of a hobby for you.'

9

Meres said, 'You did rather a good job.'

The bald man said, 'Thanks.' Nutter Bradley said nothing.

'Really rather a good one,' said Meres, and waited. With Bradley it was always easy, but it was also fun.

'What do you mean, really rather good?' said Bradley, his voice a parody of Meres's accented drawl. 'It was bloody perfect.'

'Well no. Not precisely that,' said Meres.

'What went wrong then? Go on. Tell me. What went wrong?'

'You've seen the papers?'

'Of course,' Bradley said. 'They think some smelly feller did it. It's him the coppers are looking for.'

'Has it not occurred to you that *he* may be looking for *you?*'

Bradley said, 'You're talking daft.'

The bald man said, 'Hold on a minute.'

'And you save your breath for your driving, Snooks,' Bradley said.

The bald man flushed.

'Don't call me that,' he said.

'You know why we call him Snooks?' said Bradley. 'it's short for Snooker Ball. Snooker Ball Jackson. Mostly he's the white, but when he gets upset – like now – he doesn't make a bad red.'

'Belt up,' said Jackson, then to Meres: 'Why would this feller be looking for us?'

'He saw you,' said Meres. 'Didn't he?'

'I don't know,' said Jackson. 'It all happened very quick.'

'He saw you,' said Meres. 'And he was there. Maybe he was sent there. A look-out perhaps? If so – one of you was careless. Not you, Jackson, of course.'

'You're bloody blaming me,' said Bradley.

'I bloody am,' said Meres. 'Jackson was the driver, you were the look-out. Only you didn't look out. Not exactly a perfect job, old son.'

'The restaurant went up lovely,' Nutter said.

'It could hardly fail to, could it?' said Meres. 'Not with the equipment I gave you. But I don't like that witness.'

'All right,' said Nutter. 'You don't like it. But don't go on about it or I'll–'

'You'll what?'

'I'll belt you.'

Meres chuckled: a small, comfortable sound. He had got where he wanted to be at last. Snooker Ball Jackson watched him warily.

'You saying I couldn't?' said Nutter.

'I'm not saying anything,' said Meres. 'You're the one who's doing the talking.'

Nutter stood up, and Jackson said quickly, 'Seems to me we're wasting time. It's the little smelly feller we should be worrying about.'

Nutter subsided, and Meres looked at Jackson with dislike.

'You want us to start looking for him?' Jackson asked.

'No,' said Meres. 'I'll do that. It requires finesse. There's another job for you.'

He told them what it was, and when he finished Nutter began to look happy again, poor stupid bastard.

'When?' he said.

'Quite soon,' said Meres. 'I'll let you know. And do stay out of trouble till then.' He left and Nutter cursed him in a savage stream of filth. Real language, Jackson thought. Stuff I wouldn't even use in my head.

Aloud he said, 'You want to watch that feller.'

'Him? Toffee-nosed poof,' said Nutter, and the curses came again.

Jackson looked at him and wondered, What have I done to deserve you, mate? The job was all right, and the money was great, but when he worked with a firm he liked to know who they were, even a two-man firm like this one. And Nutter Bradley he didn't know at all – just foisted on him as you might say. Young tearaway. Good with a gun – he said. Been in the paratroops – he said. Liked his work, and that was the truth. He'd seen him. Made him nervous, that did. Too bloody nervous. He'd driven the car all right but he'd forgot to put his cap on. Like a bloody amateur. But he'd had more sense than to tell that feller Meres. He'd met Meres's kind before, not often thank God, there weren't that many of them, but they existed. The ultimate hard geezers. Diamond hard. Eat poor little Nutter in one mouthful, then spit him out because he didn't taste nice. Awful as Nutter was, Snooker Ball Jackson pitied him. But he wasn't daft enough to tell him so.

Getting Lonely back to his pad was like getting a drunk out of a pub before closing time. He was so nervous he shook, and the stink was appalling. Still at least it meant they got a bit of space on the tube, but when they got off it was even worse. Even with Callan beside him, Lonely jumped at every shadow. When they reached the dark little street by the pub, Callan almost had to carry him. And if Spencer Percival Fitzmaurice was waiting he'd have even less chance than the last time.

'There's somebody following us,' Lonely said. Callan stopped dead. Even scared out of his socks, Lonely was never mistaken about that. Callan waited for a pool of shadow, then looked back over his shoulder.

'I can't see anybody,' he said.

'No more can I,' said Lonely, 'but he's there.'

If Lonely couldn't spot him, he must be the best. Callan kept on going.

'Oh him,' he said. 'Don't worry about him. He's the bloke I'm working with. On account of that Blythe geezer.'

'You're scared of Blythe?'

'No, son,' said Callan. 'Not scared. Only careful.' And Lonely relaxed. Not that he understood a word of it, but it sounded crooked, and therefore made sense.

Callan got him into the flat and opened beer, and the little man was more relaxed than ever, so relaxed that he became aggrieved.

'Me,' he said. 'Mixed up with arson. That's something I don't hold with. Nasty, that is. People could get killed.'

'The restaurant was closed,' Callan said.

'But there's people lives near. Suppose they'd got caught?'

And maybe they would have been, thought Callan, if a copper hadn't been close by... And what kind of arsonist knows when a copper's on his beat?

'Maybe I ought to leave the country,' Lonely said.

Callan looked at him in wonder. Lonely, who thought you needed a passport to go to Southend. And now he talked of going abroad.

Callan said gently, 'Just give it time. It'll blow over.'

'If they catch the ones that really done it, it will,' said Lonely. He didn't sound as if he thought that

110

very likely. Neither did Callan.

They were eating supper when the phone rang. Lonely promptly wanted to go into hiding, but Callan forced him to stay in the kitchen to finish his meal, and went into the living-room to take the call.

'Hallo,' he said.

'Hold on,' said the cool, lovely voice. 'Charlie wants to speak to you.' And Callan held on.

'Callan?' said Hunter.

'Hallo, Charlie.'

'About that dentist chum of yours. I think you ought to see him tomorrow.'

'He just did my teeth,' said Callan.

'Just a friendly call,' said Hunter. 'It might be worth while... And maybe you won't feel such a fool.'

'Why not?' said Callan.

'He might be pleased to see you,' said Hunter. 'Particularly if you arrive shortly after nine to-morrow evening. Very shortly after. Will you do that?'

'If you say so, Charlie,' said Callan.

'I am saying so. It might even help your Red File problem.'

Hunter hung up, and Callan noticed without surprise, that his hand was shaking. He put the phone down, and waited till his shakes subsided. Lonely had enough to worry about without that.

'Who was it?' said Lonely.

'Mate of mine,' said Callan. 'He thinks it's about time I went to see my dentist.'

Lonely said, 'If you don't mind my saying so, Mr Callan, you got some very funny mates.'

Callan smiled. 'I don't mind, old son,' he said. 'It's true.'

Kyle got lucky early on. A good sign, that. It was about time he had a bit of luck. No trouble about recognising him, full face or profile – and the description fitted him a treat: small, agile, no visible scars. Sometimes troubled by body odour... No. That wasn't quite right. It was everybody else who was troubled... He looked at Lonely's form. Larceny, money and goods, twenty pounds. Larceny, money and goods, eighteen pounds, twenty-five pounds, nineteen pounds seven and elevenpence. Then back in 1969 his really big job, warehouse breaking. Eighty-seven pounds ten. Never violent, and rarely successful. But he'd managed to keep out of trouble for the last few years. Arson was a new line for him, too. All he'd ever done before was steal. Laboriously, in neat italic, he began to copy out Lonely's form. Maybe Walters could still find time to help him...

'Tea-leaves like that are ten a penny,' said Walters, and finished his beer. Kyle signalled for a refill.

'No, son,' Walters said. 'This is my shout.'

'You're doing me a favour,' said Kyle.

'You don't have to buy it, son,' Walters said. 'I don't mind you being independent, but what about my feelings?'

Kyle flushed. All his life he'd heard about how independent he was. But that was the polite word. Usually it was just plain bloody stubborn.

'He's never been in my manor,' Walters said, 'but I've got a few mates over where he lives. I made a few enquiries.' He took out an old envelope. 'Lives over in Notting Hill – I've got his address for you. Clean over the last five years, but that doesn't mean he's turned honest. That geezer could no more turn honest than he could change his sex.'

'Getting better?' Kyle asked.

Walters shrugged. 'Could be. He's been seen around with a hard geezer, so maybe he's got himself a minder.'

'What hard geezer?' Kyle asked.

'That's just it. From what they tell me they don't seem to do any jobs. But he's hard all right. Believe me, son. The blokes who told me are connoisseurs... So I asked them to check back. This what's his name? Lonely – he's the nervous type. Hence the smell. They don't usually go mates with villains. And the only hard geezer they could come up with was one who'd done bird with Lonely. Years ago that was. They shared a cell.'

'Is it the same one?'

Walters said, 'Could be. Nobody's all that sure. But if it is – and Lonely's with him–'

'Yes?'

'Take a few mates with you, son,' said Walters. 'Say half a dozen.'

'I've got to go out,' said Callan. Lonely took it well, considering.

'You aren't going to be long, are you?' he said.

'I hope not,' Callan said. 'Put the chain on the door. I'll ring.'

Lonely looked anxious.

'You're not going to pull a job are you?' he said. 'Not when I'm here?'

'Just going to see a mate,' said Callan.

Lonely sniffed, 'I thought I was your mate,' he said.

'You are son,' said Callan, 'but we've still got to live.'

'Oh I see,' said Lonely. 'Money in it, is there?'

'That's right.'

'You go right ahead then,' said Lonely. 'Always take care of the pence.' He made a large, and for him, untroubled gesture, and Callan left. There were eggs and beer in the fridge, and chips in the freezer, and if Mr Callan was doing the collecting, the pounds would take care of themselves...

He'd hired a sports car. Cost a bit more, and mopped up the juice, but it handled well and was nice to drive, and it wouldn't look too out of place in that Georgian square... The trouble was it handled too well. He got to where he wanted to be at half past eight. Time to find a pub with a car park and drink one cautious whisky and wonder what the hell Hunter was playing at. Watching his gaff, and setting up times and places, and telling him Blythe would be pleased to see him. And enjoying it. Callan was sure there had been enjoyment in his voice. Just like old times, when Hunter had only half-briefed him, just to see if he could figure out the rest of it for himself. And he usually could: but that was when he was set for promotion. Lord High Executioner's Chief Assistant.

He finished his drink and set off for the square. As he'd thought, it was just about crammed with cars: no room for Callan. All the same there was time, so he drove round, and just as well he did. There was a Ford Capri there, and a stocky feller

114

with a tweed cap behind the wheel, and he never took his eyes off Blythe's place; not once. Callan kept on going out of the square, and squeezed in behind two Bentleys in a space beside the church, then looked at his watch. Two minutes past nine. Maybe there was time to take a look and maybe there wasn't, but if you're cautious you can always squeeze in an extra couple of minutes. Softly, hugging the shadows, he went back to the square. The geezer with the tweed cap had parked under a street lamp, and Callan's guess was it was the only place left. As Callan watched, the geezer took his cap off, and scratched his head, but his gaze never left Blythe's surgery. He was as bald as a billiard ball. Cautiously Callan retreated, reached the corner of the square and ran, past a mews and a block of garages, to the lane behind the square, and counted off the doors till he reached it: number twenty-three, with a row of dustbins left out all ready for the morning, and just right for a geezer in a hurry who happened to want to get over a wall. Into a back-yard then, and hope to God there aren't any dogs, then to a back-door of formidable dimensions, and that would have been that short of borrowing a chopping axe, if some health fiend hadn't left the pantry window open. Slow and easy, and hope it doesn't squeak, and it doesn't, mind the bread bin and there you are inside: burglarous entry. Going mates with Lonely had its advantages.

Callan moved, cat-footed, into a kitchen: breakfast set for one, then opened the door. Not a squeak, not a decibel. He went into a corridor and stood motionless, letting his eyes distinguish against the darkness of the hall the even blacker darkness of a flight of stairs. He moved forward, then froze. From the first floor there came a little patch of light. Suddenly from above there came music, too: an orchestra that played in warm, caressing chords, and two women singing a duet. For a moment he thought a third voice joined in, but then it rang out again. The third voice was a scream, and not in the score. Callan went up the stairs, and hoped it wasn't Spencer Percival Fitzmaurice who was causing the screaming. If it was, he'd soon be screaming too.

He reached the door at last, and the music swelled, the two women's voices reached a chord of unutterable sweetness, and again the scream came. Callan risked a look round the door: Blythe in pyjamas, one hand jammed up hard behind his back, and holding it a young feller, smiling, enjoying his work... And Hunter had said don't get there before nine o'clock. But he hadn't said hand out visiting cards. Callan took his scarf from round his neck and wrapped it across his face so that only his eyes were free. He hadn't done that since he was seven years old, playing cops and robbers: and even then he'd always been a robber.

Laughing Boy said, 'I don't know what you're yelling now for, poof. This is only the warm up.' Then he pulled on Blythe's hand again, and Callan moved, erupting through the door.

No fancy stuff; he didn't need it: Laughing Boy was too intent on his work. Just a straight dash through and a chop on the arm that held Blythe's hand, then a spear-stick in the gut that immobilised him but left him just conscious enough to feel pain. Callan's hands balled into fists, and he began to beat Laughing Boy, a steady, systematic beating: controlled, careful, vicious; until over the music he could hear a voice saying, 'Black trash, white trash, nigger, fascist pig.' The voice was his own. Callan let his fists drop; he was hitting the wrong man. Laughing Boy fell to the ground.

'I don't know who you are,' said Blythe, 'but I'm extremely grateful.'

Callan turned to face him and grunted with pain. His ribs ached again from his own beating. He unwrapped the scarf from his face.

'Mr Callan,' said Blythe. 'I never expected–'

Callan looked down at the man he'd beaten.

'Who's your friend?' he asked.

Blythe rubbed the shoulder joint that had been twisted.

'I've no idea,' he said.

Callan said, 'It seems to me we have two choices. Either I can carry on where your friend left off, or we can call the police.'

Blythe said, 'Oddly enough, neither of those ideas appeals to me.'

Callan looked at him. 'Dr Blythe,' he said, 'how brave you are. What *do* you want to do with him?'

'Hurt him,' said Blythe at once, 'but you've already done that. Thank you.'

'My pleasure,' said Callan.

'Do you know, I somehow thought it was?'

Callan said, 'You've left it a little late to be astute. What do you want to do with him now?'

'Get rid of him,' said Blythe.

'You're sure?'

Blythe nodded. Callan grabbed Laughing Boy by the collar, and towed him to the stairs. He was far too heavy to carry, and anyway Callan's ribs hurt. He bumped him down the stairs and along the hallway to the front door, stuck him out in the doorway, then switched on the porch light and waited. Silence, for a minute, two, then the faintest hint of a foot-fall, the soft scrape of Laughing Boy's clothes as he was lifted, then more silence. Callan moved into the reception room and looked out of the window as a car door slammed. A Ford Capri moved out of its parking space, a tweed-capped man at the wheel. In the back seat Laughing Boy lolled, apparently drunk. When he came to he'd wish he were. There was a sound on the stairs and Callan whirled. Randy Blythe, D.D.S., wearing a kaftan and still rubbing his shoulder.

'He's gone,' said Callan. 'A friend collected him.'

'A friend?'

'Relax,' said Callan. 'They've both gone.'

'In that case,' said Blythe, 'perhaps you'll come back upstairs and join me in a drink.'

He hadn't any Chivas Regal, but his single malt was fifteen years old. In emergencies you have to learn to make do.

'No doubt this all seems a little strange to you,' said Blythe.

'Just a little.'

'On the other hand your sudden appearance seems a little strange to me.'

'Fair enough,' said Callan. 'Let's start with you.'

'Why me?' said Blythe.

'I could say because I'm stronger than you are,

118

but I won't,' said Callan. 'Let's say it's because I did you a favour.'

Blythe sighed. 'I have rarely met a more unlikeable man than you,' he said.

'One just left,' said Callan.

'All right,' said Blythe. 'All right. He came here what – fifteen minutes ago? I'd just had a bath and was playing some records. He rang the bell and forced his way in.'

'He knew you were alone?' Callan asked.

'He must have done,' said Blythe.

'You aren't always, Randy, now are you?'

Blythe said, 'You really are detestable, you know. As a matter of fact I quite often entertain friends at this hour. I can only assume he was watching my house.'

'It would seem,' said Callan, 'a reasonable suspicion.'

Blythe looked at him.

'I think you're at your worst when you're ironic,' he said, and went back to rubbing his shoulder.

'Who was he?' said Callan.

Blythe said, 'We weren't exactly introduced.'

'He must have said something.'

'He said, "Hello poof",' said Blythe, 'then he hit me in the stomach and began to twist my arm. Then he said, "Keep away from her poof. Her family don't like it." Then he said, "I don't know what you're yelling now for, poof. This is just the warm-up", then you arrived.'

Callan said, 'Keep away from her. Her family don't like it... Who would that be?'

Blythe said at once: 'Sophie.'

'I thought her daughter was in Crete.'

'Her cousin isn't.'

'You think her cousin hired that young tear-away?'

'I'm sure of it,' said Blythe. 'You haven't met him, Callan. I have. He's – quite ruthless. And no-body's fool, believe me. The form of words that young thug used would implicate nobody. That's why Vardakis told him to use them.'

Callan said, 'You were a mug to have him thrown out. You could have called the coppers.'

'Could I?' said Blythe. 'He would probably say I invited him here.' He hesitated. 'It's happened before, you know. When I did.'

Callan said, 'You're up a gum tree then, aren't you?'

'Am I?'

'Well of course you are. You can't go on with this thing.'

Blythe said impatiently, 'Of course I can. Var-dakis won't interfere once we start the operation. Helena's a *relative;* his cousin's child.'

'Dr Blythe, Dr Blythe,' said Callan. 'Your late caller was nothing. An amateur. Once you get over this you'll be mixing with the pros – and they'll really hurt you.'

Blythe said, 'If you don't mind, we'll change the subject... Why are you here?'

'I came,' said Callan, 'to tell you I've changed my mind. Maybe I'll take the job, but it'll cost a bit more than ten thousand pounds.'

'Sophie told me the things you said,' said Blythe. 'Too many people in the know, an utter lack of security. That hasn't changed, Callan. Why have you?'

'I need the money,' said Callan.

'And you didn't two days ago?'

'I didn't think I did,' said Callan. 'I was wrong.'

'You're not trying to tell me that somebody robbed you of your little all?' Callan made no answer, and Blythe tried again. 'Blackmail. Can it be that Callan is being blackmailed? But how terribly brave Callan's blackmailer must be.'

'Not brave,' said Callan. 'Out of reach. I'll take the job for fifteen thousand quid.'

'We can still only offer ten per cent in advance,' said Blythe. 'Even if we do accept your figure.'

Callan shrugged. 'That's all right. He'll wait a week.'

'A week?' Blythe tried to hide the dismay in his voice, and failed dismally.

'The quicker the better,' Callan said. 'For both of us.'

'I'll have to telephone,' said Blythe.

'The Parnassos?'

'That really isn't your business, Callan.'

He moved to the door, and Callan blocked him off.

'When did you get back from Paris?' he asked. Blythe said nothing. 'Believe me, this is important,' Callan said.

'I came back late this afternoon.'

'And your appointments?'

'My receptionist cancelled them. She let it be known that I had a severe cold. Nobody wants a dentist who's liable to sneeze. What is all this?'

'You can't phone the Parnassos,' Calian said. 'It was burnt out on Thursday night.'

'Burnt out?'

121

'Petrol bomb,' said Callan. 'It did a nice, quick job.'

'Oh my God,' said Blythe. 'All those dear people.' His face was agonised.

'Thursday,' said Callan. 'Early closing. The place was empty.' Slowly, the agony died, and was replaced by bewilderment.

'But Sophie can't have known,' he said. 'She didn't tell me–' He stopped, then looked at Callan. 'I still have to phone,' he said. 'Help yourself to another drink.'

Callan let him go. Paris he thought. On a direct line. God knows if it's bugged or not. Since Hunter's involved, it probably is. Ah well, Randy had made so many mistakes one more wouldn't hurt him. He looked around the room. Nice, very nice.

Dark blue velvet curtains, pale blue velvet sofa and chairs, the original stuccoed ceiling lovingly preserved. And everywhere books, big, fat, expensive books. Byron and Sir Arthur Evans and translations of Euripides: lives of Venizelos and histories of the Greek War of Independence: coffee-table stuff with pictures of Delphi, the Parthenon, Epidauros, books on Greek statuary, books on Greek vases. Blythe was nuts on Greece, all right. Callan went back to the record-player, and looked at the record he'd heard when he first came in. *Der Rosenkavalier*', he read. 'Richard Strauss.' He pushed the appropriate button, and the music began again; rich, voluptuous, yearning: in the women's voices a sexuality that came very close to parody. It didn't seem to Callan to have much to do with Greece, but it made good listen-

122

ing. It was still playing when Blythe came back. He said at once, 'Why are you playing that?'

'Does it scare you?' Callan asked, and Blythe nodded. 'It should. That's why I played it.'

'You want me out of this,' said Blythe. 'Why?'

'You've got a lot of guts,' said Callan, 'but you bruise too easily.'

Blythe said, 'I don't suppose I'll like *Der Rosenkavalier* ever again. A pity. It used to be my favourite. I suppose that's because in a way it's homosexual too.'

'You're kidding,' said Callan.

'The contralto,' Blythe said. 'She's supposed to be a boy – a page. The soprano – the marshal's wife – is in love with him. Or her... And what do you like, Callan? Sousa marches?'

'I like what I know,' said Callan. 'So tell me about the phone call.'

'We'll go to fifteen thousand,' said Blythe. 'But you'll have to take the ten per cent in pounds sterling. The rest you can have in any currency you like.'

'Fair enough,' said Callan. 'Do I do it alone?'

Blythe said, 'There'll be a contact in Crete. Otherwise yes.' He hesitated. 'I phoned Paris, you know.'

Callan said, 'I somehow thought you might.'

'That dreary irony again,' said Blythe 'Sophie will come over here and brief you herself tomorrow.'

Callan said, 'Did you ask her about the Parnassos?' Blythe nodded. 'Did she know?' Blythe nodded again. 'Why didn't she tell you?'

'She seems to have taken your remarks about

security to heart.'

'She left it a bit late,' Callan said.

'You still have doubts about the job then?'

'Not if I do it my way,' said Callan. 'And it's the only way I'll do it.'

'I'm sure Sophie will be delighted to hear it.'

Callan looked around the room. 'Let me ask you something,' he said.

'If it's relevant.'

Callan said, 'It's relevant, all right. How did you get into this Greek thing? Boy friend?'

'Certainly not,' said Blythe. 'Greece has always been an ideal to me. Everything about it. They invented democracy; they perfected art. In later times they fought for their liberty in the face of the most appalling persecution. Against the Turks, and against Hitler, too. And the struggle still goes on... I love their food, their wine, their language, their way of life. It is true that in classical times their sexual habits were very close to my own, but that has nothing to do with it. Nothing at all... I have always loved Greece. I always will.'

The speech came out like a set-piece, and it probably was: an amalgam of stuff he'd done at lectures (The Literary Society are lucky enough to have with us tonight that well-known Hellenophile) and the kind of parties the Groper went to. But it was sincere for all that, Callan thought. He meant every word, or thought he did. Even the bit about sexual habits.

'So that's why you don't mind getting hurt,' he said.

'I mind very much,' said Blythe. 'I should mind even more being killed. But I would take that risk

124

if it were asked of me. We all have to die at some time, Callan. It would make more sense if one died for a purpose.'

And there he goes again, thought Callan. Putting me down.

'Have another?' Blythe asked.

'No thanks,' said Callan. 'I better be off.'

Blythe poured one for himself.

'Two things,' Callan said. 'First – you don't ask me how I got into the house.'

'I assumed that our friend hadn't closed the door properly.'

'Wrong,' said Callan. 'I came in through the back window.'

'May I ask why?'

'Because I didn't want anybody to see me.' He watched as Blythe gulped at his drink. 'You'd better lock up properly after I've gone.'

'And the other thing?'

'When do I see Sophie Kollonaki?'

'Kensington Mansions,' said Blythe. 'Number forty-four. Any time after two o'clock.'

'What name?'

'Her own of course,' said Blythe, and drank again.

Callan left him, and marvelled. No matter how often he thought he'd got used to the feller, Blythe could always produce one more surprise.

10

'And that's about it, sir,' said Kyle.

The inspector said, 'You have been busy, haven't you?' Kyle waited. This could be the old boy's idea of a reprimand, or it could be a joke.

'I like it,' the inspector said, and then added: 'Got you down, didn't it?'

'Sir?'

'Losing chummy like that. It bothered you. Well, so it should have. But you did do something about it, and that's what I like.' He looked again at the laboriously typed report. 'Two names to look for, and the smelly one's address. We've got a good chance on this one. You've done well.'

'Detective Sergeant Walters showed me how to go on, sir,' said Kyle.

'I'll thank him too,' said the inspector, 'but at least you did what he told you.' He gathered up the sheets of the report.

'All right, Kyle,' he said. 'I'll pass this on to C.I.D.'

But Kyle still lingered.

'Sir—' he said.

'Well?' the inspector said. 'Going to be greedy are you? Want to be in on the kill?'

'I'd like to, sir,' said Kyle. 'If it's possible.'

'See what I can do,' said the inspector. 'Now you get back on duty.'

Good boy, he thought. Used his initiative. And

126

didn't mind giving up his free time to see a thing through. Stubborn, too. Ought to do well if he stuck at it... He picked up the report and walked along the corridor. Bert was usually about at that time in the evening. The big stuff wouldn't start for an hour at least. He knocked on the door and went in. Detective Inspector Mather glared, then relaxed.

'Oh it's you,' he said. 'Come in, Harry. What can I do for you?'

The inspector put the report on his desk. 'Take a look at that,' he said.

Mather leafed through it quickly.

'Young Kyle.' he said. 'Walters told me what he was up to. He's done all right.' He let the papers drop, and the inspector knew at once that something was wrong.

'You'll put out an "all stations", won't you?' he said.

'We'll see, Harry... We'll see.'

'What d'you mean, we'll see?' the inspector said. 'Do you want Kyle to pick chummy up himself?'

'No,' Mather said. 'I don't.'

'For God's sake, man. You're not trying to tell me you're jealous because Kyle acted on his own?'

'No,' Mather said, 'I'm not. He's done well and I admit it. The thing is, Harry, this Lonely mightn't be the one that did it.'

'I know that. Kyle knows it too. He says so in his report. But even if he's innocent, this Lonely probably saw who did it.'

'I know,' said Mather. 'I know.'

'This is arson, Bert. On your patch. Are you

saying you're going to do nothing about it?'

Again Bert Mather glared, and fought for control.

'I'm saying I've been told,' said Mather.

'Told what, for God's sake?'

'To lay off.'

'But who on earth could do that to you?'

'Save your breath, Harry,' said Mather. 'I've also been told to keep my mouth shut.'

But Harry didn't save his breath. Never could, never would. Argue and argue, that was Harry, and who could blame him when it was one of his own lads? All the same, Mather was glad when he went. He waited till the door shut and picked up the telephone.

'Get me Special Branch,' he said, and waited, and went through channels, and finally got through.

Detective Superintendent Murdoch said, 'Of course it's embarrassing. I'm embarrassed, you're embarrassed, we're all embarrassed.'

'But Constable Kyle found out who it is, sir,' Mather said. 'Little tea-leaf known as Lonely—'

Murdoch said, 'I know who it is.'

'We're talking about arson,' said Mather. 'On my patch.'

'That makes it worse, I suppose.'

'It does to me, sir. And now we've got a lead.'

'Lonely didn't do it,' said Murdoch.

'He might have seen who did. I'm not saying we should arrest him—'

'Good,' said Murdoch, 'because you're not going to.'

'Look, sir,' said Mather, 'I've just had Kyle's

inspector in. He's hopping mad.'

'Very right and proper,' said Murdoch. 'So long as he doesn't do anything, and you don't, and Constable Kyle doesn't. Lay off, inspector.'

'I'll want that in writing, sir.'

'You'll get it,' Murdoch hung up, and scowled at the telephone. He hated the telephone, hated what he'd just said, hated his job. But he'd done it. Chain of command, he thought. Kyle goes to his inspector, and he goes to Mather, and Mather comes to me. And now it's my turn. He picked up another phone, and dialled the number that he'd had to memorise the first day on this job.

'Yes?' the woman's voice said.

'Let me speak to Charlie please,' he said. 'This is Murdoch.'

'Charlie isn't available at the moment. Can I take a message?'

'Yes,' said Murdoch. 'Tell him I did what he asked.'

'Callan beat Bradley, you say,' said Hunter.

'Quite efficiently,' said Meres. 'He's in rather a mess.'

'Yes,' said Hunter. 'He would be if Callan beat him. He had quite a lot of venom to work off. Did Bradley get a good look at him?'

'No, sir,' said Meres. 'He kept on talking about a bunch of masked tearaways. It took him quite some time to admit to one man with a scarf over his face.'

'Has he any idea what Callan looks like?'

'I doubt it, sir. Pain does rather distort one's faculties. I get the impression of a sort of giant.'

'Spencer Percival Fitzmaurice.' Hunter paused. 'How did Bradley escape?'

'He didn't, sir. Callan let him go. Rather careless, wouldn't you say?'

'Careless?' Hunter considered the word. 'I wonder, Toby. I wonder.'

Lonely was so glad to see him back he got up first and made the breakfast. And that suited Callan fine. Regular little marvel with the frying pan was Lonely. He soaked in the bath and looked at his bruises. They'd turned brown now, not so puffy, but still with a lot of sting left in them. Noticeable too. When he went to Crete he wouldn't be doing any sun-bathing. Callan let some water out of the bath then turned on the hot tap again. It was the only thing that eased the bloody sting. Outside he could hear Lonely yelling.

'Come in,' he yelled back. 'I can't hear a blind word you're saying.'

Lonely came into the bathroom reluctantly, embarrassed as always in the presence of nakedness.

'Mr Callan,' he said. 'I can't find the bread.'

'Second shelf in the larder,' said Callan, then looked up. Lonely was staring at him, horrified.

'Now don't start, for God's sake,' said Callan. 'This is a bloody bathroom.'

'Oh my Gawd,' said Lonely. 'Mr Callan – what happened?'

'I got duffed,' said Callan.

'*You?*' The incredulity in the little man's voice should have been balm, but the ache went on just the same.

'It's possible,' said Callan. 'Believe me.'

'Yeah,' said Lonely. 'I can see it is... Was it last night?'

'Don't be daft,' said Callan. 'Last night I went to the dentist. I told you. This was Thursday.'

'And you come over and fetched me here after that?' said Lonely. 'You're a good mate, Mr Callan.'

Eggs and bacon and fried bread, then toast and marmalade and about a gallon of tea. Lonely really knew about breakfasts. He knew all about eating them too, thought Callan, watching him butter his fourth slice of toast.

Very gently he said, 'Now don't get excited. I just want to ask you something.' Lonely spread marmalade on the butter, making a slab an inch thick. 'This feller who drove the Capri – how bald was he?'

'Bald as he could be,' said Lonely. 'Head like an ostrich egg.'

'And the young bloke with him,' said Callan. 'Black-haired, you said, pale-looking?'

'No I never,' said Lonely. 'He was blondy – and he had a sun tan.' He stopped chewing. 'Them what duffed you,' he said. 'It doesn't have nothing to do with the petrol bomb, does it?'

Callan was grateful for the thought that it took more than one, but even so, he lied.

'Of course not,' he said. 'I told you. This was before.'

'Who done it then?'

'Old grudge,' said Callan. 'Nothing to do with you.'... And he'd make sure that wasn't a lie.

Lonely said uneasily, 'Are you going to do anything about it?'

131

'I might,' said Callan. 'If I ever get the chance – and it's the right chance. But don't you worry, old son. You won't be there when it happens.'

So that kept him quiet until lunch time, but when Callan told him he was going out after lunch, the uproar started all over again. Something would have to be done about Baldy and Laughing Boy, thought Callan. The noise was getting him down.

Another wide street, and again tree-lined. Nice view too: Royal Gardens, Royal Palace, and a copper on the gate who gave him the beady eye as he went through... Callan walked past the great houses, every single one of them conversion jobs now, except the embassies and consulates. Number 44 was one of the biggest of the lot, with a kind of obliging feller in the hall with a smile on his face and a gun under his armpit who was only too happy to ring up and make sure that Mrs Kollonaki really was expecting Mr Callan. And when he found out Callan was expected, you'd have thought it was his birthday he was so happy.

'Straight up to the second floor, Mr Callan,' he said. 'You'll be met.' He was too, by another butler, a short, stocky one this time, in a white mess jacket. Callan looked at his hands. They'd done rather more, he thought, than polish silver...

It seemed she had a whole floor. Not quite so good as Paris perhaps, but if you only visited a place two or three times a year you had to be prepared to rough it a little. Callan followed the butler down a maze of corridors. Everywhere he looked there were pictures. Most of them looked old, and all of them looked expensive. The butler reached a door at last, tapped on it softly, and went in.

'Mr Callan,' he said. His voice was accented, low-pitched, a little hoarse. Not exactly a butler's voice, thought Callan, but dead on for a fighter's. He went in, and the butler shut the door behind him.

This time she wore white, and it should have been murder for a woman of her age, but it wasn't. Nothing could be. She made no move to shake hands.

'I thought I'd never see you again,' she said.

'Me, too,' said Callan. 'Life's full of surprises.'

'Can I offer you something? Coffee? A drink?'

'No thanks,' said Callan.

'You wish to be businesslike? Very well.' She tossed an envelope to him. 'Fifteen hundred pounds. Count it please.'

Callan opened and counted. One hundred tenners and one hundred fivers, and all used notes. Nice touch.

'Just right,' he said.

'How would you like the rest of it?'

'Swiss francs,' said Callan. 'In a Swiss bank.'

'Very well. Now let me tell you how you will earn it.' Callan waited. For once her fluency had left her. She seemed to have trouble getting started.

At last she said, 'My daughter is in a village called Kronis. My father's farm is there. She looks after it – but she's not allowed to live there. She boards with a family called Polybios, who are great friends of the Colonels. My cousin pays for her board – far, far more than they deserve. You

133

will not contact any of the Polybios family.'

'I've got to make contact with somebody,' said Callan.

'Of course.' She became impatient, and with that her fluency returned. 'You will talk with a man called Dimitri. He works for Polybios.'

'Your cousin paying him too?'

'Dimitri neither seeks nor expects money,' she said. 'He is one of us.' She scowled at Callan. A few hundred years ago, he thought, she'd have had me beheaded.

'You will devise a way to get my daughter out of Polyhios's house' – just like that, thought Callan – 'and Dimitri will tell you where there is a motor-boat waiting. You will then go to Izmir, in Turkey.'

'Does she have a passport?' Callan asked.

'She does. I will give you an address you must go to in Izmir. Once you have delivered her there, your work is finished. Do you have a gun?'

Callan lied, frankly and openly.

'No,' he said.

'A gun will be provided also.'

'I'm not taking any guns into Crete,' said Callan.

Again the impatience. 'A gun will be provided in Crete,' she said. 'Have you any questions?'

Only a million, thought Callan. This thing's so chancy it's hysterical. 'Not yet,' he said, 'but I would like to see a photograph of your daughter again.'

'I have some here.'

He took them. Studio portraits, profile and full face. That made things easier.

'Here are the addresses,' she said. 'You will memorise them, then burn them. In front of me.'

Callan took the sheet of paper and concentrated. Three minutes later the addresses were ash in an ash-tray.

'Now give me back the photographs,' she said.

Callan said firmly, 'Tomorrow. I've got to get to know this face really well.'

'Tomorrow then,' she said. 'But you will bring them to me yourself.' She rose. 'I think our business is finished.'

'Not quite,' said Callan. 'There's the money.'

'I have told you will be paid.'

'And I believe you. I'm just going to tell you how. A cheque dated two weeks from now, in any Swiss bank you choose. When they tell me it's in, I'll leave.'

'Very well.' Again she waited for him to go, but Callan made no move.

'Now it's question time,' he said. 'How strong is the Polybios house?'

'It is old,' she said. 'In the old days they built houses like fortresses. It is strong.'

'Good locks?'

'Now they will be the best,' she said.

'Another question,' said Callan. 'Why the gun?'

'Surely that is obvious,' she said. 'There may well be opposition.'

'And if there is I'm to kill it?' She said nothing. 'Whatever happens, Mme Kollonaki,' said Callan, 'I'll handle it my way.' Again no answer. 'Just one more question, then I'll go.' That didn't exactly break her heart.

'Very well,' she said.

135

'Why me?' said Callan. 'Why not leave it all to Dimitri? Surely he's got friends.'

She hesitated. 'He has already offered to do this,' she said at last. 'I would not allow it. The risk would be too great. Besides he is of more use to me where he is.'

'I'm expendable, he's not?'

'A computer in Moscow told me you could do this,' she said, 'and I believe it. Also – I think you are forgetting the fifteen thousand pounds.'

'Looks to me like I'm going to earn them,' said Callan. 'Especially if they have petrol bombs in Crete.'

She flinched then.

'That will be taken care of,' she said, 'but it is no concern of yours. Your business is to get my daughter back – and nothing more.'

This time he left. Amateurs, he thought. All the same. Dead keen for you to hurt somebody, but as soon as they got hurt themselves they start yelling. Well he'd yelled too when Fitzmaurice got his hands on him, but he'd long ago relinquished thoughts of revenge. It only made you more vulnerable... Callan turned a corner, and found he was facing the butler.

'If you please, sir,' the butler said, 'Mr Vardakis would like to speak to you.'

They sounded like words he'd memorised: they also sounded like a command.

'O.K.,' said Callan. 'After you.'

The butler led off, but he didn't like having Callan behind him. That made him vulnerable too. When they reached the appropriate door, his face had lost some of its impassivity. He knocked

136

and went in, and Callan followed slowly. The door was interesting. Mahogany, of course, and expensive, but two layers of mahogany, and sheet steel in the middle of the sandwich. And then the lock – a Manton, and triple action. There were no better locks made. Callan had once been apprenticed to a locksmith, and he knew. He went into the room, and the man behind the desk rose, then looked at the butler. Callan looked too. He was poised like a fighter.

'All right, Theo, you can go,' he said. 'Come and sit down, Mr Callan.'

The butler left, and Callan sat down: a low chair, too low, so that he found himself looking up at Vardakis. Ah well, it was what the other man had intended. Big shoulders, Vardakis had, and a barrel chest, but he wasn't a tall man. Callan doubted if he were as tall as his cousin Sophie. Looking down on people must be a treat for him.

'Can I offer you something?' Vardakis asked. 'Coffee, a drink?'

So hospitality runs in the family, thought Callan. 'No thanks,' he said.

'You are surprised to see me here?'

'Not particularly,' said Callan. 'I had a feeling the place belonged to you.'

'Sophie has told you about me?'

'A little.'

'I owe her a great deal,' Vardakis said. 'Far more than she will let me pay. But I can look after her, protect her. And I do.' Callan said nothing. 'I will not allow her to be hurt, Mr Callan.' Again no answer. Vardakis sighed.

'Mr Callan,' he said, 'the whole point of a

dialogue is that two people participate. I did not invite you here to listen to a speech from me.'

Callan looked around the room. More pictures: the most expensive yet by the look of them, and probably a safe behind one, and an alarm that would go off as soon as you touched the frame. And the rest all functional: work table, desk, angle-light: the only luxury the chair he sat in and that was too low. Maybe there was symbolism in that.

'Mr Callan,' said Vardakis, 'it is now your turn to speak.'

'You seem to think,' said Callan, 'that I want to play your rules.'

'You will explain that, please.'

The request that came out like a command: it was obvious who'd taught Theo what to say.

'You know very well,' said Callan. 'If I talk you'll ask questions and if I answer them there'll be more questions, and before we know where you are you'll have a nice little interrogation going.'

Vardakis gave a great bull bellow of laughter that held no amusement at all. 'Interrogation?' he said. 'I haven't done that for years. But when I did, it was not in places like this.' Callan stayed silent.

'I take it you are afraid that I will ask what you discussed with my cousin. You are wrong. I *know* what you discussed with my cousin.'

'I know that,' said Callan.

'I find that hard to believe.'

'"Can I offer you something?"' Callan quoted. '"Coffee? A drink?" Her very words, Mr Vardakis. You slipped up there.'

Vardakis flushed. 'I do not wish to spy on her,' he said, 'but she must be protected. I have no

138

choice.' He waited. 'You do not wish to make a moral judgment?'

'No.'

'That is something to be grateful for.' He struck his hand on the desk. 'So. You are going to Crete to rescue Helena – and all you ask in return is a Swiss bank account. When you get to Crete you will be given a gun – and the suggestion is that you will use it.'

'Her suggestion,' said Callan.

Vardakis shrugged. 'There is one inescapable fact about guns,' he said. 'They go off. Particularly when they are in the hands of a man like you.' Again he waited. 'This silence of yours is childish,' he said, and waited once more. The flush came again. 'I could have you stopped,' he said at last. 'Even better, I could have you arrested when you reach Crete. Are you familiar with our prisons, Mr Callan?'

'Did you have your cousin bugged in Paris, too?' said Callan. 'Because if you did you heard her say that this is the one enterprise of hers you wouldn't dream of hindering, because Helena Kollonaki is family, Mr Vardakis, and you're a great one for family.' This time it was Callan's turn to wait. 'Are you telling me your cousin's lying?' Callan asked.

'I should beat you for that,' said Vardakis, 'or have you beaten.'

'Keep the butler for the rough work, do you?' Callan asked.

'We all get old,' said Vardakis. 'Although perhaps "all" is an overstatement. In your own case for example.'

'All right, you're a hard man,' Callan said. 'You

can have me taken care of. All right. But you haven't answered the question. Is your cousin lying, or did you lie to her?'

'Neither,' said Vardakis. 'I should like Helena to be here – if it were possible.'

'Then why pick on me?' said Callan. 'That's what I'm here for.'

'Because I don't trust you.'

'Then find somebody else.'

'You are being absurd,' said Vardakis. 'You are the one Sophie picked: the one the K.G.B. recommended.'

'Is that what bothers you?'

'No,' said Vardakis. 'I know you never belonged to the K.G.B. What bothers me is something I understand very well. Money.'

'You know the arrangement. If I fail, I don't get paid – apart from my ten per cent.'

'I said Helena should be set free, if it were possible. Unfortunately it is not,' said Vardakis. 'That is why I think ten per cent is too low a price for failure.'

'How high would you estimate failure, Mr Vardakis?'

Vardakis said, 'Fifty thousand pounds. If it were seen that you had tried – really tried – and failed, I think fifty thousand pounds would cover it.'

'And how could it be seen that I had really tried?'

'If someone were killed, for example.'

'Polybios?'

'No. Not Polybios... Dimitri would be better. Even the memory of Dimitri upsets my cousin.'

Callan said, 'Let's hope your cousin isn't bug-

140

ging you.'

'I have made absolutely sure that she is not,' Vardakis said. He was quite serious.

'Just how do you square all this with your family feelings?' said Callan.

'Quite simply. If you fail, Sophie's political aspirations fail also. In a year or two, somebody else will take her place – and Sophie is not the one to take a second rôle. When that happens – I have friends in Athens. Important friends. Helena's release can be arranged.'

'So why not just pay me not to go?'

'She would send somebody else,' said Vardakis. 'But if you try and fail – she will give up, Mr Callan. She must. You are the best. Well, Mr Callan? Five thousand now – and forty-five thousand when you fail?'

'You're on,' said Callan.

'I have it here,' said Vardakis. 'Three thousand five hundred pounds in Swiss francs. The rest will be paid into a Swiss bank – just as you arranged with my cousin.'

'Three thousand five hundred?'

'My cousin has already given you fifteen hundred.'

'And I'm keeping it,' said Callan. 'And five thousand from you. It's your murder, Mr Vardakis. You pay for it.'

Vardarkis sat like a stone man, then reached into a drawer and handed over an envelope.

'Right,' said Callan. 'I'll wait for confirmation for the rest, then I'll go to Crete and fail.'

'Be sure you do,' Vardakis said.

'You can rely on me,' said Callan.

'I can do better than that,' said Vardakis. 'If you try to cheat me I can destroy you.'

Outside the butler was waiting, and this time he didn't look so worried as he walked ahead. They probably had some sort of signal arranged, Callan thought. If Callan turns nasty come in and duff him, and bring a couple of footmen to hold him while you do it... He went down in the lift and past the security man, who smiled and wished him goodbye. Over an hour among all that money: no wonder he rated a smile. You don't know the half of it, friend, thought Callan, and got into his car. The next problem, he supposed, was Lonely, but he was wrong. He drove as always, wary of tails, but if the opposition have the time and money to spare, enough cars, enough men, they can always hang on to you no matter how good you are. All you could do was be careful, and follow the drill, and that Callan did. There was one souped up mini he didn't much like the look of, but he lost it on the Bayswater Road, then used the back doubles till he felt easier again. Park in the side road, he thought, then have a chat with Lonely. Time I had a word with him anyway.

He had left the car and was walking down the road when he heard it: the metallic clink of metal on stone. The high crack of the gun sounded when he was already on his way to the ground, rolling over and over to the shelter of a lamp-post; the only shelter there was. Callan huddled and peered and couldn't see a bloody thing, then again the sharp, high crack sounded, a bullet chipped into the wall behind him, and ricocheted screaming.

Callan huddled closer into the lamp-post, and knew it was a waste of time. He hadn't a hope in hell. A minute, two, and nothing happened. Callan watched the sweep hand of his watch make one more revolution, then very cautiously moved up into a crouch. Still nothing. He counted ten then stood up: his whole body seemed to be vibrating, wincing at the thought of the bullet's impact. Callan moved back, and looked at the mark the bullets had made, one only inches to his right, the other a great gash in the brick wall just above his head. The bastard could shoot all right. He went back to the car. Lonely would have to wait; it was time to call on Hunter... As soon as his hands stopped shaking.

'Shot at you?' said Hunter.

'Twice,' said Callan. 'My guess is it was a rifle. It was too bloody accurate for a pistol.'

'You think it was some kind of warning then?'

'Yeah,' said Callan. 'I do.' He thought for a minute then said, 'I suppose this does come as a surprise to you?'

'My dear Callan, what must you think of me? Of course it's a surprise.' He looked at Callan's face. 'You're thinking of Fitzmaurice? But then you had broken the rules. This time you haven't, so far as I know. And in any case, why should I encourage anyone to shoot at you?'

'Not at me,' said Callan. 'Past me. They wouldn't have hit me unless you said so.'

Hunter affected bewilderment. 'Who wouldn't?' he said. 'Meres perhaps? My dear Callan, I assure you–'

'No,' said Callan. 'Not Meres. More like a young, blond fellow with a sun-tan. He's got a bald-headed mate who's a possible, but I think he just drives cars.'

'How would I get to know such people?'

'You know me,' said Callan.

'A fair young man and a bald one,' Hunter said.

'That's right,' said Callan. 'They threw a petrol bomb into the Parnassos. The blond geezer's a bit more versatile than that, though. He was beating up Blythe when I went to see him.'

'You didn't report that,' Hunter said.

'I thought you already knew. Come off it, Hunter. Get there just after nine you said. And the beating up started at nine sharp.'

Hunter gave up. 'You hurt the young man quite severely, I understand,' he said. 'I hope Blythe was grateful?'

'Yeah,' said Callan. 'He took me back. The return of the prodigal. Fifteen thousand quid.'

'Then it did help,' said Hunter. 'I'm glad.'

'Suppose he'd beaten me?' Callan asked.

'I considered the contingency unlikely,' said Hunter. 'But if he had you would have been of no further use to us.'

'I'm glad I passed the test,' said Callan, then: 'Hunter – why are you doing this?'

'Ah,' said Hunter, 'we're back to "why" are we? You know that's not allowed. There are reasons, Callan. Accept them.'

'And accept being shot at?'

'That will be investigated. I have no reason – at the moment – to hold the blond young man responsible. Tell me about Sophie Kollanaki.'

Callan told him. When he had finished Hunter said, 'Dear me. She does want rather a lot for fifteen thousand pounds.'

'Oh I can do better than that,' Callan said, and told him about Vardakis's offer. For once Hunter looked surprised. Callan enjoyed that.

'And you are to kill this er – Dimitri?'

'That's what he said. That'll prove I tried.'

'For an amateur he does rather go to extremes,' said Hunter. 'Which offer will you accept?'

'Yours,' said Callan. 'I don't like being in a Red File. And I won't kill for money.'

'For once you're being sensible. Did Sophie discuss a modus operandi?'

Callan said, '"Just go," she said. "Contact Dimitri. Get the girl. Take a motor-boat to Izmir. Just like that."'

'You have an alternative suggestion, I hope?'

'Yeah,' said Callan. He explained it, and Hunter listened in absorbed silence, then stayed silent till after Callan had finished.

At last he said, 'Excellent. I'll get it in hand.' He reached out to the intercom.

'There's just one more thing,' Callan said.

Hunter thought for a minute. 'Your odoriferous little friend?'

'That's right,' said Callan. 'Lonely.'

'You really want him with you on this jaunt?'

'Of course I don't,' said Callan. 'But what choice have I got? If I leave him here he'll get nicked for arson.'

'I should use my best efforts to prevent that.'

'Maybe you would,' said Callan. 'But I've got no guarantees you'd succeed, have I?'

145

'A guarantee is out of the question,' said Hunter. 'Not without blowing your cover, and that I will not do.'

'There you are then,' Callan said. 'Besides, I might need him.'

'How could you possibly–'

'The locks in the Polybios house are the best there are, according to Sophie Kollonaki. Lonely'll earn his keep.'

'Very well,' said Hunter. 'I'll sanction it.'

Callan rose. 'I'd better be off then,' he said. 'You'll let me know when it's ready?'

'Of course,' said Hunter. 'But how in the world will you persuade that deplorable little man to go to Crete?'

11

Lonely had made steak and kidney pudding that night, and apple tart and custard to follow. Callan was loud in its praise, and Lonely smiled.

'Ta, Mr Callan,' he said. 'The only thing is going to the shops. Puts the wind up me that does. And for a steak and kidney pudding you got to have everything fresh.'

'Ah,' said Callan. 'I've been thinking about that.'

'You mean like use frozen suet, Mr Callan?'

Firmly Callan reminded himself that with Lonely one must go calmly and gently. 'No,' he said. 'Not quite like that.'

'Cos I couldn't,' said Lonely. 'Really I couldn't.

Especially when I'm cooking for you. I mean it's not as if I know whether you can even *get* frozen suet. I never seen it on the telly.'

'Why don't you–' Callan began, and found that he was yelling. Calmly, he told himself, gently.

'Why don't you get yourself a beer out of the fridge?'

'Oh – ta, Mr Callan,' said Lonely, and went to the kitchen. Callan poured himself a Scotch. For Gawd's sake tell him quickly, he told himself, before he tells me how his grandma stole her recipes from Mrs Beeton. Lonely came back with his beer.

'Cheers, Mr Callan,' he said.

'Cheers. Now what I'm on about, old son–'

'You can get them ready made,' Lonely said. 'Just put them in the oven and warm them up. But they don't taste the same.'

'Will you for Gawd's sake belt up about your bloody puddings?' said Callan, and thought, Oh my God. Now I've hurt his feelings. 'Sorry,' he said. 'Forget I said that. I've had a lot on my mind recently.'

'That's all right, Mr Callan,' Lonely said. 'And you got duffed an' all. Bad for the nerves, that is.'

'I thought you were looking a bit peaky, too,' said Callan.

'That's the arson,' said Lonely. 'Makes it worse when you're innocent.'

Later, thought Callan. I'll work that one out later.

'Need a holiday,' he said. 'The pair of us.'

'A holiday?'

'Yeah,' said Callan. 'Sunshine, sea breezes, good

food. Nothing to do but relax. Do us a power of good.'

'But, Mr Callan,' said Lonely, not without pride, 'I'm a wanted man.'

'Yes, but you're wanted here, aren't you? I'm saying we should go somewhere else where you're not wanted.'

'They'd nick me in Margate or Brighton just the same.'

Gently, Callan told himself, calmly. 'How about somewhere further away?' he asked.

Lonely thought hard. 'Scotland?' he said. 'You won't get much sun up there.'

'Abroad,' said Callan. 'I'm saying we should go abroad.'

'Out of England?' Lonely was horrified.

Calmly, Callan; gently. 'That's right,' said Callan. 'Out of England. Away from all those nasty rozzers. After all, you suggested it yourself.'

'Maybe I did,' said Lonely, 'but I didn't mean it.'

'I've been to a travel agency,' said Callan. 'This looked like a good place.' He threw some folders on the table, and Lonely picked them up.

'Crete?' he said. 'But isn't that like Greece?'

'Sunshine,' said Callan. 'Sea breezes. Good food–'

'You're wrong there, Mr Callan,' Lonely said. 'I had Greek food in that Parnassos place. 'orrible it was. If you ask me it was a customer burned it down.

'They have special food for tourists,' said Callan. 'It says so in the brochure.'

Lonely looked, and relented. 'So it does,' he

said. 'Some of them birds aren't bad either.' He looked again. Suddenly it was all off.

'A hundred and fifty quid for two weeks,' he said. 'I haven't got no hundred and fifty quid for no fortnight's holiday.'

'I have,' said Callan. 'I'll treat you.'

Lonely looked at him, awed by such largesse.

'You're going to pay for me holiday?'

'That's right,' Callan said.

'You *are* a good mate, Mr Callan,' said Lonely.

Now don't you start feeling rotten, Callan told himself. You're in a red file, mate.

Kyle's mum said, 'I don't know what's the matter with you. I really don't. Has my cooking gone off, or something?'

Kyle looked at the Irish stew she'd made: just about perfect.

'No, mum,' he said.

'Then eat it.'

'I'm not hungry,' he said. She looked at him fiercely, then softened.

'Your dad was just the same,' she said. 'A worrier. What is it? That smelly feller?'

'They've dropped it,' said Kyle. 'Nobody's bothered.'

'Then why should you be bothered then?'

'It was me that saw him,' said Kyle. 'And lost him.'

'Proud,' she said. 'And stubborn too. Just like your dad ... Scotsmen.' But there was no scorn in her voice, only a pride of her own.

'You'll have to find him on your own,' she said. 'Or would that get you into trouble?'

'I don't see how it could,' said Kyle. 'Not if I brought him in. But where would I start looking?'

'I thought you said he'd got relatives?'

'Thousands of them,' said Kyle. 'And all bent. It could take years.'

'You got anything better to do?... You think about it.'

Kyle thought, then pulled his plate towards him, picked up his fork. 'No, mum,' he said, 'I haven't.'

He hadn't seen Beasley for years, and that was fine. He hated Beasley. Hated his greasy crawling, his total dishonesty, his contempt for every living male. Not that you could blame him for that: Beasley was in the porn business... But hate him or not, he had to see him. For what he wanted, Beasley was the best... Out in Kensington now, the flash part: big studio with a flat to go with it. And parties, no doubt, and a few drags on a ciggy laced with Acapulco gold, just to get things started. It looked as if Beasley was big time now; too big to do poor old Callan a favour, but Callan doubted it. Beasley had always been terrified of Callan, and whatever else about him had changed, Callan was sure that hadn't. He looked at the name-plate: black wood, white, Gothic script: Drysdale Beasley, then underneath, in smaller lettering, 'By appointment only'. Ah well. Rules were made to be broken. Callan rang the bell.

It was opened at last by a blonde in a kaftan: nice blonde, young, pretty: nice kaftan, expensive, new, but both blonde and kaftan were just a little bit dirty.

'You're terribly late,' she said, then stopped.

'Beasley, please,' said Callan.

'I take it you can read,' said the blonde.

'Without even moving my lips,' said Callan.

'Then read that,' she said, and pointed to the notice, 'then piss off.'

She started to slam the door, but Callan's arm moved faster, holding it back.

'He'll see me,' said Callan. 'You better believe that, darling.'

'I'm warning you,' she said, 'we've got protection.'

'Go on the way you're going and you won't need it,' Callan said, and leaned on the door. 'The name is Callan.' She opened her mouth to yell. 'Do that and I'll belt you.' Her mouth closed. 'Now you just lead the way.'

She hesitated. Ordinary feller, ordinary voice, not even particularly big. It was the eyes, she thought. Flat, expressionless. They told you nothing. They never would, no matter what he was doing to you.

'You're sure he wants to see you?' she said.

'We're old chums,' said Callan, and stepped inside. 'After you.'

Nice corridor, real parquet flooring, and the blonde's heels clattered as she walked. Callan made no sound. Up to a big door of heavy wood, and she tapped once, gently. Callan reached across her and hit it with his flat hand. It boomed like a drum. He looked at the blonde: suddenly she looked happier. Could it be that there was a surprise for him?

He moved back slightly, his weight evenly balanced, his hands open at his sides. Anyone, he

151

thought, anyone at all, except Spencer Percival Fitzmaurice, then the door opened, and he saw the opposition, big and beautiful, and clad in black leather that must have cost more than Lonely's holiday.

'He pushed his way in, Larry,' said the blonde, 'Said he has to see Dry.'

Larry looked pleased. The big hands clenched, the muscles rippled beneath the leather.

'I think you need a lesson, friend,' he said.

Callan kicked him in the stomach, the terrible karate kick with the edge of the foot that slices like a blade. Larry retched, and fell on his knees.

'I think I've had one,' said Callan, and waited. But Larry had no more to say: it was the blonde who leaped at him, finger nails like talons, her voice screaming out a steady stream of filth. Callan ducked under the finger nails, then slapped her open-handed. She stumbled into Larry and fell, and Callan pushed open the door.

It was party time, all right. Champagne and Scotch, and pot by the smell of it, and probably speed and LSD as well, for the ones who were feeling bashful. Not that any of them looked it. Birds with whips and fellers with whips, and a bloke tied to a cross and two birds working on him, and Beasley in what looked like a monk's habit, busy among the strobe lights, clicking away. Even the blonde's screams hadn't bothered them. Why should they? Callan thought. Some of them were doing quite a bit of screaming themselves, especially the bloke on the cross.

'I'm sorry to break in on you like this,' Callan said, and suddenly the whole sickening tableau

152

stilled. It was like seeing some monstrous engine running down. Beasley turned, and the tassels of his habit slapped into the girl nearest him. She gasped, and a red mark glowed on her naked thigh. Weighted with metal, Callan thought. You really are a lovely person.

'Hi, Dry,' he said.

'Why it's Mr Callan,' Beasley said. 'Don't tell me you've come to join in our frolics?'

'Nice of you, Dry,' Callan said. 'But I've just had frolics of my own.'

The blonde pushed past him.

'He kicked Larry,' she said. 'In the stomach.'

'Oh my God,' said Beasley. 'Don't tell me he's bruised.'

He came up to the door, tassels swinging and looked down on Larry, now kneeling on the floor and groaning. He bent and tugged at a zipper and the leather split. Larry was bruised all right. Beasley looked across at the blonde: her face red where Callan had slapped it.

'I wish you wouldn't damage them,' he said. 'They're expensive.' His hand moved to the cord at his waist, the tassels swung.

'Try it,' said Callan, 'and I'll damage you.' The hands dropped.

'What do you want?' Beasley said.

Callan hauled Larry into the studio, then shut and locked the door on the scene inside. Already someone was giggling.

'Your best work,' he said.

'That? I've retired,' said Beasley. 'There's lots more money in porn.'

'You're making a come-back,' said Callan.

'If you go now I won't have you punished,' Beasley said. 'If not—'

'Look at me, Dry.' Slowly, reluctantly, Beasley looked at him. Callan waited, and the fear came.

'Got a firm minding you, have you?' Beasley nodded. 'Do you know what would happen if you set them on me?'

Beasley made one more try. 'Don't tell me you'd kill them?'

'Just that,' said Callan. 'Them and you. Do you believe me, Dry?'

'I believe you. But one day—'

'Now now,' said Callan. 'Let's be nice. You do me a favour, and I won't say anything about your jolly fun in there. How's that?'

'What do you want done?' said Beasley.

'A passport,' said Callan. 'And quick.' Beasley opened his mouth. 'And don't try to tell me you haven't got any or I'll wrap that tassel round you.'

'Do you have a photograph?' Callan showed him.

'Yes,' said Beasley. 'It'll do. All right, leave it here and—'

'You're not listening, Dry,' said Callan. 'I said quick. Like now.'

Inevitably Beasley began to protest, and equally inevitably, the protest lacked conviction.

'You'll have to pay for it,' he said at last.

'Of course I will,' said Callan. 'Think I'm a crook? We can't have you losing money, can we? Going rate, Dry. Fifty quid.'

'Fifty quid?'

'You'd better hurry up,' Callan said, 'or the frolickers'll catch cold.'

It took an hour, and it was a beautiful job. Callan handed over the fifty. 'There you are, Dry,' he said. 'Cash on the nail. I bet you don't get many customers like me.'

'My God no,' said Beasley.

Next stop was the Vardakis house, to return the photographs, and collect another big smile from the security man. If she was pleased to see him she managed to hide it, but she was glad to get the photographs back.

'You think you will know my daughter?'

'I'll know her,' said Callan.

'And Dimitri? You know where to reach him?' Callan nodded. 'Neither of them must be harmed,' she said.

'That's up to them,' said Callan. 'I'll do my best, but I don't give guarantees.'

She sighed. 'Please tell me the addresses you memorised,' she said, and Callan did so: no hesitation, no mistakes.

'When do you go?' she asked.

'As soon as I hear from Switzerland.'

'Which flight?'

'No,' said Callan. 'Question time's over, Mme Kollonaki. All you do now is sit and wait.'

'Yes,' she said. 'I suppose it is like that. Good luck, Mr Callan. Bring my daughter back to me.'

This time the butler took him straight to the lift.

Lonely's place then, to pick up his birth certificate, since Lonely was too frightened to pick it up himself. In the blue vase on the mantelpiece, the little man had said. There were nine blue vases on the mantelpiece, but he found it at last

155

– in the green vase on top of the telly. Then back to his place to coax and chivvy Lonely to have his photograph taken, and finally succeeded when he told him they had machines that did it nowadays without the aid of nosy photographers. Over to Petty France then, and Lonely still terrified, till he found you had to wait in a queue just like the dole, then for some reason it wasn't so bad. He looked round the crowded room, almost happily.

'All these geezers,' he said. 'They'd have a hard job finding me among this lot.'

'They wouldn't even try,' said Callan.

He jibbed a bit when he found he had to pay, but Callan got the money out of him. He would have jibbed even more if he'd found out that the usual waiting time for a passport was ten days, but he didn't. And anyway, his would come by return of post: Hunter would see to that.

And after that, all he had to do was wait for two letters from Zurich that came promptly enough. At least they weren't from the same bank: even a Swiss banker might raise his eyebrows at two post-dated cheques. But Herr Heller and Herr Schiff were both happy to advise him... He sent Lonely out to buy some rather more sportive gear that would make him a little more acceptable in his rôle of happy holidaymaker, and paid a final call on Hunter: listened, memorised, and promised to obey. Both men knew that he would keep his word: the red file was a massive incentive.

The plane left from Gatwick; Lonely was a little affronted by this. Heathrow, his researches told him, had more class. But he cheered up when he

156

got to the duty-free shop. He had Callan's allowance of cigarettes as well as his own, and he bought four different kinds of after-shave. His preoccupation with personal freshness had always been well above the average, and with reason, Callan thought. Let's hope he doesn't have to use them all... But the hope, he knew, was unjustified. Still, for Lonely at least it really was a holiday. He enjoyed the drinks in little bottles, the prettiness of the air-hostesses; even the food. But then Lonely carefree could enjoy anything. Mercifully the take-off had been smooth. There hadn't even been a whiff.

'Them gits at passport control hardly even looked at me,' he said contemptuously. 'It just goes to show, Mr Callan.'

'Show what?' Callan asked.

'Play it big and you get away with it,' said Lonely.

Callan looked at him. Green, light-weight trousers, lemon-coloured shirt, snap brim straw hat. Big Time Lonely.

'We've got it made, son,' he said, and Lonely sighed, contented, and rang for more booze.

Heraklion didn't bother him. The airport was busy and full, a miniature Gatwick, and the city was bustling enough to relax him. Only the heat surprised him. It had obviously been hot for so long, was going to go on being hot, and nobody acted surprised. Not like England at all... But when the coach left the town behind them and headed out into the countryside, Lonely began to be alarmed. It was superb countryside: vineyards and sheep pasture, little white cubes of cottages

157

spangled with flowers, and always the mountains beyond: soaring, beautiful, immense. But Lonely had no taste for landscape. It left him too exposed: better, far better, the crowded anonymity of a London street.

'Is it all like this, Mr Callan?' he asked.

Callan was looking out for the village of Kronis.

'Yeah,' he said. 'Beautiful, isn't it?'

Lonely was appalled.

'You mean where we're going,' he said. 'It's all empty like this?'

Callan looked at him and understood.

'No, son,' he said. 'Where we're going's a town.'

'With streets and that?'

'Streets and caffs and a cinema and shops,' said Callan.

Lonely relaxed.

The bus skirted a horse-drawn cart that might have been made during the Venetian occupation, then slowed down for the village. Kronis. One long street that straggled to the sea, one caff, a little domed church, and every house built solid enough to withstand a siege: rough-hewn, white-washed stone, tiny windows, heavy, olive-wood doors. Whatever money he collected, he would have earned it. The bus accelerated out into the countryside once more, and they passed more vines, more conifers, and came back to the sea: a shiny, glittering sapphire sea, even bluer than in the brochures. Then a strip of sand, and the first of the hotels, a great white shaft of holidaymakers' hutches. Not their hotel, though Sophie Kollonaki had suggested it. Close to Kronis, she had said, and that was just the trouble. It was too bloody close... On along the sea road, winding round smooth-towering cliffs; the sea still glittering beneath them, then more hotels, and a sprawling, untidy town: cars and people and donkeys, tiny, domed churches, caffs and music, and Lonely getting happier by the minute.

Then the town ended, and Lonely looked worried once more, but not for long. A few more cliffs, a few more pines, a few more glimpses of the sea, and they had reached their hotel. Lonely looked about him.

'Cor, Mr Callan,' he said, 'this is something like.'

A garden neatly landscaped, its focal point a swimming pool, and all around, little white cubes of guest cottages, thinner, less enduring replicas of the peasant houses they had passed, but tactful in that exquisite setting; even appropriate. To one side the main hotel building, long and low, already half-obscured by pine-trees: to the other a sandy bay that curved in a smooth arc back to Kronis and above it as always the mountains, harsh, barren, majestic.

Callan and Lonely got out with the others, and they went in to register. Lonely loved it: the sleekness of the well-polished wood, the cool, dim bar, and fat, upholstered furniture. He didn't even protest when they took his passport. Mr Callan was in charge: there wouldn't be any trouble... They registered and a bell-boy took their luggage and led them to their cottage, opened curtains, showed them the bathroom, and Callan gave him money. To the manner born, thought Lonely. You can tell Mr Callan's lived. The bell-boy left, and they looked at the cottage: your holiday home from home, the brochure said. A twin-bedded room, a tiny patio, looking out to the sea, a bathroom and toilet, *and* a shower. Keeping clean would be dead easy in a place like this. And everywhere there were flowers: roses, carnations, geraniums, honeysuckle: great splashes of colour against white-washed walls.

'We'd better unpack,' Callan said, and looked unwillingly at his suitcase.

'Why don't you let me, Mr Callan,' said Lonely, 'You just sit down and relax.'

'If you wouldn't mind–' said Callan.

'Pleasure,' Lonely said.

'What I'd like to do is take a walk round. Get to know the place.'

'You go right ahead, Mr Callan,' said Lonely.

'Tell you what,' said Callan. 'You unpack and join me in the bar and I'll buy you a drink.'

He didn't walk far. He'd studied the lay-out of the hotel in Hunter's office, and the man he had to see would be in the bar, waiting, and probably nervous, as Hunter's couriers so often were. He used all kinds, and they were nearly all amateurs: they had to be. That way their cover was immaculate; but it did mean they got edgy. Callan stopped and picked a rose, then went into the bar: a handful of Germans, boiled in the heat like lobsters, but tireless: drinking beer, planning tomorrow's excursion, tonight's dinner. A brace of honeymoon couples, seated at tables, absorbed only in each other, and his man, all by himself, sipping ouzo and reading the *Journal of Hellenic Studies,* and looking just the man to do just that.

160

A scholar all right, but young and sun-tanned, just as Hunter said he would be. White shirt, grey slacks, a ring on the little finger of his left hand and the work bag that Cretans used to carry and all the souvenir shops sell: a square of woven wool with a long, plaited wool strap. Blue and white in an abstract design. That was his man all right. He even had the worried look. Callan stood beside him, laid the rose to the right of the ashtray and ordered whisky. Reluctantly the scholar took his nose out of the journal and looked at the rose.

'Pretty,' he said.

'Yeah,' said Callan. 'It had fallen off. Seemed a pity to leave it lying.' He sipped at his drink.

'The flowers in Crete really are rather lovely,' said the scholar, and went back to his book: contact made. Callan continued to sip his whisky, and the scholar knocked back his ouzo and picked up his work bag, then said: 'I wonder – have you seen the scarlet lilies here? They are rather splendid.'

'I've just arrived,' said Callan.

'I could point them out to you if you like.'

'You're very kind,' Callan said. And very nervous. Nobody should get as tense as that over horticulture. Better hurry up and get it over.

They went outside, and Callan admired the scarlet lilies as the scholar and he walked to the car port, and the scholar thrust the bag at Callan.

'Here,' he said.

Callan looked round. There was no one sight. He took the bag, felt the weight of metal inside it.

'Take it easy,' he said.

'Easy?' said the scholar. 'I hate this. You can tell

161

Charlie from me it's the last time. Absolutely the last.'

'But it isn't,' Callan said.

'I'm telling you–' the scholar said.

'No,' said Callan. 'I'm telling you. You're on stand-by.'

'But I've got a dig at Mount Dicte tomorrow.'

'You're not up to it,' said Callan, and his voice hardened. 'Believe me you're not.'

'And just what do you suggest is wrong with me?'

'Seeing you're so keen on flowers,' Callan said, 'you could be coming down with hay-fever.'

12

When Lonely came to the bar, Callan was deep in conversation with a Greek feller, but he bought the little man a beer. Lonely looked at the bottle, saw that it was Greek and feared the worst. To his surprise he liked it, and sat drinking happily while Callan signed papers and counted out money. Leave it to Mr Callan, he thought, whatever it is, he knows what he's doing. Then the Greek feller left and Callan ordered him another beer.

'We've just hired ourselves a car,' he said. 'Fiat. It's out there in the car-port.'

'A car?' said Lonely. From the amazement in his voice it could have been an elephant complete with howdah. 'What do we want a car for, Mr Callan?'

'Oh, I don't know,' said Callan. 'Get about a bit. Trip to the town.'

'They got a bus goes to town,' said Lonely. 'There's a notice up in our gaff – gives you the times and that.'

'We don't want to queue for buses when we're on holiday, now do we?'

Lonely said, 'You really do know how to live, Mr Callan.' He looked at the work bag. 'That yours?' he said.

'Yeah,' said Callan. 'I got it at the souvenir shop. Like it?'

'Pretty,' said Lonely. 'You don't think it makes you look a bit poofy?'

'Not me,' Callan said. 'It's a present for the Groper... Fancy a run into town before dinner?'

'Smashing,' said Lonely, and picked up his glass.

'Don't choke yourself,' Callan said. 'I want a wash anyway. See you back here.'

He had to check what was in the bag, too, but if Hunter had laid it on, it ought to be right, and it was. A nice little set of burglar's tools, probes, skeleton keys, twirls; in a little zip bag that should have held an electric razor. Lonely had never owned anything as good as this. He'd have a hell of a time getting them back from him when the job was over.

They found a café by the little harbour, and Lonely noted with approval that the same beer was a drachma cheaper than at the hotel. For the rest he was quite content just to sit and watch the world go by.

'There's a fridge in our room, Mr Callan,' he said. 'Did you notice?'

'We should put some of that beer in it,' said Callan.

'They got off-licences here then?'

'Of course,' said Callan, and rose. 'I'll go and get you some.' He picked up the bag. 'You just stay there and take it easy.'

A square with a fountain, Sophie Kollonaki had said, with a barber's on one corner. Turn up the side-street, past a souvenir shop, and a photographer's, and there it was: small, dark, and crammed with stuff: fruit and vegetables and wine and honey and beer: sweets, cakes, soft drinks, cheese: great sacks of nuts and rice and wheat. There wasn't a hell of a lot of room for people, but it was crammed even so: more beef-red Germans buying like squirrels storing it away for winter, and waited on by a stocky man with a chest like a wine barrel... Fifty, Sophie had said: but he didn't look it. Hands like steel grabs, and a scar across the back of the left one, a scar like the letter 'L'. Callan looked in the photographer's window until the Germans left, then moved in quick. The man looked at him: his eyes were of a blue so dark as to seem almost black: hard, wary eyes. You've done bird, mate, thought Callan.

'You're Dimitri,' he said aloud.

'What makes you think so?' The voice was deep, booming from that barrel chest.

'A lady in London,' said Callan. 'Her name is Sophie.'

Dimitri gestured to a curtained doorway.

'We better go in there,' he said.

164

'We will,' said Callan, 'if you can tell me my name.'

'Callan,' Dimitri said. 'Mr David Callan.'

Callan followed him in.

The room held far too much furniture, a great deal of stock the shop couldn't hold, a radio blaring bouzouki and a caged canary that even so managed to hold its own. In the midst of it a fat woman placidly dozed. Dimitri shook her awake and she went out to mind the shop.

'My sister,' Dimitri said. 'I come to see her when I have time off. You came to collect something?'

Callan nodded.

'This maybe?'

His hands reached behind his chair, and came up holding a revolver. He held it by the butt and its barrel was aimed at Callan's heart. His hand was perfectly steady.

'Sophie didn't say you'd give it to me one bullet at a time,' said Callan.

'Maybe I don't give it to you at all,' said Dimitri. 'I think Sophie makes a mistake this time.'

'What's wrong with wanting her daughter back?'

'Nothing,' said Dimitri. 'But why should she send you? I am here.' The pride in his voice was unmistakable.

'She won't risk you,' said Callan.

'But she will risk you?'

'That's right,' said Callan. 'All I'm costing her is money.'

Dimitri laughed then, and threw the gun to Callan.

'Perhaps you can tell what this is,' he said.

'Colt Python revolver,' Callan said. 'Two and a half inch barrel. Takes .357 magnum or .38 special shells. Ramp front-sight, notch rear-sight.'

'You know a gun when you see one,' said Dimitri. 'Maybe I ought to give you some shells.' He handed over a box of magnum shells, and watched, placid as his sister, as Callan loaded the gun.

'How much would that gun cost in America?' he asked.

Callan said, 'I don't know. About a hundred and fifty dollars.'

'Over here you could weigh it in diamonds,' said Dimitri, 'I should like it back when you are finished with it.'

'You'll get it.' Callan put gun and shells in the work bag. 'When do we do the job?'

'Maybe Wednesday,' Dimitri said. 'Maybe next week.'

'Why the maybes?'

'Polybios's old mother is ill,' said Dimitri. 'She lives at the other end of the island. We'll use one of the nights he takes his wife to visit her. I'll let you know when he makes up his mind.'

Callan said, 'If it's all the same to you – no phone calls.'

Dimitri chuckled. 'I think I'm beginning to like you after all,' he said. 'Don't worry. I'll make contact.'

Lonely was happy enough where Callan had left him: the caff had plenty of beer. All the same it was nice to see the bag full of bottles; nice of Mr Callan to carry the bag. They walked to the car, and Callan stowed his bag carefully on the

166

back seat.

'Funny, isn't it?' Lonely said.

'What is?'

'The way these Greeks drive on the wrong side of the road. Put the steering wheel on the wrong side of the car, too.'

'You know what's even funnier,' said Callan. 'All over the world they drive on the wrong side of the road. We're the only ones who do it right.'

'Just goes to show,' said Lonely. 'You can't beat good old England.'

Callan drove off.

'That caff,' Lonely said. 'Nice that. Sitting outside. Next door to a jewellers too. Lovely stuff there. Bulls' heads in gold, and a big gold thing with like bees crawling over it.'

'A honeycomb,' said Callan.

'Beg pardon, Mr Callan?'

'That big gold thing. It's called a honeycomb.' But Lonely was impervious to enlightenment.

'The bees was gold too,' he said. 'Eighteen carat easy. Lovely tickle that would be.'

'I thought you were supposed to be resting,' said Callan.

'I was only talking,' said Lonely. 'You know I wouldn't do anything to get you into trouble.'

Grimly Kyle worked through the list of Lonely's relatives: surly uncles, shrill and vituperative aunts. Singly and in chorus, the answer was the same: they didn't know where Lonely was, and even if they did they wouldn't go telling no coppers. To persevere in the face of such opposition seemed hopeless: but to give in was unthinkable. By the time he got to Cousin Alfred's he'd had time to revise his technique.

'I never,' said Cousin Alfred grandly, 'grass to the fuzz.' Then he added for emphasis: 'No way.'

'Suit yourself,' said Kyle and turned to go. 'It's his money.'

'Money?' The word had its own charisma for Cousin Alfred.

'If he can prove ownership that is. Wallet with his name on it.'

'Wallet?' No charisma this time. Kyle gathered that Lonely was not one for wallets, but Cousin Alfred made a recovery. 'Oh yeah. He did say he'd lost his. Lot in it, was there?'

'Fifty quid,' said Kyle, and Cousin Alfred whistled. 'Pity you don't talk to coppers. He might be glad of that money.'

'Now wait a minute,' Cousin Alfred said. 'If it's a matter of lost property – that's different. Trouble is I don't know.' He thought for a moment, a process as painful as it was laborious. 'I saw him make a phone call once though.' Unhesitatingly, he reeled off the number. Bent to a man, thought Kyle. Even steal each other's privacy. Thank God he was stupid, too: stupid enough not to ask who'd put Kyle on to him.

'Thanks,' said Kyle, and turned to go.

'Here,' said Cousin Alfred. 'You won't forget to tell Lonely it was me that told you?' Cousin Alfred said.

'I won't.'

'Lonely's never been one to forget his relations, specially when they've done him a favour. There ought to be money in this.'

Kyle remembered the hard man Lonely went mates with.

Or a bloody good hiding, he thought.

'You find our landscape beautiful?'

Callan looked from the sea that gleamed silver on black, to the mountains across the bay. By moonlight they too were shadowed silver; the mountains of the moon indeed.

'Beautiful?' said Callan. 'But it's more than that.' He sought the word. 'It's – pure.'

Dimitri said, 'It was... It will be again.' He was back to the job. 'It will be Friday,' he said. 'Polybios has gone to his mother. His wife will join him there. You will take her on Friday night. Eight o'clock. The boat will be ready... You can manage a boat?'

And there it was again: the amateur bit. All this way before they asked if he could manage a boat.

'I can,' he said. 'Where will you get it from?'

'Polybios,' said Dimitri, and Callan laughed. It was a nice touch.

'What happens to you?'

'I shall be in the house,' said Dimitri. 'I shall try to resist – and you will knock me unconscious.' He looked hard at Callan.

'O.K.,' said Callan.

'I mean it,' said Dimitri.

'So do I. Tell me about the locks on the house.'

'Mantons,' said Dimitri. 'Double action.' Callan gave a grunt of satisfaction. Double action Mantons were bastards, but at least they were English bastards. 'You can manage them also?' Dimitri asked.

'I've brought a mate for that.'

'A mate? A friend?' Callan nodded. 'Nothing was said about a friend of yours.'

'That's security for you,' said Callan.

'I am not sure that I can authorise—'

'If you want Manton locks opened, he's in,' said Callan.

Dimitri sighed, but there was no more argument. Instead he talked of the lay-out of the Polybios house, the way to the beach where the launch would be waiting, the necessity for punctuality – and silence. And Callan agreed with every word. It was a pity that Vardakis wanted Dimitri dead. He seemed to know his stuff.

'That is all, I think,' he said at last. 'Good luck, Mr Callan. All will be in readiness. I swear it on the grave of my mother.'

Callan watched him leave till he disappeared among the rocks, then listened to the putt of the two-stroke as he rode back to Kronis. He wished Dimitri hadn't said those last words. Until then he'd been inclined to believe him...

He went back to the hotel, collected their passports, then to their room, moving softly through the garden. From the main building came the sound of beat music, but distance muted it: he could still hear the whisper of a tideless sea... He hoped it would stay like that. Callan would bet money that Lonely was a lousy sailor. Carefully he made his way to the little patio, and checked the trough of flowers that held the gun and the burglar's kit, then went inside. Lonely was asleep and even in his sleep he was smiling. Poor little perisher, thought Callan. He wouldn't be smiling tomorrow.

'We bugged Callan's flat as soon as he left,' said Meres.

'An excellent precaution,' said Hunter.

'Somebody keeps ringing it,' Meres said. 'At fairly regular intervals. Say three times an hour.'

'Your friends?' asked Hunter.

'I think it most unlikely they would have the number,' said Meres. 'Certainly not from me, sir.'

'You'd better have the call traced,' Hunter said.

'I have that in mind, sir,' Meres said. 'What action do you want me to take?'

'Trace the call and well see,' Hunter said.

Kyle put the phone down.

'At least it doesn't cost us anything,' said his mother. 'Not when there's no answer.'

Kyle dialled one hundred, and asked the operator for the supervisor.

'Supervisor here,' the voice said.

'Good evening,' said Kyle. 'This is Kent Street police-station.'

'Andy!' his mother said. He waved her to silence. 'We're trying to trace an address from a phone number... Yes... Quite important. Suspected arson.' He gave the number.

'Hold on a moment, will you?' the supervisor said. Kyle covered the mouthpiece.

'Pencil and paper, please, mum,' he said.

'Andy, you can't *do* this.'

'Pencil and paper,' he said again, and she fetched them. Just like his father. No stopping him.

The supervisor came back, and Kyle wrote it

down and thanked her, the bland, impersonal thanks of the man on duty.

As he hung up his mother said, 'It'll mean your job.'

'Not if I get him,' said Kyle.

Callan watched Lonely finish off breakfast. Rolls, toast, croissants, honey, jam: Lonely scoffed the lot, then poured out the last of the coffee and lit a cigarette.

'Pity there wasn't no bacon and eggs,' he said.

'I reckon you'll live till lunch-time,' Callan said. 'What d'you fancy doing?'

Lonely shrugged. 'Whatever you say, Mr Callan,' he said. 'That's fine with me.'

'Honestly?'

'Of course,' said Lonely.

'In that case let's have a drive round,' said Callan, and Lonely saw nothing wrong with that. It was too early for beer anyway...

At least Kronis didn't have any parking problems. You just left your car where you stopped. Callan pulled in to its tiny square just as a tourist coach pulled out. He turned in his seat and looked at the Polybios house. Just like the others, apart from the locks. A bit bigger maybe, in a little better state of repair, but just as solid, just as much a mini-prison. On the upstairs balcony a girl was watering flowers, a pretty girl with black hair and honey skin: the girl he had come to lift... Callan got out, and Lonely followed, as Callan headed across the square.

'You're going the wrong way,' he said. 'The caff's over there.'

'We're going to the church,' said Callan.

'The church?' Lonely couldn't have been more horrified if he'd said brothel.

Callan lifted his guide-book.

'It's educational,' he said. 'They've got pictures called ikons – hundreds of years old.'

Lonely sighed and submitted. After all, he'd given his word.

The church was cool, old and quite tiny. Something to do with the Turks, Callan remembered. No big buildings for Greeks. They might get together and start something. The cleanliness of it too was intriguing: the golden stone might have been cut yesterday, instead of eight hundred years ago. He moved softly, for people were praying, kneeling not just towards the high altar and Christ Pantocrator, but to the tiny pictures on the walls of the church: Saint George and the Dragon, Christ Crucified, Saint Peter with his keys, Mother and Child, each set in frames of heavy gold, some of them with beaten gold or silver worked into the painting, some of them set with precious stones. Callan sat before an ikon of the Last Supper: an elegant composition incredible in so tiny a frame. Lonely joined him, and he too studied the frame: gold thick as his thumb at the corners, and at each corner a tiny cross in rubies and pearls.

'Another tickle?' said Callan.

Lonely looked shocked.

'I wouldn't do no churches, Mr Callan,' he said. 'Unlucky that is.' But he went on looking.

There was a whisper of movement, and the girl came in. With her was a stocky woman with muscles like a wrestler: Mrs Polybios. The girl

173

wore white: Mrs Polybios was in unrelieved black, but not the black that peasant women wore. This was smart stuff, good material: probably came from Athens. Mr Polybios was doing all right, thought Callan, and Helena Kollonaki was doing even better. That cool white sheath didn't even come from Athens: it had Paris written all over it. She and her mother might be separated, but they used the same couturier... The woman in black knelt before the image of Christ Pantocrator, then muttered fiercely to Helena. Reluctantly, she knelt beside her. Mrs Polybios put a lot of muscle into her praying. The girl beside her was as still as a stone.

'You like the pictures?'

Callan looked up. A man in uniform: hard cloth, well-cut, boots polished, tie exactly knotted. A copper. Well, it made sense. Wherever Helena went, the coppers wouldn't be far away.

'Very nice,' said Callan at his most refined. 'Very nice indeed.'

He reached out a restraining hand to Lonely, whose only instinct in the presence of policemen was flight.

'My friend and I were just saying how nice they are.' He turned and looked at Lonely. 'Weren't we?'

Somehow Lonely calmed down enough to say, 'That's right.'

'You are staying here in Kronis?'

'Here?' said Callan, and succeeded in looking affronted. 'Oh dear me no. We just drove over from the Royal Palace Hotel. Your pictures are in the book, you know.' He flourished his guide-book. 'I believe you call them ikons,' he added kindly.

'I think you are wise,' the policeman said. 'There is nothing of interest in Kronis – apart from our ikons of course.' He nodded and left, and soon Callan and Lonely left too. Lonely was all for it. As they went to the hired Fiat Callan looked at the Polybios house once more. A dog lay panting in the shade of the verandah: a big surly mongrel with teeth like broken swords.

Lonely said, 'That rozzer's still about.'

'Of course he is.' Callan was soothing. 'He lives here.'

'What did he want to come and speak to us for?' Lonely was indignant.

'I expect he was just being friendly.'

'I don't want to get friendly with no rozzers,' said Lonely. 'Especially when I'm on holiday.'

'How about a drink?' said Callan, and drove him to Heraklion. Cars and buses and crowds had their usual calming effect, and so did beer. By the time Callan took him to lunch, Lonely was fine. It was a good lunch; with more beer for Lonely and wine without turpentine for Callan. Methodically Lonely ate his way through taramosalata, grilled fish, lamb stew, salad, cheese and Turkish Delight, then settled down to Greek coffee, thick and honey-sweet. He even liked that. 'Better than the Parnassos, Mr Callan,' he said.

Callan looked at the bill. 'It should be,' he said.

'Blimey,' said Lonely, 'this lot must be costing you a fortune.'

'That's all right,' said Callan. 'You can pay me back some time.' Maybe sooner than you think.

Lonely finished his coffee and belched delicately. 'What were you thinking of doing now, Mr Callan?'

'Looking at ruins,' said Callan. Lonely's face fell. 'You don't have to come if you don't want to.'

Lonely said, 'if you don't mind, Mr Callan. There's a square back there with like a lion in the middle. Got benches and that. You can buy English papers there. I saw them. I think I'll go there and have a read and a kip.'

'You sure you'll be all right?' Callan asked.

'Course I will.'

'You – you are enjoying yourself?' Callan asked.

'Never had such a good time in me life,' said Lonely. 'You're a real mate, Mr Callan.'

Callan watched him go; white shirt today, and pale blue slacks, snap-brimmed hat pulled jauntily to one side. His mate. His mucker. If only he'd stop being so grateful.

13

Callan parked the Fiat, and walked past Evans's house, the Villa Ariadne, an uncompromising Victorian slab refusing to become Levantine. He looked at the garden: pines and oleanders and palms set with fragments of ancient statuary, most of it broken. An archaeologist's garden. But then Evans had been an archaeologist; *the* archaeologist, for Crete: the man who had discovered the palace of Minos and built his villa nearby so that he could work on it. An upright, an eminent Victorian, thought Callan. Today's archaeologists were rather different.

He walked on to the site of Knossos, the Palace of Minos: past the car-park and the fizzy drink stands to the ticket-office. Callan paid and went in; a hundred other people were doing the same. He paused by the bronze head of Evans by the entrance, but it was too early by far. There was no sign of his archaeologist. He walked on and into the labyrinth, and all around him earnest little groups clustered round lecturing guides. The thing was immense. Porticoes, corridors, colonnades, tier piled on tier, ancient stone supported by stone almost new. And everywhere colour and paint: the massive, squat supporting pillars as red as the wine he had drunk at lunch. And the inside had all been painted too, and the reproductions of the originals were still there: simple, arrogant, superb. But the vastness of the thing was oppressive; the vastness of a labyrinth, with the overtones of fear all mazes have. Through gaps in the pavement, crevices in the walls, he could see plants growing, the golden discs of flowers: in a courtyard swallows weaved patterns in air. Callan felt heartened and went to look for his scholar, and sure enough he was there by Evans's statue, and dead on time.

'It's good of you to find the time to show me round,' said Callan.

The archaeologist gave him a look of pure hate. 'Not at all,' he said.

More tourists passed them: meek sheep chivvied by sheepdog guides: so much to see, so little

177

time to see it.

'I suggest we go to the House of the Sacrificed Oxen,' the archaeologist said. 'It has rather a decent altar and it may not be quite so crowded.'

He led the way through the labyrinth like a man going from home to his local, and when they reached the house it was deserted. The altar was there all right, but his guide was in no mood to talk about it.

'I told you I wouldn't do anything else,' he said.

'No,' said Callan. 'You told me to tell Charlie that the delivery you made was the last one. Absolutely the last. Do you really want me to tell him that?'

'Look, Mr – I've no idea what your name is.'

'That's right,' said Callan. 'You haven't. But I know what yours is.'

'I'd be obliged if you won't use it. Not here, not anywhere.'

'Not unless I have to,' said Callan.

'I got into this because I was asked to,' the other man said. 'Decent old boy took me to lunch at his club. Talked about the security of our country, told me what a contribution I could make.' He looked at Callan, bewildered. 'I liked him. I actually liked him – and I did what he asked. I thought it was the right thing to do, God help me.'

'This isn't my business,' Callan said. 'What I want is–'

'Please,' the archaeologist said. 'Let me finish. You're the only person on the island I *can* talk to about this.'

'All right,' Callan said. 'But make it quick.'

'Then I met some chap who worked for Charlie.

178

Some kind of paymaster. He told me he was authorised to pay me expenses – just to reimburse me, he said. What I was doing for Charlie cost money, and there was no reason why I should lose by it.'

'Well, was there?'

'It didn't work like that,' the archaeologist said. 'The money got bigger and bigger. I tried to send it back, but I didn't know where. I even went to the old boy at the club. He said he didn't know what I was talking about. Then the paymaster came back. He made me sign a receipt.'

'Made you?'

'He had some kind of thug with him,' said the archaeologist. 'A brute from a public school.'

Meres, Callan thought, what a busy little bee you are.

'Only it wasn't a receipt, it was a contract,' the archaeologist said. 'I'd signed on to be a spy.'

'I doubt if Charlie could enforce it,' said Callan.

'He doesn't have to.' The man was very close to tears. 'I'm an archaeologist. My peers say I'm a good one. With luck I could go a very long way indeed – and it's my whole life. Do you believe that?'

'Yeah,' said Callan. 'I believe it. Go on.'

'In the good old Edwardian era quite a few chaps like me were spies – in an unofficial sort of way. And everybody thought it was fine. Jolly good sports doing a little amateur espionage to protect the good old Empire. But always in a very gentlemanly way. What I've helped to do has never been gentlemanly.'

179

'You've no idea what you've helped to do,' said Callan. 'You're just a courier.'

'Nobody told me. No... But I'm not a fool. I know what I've done all right – just as I'll know what you've done – and what my share in it was.'

Callan moved a little closer. This could turn out to be nasty.

'You want out, is that it?' he said.

'That's it.'

'And how do you propose to set about it?'

Discretion, Hunter had said, but use your initiative if it should be necessary. Initiative was a nice, bland word. It held no hint of the sound the hand made bruising flesh, breaking bone, and Callan did not want to kill this man. But Hunter had been aware of that one too. If he went on like this and Callan let him live, then Callan himself would die – or even worse, face interrogation: and Hunter knew it.

'How can I?' said the archaeologist. 'There's nothing I can do.'

'Yes there is,' said Callan, 'and you know there is. You're not a fool. You said so yourself.'

'You mean go to the Greek police and confess?'

'That's right.'

'I thought of it,' the archaeologist said, 'but it really isn't on, you know.' Callan waited. 'I'd be ruined professionally. I couldn't stand that.'

Callan relaxed, a very little, and found that the other man was staring at him.

'How very odd,' he said. 'You're perspiring. I thought it was quite cool in here.'

Not perspiring, mate. Sweating. On account of I thought I was going to kill you.

'You were told to get a boat,' said Callan.

'I did get one. Rather a nice one. Twin diesel. Fifty feet.'

'Charter job?'

'That's right. To a person named Robertson. I take it that's a fictitious name.' Callan ignored it.

'Where is it now?' he asked.

'Aghios Nikolaos harbour.'

'You could have told me yesterday,' Callan said.

'I hadn't got it yesterday.' The archaeologist was impatient. 'There aren't many boats like that to be had here.' He reached in his pocket, handed over papers. 'Here,' he said. 'Now for God's sake leave me alone.'

'Who saw you do it?'

'Nobody. I got a friend of mine to do it. A German... He's gone back home... I told him I was trying to get round currency restrictions.' The archaeologist hesitated. 'He was a good friend – but I don't think he is any more.'

Kyle tried the door-handle again. The door was still locked. Methodically he set to work on the knocker, slamming it down as only a policeman can, but there was no joy. He banged even harder: at least it helped his frustration.

Behind him a voice said, 'I rather think Mr Callan's away.'

Kyle turned. The card by her door read 'Miss Eileen Brewis'. She was tall, neatly dressed, prim.

'He hasn't left his milk bottles out for two days,' she said.

And you have an eye for such things, I don't doubt, thought Kyle.

'Did he have a friend with him?' Kyle asked.

'He did come back with someone a few days ago,' Miss Brewis said. 'Rather a low type I thought. Not like Mr Callan at all. I don't know if he stayed,' she said regretfully.

'A small man, wearing a raincoat and a dark blue suit?'

'That's right,' she said. 'Very shabby I thought. Still he had made some attempt to smarten himself up.'

'Indeed?'

'His cap,' she said. 'It looked quite new. You're not a debt collector by any chance?'

'No,' said Kyle. 'I'm a policeman.'

At once she began to shut the door. Kyle spoke quietly.

'Just a little matter of lost property,' Kyle said. 'Nothing – er – criminal.'

'Mr Callan never mentioned any lost property to me,' she said. It was a black mark for Callan, obviously.

'I wonder if you'd mind describing him?'

She didn't mind at all. Medium height, good shoulders, quite a pleasant smile. On and on she went and the picture grew clearer by the minute. She fancied this Callan all right. She doesn't know he's a hard one. Kyle thought, but he had no doubt that he was Lonely's hard friend. The name was different, but the hard ones often changed their names. They couldn't change their faces – or their bodies.

'Do you happen to know what he does for a living?'

'His hours are irregular,' she said, and there was

another black mark. 'And that is all I can tell you. I fail to see what it has to do with lost property.'

Kyle smiled his most boyish smile.

'Just trying to find out when he would be in,' he said.

'Mr Callan is quite unpredictable, I'm afraid,' she said. 'If there's nothing further—'

'Thank you. You've been very kind.'

The door shut firmly and Kyle heard the chain go on, boyish smile or no boyish smile.

He went down the stairs and crossed the road to join the bus queue. The man in front of him buried his nose in his paper and didn't look up. That bastard Meres, he thought. Calling me in on my rest day just to keep tabs on a copper... Across the road a second man got into the phone box and dialled, then waited for the cold, beautiful voice.

'Yes?'

'Let me speak to Charlie please,' he said.

Time to go to the Heraklion museum, Callan thought. If you want to look like a tourist, act like a tourist. So he went and looked and marvelled at the wonders the Cretans had achieved, three and a half millennia ago: paintings and pottery, jewellery, gold work, rings; all of it beautiful. And everywhere one looked, two reiterated themes: bulls and double axes. Bulls that were heads only, like the one Vardakis owned, or great, elaborate paintings of dancers leaping over them in a ritual that seemed even more dangerous than the torero's. Massive axes of bronze, each with the same broad, double blade, or tiny ones of gold, some worked in

183

a stipple design on other gold objects, but all of them of an amazing craftsmanship when you thought of what they had to work with. All of it valuable too, if the locks on the display cases were anything to go by... Callan looked at his watch. It was time to visit another craftsman.

He slumbered peacefully by the fountain. The Saracens had built the city, Byzantines, then Venetians, then Turks had succeeded them, building, adding, enriching, till at last the Greeks took back what was their own. Eleven hundred years of history lay around him, and Lonely slept. Gently Callan touched him, and Lonely came awake at once, alert and wary.

'Oh it's you, Mr Callan,' he said. 'I must have nodded off. Had a good time?'

'Smashing,' said Callan, 'and you?'

Lonely picked up a pile of papers. 'Great,' he said. 'These are all the English ones they had – and there's nothing about the arson. What'll we do now?'

'Mystery tour,' said Callan. 'I've got a bit of a surprise for you.'

They drove out past the enormous fortifications the Venetians had made, and Lonely asked who had built them. Callan told him.

'I don't mean that, Mr Callan,' Lonely said. 'I mean who hauled the stone and that?'

Callan shrugged. 'Prisoners probably.'

Lonely looked at a towering bastion, its walls five yards thick.

'I'm glad I wasn't in their nick,' he said. Callan took the road to Aghios Nikolaos. 'Funny thing,' Lonely went on. Callan waited. 'When I was reading the papers.'

'Get on with it,' said Callan.

'Must have been nodding off,' said Lonely. 'Dreaming like. I thought I saw that blondy feller. Daft isn't it? I mean what would he want to come here for?'

Callan said carefully, 'There's no accounting for dreams.'

But he kept his eyes open when they drove through Kronis, and even when he saw that the square was empty he didn't relax.

Kyle was telling his mum all about it when the knock at the door sounded. She was having a good old giggle at his description of Miss Brewis but she was up and out, even so, before Kyle could get to his feet. She didn't believe in men opening doors, or so she said. Kyle thought the truth was that she was nosey, like all women, but in a nice, friendly sort of way... She wasn't giggling when she came back.

'Andy,' she said. 'It's your inspector.'

Kyle looked at the older man's face.

'All right, mum,' he said. 'You get off to bingo.'

She didn't move: her eyes were on the inspector's face.

'There's – nothing wrong, is there?' she said.

'Just dropped in for a chat,' the inspector said. 'Police business. It *is* confidential, Mrs Kyle. If you don't mind.'

She had to leave; she knew that: but she wasn't going off to bingo, not when her son had that look on his face. She turned to Kyle. 'I'll be in the kitchen if you want me,' she said, and left.

Kyle motioned to a chair.

'Sit down, sir,' he said. The inspector did so, and Kyle waited.

'I understand you've been working on your off-time,' the inspector said at last.

Kyle looked at him, surprised. 'That's right, sir.'

'Trying to trace this Lonely.' Kyle waited. 'Going round his relatives. Good idea that.'

'Thank you, sir,' said Kyle. 'As a matter of fact–'

'Wait,' the inspector said. 'Let me finish. You managed to get a phone number, right? And an address. In fact you've just come back from that address.'

This time Kyle wasn't surprised: he was amazed.

'That's right, sir,' he said. He paused, then asked, 'Have you been having me followed, sir?'

'Not me,' the inspector said, 'but somebody has.'

'Of all the bloody nerve,' said Kyle. 'Look, sir, I–'

'I know, I know,' the inspector said, 'but for God's sake let me finish. You went to a certain flat and there was nobody in. Right? But the woman next door likes to gossip and she told you a few things.'

'A feller with form lives there,' said Kyle. 'She gave me a good description and I'm sure of it. His name is–'

'I don't want to know his name,' said the inspector, 'and I want you to forget it.'

'Forget it?'

'That's right. You never went to that block of flats, you never talked to that woman.'

'But, sir–'

186

'And you can forget about Lonely, too. For what it's worth I'm told he didn't do that arson job, but whether he did or not – forget him. And I'll forget you let him go.' He waited, but there was no answer. 'That's an order, Kyle.' He waited again, watching Kyle's face. Obstinate young devil, he thought, but smart, too: thinking it through before he answers.

'With respect, sir,' said Kyle, 'I don't think you can give me an order like that.'

'Can't I?'

'No, sir. I saw, this man Lonely. Nobody else did. He was very close to that fire – and running. He's a criminal, consorting with a criminal. I – we have no right to forget about him.'

'He didn't do it.'

Doggedly Kyle said, 'That's not what you said before, sir. You said, "For what it's worth I'm told he didn't do it." Doesn't sound as if you believe it, sir.'

'Never mind what I believe,' the inspector said, then stopped. This was a good lad with brains. Shouting at him wouldn't stop him thinking. 'Look, Kyle,' he said, 'I can't tell you much because I don't know much. But I can tell you this. I was ordered to tell you to lay off.'

'Can I ask by whom, sir?'

'I don't see why not. It was a Detective Chief Superintendent from Special Branch. Go yourself, he said, and tell Kyle to stop meddling. And that's exactly what I've done. Lay off, Kyle.' He waited. 'Well?'

'I heard you, sir,' said Kyle.

'Of course you did,' the inspector said. 'You're

not deaf... Will you do what you're told?'

'I'll think about it, sir.'

It was said deferentially, with quiet politeness; but it was said. For the first time in the inspector's career a subordinate had questioned a direct command. 'This won't do you any good, Kyle,' he said.

Kyle said, 'I don't think it's doing any of us any good, sir.'

Callan left Lonely at his favourite café, drinking beer, then walked to the little harbour, handed over papers, and took possession of his yacht. Six berths, saloon, galley, wheelhouse, bathroom, showers. Hunter was really doing things in style. White paint glittering, brass shining, Greek flag flying aft. M.Y. *Galatea*, Piraeus. He checked the oil tanks, and they were full: the hold was crammed with extra fuel. Fast and yet heavy, ready for open seas, and good for a thousand miles at least – unless the Greeks called out their navy... He checked the stores: water tanks full, cupboards full of cans, fish and meat in the freezer; wine in the racks, beer in the fridge, scotch and gin in the saloon. How well the rich lived... He went back to the café, to collect Lonely. The little man had made a discovery: the caff sold chips.

'Course they're not as good as you get at home,' said Lonely. 'I reckon it's the fat. Still, they're not bad, considering.' He held the paper bag out to Callan. 'Have one?'

'No thanks,' said Callan. 'I want to show you the surprise.'

Lonely was still clutching his bag of chips when Callan reached the harbour and went aboard the

188

Galatea. He looked round; Lonely was still ashore.

'Come on,' he said, but Lonely hung back.

'Mr Callan, you shouldn't,' he said.

'Belt up and get aboard,' said Callan, and Lonely didn't hesitate. When Mr Callan used that tone of voice, you did what he said. But even then, standing by the wheel-house, he made one last try.

'Mr Callan, you mustn't,' he said. 'Suppose the owner comes?'

Callan took keys from his pocket, went into the wheel-house.

'Suppose he does?'

The engines caught and fired: a low and pleasing purr. Lonely settled into the wheel-house after Callan.

'We'll be done for piracy,' he said.

Not if we're lucky, Callan thought.

'You're wrong there,' he said. 'I've hired her.'

Lonely looked at him, astounded.

'You've hired this?' he said.

'That's right.'

'But it must have cost a mint.'

'Never you mind what it cost,' said Callan.

'But I do mind,' Lonely said. 'I mean it's all very well you treating me to a holiday, Mr Callan. But this—'

'Always live well when you can,' said Callan.

'But that's what I mean,' said Lonely. 'Last week you was working on the roads. Where on earth did you get the money?' He broke off, aghast at his own insolence. 'I'm sorry, Mr Callan.'

'That's all right,' said Callan. 'I've got a mate that's got a lot of money and I've given him a bit of a hand from time to time. Know what I mean?'

189

Lonely hadn't the remotest idea, and he was glad of it.

'And this geezer slipped you a few quid?'

'That's right,' said Callan. '"Go and get yourself some sun," he said. "Do things in style."'

Lonely looked about him.

'You're certainly doing that,' he said. Callan switched off the engine.

'Come and have a look round,' he said.

Lonely was enchanted: the showers and toilets really worked, the bathroom even contained bath salts, and with a galley like that even roly-poly pudding was possible.

'More like a house than a boat,' he said. 'Bigger than any house I ever lived in.'

Callan showed another marvel: a fridge fully stocked: there was even beer.

'Help yourself,' he said, and Lonely sprawled on the settee, lordly, at ease.

'This is the life all right,' he said, 'but isn't it a bit big for a drive round the harbour?'

'I thought,' Callan said, 'we might go a bit further than that.'

'Just as you say, Mr Callan,' Lonely said. 'You're the skipper.'

Better get up topside, thought Callan. When I break the bad news we'll need all the fresh air we can get.

They went out of the harbour and into the bay. The *Galatea* handled like a dream. Even one-handed he could take her anywhere he wanted – so long as the weather stayed like this, anyway: no wind, almost no swell: mill-pond calm. Even Lonely was enjoying it... He opened her up a bit, and the twin diesels moved on from a purr to a muted roar, the speedo needle slid smoothly up and over till they reached the other end of the bay and the village of Kronis lay before them, a straggle of building blocks that enlarged slowly into houses. Kronis, too, had a little harbour, a mole that jutted across the bay's curve to provide still water for a couple of fishing caiques and a power-boat. The Polybios boat; not quite so big and heavy as the *Galatea,* but big enough. She would do. Callan eased off, and glanced idly at her, then swung the helm over, fed more power, and set off into the shining, translucent blue. Aghios Nikolaos had dwindled to a line of headlands when he eased off once more.

'This is the life,' said Lonely, and lay at ease on a rubber mattress on the deck. 'I reckon even millionaires don't live better than this.'

'Life of Riley,' said Callan. 'You know I've been thinking – about that honeycomb.'

'The gold one in the jewellers?'

'That's the one... I reckon we could nick it if we put our minds to it.'

Lonely took it in his stride.

'Certainly we could,' he said, 'only we'd need me tools to do a jeweller's and how would we get it off the island anyway?' He settled down on the mattress. 'Pity.'

'All the same,' said Callan, 'it seems a shame to come all this way and not do a job. How much you reckon we could get for that honeycomb?'

'Five thousand, maybe seven,' said Lonely. *'If* we could nick it. Big job that would be... Real class.'

'I know where we could get more than that.'

'Not the church,' said Lonely. 'I told you. Mr Callan. Robbing churches is unlucky.'

'Not the church,' said Callan. 'A bird.'

'Robbing a bird?'

'No. Not robbing her,' Callan said. 'Lifting her.'

'Kidnapping?'

Callan thought for a moment. 'You could put it like that,' he said.

The little man was horrified.

'We could get years and years for kidnapping,' he said. 'Life even.'

And maybe even worse than life: death.

'We could get fifteen thousand quid,' said Callan.

'Millionaire's daughter, is she?' Lonely asked.

'No,' said Callan. 'Just a relative.'

'Fifteen thousand,' said Lonely. 'Gawd. I've never even seen fifteen thousand.'

'Nice easy tickle,' said Callan. 'Say half an hour's light work and five grand of it's yours. Take care of your old age.'

'I daresay it would,' Lonely said regretfully. 'But I don't hold with kidnapping, Mr Callan. Never did. It's cruel.' He looked reproachfully at Callan. 'I never thought you would hold with it neither.'

It was time, Callan realised, for a fairy-story.

Once upon a time, it appeared, there was a beautiful princess called Helena. Her widowed mother loved her, and her rich relative loved her, and she was very, very happy, till the wicked ogre Polybios one day stole her away and locked her up in his castle. The beautiful princess wept: the

192

millionaire grieved, her mother mourned, for the sun had gone out of their lives. Then one day two handsome princes came along, and broke into the ogre's castle, carried off the princess and gave her back to her mother. How happy they were to be re-united, and how happy the millionaire was too. He rewarded the handsome princes with ducats and louis d'or and pieces of eight, to the value of fifteen thousand nicker, in any currency they cared to name.

'Yeah, I daresay,' said Lonely. 'But how would we get her off the island?'

'By boat.' said Callan. 'This boat.'

'Cor,' said Lonely. 'I never thought of that. Be our good deed, wouldn't it? Like Robin Hood.'

'Exactly like Robin Hood,' said Callan.

'I still don't see what you need me for,' said Lonely. 'Sounds more like a job for a couple of heavies.'

'One heavy,' said Callan. 'Me. I'll take care of the rough work.'

Lonely stiffened. 'If there is any,' he added hastily. 'There shouldn't be – not if you'll help me.'

'Doing what?'

'Opening up Polybios's drum. The locks could be a bit tricky.'

'What kind of locks, Mr Callan?'

'Mantons,' said Callan.

Lonely's sigh was equal parts of regret and relief.

'There you are then,' he said. 'We're back where we started. I couldn't do no Manton locks without tools.'

'I've got tools,' said Callan.

Lonely sat up as if Callan had rammed a spike in him.

'You brought them here?'

'No,' said Callan. 'A mate of mine got them for me.'

'I thought you didn't have no mates here.'

'So did I,' said Callan. 'I was wrong.'

Lonely clutched at one more straw.

'I couldn't work with no foreign gear,' he said.

'Don't worry,' said Callan. 'You could work with this stuff. It's the best I've ever seen. Tell you what – you have a look at it and make up your mind then. O.K.?'

'O.K.,' said Lonely, and had a flash of inspiration. 'If you want to know what I think, Mr Callan,' he said severely, 'I think you knew about all this before we even got here.'

'You're right,' said Callan.

'I don't think that's very nice,' Lonely said.

'You mean you don't want five thousand quid?'

On reflection, Lonely thought that perhaps he did. But it didn't make him look any happier.

14

Vardakis knocked at Sophie's door and said, 'It's Michael.'

Never once, she thought, not one single time since he turned away from me and what I fight for, had he ever been anything but polite.

'Come in,' she said.

He was carrying a box, gift-wrapped in expensive paper. Oh God, she thought; more presents. Then she saw that the wrapping was torn.

'I thought you might like to see this,' he said, and put it on a table. She went to it, and he pulled back the lid of the box. Inside were a series of flat slabs, a clock movement, and a battery. For once Sophie Kollonaki lost her composure. She grabbed the box and ran for the window. It was the sound of his laughter that stopped her: it was harsh and jeering, but there was amusement in it too.

'Always the heroine,' he said, 'but it isn't necessary this time, Sophie.' He went up to her, pushed one of his short, stubby fingers into the box: flicked at a dangling wire.

'It's been immobilised.'

He took it from her; put it back on the table.

'Who?' she said. 'Who would–'

'I thought I'd ask you that,' Vardakis said.

'You really think I would send you that?'

'Of course not. But you have friends who might.' She gave no answer. 'Not very good friends though. Eh, Sophie?'

'I don't understand you,' she said.

'It was addressed to me,' said Vardakis, 'but surely your friends know that you're here too? Supposing you'd been with me – and I opened it – and it went off?'

He picked up the box again, and left her. For the first time since her husband died, Sophie Kollonaki thought that she might cry.

Vardakis went back to his office. The tall, elegant young man seemed not to have moved since he left him. He still seemed calm and relaxed, but then he'd even seemed calm and relaxed when he'd immobilised the bomb.

'I'm most grateful to you, Mr Meres,' Vardakis said. 'It was lucky for me you were here when that nastiness–' he nodded at the box – 'was delivered.'

'All part of the service,' Meres said.

'No,' said Vardakis, 'I think not. For this you deserve a bonus.' He took out a cheque-book and began to write. 'My life is still precious to me.' He considered carefully, then wrote in an amount. 'Sophie's also.' He handed over the cheque.

'You've talked to her?'

'She didn't know,' Vardakis said. 'I am quite certain that she didn't know.'

Callan docked the cruiser, and began to coax Lonely into taking the bus back to the hotel. It wasn't all that difficult: sun, sea air and beer had taken their toll. A kip before dinner was just what Lonely needed. He caught the bus, and learned with delight that he didn't have to pay. Mr Callan certainly knew his way around... Callan went to the café, ordered whisky, and waited. Lonely hadn't been dreaming; they'd been sent reinforcements from England: reinforcements he didn't need, didn't want come to that, but they were here, and contact had to be made.

Better to make it in the open air with a few hundred witnesses walking about. Much better. He sipped at the whisky and watched the endless procession moving by. Girls in shorts, in jeans, in long skirts slashed to the thigh; a fat man in a yellow shirt, a skinny man in a shirt of red and purple check; old, Cretan women in enveloping black, who treated the harsh sunlight as if it wasn't there. He began to think about Lonely.

He couldn't risk him on the boat. No chance. He'd nearly gone overboard trying to tie her up when the engines were stilled. Once they hit open seas Lonely wouldn't even be a passenger: he'd be a patient. No, Lonely couldn't go home by the scenic route. If the girl knew her way around a boat they'd be all right: if she didn't – he'd have to manage somehow... A shadow fell across the table, and Callan looked up, un-hurried. The geezer had found him: might as well get it over with.

'Oh my Gawd,' said Callan, 'what are you doing here?'

Randolph Blythe said, 'I thought I might buy you a drink.'

Gorgeous, Randy was. An absolute knock-out. White slacks, cherry red shirt, white straw hat with a cherry red band, red and white worry beads on his wrist. A feast for the eye.

'Whisky,' said Callan. He reckoned he was going to need it. Blythe ordered in a fast sputter of Greek that didn't make him any less conspicuous. Tourists talk English, and shout to make them-selves understood. The waiter brought whisky for Callan and ouzo for Blythe.

'Cheers,' Blythe said.

'Cheers,' said Callan. 'It's funny the way you and I keep running into each other, isn't it?'

'Ah,' said Blythe, 'I was going to talk to you about that.'

'Somehow,' said Callan, 'I rather thought you were.'

'I hate to say this,' said Blythe, 'but Sophie doesn't quite trust you. Not totally.'

'And that's why you're here?'

'That's why.'

'To make sure I do the job right?'

Blythe inclined his head: a gracious nod of assent that turned halfway into a dip in the ouzo.

'Precisely,' he said.

And just how do you intend to do that, Callan wondered, and found that he didn't want to know the answer.

'Why doesn't she trust me?' he asked.

'She found out that you'd talked with her cousin.' Callan stayed silent. 'It's no good denying it, Callan.'

'I'm not denying it,' said Callan.

'Well then?' Blythe seemed surprised to meet with no denials. 'When do we – er – do it?'

Just like that, thought Callan. I tell you the time, the place and the loved one so you've got them all ready to spill when the rozzers pick you up.

'All in good time,' said Callan. 'I'll let you know when I'm ready.' He finished his whisky. 'Where are you staying?'

'Your hotel.'

'Sophie told you about that, too?'

'Well of course she did,' said Blythe. 'She knows she can trust me... Oh I'm sorry. I didn't mean–'

Callan hardly heard him. 'How did you get here?' he asked.

'Charter flight,' said Blythe. 'From the Association of Archaeology. It's really an excellent cover. More than eighty of us. And another lot due in tomorrow from Manchester. I won't be all that conspicuous, you know.'

'Do the planes go back empty?'

'I don't know,' said Blythe. 'They're quite adequately paid for, you know. Why do you ask?' He looked suddenly alarmed. 'You can't possibly take Helena out on a charter plane.'

'Of course I can't,' said Callan. 'We wouldn't have a hope in hell. I was just curious.'

Blythe looked relieved. 'Have another drink,' he said.

'No thanks.'

'Well do you know,' said Blythe, 'I rather think I will,' and shouted again in his fast, fluent Greek. Callan left him to it.

Kyle walked back from the gym, his body pleasantly weary. One good thing about the ten till six shift, he thought: it left most of your evening free and you copped a good lie-in the next morning, and after a training session, you needed it. Judo was important in his job: it kept you fit and maybe it would come in handy, too, but after an evening with his instructor he was ready for his kip, and his supper. Even the thought of it made him step out more briskly.

The car slowed up beside him, and the driver leaned across, wound down the passenger window. Lost, thought Kyle. In a car like that he would be lost, round here.

'Mr Kyle?' the voice said. Smooth voice, posh voice. What his mum would call a real gentleman's voice. I was wrong, he thought. Not lost.

But I don't know you.

'Yes?' he said.

'I'm afraid there's been an accident,' the posh voice said. 'Your mother. Hop in the back and I'll take you to her.'

'An accident?'

'Yes. If you don't mind, Mr Kyle. It is rather urgent.'

Kyle got in, and the car moved off again before he'd even shut the door. In the darkness beside him a man stirred and leaned forward, and Kyle found that he was sitting beside a large and powerful negro.

'There, there, Mr Kyle,' the negro said. 'You just take it easy. I'm sure everything is going to be all right.'

The driver said, 'I hope so,' and Kyle began to worry about his voice. It should have been worried and concerned, if the words were to make any sense. Instead, it was enthusiastic, even zestful.

'Of course it is,' the negro said. 'Your mammy will be just fine.'

'We'll see,' the driver said, and the car moved faster.

'Where is she?' Kyle asked.

'Not far,' the negro said. 'Just don't worry, my friend.'

But Kyle had begun to worry a great deal.

'Look here – who are you?' he asked.

'Couple of passers-by,' said the Negro. 'Doing our good deed for the day.'

The car moved on past the houses and pubs to the silence of a park.

'Hit and run,' the driver said. 'Nobody seems to

have any conscience these days, do they?'

The car slowed, stopped. 'Out you go. I'm afraid we'll have to walk it from here.'

Kyle got out, moving warily. Instinct was urging him to run away, but instinct was being foolish, as usual. He was a young, fit man, a trained man, skilled in judo, and more than that, he was a copper. If these two were up to something, it was his duty to find out what it was... The negro and posh voice were out of the car in a flash, and herding him with the same unobtrusive skill he'd seen used by two veteran policemen winkling the one real agitator out of a noisy crowd. The two men walked Kyle into the dimness of the park, and he stopped by a grove of trees.

'I don't believe you,' he said. 'I don't believe my mother's had an accident.'

'Not yet,' said posh voice.

'There,' said the negro. 'Isn't that nice?'

'What the hell are you on about?' said Kyle.

'This is a warning,' posh voice said. 'Stick to your job and do what you're told. Otherwise—'

'Otherwise accidents *will* happen,' said the negro.

'You don't scare me,' Kyle said.

'Of course not,' posh voice said. 'You're big and tough and terribly brave, I'm sure. It would be a waste of time trying to frighten *you* – but we might frighten your mother.'

Kyle went for him then, ignoring the negro. For him the negro didn't even exist at that moment: there was only this sneering bastard threatening his mother. But even then Kyle didn't quite give way. He went in as his instructor had taught him, feet right, hands right, a hundred and eighty pounds of muscle and bone: and the elegant man swayed just enough to make him miss his beat, then countered with the filthiest, most appalling blow that Kyle had ever heard of. Kyle went down screaming, and the elegant man drew back his foot once more, but the negro moved even faster. A large black hand chopped down behind Kyle's ear, and the screaming stopped.

'Damn you, Spencer,' said Meres.

'Mr Hunter's orders,' Spencer Percival Fitzmaurice said. 'Once you look like you're enjoying it, the party's over.'

'I only hit him once,' Meres said.

'The way he was yelling,' said Fitzmaurice, 'I reckon that's enough.'

Callan went back to his bungalow and checked that his flower-pots were untouched. The little man lay on his bed, snoring lustily. Stacked neatly by the refrigerator were four more empty beer cans: when Lonely was worried he turned automatically to beer... I'll have to get him off it tomorrow, thought Callan, but tonight I'd sooner have his snores than his smell. He walked out without a sound, and made his way to the sea again, striding out along the bay. The sun was setting with the swiftness he would never get used to, but away to his left, from the road, he sensed a sudden flush of rose-pink light. Binoculars, he thought, and kept on walking, not looking again, then settled at last on the sand, his back against a rock, his plaited straw hat tilted to shade his eyes. The Colt Python was still in its flower-pot, and a fat lot of bloody use it was there, but if he had a date it was up to him to keep it. He couldn't ask the other party to wait while he went back to fetch his gun.

Callan eased his shoulders back against the rock, let one hand flop on to the sand, feeling it yield to his fingers. Slowly his body relaxed into the posture of sleep, and he watched himself being stalked and awarded marks for it: high ones. This geezer was good, no doubt about it. Coming in out of the sunset, using all the cover there was, then moving in on him from behind before he was too close to be recognised. Very high marks indeed, old son, thought Callan, and I only hope your intentions are honourable.

Behind him a voice said, 'Don't move. I've got a gun on you.' Callan stayed as he was, breathing as if asleep. 'Clever sod,' the voice said. 'I know you're awake.' Callan kept up the deep, even breathing, and heard the other man restless, fidgeting, then moving slowly round to face him. Through the hat's plaited straw Callan looked, without surprise, at the young blond man who had thrown a petrol bomb, and duffed poor Randy Blythe. He was holding a .380 Browning Standard Automatic. For himself Callan preferred the Colt Python, but the Browning was a hell of a good gun, and the other man held it as if somebody had taught him how.

'Blimey,' blondy said. 'You really are asleep. You ask me you're past it, dad.' He drew back his foot to kick, and as he did so Callan's hand moved, hard, dry, stinging sand bit into blondy's face and eyes, and even as blondy's left hand went up to his face, Callan rolled over, grabbed his wrist, struck with the edge of his hand at the elbow. Blondy gasped and the Browning fell, and Callan scooped it up and waited. There was no hurry. For the next five minutes blondy was too busy wiping sand from his eyes to be capable of anything else. That, and swearing. He did a good job of swearing, even better than his stalking. Callan heard him out in silence: there was nothing in it for him.

When the other man could see again, he found he was looking down the barrel of the gun.

'You're full of tricks, aren't you?' he said.

'What's your name, son?' Callan asked.

'Find out.'

'I asked you nicely,' said Callan. 'Didn't I ask you nicely?' The Browning moved down to the other man's stomach. 'If I have to find out it may not be so nice.'

Slowly, reluctantly, the other man said, 'Bradley.'

'Got a first name?' said Callan. 'Or didn't your parents bother?'

'People call me Nutter,' said Bradley.

'I'm not surprised,' said Callan. All the same he looked warily at that thick, if well-shaped, head. In the kind of brawling Bradley was used to it would make a formidable weapon.

'We do seem to meet in the most unfortunate circumstances,' he said, and thought: At least Randy usually buys me a drink.

'I've never seen you before,' said Bradley.

'We both know that's a lie,' Callan said amiably. 'I duffed you, son, don't you remember? The night you were supposed to duff a dentist.'

Bradley remembered all right: his eyes were glittering with hate. Waste of time, hating people. It sapped your energy and made you vulnerable. Nutter had a lot to learn – if he wasn't too thick to learn anything.

'Sit down,' said Callan. 'On the sand. And put your hands where I can see them.' It took time, but at last Bradley did as he was told. Callan perched on the rock and stuck the Browning in his waistband.

'What are you doing here, son?' he asked.

'Don't call me son.'

'Why not?' said Callan. 'You called me dad. Fair's fair.'

'All right,' said Bradley. 'All right. You've beaten me twice.' He stopped there, biting off words, and Callan had no doubt of what they would have been: There'll be a third time, so watch it.

'What you doing here?' Callan asked.

'Come to see you.'

'With a gun in your hand?'

'That was a try-out,' said Bradley. 'Just to see if you were any good.' Callan waited. 'The Big Man sent me.' Still Callan waited. 'You're not trying to con me you don't know who the boss is?'

'No,' said Callan. 'I'm wondering if you do.'

'No names,' said Bradley. 'He said not to use names.'

Sensible Mr Vardakis, thought Callan.

'He said to tell you he's got a flat in London and a house in Paris, and they've both got trees outside. All right?'

'Fine,' said Callan.

'I'm in same as you,' said Bradley. 'So don't you

try telling me different.'

'I'm not trying anything, son,' said Callan.

But this time even the word 'son' lost its power to wound.

'You'd better not,' Bradley said. 'He doesn't trust you, dad – that's why he's sent me to keep an eye on you.'

Snap, thought Callan. Two in one day.

'So what are you going to do about it?'

'Come with you,' said Bradley. 'I'm your reinforcements, dad.'

'You got any experience of this kind of thing?'

'I've been around,' said Bradley.

'Doing what?'

And that was all it took: out it came. Very proud of himself, Mr Bradley was. Teenage tearaway, then a spell in the paratroops, then a freelance doing the heavy. Never an idle moment.

'My mates thought I was barmy joining the paratroops,' he said. 'Best move I ever made. Weapon training, unarmed combat, getting you fit – and not just for free, they pay you for it.'

'So that's where you learned to handle a gun?'

'That's where,' said Bradley. 'The best training you can get, mate.'

Well perhaps not the very best, thought Callan, but good enough.

'So when do we start?'

Oh gorblimey, another one. Wants the whole modus operandi just like that.

'I don't know that you start at all,' said Callan.

Bradley grinned. It didn't make the brutal, handsome face any kinder. 'The Big Man thought you might say that,' he said. 'He gave me a message for you. Either you take me with you or the deal's off.' Callan said nothing. 'And if it's off he'll shop you, Callan. He told me so.'

'All right,' said Callan. 'Where are you staying?'

'At the Miramar,' Bradley said. 'Just down the road.'

'I'll let you know when we're ready to move.'

'You'd better,' said Bradley. 'I'll be watching you. Now give me my gun back.'

One thing about this idiot, Callan thought. He certainly recovers quickly.

He took out the gun, and it pointed briefly to the space between Bradley's eyes, and the boy didn't even seem to notice, just held out his hand imperatively. He-Who-Must-Be-Obeyed. Callan swivelled the gun by its trigger guard so that it lay in his hand butt uppermost, then released the catch, took out the magazine, and gave Bradley the empty gun.

'And the ammo,' said Bradley.

'Maybe later,' said Callan, 'if you're a good boy.'

'The Big Man said–'

'The Big Man seems to have said a lot of things,' said Callan. 'I don't think you've told me all of them. Later I said, and later I meant.'

He stood up and walked away. Behind him Bradley was swearing, but that was no novelty. He used all the same words as last time.

Lonely was hungry. Rest and sea air always got him like that, he explained, and proceeded to work his way through the menu, and Callan watched and marvelled. When Lonely was hungry he could eat like three navvies, and still not put on an ounce. The dining-room was cool and dimly lit, and except for their own table, the waiters weren't overworked. Callan watched the diners slowly drifting in, fresh from their showers, ready for an evening's fun and frolic. Blythe was one of them – elegant in pale pink slacks and a white silk shirt. He's had time to change, Callan thought. I hope he had the sense to take a shower too. He looked at Lonely: the little man had eyes only for his plate.

'Mate of yours just came in,' he said.

Lonely looked up and followed Callan's gaze 'Blimey,' said Lonely, 'what's he doing here?'

'Being nosey,' said Callan.

Lonely put down his knife and fork.

'You mean *he's* in on this lark?' Callan nodded. 'I never said I'd work with no amateurs, Mr Callan. Asking for trouble that is.'

'Don't worry,' said Callan. 'He won't bother you.'

'Him?' said Lonely. 'I'd like to see him try.'

'Maybe I'd better have a word with him – tell him he's not wanted. You don't mind if I leave you for a moment, old son?'

Lonely picked up his knife and fork. 'Help yourself, Mr Callan,' he said. 'I've still got me pudding to come.'

Callan moved between the tables to where Blythe sat in solitary state. His waiter, Callan noticed, was the most handsome in the room, and Blythe was speaking to him in Greek. The waiter didn't seem to be enjoying what Blythe was saying.

'Mr Blythe, isn't it?' said Callan.

208

Reluctantly Blythe looked away from the waiter, who left at once.

'Yes?'

'We shared a table at a café earlier. You remember? My name's Callan.'

Blythe looked nervously at the next table, where six Germans were putting it away almost as steadily as Lonely. Again like Lonely, they too had eyes only for their plates. Blythe took a quick gulp of wine, and put the glass down heavily. A red stain spread across the cloth, and Callan wondered how much more he'd shifted.

'Yes,' said Blythe. 'I remember you.'

'Maybe you remember somebody else,' said Callan. 'A young blond feller who tried to duff you.'

'I'll never forget him,' Blythe said. 'But is it wise to talk about him now?'

'I think so,' said Callan. 'He's here in Crete.'

15

The ward Kyle was in was small, over-crowded and noisy. Men coughed over illicit cigarettes, argued over card-games, laughed at the comedians on television and nothing the sister said could make them chuck it for more than a couple of minutes. Only matron could do that, but then matron could do anything, thought Kyle. Crack nuts with her eyebrows that one. And that reminded him, and the pain started again. He looked at the inspector, the weathered face more brick-red than ever against the yellow cloth of the screen they'd put round his bed.

'You're sure that's all you can remember?' the inspector said.

'That's all, sir.'

'Just two fellers came out of the park and gave you a hiding?'

'Yes, sir.'

'They didn't say anything?'

'No, sir.'

'Didn't call you names, didn't call you copper? Fuzz? Nothing like that?'

'All they did was kick me, sir – where it hurts.'

'They didn't steal anything of yours – you know that?' Kyle nodded. The inspector paused, but Kyle said nothing. 'Have you been making enemies, Kyle?' The brick-red colour deepened. Of all the damn fool questions. Obviously the poor bastard had been making enemies.

'None that I know of, sir.'

'It doesn't make sense,' the inspector said.

'Couple of maniacs,' said Kyle.

'Nut cases don't usually go about in pairs,' said the inspector. 'Can't you remember anything about them?'

'No, sir.'

'Think about them one at a time. Dark? Fair? Short? Tall? Clean-shaven? Moustache? Glasses?'

'It was very dark there, sir. The street light's not too good and they moved so quick–'

'They must have,' the inspector said. 'Your instructor reckons you're pretty good at judo. Seems to think it would take a couple of trained

210

men to handle you like that.'

Kyle said, 'It was all so sudden, you see, sir. They just came out of the park and lammed into me.'

'And what were you doing near the park anyway?'

'Just taking a walk, sir.'

'Not meeting a girl by any chance? A girl with a couple of brothers?'

'No, sir.'

'Know a girl like that?' Kyle shook his head. 'Nothing to do with me if you do. Except I want those two, Kyle. They beat you up and I want them.'

'Me too, sir.'

But he didn't sound as if he meant it.

It was a treat to deal with a real pro for a change, and Dimitri was all of that. One moment Callan and Lonely were alone in their room, the next he was with them, quiet and easy moving, handling his bulk with skill learned years ago, now taken for granted. Lonely jumped up, terrified, and moved instinctively towards Callan.

'Don't start getting nervous,' Callan said. 'He's a good guy.' He turned to Dimitri. 'Nice of you to drop in. Have a drink?'

'Beer,' said Dimitri, and Lonely scuttled off to get it.

'How did you get in here?' Callan asked.

Dimitri grinned. 'In Crete everybody has a relative in the hotel business. Here I've got two nephews – my sister's boys. One's a chef. It's only right I should visit them sometimes.' The grin broadened. 'He's a very good chef.'

Lonely handed him a beer, and Dimitri said, 'Thank you,' and took a healthy swig. 'Friday,' he said. 'Definitely Friday.'

'Polybios will be gone then?'

'He leaves tomorrow.'

'Then why not tomorrow?'

'Because on Friday Captain Vlassos will be going on leave.'

'He's that copper in the village?' Dimitri nodded. 'Won't they send a replacement?'

'Not till Saturday. So you see, Friday is the best chance of all.' He turned to look at Lonely, who still stayed very close to Callan.

'This is your locksmith?' Callan nodded. 'I hope he is a good one?'

'The best,' said Callan, and Lonely smirked.

'Double action Mantons,' Dimitri said. 'I hope our friend here warned you.'

'They won't–' Lonely's voice was a squeak, and he coughed and tried again. 'They won't be no problem.'

'You have tools then?'

Before Lonely could speak, Callan answered for him.

'Never mind what he's got,' Callan said. 'We'll do our job.'

'I'm sorry if I sound inquisitive,' said Dimitri, 'but I have to be sure that this will go perfectly. There is so much at stake–'

'We don't guarantee perfection,' said Callan. 'Nobody can. But we do our best. It's the only way we get paid – and we both like money.'

Dimitri said, 'Only get Helena out and you will

212

be paid. You agree to Friday?'

'Like you said, it's the best chance of all,' said Callan.

Dimitri knocked back the rest of his beer, and sighed in content. 'Midnight – if that will suit you?'

'Later,' said Callan. 'Three in the morning – Saturday morning.'

'But that is less than three hours before dawn.'

'We don't need three hours,' said Callan. 'More like three minutes.'

'Very well then,' Dimitri said. '0300 hours.' He smiled at that, remembering. 'It is what your officers used to say – during the war. You will not forget that I must be knocked unconscious?'

'I won't forget,' said Callan.

'That is essential,' Dimitri said. 'It is not essential to kill me.'

'It isn't essential to kill anybody,' said Callan, and thought for a moment that the big man was going to argue, just on general principles. When it came to killing, Dimitri's list would be a long one, Callan was sure. But in the end all he did was rise, neat and contained as ever, set down his beer glass and leave. Lonely opened his mouth to speak, and Callan clapped his hand over it.

'Get yourself a beer,' he said, and went out to their tiny balcony. But Dimitri was gone. The moon was up, and from most of the bungalows light still blazed, but there was no sign of Dimitri. Dealing with a professional did have its advantages. He took the tool-kit the archaeologist had given him from its hiding place, and went back to Lonely.

'Something up then, Mr Callan?' Lonely asked.

Callan sniffed, but the only scent in the room was that of roses. Keep it like that, he thought. Break it gently.

'I thought you might be interested in this,' he said and handed over the tool-kit. Lonely looked at him as if it was Christmas.

'Cor,' he said, 'I never had anything like this before, Mr Callan. Where d'you get it?'

'Never mind,' said Callan. 'Think you could open a Manton with it?'

Lonely rummaged happily among pick-locks and twirls. 'With this lot,' he said, 'I could open the Bank of England.'

Callan went out to the verandah, and came back with the Colt Python revolver.

'I got a present too,' he said. Lonely looked at it warily, but still there was no smell. He'd seen a gun in Callan's hands too many times for that.

'You said it wasn't essential to kill anybody,' he said cautiously.

'It's not,' said Callan, 'but this makes sure that everybody has the same idea.'

He began to check the gun, and they worked on in companionable silence, two craftsmen busy with familiar tools.

Callan said at last: 'At least we don't have to worry about that blondy geezer.'

Lonely tried a twirl on the bathroom door: it opened no trouble at all. 'That's right,' he said. 'He's two thousand miles away.'

'Well no,' said Callan. 'He's a bit nearer than that.'

'I was never no good at geography,' said Lonely.

'How far away is he then?'

'About a mile and a quarter.'

The smell came then: real vintage Lonely.

'A mile and a quarter? And you say we got nothing to worry about?' he yelled. 'Look, Mr Callan–'

'Keep your voice down,' said Callan. His own voice was low and even-pitched, but Lonely was silent at once.

'Just listen,' said Callan. 'That's all I want you to do.' As he spoke his fingers fed bullets into the gun, assembled it, cocked it, put it in his pants' waist-band. 'You do as I say, and it's a doddle. I mean that, old son. Nutter Bradley can't hurt you.'

'Who?'

'The blondy geezer,' said Callan. 'He can't hurt you. Nobody can if you stick with me and I've got this.' His hand moved and the gun flicked out, quick and terrible.

'You've got to trust me, son.'

'Oh I do,' said Lonely. 'You're the best minder I ever had. Only what I don't understand is – what's this Nutter come here for?'

For Lonely, explanations had to be quick and simple. Accuracy came well down on the list.

'To shop us, son,' said Callan.

'You won't let him, will you?'

Callan looked hurt. 'You think we came all this way just to get done?'

'Well what we going to do then?' Lonely asked.

'Shop him,' said Callan.

'No fighting?'

'Not if I can help it,' said Callan.

'I don't want you to think I'm being a nuisance,' Lonely said, 'but I can't do my best work when there's fighting. Fighting puts me off.'

'If we do this right,' said Callan, 'you'll be nicely out of the way before the punch-up starts.'

Lonely began to relax, and with the relaxation came puzzlement.

'Another thing,' he said, 'that Blythe geezer. I thought you said that Nutter was duffing him.'

'I did,' said Callan.

'Well they can't be on the same side then, can they?'

'They're not,' said Callan. 'But they both want the same thing.'

'That bird we're going to lift?'

That wasn't the right answer at all, but Lonely had worries enough for one night.

'That's right,' Callan said.

'That makes you, me, Nutter and Blythe – all after her. And Dimitri.' He paused. 'I suppose Dimitri's on our side?'

'Of course,' said Callan, who could lie as well as the next man. Dimitri should be on their side, no question, but if he was, why had he not told him about the dog?

Callan said, 'I hate the waiting around before a job.'

'Me too,' said Lonely. 'It's worst part, the waiting.'

And the imagining, he thought, and the thinking about it. Imagining the rozzers got you, thinking about a Greek nick and what they might do if they put you inside.

'Tell you what,' said Callan. 'Why don't we do this job tomorrow instead? Get it over with?'

'Cos Dimitri said that copper would be there

216

tomorrow,' said Lonely. 'Don't you remember?'

'One copper,' said Callan. 'He'll be no problem. Better than sitting here worrying for the next few days.'

'What about Dimitri? You going to let him know?'

'Of course,' lied Callan.

Lonely sighed. 'Suit yourself, Mr Callan,' he said. 'You're the boss. Only I do wish you'd tell me the truth sometimes.'

Most of the flats in the area started on the first floor: the ground floor and basements were given over to commerce: Greek restaurants, Greek cafés, Greek butchers and grocers, tobacconists who sold Greek newspapers and magazines. It was a shabby neighbourhood, but the Greek craving for colour was there: blue, red and yellow paint crudely applied, jam jars and milk bottles filled with bright, cheap flowers, marigolds and Michaelmas daisies and the odd wilting carnation. The Greek noise was there too; car horns and radios blared, men and women yelled at each other like enemies even if they were saying good-morning.

Meres detested it. Noise and colour alike were crude, and lacking in subtlety. Life here was for the most part poor, and uncomplicatedly happy. He detested that too. The job now, that was another matter. Pick-ups were chancy affairs, and sometimes the man you had to pick up was naughty and had to be rebuked, and that could be fun, and even if he came quietly he was usually terrified, and that too was not unamusing. He

217

shifted more comfortably on the seat of the big old Chevrolet, and the feeling of detestation returned. A spade car, with weirdly psychedelic paintwork, and driven by Spencer Percival Fitzmaurice. Meres wondered if it actually *amused* Hunter to partner him with a West Indian. Not that it was a bad cover: there were plenty of West Indians in the street. They even liked Greek food.

Fitzmaurice said, 'We's jest about here, massa.'

Wearily Meres said, 'Cut that out.' He'd said it many times before.

'Yassuh,' said Fitzmaurice, and slid the car into an empty space. Whatever else he was, Meres thought, he was a bloody good driver, and opened the door.

'Steady on, old boy,' Fitzmaurice said. 'You're not going in there alone, are you?'

'Yes,' said Meres. 'I am.'

'But it's madness,' Fitzmaurice said. 'Facing a horde of bally savages all on your own.'

Meres slammed the door. Fitzmaurice wound down the window and shook his hand. 'Well cheerio, old boy,' he said. 'Pip pip, toodleoo and all that sort of rot,'

Meres pulled his hand away and Fitzmaurice watched him push a blue-framed door, with canary yellow panels. It would be open, Hunter had said, and it was. Meres went inside.

One day, Mr Meres sah, Fitzmaurice thought, you's gwine to find out we ain't all Uncle Toms: not even when we is on yo side...

Stairs covered with worn linoleum, but the banisters painted a screaming crimson. Meres went up in silence to the first floor. The door on

218

the left, Hunter had said. Knock twice and ask for Nicky. If he doesn't answer go in anyway. He'll be asleep and the door won't be locked. Meres took out a Smith and Wesson .38 with a two-inch barrel. Good enough for close work, and it didn't spoil the fit of his suit. He knocked twice, softly, and no one answered. Meres breathed deeply and evenly, and grasped the door-knob in his handkerchief, and twisted. The door swung open, and there was Nicky, asleep. Meres found this pleasing; sleeping people were so vulnerable, and this one, he thought, would be vulnerable at any time: young and slight, and intelligent by the look of him, and in all probability far too imaginative. Meres picked up a water-glass left handed, and threw its contents into Nicky's face. Nicky sat up, spluttering, and found he was looking into the barrel of a Smith and Wesson .38.

'Let's both be quiet as tiny mice,' Meres said softly, 'otherwise this thing will go off.'

Nicky lay back, terrified.

'Get up and get dressed,' said Meres, and the boy did as he was bid, pulling on a T-shirt and jeans on top of his underclothes, thrusting his feet into sandals.

Meres moved behind him, put the muzzle of his revolver to the nape of the boy's neck. Nicky shuddered.

'Hands in your pockets,' said Meres, and the boy obeyed.

'Now downstairs on our tippy-toes.'

It was so easy. The little creature did exactly as he was told, and when they reached the side-door Meres holstered the gun, grabbed him as if he

219

were helping a drunk, and ran him into the car, sandwiching him between Fitzmaurice and himself on the front bench seat. Fitzmaurice eased the car into the traffic, then flicked a look at the terrified, bewildered face.

'You're going to talk to Charlie, white boy,' he said, 'and I don't think you're going to like it. You aren't going to like it at all.'

'Do you expect me to stay in this bijou little chalet all day?' said Blythe.

'Would you sooner Bradley saw you?' asked Callan.

Blythe gave a long-suffering sigh.

'But how am I to explain it?' he asked. 'I'm supposed to be on holiday.'

'Tummy upset,' said Callan.

'Oh very well.' Blythe's gaze wandered to the refrigerator. 'Care for a drink?'

'Not when I'm working,' said Callan.

Blythe took bottled water from the refrigerator, and reached for the ouzo.

'If I were you I'd take it easy,' Callan said. 'You're working too.'

'You mean it's tonight?' Blythe asked, and Callan nodded. 'Just a small one,' said Blythe. 'I won't have too much. I promise.'

Callan looked at the litter of bottles on Blythe's dressing table. Headache pills, hangover pills, stomach pills, sleeping pills. He picked up the last bottle and looked at the formula.

'Any good?' he asked.

'Excellent,' said Blythe, and sipped cautiously at the ouzo. 'You can only get them on prescription of course. They are rather strong.'

'Dangerous?'

'In excess.' Blythe looked at his drink and grimaced. 'Like everything else.'

'How much is dangerous?'

'For an adult? Seven tablets – ten perhaps. It would depend on the state of his heart.'

Callan shook the tablets from the bottle and counted them. Fifteen tablets. 'This lot would kill any man?'

'Undoubtedly,' said Blythe.

They wouldn't do a dog any good either. Callan put the tablets back, and pocketed the bottle.

'You could ask,' said Blythe. 'You could even tell me why you want them.'

'I stole them,' said Callan. 'If you get nicked that's all you know.'

'If I get captured you mean?'

'It'll be rough,' said Callan. 'Have you any idea how rough it'll be?'

Blythe nodded. 'I've been told,' he said.

'You still want to go through with it?'

'I must,' said Blythe. 'I believe in this.' He went to the bathroom, and poured what was left in his glass down the sink. There wasn't much. 'Tell me what I must do,' he said, and Callan told him.

Blythe thought it over. 'It doesn't seem much,' he said at last.

'It's enough,' said Callan.

'I really do want to help,' said Blythe.

'You'll be helping. Got your air ticket?'

'Of course.' Callan held out his hand, and Blythe handed it over. Callan put it in his pocket.

'You won't need it,' Callan said.

221

'Will you?'

'Diversion,' said Callan, and Blythe was too scared to ask what the hell he was on about.

A busy morning. Busy busy. Into Heraklion with Lonely to have Blythe's ticket transferred to the Manchester flight, send a telegram, and hire a scooter for Lonely. Make Lonely drive a car and he was reduced at once to a kind of dangerous terror, like a rabbit with a machine-gun, but give him a bike and he was hell on wheels. Take him to a caff after that, and buy him beer, and tell him about his getaway.

'What's an archaeologist?' Lonely asked.

'A sort of scholar,' said Callan.

'I can't be a scholar,' said Lonely. 'Suppose the rest of them start talking to me.'

'Tell them you've got laryngitis,' said Callan.

'What's laryngitis?'

'It's something wrong with your throat,' said Callan. 'And there will be if you don't belt up.'

'So I just go back to London then?' said Lonely. 'But how can I, Mr Callan? I'm a wanted man.'

'This plane's going to Manchester,' said Callan.

Lonely looked alarmed. 'I never been there in my life,' he said.

'It's a city, isn't it?' said Callan. 'It's got caffs and pubs and chip-shops. You'll manage.'

'How long, Mr Callan?'

'Few days,' said Callan. 'Don't worry son. I'll look after you. I've got a place there all lined up for you.'

'You sure?' said Lonely.

Callan knew his duty: he licked his finger then

made the appropriate actions. 'See this wet, see this dry, cross my heart and hope to die,' he said. Lonely was content.

Nutter Bradley wasn't. He said so, over and over in the bar of his hotel. 'It's too soon,' he said. 'I've just got here.'

'Found a bird, have you?' said Callan.

'You can't mix business with pleasure,' Bradley quoted. 'Don't you believe it. I *always* mix business with pleasure.'

'I think you're scared,' said Callan. Bradley stood up. 'Sit down,' Callan said. 'We can't fight here.' Bradley sat.

'One day, dad,' he said. 'One day...'

'When you've got your nerve back,' said Callan. 'Looks as if it's going to be a long wait.'

Bradley sat in silence, and Callan waited. He'd worked with Bradleys before: lots of them. They were never easy. For the small things, the safe things, fine: but when it came to the big jobs they needed days to get their nerve up, and even then you couldn't trust them: they got reckless, and a bit greedy too. Liked to see the blood flow. Ah well, it would all depend on the timing.

'You're a cold bastard, aren't you?' Bradley said, and still Callan waited. 'All right, sod you. What do I have to do?'

Callan told him, and Bradley began to relax, one muscle at a time.

'Suits me,' he said. 'If you *want* to do all the rough work—'

'I don't,' said Callan. 'But I'm the only one who can get it done.'

'Fair enough.' Bradley gestured for more drinks.

223

'So I'm the rearguard, is that it?'

'That's it,' said Callan. 'You seen the village?'

Bradley nodded. 'Drove through yesterday.'

'Know the house?'

'Yeah. Top end of the village.'

'You can move quiet when you want to,' said Callan. 'See that you do.' He took the glass of wine the waiter brought him. 'Quiet in, and quiet out,' said Callan. 'And nobody gets hurt.' This time it was Bradley who stayed silent. 'You heard me.'

'All right,' said Bradley. 'I heard you. I was thinking about the Polybios boat.'

'The Big Man knows about that?'

'The Big Man knows about everything, mate. And don't you forget it.'

'What about the boat?'

'Suppose they move it?'

'Then it's off,' said Callan. 'If we don't get a boat we haven't a prayer.'

'We could get another boat,' Bradley said.

'Not today we couldn't,' said Callan.

Bradley looked even more relieved. That would never do.

'Don't you worry, son,' said Callan. 'The police will be watching that boat just like they watch the house.'

'Bastard,' said Bradley.

Callan rose.

'Hold on,' said Bradley. 'What about my ammo?'

'All in good time,' Callan said.

Hunter said, 'I understand you were once a medical student. That will make things a lot easier.'

Nicky remembered what he had been taught to

224

do if this happened, and said nothing.

'You're expecting a beating, of course,' said Hunter. 'Men punching you in the kidneys, rubber hoses, that sort of thing. Cigarette burns perhaps, electric shocks to the testicles.'

Nicky willed himself not to speak.

'We don't do that,' Hunter said. 'We don't have to. It's messy, gratuitously cruel, and really not terribly reliable. I daresay that surprises you.' He waited, and again Nicky fought to achieve silence. 'The trouble is that once a man is totally broken, even he himself is never quite sure what the truth is, no matter how much he may want to tell it...' He broke off with the donnish petulance of a lecturer side-tracked into irrelevance. 'Now where was I? Oh yes. Your career as a medical student. How long had you been studying?'

He waited, and Nicky stayed silent.

'My dear boy, there is really no point in this,' said Hunter, and consulted a yellow-backed file. 'You're extremely well documented, you know. By the by, are you familiar with my filing system? No of course not. How could you be? At the moment you're in a yellow file – surveillance only. If things should go awry – and I do trust they will not – a red one will be substituted. The symbolism is obvious, as I'm sure you'll agree. Red is for elimination.'

Nicky shifted in his chair, but Hunter was immersed in the file and did not look up.

'University of Athens,' he read. 'Final year. My poor chap, you have been unlucky in life. But at least you'll understand what Snell will have to say. Snell is our resident psychiatrist – interrogation techniques and so on. Don't bother memorising the name by-the-by; it's quite untraceable. He is also a qualified doctor. I'm sure you'll he most interested in what he has to tell you about his methods of work.' He waited, then added, 'Interested, and perfectly appalled.'

There was a knock at the door, and Meres came in.

'Is Snell ready?' Hunter asked.

'He asked for another five minutes, sir,' said Meres.

'Very well.' Hunter went to the drinks cabinet, and turned back to Nicky. 'My dear boy, I'm awfully sorry,' he said. 'Would you like a drink?'

This time Nicky, spoke.

'Whisky,' he said. 'Neat.'

16

The ward was as noisy as ever, and this time there were no screens round the bed. There wasn't even the illusion of privacy. But then Detective Sergeant Walters hadn't come officially, just stopped by with a few magazines and a bag of fruit with a bottle of beer at the bottom.

'It's very nice of you, sergeant,' said Kyle.

'Better not call me that any more,' said Walters. 'My retirement's through.' He sat for a moment, then said, 'Sit on your arse for forty years, and hang your hat on a pension.'

Kyle looked bewildered. 'A real clever poet

wrote that. Educated man, too. Only bit of poetry I ever remembered. Not that I did much sitting.'

'What'll you do now then?' Kyle asked.

'Bit of a holiday,' said Walters, 'then one of those security firms I suppose. No good being idle, not on my pension.' He plucked a grape from the bunch he had brought, and munched reflectively.

'Sorry to hear about your trouble,' he said. We all were.'

'Thanks,' said Kyle.

'Nothing worse than these mad kick and run bastards. 'They're murder to trace. I mean without a description where are you?'

'I know it sounds daft,' said Kyle. 'But I told the inspector–'

'Yes,' said Walters, companionable as ever, 'I saw the report. I suppose you had your reasons for lying, but I'm damned if I can see what they were.'

Kyle said carefully, 'I don't know what you're talking about and I don't care.'

'Then I'll tell you,' said Walters.

'Don't bother. Just take your bloody fruit and go home.'

'It was all in the timing,' said Walters. 'You slipped up badly there, lad. But the pain you were in – I don't suppose you were in any shape to work it out properly.'

Kyle wanted more than anything else in the world for Walters to go away, but the old bastard was on to something – he could feel it – and he had to know what it was. 'All right,' he said wearily. 'Let's have it. Whatever it is.'

'The trouble is you're a copper,' Walters said.

We know you and we like you and you're good at your job. Why should we doubt what *you* tell us? No reason. So we don't check. Only I remembered a couple of things and I did check.'

'Check what?'

'What time you left the gym, what time you were found by the park. You couldn't have got there on foot in that time – not if you were an Olympic gold medallist.' He took another grape. 'So it had to be a car. You were taken there, son. Taken for a ride as you might say.' He grimaced. Either the grape or the joke was sour. 'That means the odds are that you did see whoever it was. And that makes another lie. And why two men? Why not three, four, a whole gang? My guess is because there really were two – and you were in such a bad way you let it slip out.'

'You said you remembered a couple of things,' said Kyle. 'What were they?'

Walters nodded approvingly. 'That's good,' he said. 'That's using your head. I'll tell you what they were. You asked me about a smelly feller – and you were told to lay off.'

'Who told you that?'

'Nobody,' said Walters. 'But you must have been – because I was told to lay off.'

'And you think that's why I'm here now?'

'We've got the means all right,' said Walters. 'A tearaway's boot. And the opportunity. A car – and a nice dark place. My way we've got the motive as well. You didn't do what you were told.'

'Have you told anybody else this?' Kyle asked.

'Why should I?' said Walters. 'I've retired.'

'Then why tell me?'

'Being retired doesn't mean I've stopped being nosy,' said Walters. 'What in the world possessed you to get into that car?'

'My mum,' said Kyle. 'They said she'd had an accident.'

Walters selected another grape. 'I bet that's not all they said about your mum,' he said.

Kyle looked at him. The clear young eyes held an expression they rarely contained: uncertainty.

'What am I going to do, Mr Walters?' he asked.

Lonely had been passing the time by practising with his tool-kit. Over lunch he informed Callan proudly that he could open up every drum in the place.

'In fact I been thinking, Mr Callan,' he said. 'If we set off early we could do that jeweller's before we went to your bird's place.'

Callan vetoed this: they'd have quite enough to do that night without stealing gold honeycombs. He ordered veal, and made Lonely order it too. When it came he wrapped it in his napkin, and pocketed it, surreptitiously, and made Lonely do the same. Lonely obeyed without hesitation. You didn't argue with Mr Callan. All the same, you couldn't help wondering sometimes...

After lunch he spent time telling Lonely how to get on in the aircraft on his own. It took time, and it took patience, but eventually he got there.

'The only thing,' said Lonely, 'they'll see my name on my passport.'

'No they won't,' said Callan. 'All they'll do is look at the photograph. The name they'll worry about is the one on your ticket.'

'But that isn't my name.'

Slowly Callan said, 'I know it's not. It's Blythe's name. And Blythe's supposed to be ill. He's had a doctor to see him, just to make sure. That's why he's going home.'

'But he isn't going home, Mr Callan,' said Lonely. 'I am.'

Callan sighed. 'You're Blythe,' he said. 'You've got laryngitis and you can't speak – but you're Blythe till you get to Manchester.'

'But what if they pick up the real Blythe?'

'They won't,' said Callan. 'Not till you're home and dry.'

'But what about him?' Lonely persisted.

'It'll be rough,' said Callan, 'and he thinks he knows it. But he doesn't. He has no idea at all...'

But he went to see the patient anyway. Keep him happy, keep him smiling, and above all keep him thinking it was going to work... Blythe was in bed, elegant in pyjamas of pale blue silk, his battery of pills reinforced by an enormous bottle of a pink mixture with white sediment. It looked vile.

'The doctor's been then?' Callan asked.

'As you see,' said Blythe. 'He left me this. It tastes revolting.'

'Why do you take it then?'

'Because my stomach *is* upset,' said Blythe. Callan smiled: he couldn't help it. 'Don't you dare laugh at me,' Blythe yelled. 'I couldn't bear it.'

The panic in his voice was as obvious as Lonely's smell.

'You want out, Randy?' Callan asked.

'Can you do it without me?'

Callan shook his head. 'Not a chance,' he said. And it was true. If Blythe was out, Callan couldn't risk Lonely, and without Lonely they couldn't move. He waited.

At last Blythe said, 'I thought you would say that.'

'It's true,' said Callan.

Blythe looked at him, weighing the honesty of his words.

'You really mean that,' he said. Pride stirred in him, flickered, then died under the wash of fear.

'If only I could have a drink,' he said.

'Why don't you?' said Callan.

'It makes me sick,' Blythe said.

It was appalling. Unbelievable should have been the word, but he had to believe it. He'd been shown the stuff they used: the laboratory, clinically clean, the drugs and hypodermics, the very textbook references. And the rats. Snell was still experimenting with the rats, pushing his technique further and further. Nicky had always hated and feared rats; but what Snell had done to the ones he displayed made Nicky pity them. It had even made him speak.

'They should be destroyed,' he said.

Snell looked up at him, a mild man with a mild voice, blinking through glittering spectacles.

'They will be,' he said, 'when I've finished with them.'

The rats had never stopped their crazy, obsessive gyrations, and Snell had gone on talking: about the strain on the heart, the withdrawal from reality, the onset of madness. And he'd proved everything,

231

point by point. It could be done, and it would be done. Nicky didn't doubt that for a moment. This small, clever, humourless man would do exactly what the one called Hunter told him, and watch its results with the same detached, objective interest that he had bestowed on the rats. On one terrible night Nicky had been punched, kicked, beaten with clubs, and he had endured. But this was different. This couldn't fail to work: it was scientifically infallible. The only way not to tell was to escape. Nicky moved in his chair in the tiny, cell-like room, and Fitzmaurice moved to face him.

'Now you just take it easy, baby,' he said, and smiled. His smile was warm, friendly, humane, but Nicky was learning. Escape was impossible.

'So you went through the whole process?' said Hunter.

'In general terms,' Snell said. 'Not enough to enable him to do it himself, of course. But enough to be sure he understands.'

'And does he?'

'Oh yes,' said Snell. 'He's a very bright young man. Really a first-class mind.'

'Did he say anything?'

'"They should be destroyed," said Snell. 'He was referring to my rats.'

'He disliked them?'

'He pitied them,' said Snell. 'He dislikes me. Hates me might be more accurate.'

'Will he talk, do you think?'

'It's extremely likely. He's very imaginative, you know.'

Hunter said, 'There isn't a great deal of time.

You'd better have your stuff ready, just in case.'

Gently rebuking, Snell said, 'My stuff is always ready.'

Hunter leaned forward and pressed the intercom buzzer.

'I'll see the young man now,' he said.

'Would you like me to leave?' Snell asked.

'By no means,' said Hunter. 'I want you here.'

It was possible to walk by oneself after all, without the support of the black giant just behind your right shoulder. It was even possible to go into that room, to face the charming, soft-spoken man called Hunter, and stand erect. It was not possible to be unaware of Snell, mildly, objectively looking at him. Nicky's knees began to tremble.

'Get him a chair,' said Hunter, and Fitzmaurice did so. Nicky wanted to remain standing, to retain that much of courage, of honour, but the big man forced him down. Hunter clasped his hands on his desk.

'I want to talk to you about bombs,' he said. 'Or rather I want you to talk to me about them.' He paused, then added: 'To begin with.'

'You really will do this to me, won't you?' Nicky said.

'You know we will,' said Hunter.

'And then I'll tell you anyway, won't I? There's nothing I can do to stop myself.'

'My dear boy,' said Hunter, 'you are wasting time and we both know it. Unfortunately I have no time to waste. Now who will you answer: Snell, or me?'

Nicky leaned back and closed his eyes.

'Ask your questions,' he said.

Once you started kidnapping girls you never had a moment to yourself, thought Callan. Your gun to check, and your boat to check, and all your troops in need of an individual pep-talk: Lonely, terrified of Manchester, which to him seemed as remote as Ulan Bator: Blythe with his unreliable tummy and even less reliable bowels: and Bradley screaming for his ammo, and either unable or unwilling to think about anything else until it had been restored to him.

'You're sure you know what to do?' Callan asked.

'Yeah yeah.'

'All right then,' said Callan. 'Tell me.'

'Get there for midnight.'

'Get where for midnight?'

'Up in the hills above the house,' said Bradley. 'When I get your signal I come on down.'

'What signal?'

'Light switch,' said Bradley. 'On – off three times.' He looked into Callan's face, saw the tension.

'You worry too much,' he said.

'I bet the Big Man doesn't think so,' said Callan.

From Bradley's hotel he went to the boat, and checked it for the last time: fuel and supplies all he needed, the engines running like silk. He waited till dark, then ran her out into the bay and anchored, riding lights just as they should be: the millionaire playboy kipping down for the night. Through a pair of night-glasses he looked at the arc of the bay that contained the village of Kronis. The thin moon showed him a group of men joking, talking by the two caques, another group by the café in the square, and women in doorways, knitting, gossiping, yelling at children playing in the streets. All the houses gleamed with light: the Polybios house, remote on the hill, glowed like a beacon from its lower storey. Dinner time, thought Callan, and transferred the glasses to the Polybios boat. None of the fishermen went near it, but once a policeman came down from the village and checked its moorings. The fishermen ignored him, and he ignored them. That, Callan thought, was just as it should be. He went to the galley, found a tin of baked beans, and ate them cold from the tin. Fuel. When the thing started you had to keep going, and for that you need energy, and that means fuel, and if all you've got time for is cold baked beans well get them down you.

He wondered if Blythe had ever eaten cold baked beans: ever could come to that. And from there his thoughts turned to Bradley, and his fist clenched over the ammo. Maybe he should have done something about those shells: given them back after he'd taken the powder out... But that wasn't on without a vice to hold them, and in any case, Bradley wasn't a novice. Even if Callan had managed to get at them, he would know... In straggling groups the men by the boats began to move back to the village, the café emptied. Dinner time, thought Callan, and tossed the empty can of beans overboard. He waited again. Very faintly he could hear the voices of women calling their kids in from play. This was a community that wouldn't sit up late: small farmers, doing a bit of fishing on the side, they needed all the daylight they could get... He waited a little longer, then checked once more. Fuel and stores were still fine, and why wouldn't they be? But the day you forgot to double-check was the day things went wrong. He went over the rubber dinghy on deck: inflated full, no sign of a leak, and the outboard he knew was working a treat. He'd tested it... Paddles, oh my God. He'd forgotten about the paddles. But there they were tucked away in a flap-pocket in the dinghy's hull. He took out the Colt Python, spun the chamber, checked it for the last time and put it in a locker on the well-deck. The equipment was perfect: only he was fallible.

Slowly clouds began to gather, dimming the moon. That was a bonus he hadn't hoped for, but with cohorts like his he could do with a bonus. Callan took off his shirt and trousers: beneath them he wore a pair of swimming trunks. Silently, without a splash, he lowered himself into the water and struck out for the hotel beach. The sea was easy, calm, the little wavelets soft as sighs. Another bonus: he would need all he could get... When he reached the shore he looked at his watch, and the time glowed up at him, three minutes past ten. Water resistant to seventy feet, the guarantee said: well at least it was still going. He turned and looked back at the village. Already some houses were in darkness...

Lonely was nervous. Well, you expected that: Callan was nervous himself. But at least the little man wasn't drinking. Or smelling. Not yet. He looked a little shaken though, when Callan

236

walked in in swimming trunks.

'Been for a swim, Mr Callan?' he asked.

Gently, Callan told himself; nicely. Don't make him worse than he is.

'That's right,' he said, and fetched a towel from the bathroom, began to dry himself.

'You'll catch your death,' said Lonely.

'Don't you believe it,' Callan said. 'It's like a warm bath.'

'I was beginning to think you'd got lost,' said Lonely. 'Or maybe the job was off.'

'It's on,' said Callan.

Lonely sighed, but said nothing. Callan went to the fridge and took out the two pieces of veal left over from lunch, began pressing Blythe's sleeping tablets into them.

'Feeling peckish, Mr Callan?'

Callan said. 'This house we're going to. There's a dog there. This'll put him to sleep.'

'Oh,' said Lonely. 'Oh I see.' Then his face looked grave. 'That Dimitri should have told us there was a dog there. You can never rely on foreigners.'

You can say that again, mate.

Lonely went over to the fridge, and carefully wiped the handle with a towel where Callan had touched it.

'If you don't mind being careful what you touch, Mr Callan,' he said. 'Only I've wiped the place off.'

'All of it?' Lonely nodded. 'What a busy little bee you are,' said Callan.

'No point in being nicked if we don't have to be,' said Lonely.

You can say that again too.

Callan looked at his watch: twenty past. There was still plenty of time.

'You know where you're going?' said Callan.

'Yes, Mr Callan. Them like plants at the bottom of the garden.'

Them like plants were vines, but Callan let it go.

'And go easy with that scooter. Don't get close enough for them to hear you.'

'You know me, Mr Callan.'

And indeed I do, thought Callan. You're scared but you're a craftsman. You'll do it right.

'You know I been thinking,' said Lonely. 'Clever of them to put that bird on an island, wasn't it?'

'Was it?'

'Of course,' said Lonely. 'Look how dodgy it is to get her off. I call that clever.'

Callan gave him the veal.

'You better take care of that,' he said. 'Mind you don't eat it.'

'Not even with chips,' said Lonely.

'I'd better be off then,' Callan said, and picked up the keys of the Fiat. 'Mind how you go, old son.'

'Aren't you going to put no clothes on?'

Callan said, 'You're forgetting. I'm going by boat.'

'Oh,' said Lonely. 'That's right... Good luck, Mr Callan.'

He smiled, but the smell was very near.

'Relax,' said Callan. 'You're on your holidays.'

He went to Blythe's chalet. The dentist was dressed in a black shirt and dark grey slacks, as

Callan had told him, but his face was blotchy and he looked ill. By the looks of the bottle he'd been hitting the medicine as if it were ouzo. He looked up at Callan.

'Good God,' he said.

'Don't worry,' said Callan. 'I haven't come courting.'

'Please don't take it amiss, but you do rather relieve my mind.' He tried to smile, and failed. 'It's time?'

'Yes,' said Callan, and gave him the car-keys.

'Oh dear,' said Blythe.

'When you leave the car,' Callan said, 'wipe off everything you touch with your handkerchief.' Blythe looked bewildered. 'Fingerprints.'

'I've never been finger-printed in my life.'

'You will be,' said Callan, 'if you don't wipe off that car.'

Blythe said, 'It's real, isn't it? I mean it's really going to happen.'

'That's right,' said Callan.

'I don't think I can do it.'

'You know where to go, don't you?'

'I wait by the big rock above the house, then go into the vineyard when the little man's opened the door.'

'Well then?'

'It isn't that,' said Blythe. He looked down at his hands: they were shaking. 'I'm afraid,' he said.

'We're all afraid,' said Callan. 'We'll still do it.'

He went out then, and down to the shore. Behind him the hotel was a blaze of light, a rock-group blared, but cloud still covered the moon and there were few lights in the village. He went into the water, swimming steadily towards the *Gala-tea's* riding lights, climbed up silently by the anchor chain aft. Quickly he dried himself and dressed. Another look at his watch. Ten fifty-five. Five minutes to go. He went to the locker and got out the Colt Python, checking it by touch in the near darkness, then looked out once again towards the village. The cafe lights still burned, and one or two others. He concentrated on the Polybios house: only one light there, and as he watched it disappeared, like an eye shutting. Callan hauled the dinghy to the side, let it go into the sea. It hit the water with a hard smashing sound that shattered the silence, and held on to the painter, waited and watched. There was no reaction at all. He stuck the Python in his trousers' waist-band, then lowered himself into the dinghy, took a paddle and shoved off. As he did so he heard, very faintly, the putt-putt sound of a motor scooter from the hotel. At least one of his cohorts was going into battle, he thought, and hoped to God the other one could find the nerve to come too.

17

Hunter ran back the tape and switched on. It really had gone rather well. Snell had been right, as he usually was in such matters. The boy had too much knowledge and too much imagination to withstand what he had been shown.

Nicky's voice said: 'There's nothing I can do to

stop myself.'

His own voice answered: 'My dear boy, you are wasting time and we both know it. Unfortunately I have no time to waste. Now who will you answer: Snell, or me?'

There was a silence then. The silence, he supposed, of heartbreak for a cause once fought for, lived for, and now about to be betrayed. It was none of his business.

Nicky's voice said: 'Ask your questions.'

'Why did you send a bomb to Vardakis?'

'He sent one to us.'

'Indeed? Tell me about it.'

Nicky's voice came back impatiently: 'Why do you pretend you don't know?' More silence then: 'Oh very well. He threw a bomb into our headquarters.'

'The Parnassos Restaurant?'

'Yes. He burnt it down.'

'Vardakis did this?'

'Please,' Nicky's voice said. 'Don't make fun of me. Not after what you've done... I mean he hired people.'

'Who were they?'

'I've no idea,' said Nicky. The fact that he didn't know an answer panicked him. 'I swear I've no idea.'

Hunter switched off then, and looked at Meres.

'It seemed to me that he was telling the truth,' he said. 'I took him over and round it several times. He really does have no idea – although his group would very much like to. You really did handle that rather well, Toby.'

'Thank you, sir.'

'Then we talked about the other bomb – the one they sent to Vardakis. He's really rather a talented youth. He made it himself... It impressed you, I gather?'

'It was quite adequately lethal, sir,' said Meres. 'I didn't exactly enjoy immobilising it.'

'I should imagine not... He hates Vardakis, you know. They all do.'

'So I should suppose, sir,' Meres said.

'Should you?' Hunter considered. 'With respect, Toby, I rather doubt it. In this country we don't seem to hate any more... Or love, for that matter. We've lost the talent for it – and the taste come to that. Hatred seems to belong to less complicated societies than ours. They work at it, you know. They're even prepared to risk danger for it.'

'I can see that they regard Vardakis as a class enemy, sir–'

'So am I, Toby. So are you. But to them he is much more than that.'

Meres hated these symposia with Hunter, playing straight man so that Hunter could think out loud, but it would never do to show it.

Deferentially he said, 'What is he then, sir?'

'A traitor.' Hunter considered the word. 'It was an Edwardian who said that he would far rather betray his friend than betray his country. You, I feel sure, regard that as liberal nonsense.'

'I do, sir.'

'So does Nicky... Although in his case one may use the word cause rather than country. It's happening all over the place, don't you think? Self-appointed judges, juries, executioners. All over the world... It keeps us in business.'

Meres shifted in his chair: another minute and the old boy would be crying.

'Vardakis had been a friend,' Hunter said. 'A good friend. In the days when they fought the Germans. He was one of them: their leader in fact. They needed him. He, it seems, did not need them. He went after money instead, and left them to their own devices. Without Vardakis they didn't manage terribly well.'

'But Nicky wouldn't even have been born then, sir,' said Meres.

'It would seem that in certain societies it is still possible to inherit hatred,' said Hunter. 'There can be no doubt of Nicky's hatred of Vardakis. One doesn't send parcel bombs for a mere whim.'

'And he had sent them a bomb too, sir.'

'To an empty restaurant. Really Vardakis has shown remarkable forbearance. They have made other attempts on him, you know.'

'I didn't know, sir.'

'Oh, of course,' said Hunter. 'Last time there was trouble here I set Callan on to watch him. But it wasn't only here, Toby. They've followed Vardakis about like bloodhounds.'

'It shouldn't have been too difficult, sir. Sophie Kollonaki usually knows where he is.'

'It seems that they had scruples about using her– Or even telling her.'

'Are you saying she didn't know, sir?'

Hunter said, 'I am.'

'But surely–'

'Vardakis would have told her? Nicky is quite convinced he did not.'

'But why not, sir?'

243

'He was afraid that if he did she might accept her party's ruling and join in the hunt. He loves her, you see. He couldn't have borne that. He couldn't have borne having to defend himself against her. This of course was absolutely splendid for Nicky and his friends. They could go on throwing bombs and pulling triggers in the certain knowledge their victim would do his damnedest to hush it up. Really to throw a bomb into an empty restaurant was a very mild reaction.'

'But he showed her the bomb they sent to him, sir,' Meres said. 'I know he did. I was there.'

'And why did he do that, I wonder?'

'It looks as if even Vardakis has had enough, sir.'

'I think it goes beyond that,' Hunter said. 'Vardakis is a very able man. A man who thinks, Toby.'

Meres took it: there was nothing else he could do.

'That bomb could have been opened anywhere in that house, and whoever was present would probably have been killed: certainly maimed. Vardakis knew it, and he deduced that Nicky's friends knew it too.'

'Did Nicky tell you the same story?' Meres asked.

'He did,' Hunter said, 'In the eyes of her friends Sophie Kollonaki has become expendable.'

Two floors below Nicky sat in his cell-like room, the door of which still bore the word 'Caretaker' in flaking paint. Compared with other cells he had known, it was luxurious. He had a wash-basin and shower stall, the bed was comfortable, the light – though he couldn't switch it off – gently shaded. But the locked door was of metal, the window barred, and they had taken away his belt and shoe-laces. Carefully he went over the room, but it had been devised by experts. It contained nothing he could use as either weapon or tool. Nicky took off his shirt: washed, and dried himself on the paper towels that were the only ones provided. These people really are careful, he thought, and picked up his shirt. Suddenly the label caught his eye: 100% nylon, he read. 'Needs no ironing.' Carefully he laid the shirt out on the bed and rolled it into a long thin rope. The loop took a little time, but he achieved it in the end, and went into the shower-stall. It had no curtain or curtain frame, but the overhead sprinkler was old and solid. He tied one end of the shirt to it, put the loop round his neck, balanced on a projecting ledge, and jumped. Every movement was recorded by a TV camera, but the guard on duty was dozing. When he woke up, Nicky was already hanging, his legs kicking convulsively. By the time they cut him down he was dead.

Callan beached the dinghy in a tiny cove a little way from the village, hauling it up into the sand. It made a soft rasping noise, but he hadn't any choice. He didn't dare risk its floating away. He looked at the ground ahead of him; rough, uneven, but nothing too tricky. He could make time without taking any chances, and just as well. It didn't do to leave Lonely too long on his own.

When he reached the vineyard he took cover at once, falling prone behind a broken stone wall. There was no sign of the little man, but that was by no means bad. Callan would have been appalled if there had been. He waited till his eyes grew used to the muted moonlight, then looked round him, quartering the ground, section by section, until at last he spotted somebody, the silver white flash of a face changing position in the cover of an ancient lemon tree. Callan drew the Colt Python and wriggled forward. He and the other feller were the only two in the vineyard: he was sure of it. And if the other feller wasn't Lonely, he'd have to be taken care of anyway. He was more than half way there when the little man called softly: 'It's all right, Mr Callan. It's me.' Callan did the rest of the distance in a crouching run, and lay prone at Lonely's side. Like Callan, the little man wore a dark shirt, denim trousers, rubber-soled shoes.

'Any trouble?' Callan whispered.

'Not up to now,' Lonely said. 'Lights is all out. Nobody stirring.'

'The dog?'

'Keeps by the house, Mr Callan. I think they got a chain on it.'

'Right,' Callan said. 'Give me the meat.'

Lonely handed it over, then Callan suddenly remembered something. Savagely he cursed himself. With Lonely you had to think of everything. and now and again you slipped, but why slip now?

'I just thought of something,' he said, keeping it calm. 'Your luggage.'

'What about it, Mr Callan?'

'You didn't bring it, did you?'

Lonely looked abashed.

'As a matter of fact I did,' he said. 'Strapped it on the scooter. I wasn't going to leave it lying round for a bunch of Greek waiters. Did I do wrong, Mr Callan?'

Callan let out his breath in a sigh of relief. 'No,' he said. 'You did fine.' He inched himself forward. 'I'd better attend to the dog.'

'Mind how you go, Mr Callan,' Lonely said. 'They got tin cans with pebbles in them strung out all over. Not that you can miss them.' He grimaced. 'Amateurs.'

As always when it came to his trade, Lonely was right. The cans were there in great festoons. It would take a blind man not to miss them. Callan eased round them and kept an eye open for more sophisticated early warning systems. There weren't any. Not in the vineyard at any rate, and not in the garden that lay between it and the house. He moved past clumps of roses and carnations, their scent heady and sweet, then crouched behind the last rose-bush before the path leading to the house. The dog lay on the patio, not moving. Callan eased himself a little to one side, and still the dog didn't stir. There was no wind to carry his scent, and Fido slept. That wouldn't do at all: he'd have to be awake to enjoy his nice snack. Callan picked up a piece of hard, dry earth, and lobbed it on to the path. The sound it made was tiny, but Fido came awake even so. The sound hadn't meant danger to him, that was obvious, but it had broken his sleep. He yawned and stretched, then sniffed at the fragments of earth. Callan wadded the veal into a tighter lump, and threw it a little further. It thumped softly on

247

to the hard earth, and the dog whimpered and moved forward, its chain rattled softly. This is it, thought Callan. If it's been trained the way it should be, it won't touch it.

Fido moved on, still suspicious, stopped and sniffed, then its head came up, teeth flashed and tore, and the meat was gone. Callan could hear the chewing, gulping sounds, then the dog moved again, sniffing at the ground, looking for more. Sorry, thought Callan, that's all there is, and that's probably too much, poor perisher. Silently, cautiously, he eased back to the vineyard while the dog still hunted roast veal.

'All set, Mr Callan?' said Lonely.

'Give me a few minutes.' He looked back from the vineyard to the road. Telephone wires. Three telephones: the café, Polybios's house – and wherever the coppers were staying. Better be safe than sorry. 'Are there any wire cutters in that kit of yours?' he asked.

'Course there are,' said Lonely. 'There's everything.'

'Nip out and cut the telephone wires then.'

Lonely demurred.

'It's high up there,' he said.

'Gawd blimey O'Reilly,' said Callan. 'Five thousand nicker and you won't even climb a pole?'

Lonely went up like a monkey, and Callan heard the soft twang of wires parting, but Lonely coming down made no sound at all.

'Good lad,' said Callan. 'I knew you could do it.' Lonely smirked. 'Now let's see how the dog's getting on.'

The two men went into the garden, and were no

more than shadows moving. Callan had been trained to this, trained by experts, but the self-taught Lonely was equally silent, equally elusive. I suppose in his way he's a minor genius, thought Callan. The only thing missing is the brain. They reached the end of the garden at last, and Callan picked out the dog, lying on its side. He tried again with a piece of dry earth and the dog made no move. He threw another, heavier piece, and the dog didn't even stir. The third one Callan aimed at the dog itself, but still there was no reaction. Cautiously, holding the Colt Python, he moved forward and bent over it. The dog wouldn't bother them that night: maybe never again.

He signalled to Lonely, but the little man was already moving up to the door, examining it with the concentration of an eminent specialist in the middle of a tricky diagnosis. He studied it, frowning, then handed Callan his kit. Callan knew a few things about opening locks himself, but with Lonely around he acted as labourer. Lonely was the craftsman. The little man selected a pencil torch, shielded the tiny beam of light with his body, and examined first the door-frame, then the locks. He moved slowly and methodically, and Callan wanted to yell at him to get on with it, but that wasn't the way and he knew it. He willed himself to patience. At last Lonely switched off the torch and delivered his diagnosis.

'Two Mantons,' he said. 'I can manage them all right, *and* the chain, but there's two bolts as well. Old 'uns by the look of them. Just iron – but it'll take time. I think I'd better take a look at the window. It'll be easier tackling them Mantons from inside anyway.'

He moved off towards the back of the house, and Callan followed. Drawing-room and living-room windows were at the front, and probably tricky. It was at the back of the house that people got careless. You bolted your door and that was that. Not this house. The windows were so tiny that Callan doubted if even Lonely could get through them, and every one was shut. Again Lonely took the pencil torch, and again he set about the same, patient diagnosis. But this time he looked cheerful.

'No need to bother about the back door,' he said. 'This'll do us. Suction cup and glass cutters, please.'

So Callan stopped being a labourer and became a nursing sister, while Doctor Lonely operated on a window. He stuck the suction cup on the glass and cut round it in a circle. The sounds he made would have roused the dog in a second, but the dog had ceased to care. Absorbed, concentrated, he worked on. He's so busy he's even forgotten to be scared, thought Callan. Lonely pulled on the suction cup and the glass came free. He handed it to Callan who put it carefully down as the little man scrambled up on the window ledge, and looked up for the fastening. His hand moved to the window, then drew back.

'Cheeky,' said Lonely. 'They got an alarm on here. Let's have the wire cutters, please.'

Callan handed them over, and Lonely worked, absorbed, then handed them back. 'Naughty, that was,' he said.

His hand moved through the hole in the glass,

the fastening clicked, and what was left of the window slid open.

'I'll just nip in and open the back door for you,' said Lonely. 'You'll never get through that.'

'Will you?' Callan asked.

'Just watch,' Lonely said.

A contortionist could have done no better. In near darkness and total silence, Lonely went through as if he were a midget. Callan handed him his tools and waited. It seemed to take a hell of a long time, but it opened at last.

'What the hell happened?' said Callan.

'Mr Callan,' said Lonely, 'there's Mantons on the back door too. *And* they're locked from the inside.'

'Well of course they are,' said Callan. 'They're not just to keep us out, they're to keep the bird in. Now come and do the front door.'

It was a treat to watch the little man find his way across a house he'd never been in before. Of course now he was inside he was niffing steadily, but his scooter ride would take care of that.

They reached the door in utter silence, and Lonely set to work. Pencil torch, twirl, and wire cutters: the front door too had an alarm wire. But Lonely cut it deftly, and laboured on, and Callan looked at the bolts on the door. Like the door itself they were massive, and made to withstand almost any shock less than a battering ram. Hand-forged, he thought, and anything up to a couple of hundred years old, and good for a couple of hundred more: and a dead loss even then if there were still any Lonelys about. Lonely probed and listened, and probed again. There was a soft double click, and one lock was loosed; the other one took no time at all. Callan reached out his hand to a bolt and Lonely pushed it away: something he'd never dare do in any other circumstances, but in these he was the boss, he knew. He took the pencil torch and examined the bolts, then used the cutters again: the bolts too were wired. You really do know your stuff, thought Callan, but even then Lonely wasn't satisfied. He gestured to Callan for the kit, and took out a tiny oil can, squirted oil with deliberate care on the bolts and hinges, checked, and squirted again. Come on, thought Callan. Come *on*. But at last he was satisfied, unhooked the chain, and opened the door. It swung in, massive and silent, and Callan and Lonely moved out like shadows, into the night air that did such wonders for Lonely's symptoms.

'A lovely job, old son,' said Callan. 'Lovely.'

Lonely smirked. 'Not bad for an encore,' he said.

'I'm obliged to you,' said Callan.

'Always ready to help a mate,' Lonely said.

'I won't forget this,' said Callan. 'Now you better be off.'

'You sure I'll be all right in Manchester, Mr Callan?'

'Course you will,' said Callan. 'I told you.'

'It's just – like – being on me own.'

'It'll only be for a few days,' Callan said. 'You do what I told you and I'll be in touch.'

'So long then, Mr Callan.'

Callan held out his hand, and Lonely took it, then turned to go.

'Oi,' said Callan.

'Yes, Mr Callan?'

'Let's have the tool-kit back,' said Callan.

Lonely sighed and handed it over, and was gone. Callan zipped it up and stowed it in his pocket. Too bad to separate a craftsman from his tools, but if Lonely had that kit he'd open up every drum in Manchester. He moved softly over to the dog, and it made no response, not even when he crouched beside it, put his hand on its body. No sound of breathing, no response at all. Dying, he thought, or maybe dead. The first casualty. He stayed by it, listening hard, and at last he heard it: the very faint putt-putt of a motor-scooter. Time to move.

18

She slept under a sheet, and nothing else. Beneath it he could see the soft roundness of her body. He moved closer and became aware of two thin straps across her shoulders, so at least she didn't sleep raw. The night was going to be embarrassing enough without that. Softly he moved to the bed-head and looked down at her face: relaxed in sleep it looked far too young and vulnerable for what had to come... You're in a red file, Callan. Get on with it.

He put one hand across her mouth and pressed. For a moment she slept on, then suddenly shot up in the bed, her body stiff with terror. Callan put his other arm round her, immobilising her as she twisted and writhed, trying to bite the hand over her mouth. Through the thin stuff of her night-gown he could feel the moist warmth of her body... This is no time to be enjoying your work, he thought. Get on with it, Callan.

'My name's Callan,' he whispered. She continued to struggle.

'Your mother sent me to get you,' said Callan. The struggling continued, and he held her more tightly, till the pain made her gasp.

'Dimitri told you I was coming,' he said. 'Callan.'

Suddenly her body relaxed, but he continued to hold her.

'You know about me, don't you? Nod your head if you do.'

Her head nodded.

'Right. Now be a good girl and I'll let you go. Are you going to be a good girl?'

Again her head nodded, and he released her, but he still stayed close.

'He – he said not till Friday,' she whispered.

'Plans have been changed.'

'But he didn't tell me,' she said.

Callan said, 'He doesn't know.' He looked at his watch. 'You better get dressed.'

She made no move.

'He must know,' she said. 'Dimitri's in charge.'

'No, love,' said Callan. 'I am.'

She got out of bed, then. The nightgown was designed for a Cretan summer, and did little to hide her. She grabbed for a robe.

'We've got to talk to him,' she said.

Callan reached for the Colt Python, and it was

in his hand: not aimed at her. Just there: ready for when it was needed. Her eyes flicked to it: dilated with fear.

'You – you've come to kill me?' she said. 'Dimitri told me you'd come to help me.'

'I've come to get you off the island,' said Callan. 'Now will you get dressed?' She moved, hesitant, towards her clothes.

'Pants and a shirt,' said Callan. 'And pack some spares.'

Still she hesitated.

'For Christ's sake,' said Callan. 'If I'd come here for rape it would have been all over by now.'

She moved away from him into a corner. He heard the soft slither of nylon, the sound of a zip, and looked up. She was wearing a dark shirt and slacks, pushing her feet into sandals with tough, rubber soles. Just as well, he thought, she's going to need them. As he watched she shoved more clothes into a small zip-bag.

'What about Euphrosyne?' she asked: at least it sounded like that.

'Who?'

Impatiently she said, 'Mrs Polybios.'

'I've locked her in,' said Callan. 'She won't bother us. Anyway she's snoring like a shunting engine.'

'Euphrosyne always snores,' she said.

'Yeah,' said Callan. 'You can't blame her husband for visiting his mum.'

She smiled, then said, 'Please may I talk to Dimitri now?'

Callan stowed away the gun.

'After you,' he said.

They passed Euphrosyne's door: the snores were rhythmical still. Softly she led the way to another door, raised her hand to knock. Callan stopped her.

'The less noise the better,' he said. And it would be interesting to see Dimitri's face when he saw that Callan had moved on the wrong day. They went into the bedroom: one plain deal chest of drawers, a wash-stand with a jug and basin, an iron-framed bed painted black. The girl's room had been pretty, even luxurious, but Callan had occupied cells better furnished than Dimitri's. The only luxury he seemed to run to was a shelf of books.

He slept in pyjamas, as neat and contained as a cat: no snoring, no sound louder than a sigh. The girl opened her mouth to speak to him, but Callan stopped her, Dimitri, he thought, wouldn't need waking. They waited in silence, then suddenly Dimitri sat up, his eyes opened.

'Helena,' he said. 'What–?'

Callan moved forward.

'Hallo, Dimitri,' he said.

Dimitri glared at him. 'This is the wrong night,' he said. 'I told you.'

'It's as good a night as any,' said Callan.

Dimitri looked at Helena. 'Euphrosyne?' he asked.

'He locked her in,' she said.

'Everything's taken care of,' said Callan. 'It's time to go.'

'Wait,' said Dimitri. 'I want to get dressed.'

'I thought you wanted me to clobber you,' said Callan.

'If I have my clothes on it will at least look as if I tried,' Dimitri said.

Callan nodded, and turned to Helena. 'Go and listen to Mrs Polybios,' he said. 'If she starts anything, come and tell me.'

She left, and Dimitri got up, poured water into the basin, then splashed it over his face.

'I'm old,' he said. 'I'm getting slow. How long were you in here before I woke up?'

'Maybe a minute,' said Callan.

'You see? Slow,' Dimitri said, and went to the chest of drawers with the old cracked mirror above it. 'Why did you change the night?'

'Transport problems,' said Callan.

'I told you the Polybios boat is ready and waiting,' Dimitri said.

'The bloke who opened up the place gets seasick,' Callan said. 'I had to make other arrangements.'

Dimitri glanced at him, then opened the chest of drawers, and once more Callan flicked out the gun, once more aimed it at nothing in particular.

'I forgot to thank you for the loan of this,' he said. 'Nice gun. Nice balance. I've been lucky. I haven't had to use it so far.'

Slowly Dimitri's huge hands went into the drawer, came out with pants, trousers, a shirt. He took off his pyjamas and dressed with the total lack of concern of a man who has shared too many cramped quarters ever to be bothered by problems of modesty. As he stooped to put on shoes Callan opened the drawer, left-handed. In it was a vast Webley revolver, British Officers' issue, World War II. It was so clean it looked as if

257

it had been made last week.

'I don't think we'll bother using that,' said Callan. 'There might be an accident.' He gestured with the Python, then put it away, and they left the room, collected Helena, and moved downstairs. Callan took care to keep the girl between him and Dimitri. When they reached the hall, the girl said, 'I don't understand.'

'What?' said Callan.

'What about Hephaistos?'

First Euphrosyne, now Hephaistos. They were going through the whole Greek pantheon.

'The dog,' Dimitri said.

'I bribed him with a piece of meat,' said Callan.

Dimitri said, 'With Hephaistos that couldn't possibly work.'

'The meat had sleeping tablets in it.'

'How much?' Dimitri asked.

'Enough,' said Callan.

'Hephaistos was my dog,' Dimitri said. 'If you've killed him I–'

'If I've killed him he'll be dead,' said Callan, 'and I'll still be wondering why you didn't tell me he was here.'

Dimitri looked at Helena.

'Because on the night we agreed he wouldn't have been here,' he said.

At least you think on your feet, old son, thought Callan.

'All right,' he said. 'I'm sorry about the dog.' He reached for the Colt Python. 'You want me to belt you now?'

'There should be one other person here,' Dimitri said.

'Sophie Kollonaki got word to you about that?'

'She did.'

Callan switched the light on and off three times. 'He'll be along in a minute.'

'In that case,' Dimitri said. 'I think I shall wait for him to knock me unconscious.' The girl gasped.

'Suit yourself,' said Callan.

They waited in silence: one minute, two, and then there was the softest of sounds outside the door, and it swung open slowly, slowly. The feel of the butt of the Colt Python was a very comforting thing... A figure swayed deftly round the door and faced them. The Browning Standard in its hand encompassed them all in a lazy arc.

'Evening all,' Nutter Bradley said.

'You tricked me,' said Dimitri. 'You lied to me.'

There now, thought Callan. And you thought you had the monopoly of tricks and lies.

Helena said, 'Dimitri, what's wrong?'

'This is not the man Sophie said she would send.'

'He lost his nerve,' said Callan. 'The way you're acting I'm not surprised. Now hurry up and get belted and let's get out of here.'

Dimitri looked at him, and acknowledged defeat.

'Very well,' he said.

He'd lived with danger for thirty years, and the way he'd lived it was a very long innings indeed, and now, in pale moonlight, nervous, forced to move too quickly, his luck ran out: he took a step towards Bradley.

'Get on with it,' he said.

'Anything you say,' said Bradley, and shot him

through the heart. The big man staggered under the bullet's impact, stumbled over a painted thin-legged chair and slid down the wall, the chair splintering beneath his weight. As he did so the girl screamed, and moved towards him.

'No,' said Bradley. The gun moved in a narrower arc between her and Callan. 'Stay where you are,' Bradley said. 'And stay quiet.'

From upstairs there came the pounding of fists on a door that would have withstood an axe, and Euphrosyne Polybios began yelling. The Browning settled on Callan.

'Let's have your gun, dad,' Bradley said.

'What is this?' said Callan. Behind Bradley the front door opened further, slowly and soundlessly, and Callan was once again grateful to Lonely.

'The girl's coming with me for the boat ride,' Bradley said. 'You stay.'

'But you can't—' said Callan.

'Watch me,' said Bradley. 'The gun, Callan.'

Callan made no move.

'Look,' Bradley said, 'I'd sooner leave you here alive. I've heard what happens to people who get interrogated here – and I want it to happen to you. But I'll kill you if I have to. Give me that gun.'

He raised his own as he spoke, and another figure appeared in the doorway behind him. It was a squat and shambling figure, and it trembled in every limb, but it kept on moving forward, and brought down a half-full bottle of medicine on the back of Bradley's head, using arm muscles developed by years of dentistry. Bradley didn't even stagger: he went down flat.

Blythe looked at the bottle.

'Thank God I didn't break it,' he said, uncorked it, and swigged. 'Christ, I feel awful,' he said, and sat down on a chair.

Helen looked at Callan.

'This is a man called Blythe,' Callan said. 'Dr Randolph Blythe. Did Dimitri tell you he would come?'

'Yes,' she said. 'He told me my mother sent him.'

Callan went up to Blythe.

'You did fine,' he said, 'and I'm grateful. I won't forget.'

Blythe mopped his forehead with his handkerchief.

'I feel sick,' he said.

Helen turned to Callan, 'Shouldn't we go now?' she asked.

Callan went to the window and looked down on the village. The gun shot had been like cannonfire, and upstairs the female gorilla was still banging and booming, but not a light showed in the village, not a glimmer. They'd learned long enough since how to mind their own business: heavy sleepers to a man.

'Randy,' he said, 'just slip upstairs and tell that bird if she doesn't belt up you'll break the door down and kill her. Tell her in Greek.'

'She'll never believe me,' Blythe said.

'Yes, she will,' said Callan. 'I'd believe you. So would our friend here.' He nodded at Bradley.

Somehow Blythe got to his feet. His knees were still trembling, but he went upstairs. Callan looked at Helena: she knelt by Dimitri and her lips moved in prayer. I could use some of that, he

261

thought. From upstairs came the sound of Blythe yelling. He sounded like Attila the Hun in a bad mood. The banging and booming stopped.

The girl looked up, and said again, 'We ought to go.'

'We'll be expected,' said Callan. He walked over to Bradley, picked up the Browning.

'But you can't stay here,' she said.

'That's right,' Callan said. 'We can't go, and we can't stay. Looks like we've got problems, love.'

Blythe came downstairs: he wasn't shaking quite so much.

'I think she heard you,' said Callan.

Blythe said, 'What do we do now?'

'Dodge the coppers.'

'I thought they'd have been here by now,' Blythe said.

'No,' said Callan. 'They're waiting at Polybios's boat.'

'But they must have heard the shot.'

'They'll still be waiting,' said Callan. He passed the automatic to Blythe. 'Do you know how to use this?' he asked.

'No,' said Blythe.

'Now's your chance to learn,' said Callan. He held up the gun. 'Slip the safety catch and pull the trigger. Nothing to it. Here.' He handed over the gun, and Blythe examined the safety catch.

'I don't think I'll do it awfully well,' he said.

'I hope you won't have to do it at all,' said Callan. He went over to Dimitri and unfastened his belt.

'Don't touch him,' Helena said.

Callan said, 'He's dead, darling. There's nothing he needs.'

He went back to Bradley, rolled him over, on his back. Tying a man's hands with a belt isn't easy, unless you've been specially trained, as Callan had been. He picked up a flower-vase, rolled Bradley back, and dripped water on him. At last he spluttered, and sat up.

'All right, son,' Callan said. 'Time to take a boat ride. On your feet.' Bradley didn't move. 'I said on your feet.'

Callan grabbed him, dragged him upright, and Bradley staggered but remained upright. 'Off we go,' said Callan. 'You first.'

'If I go they'll shoot me,' said Bradley.

'If you don't I will,' Callan said. 'What d'you bet I shoot better than they do?'

Bradley went, and Callan waited by the door, then followed. No shots, no sound from the other houses. Kronis was still asleep. Callan slipped out after Bradley, and Blythe and Helena followed: across the garden to the vineyard, then up the foothills away from the beach.

The girl said, 'We're going the wrong way.'

'This is the scenic route,' said Callan. In the distance he heard the whining scream of jet-engines beginning their climb... It looked as if one of them had made it. Bradley slowed down, and Callan forced him on. Behind him the girl moved neatly. Blythe stumbled. They reached a dip in the hills and Callan tripped Bradley, sent him rolling to the bottom of the dip and scurried down after him, checked the belt's fastening. It was still tied tight.

Callan waited till the others joined him and said,

'You stay here. You–' he nodded to Blythe, 'keep your gun on Sunny Jim here.' Bradley looked hopeful. 'If I were you I'd aim at his crotch,' said Callan. 'It's where he keeps his brains.'

He went up the other side of the dip then, and looked down at the shore, letting his eyes get used to the darkness. One was easy: crouched behind a boulder, his whole being concentrated on the path that led from the village to the shore. You haven't been at this lark long mate, Callan thought, sticking out like a sore thumb, and cramp in both legs the way you're crouching. He concentrated on the boat. One aboard her, too. Another amateur. Couldn't keep still to save his life, and maybe keeping still was the only way he could save it... At last he spotted the third one, inching his way through the shadows of the trees that lined the shore-path. The boss-man on the way back from the police-house, Callan thought. Been trying to make a phone-call and not getting any joy. All the same this one had had a few lessons: he was a lovely mover, even with a machine pistol to slow him down.

The captain reached the feller by the boulder, and clapped him on the back. Stay alert, boy, keep your eyes open and it'll be all over in no time. Well that's the theory of it, Callan thought, and moved over the brow of the dip. He went the way they'd trained him, twenty years ago, and no twig cracked, no grass rustled: the training took care of that. And the practice. More practice than he cared to remember: more than twenty years. First the commandos; then the Section. More than twenty years: almost as long as Dimitri... At the last possible moment he saw the loose stone in his way, and just, and only just, avoided it. This was no time to think of when the luck would run out. He moved on, silent, deadly; towards the man who crouched by the boulder.

Bradley said, 'You wouldn't dare use that thing, poof.'

'Wouldn't I?' said Blythe.

'Course you wouldn't,' said Bradley. 'You're shit-scared, poof.'

The girl looked away.

'Tell you another reason,' said Bradley. 'Those geezers Callan's gone looking for – there's three of them. They got guns – and they're mates of mine. You use that thing and you'd give the whole game away. Show some sense, poof. Turn me loose. I won't let them hurt you.'

Helena said in Greek, 'Make him be quiet,' and Blythe turned to her, and looked at her in surprise, as if he had forgotten she was there.

In Greek he said, 'Go and see how Callan's getting on.'

Her gaze remained hesitantly on his, then she moved off, climbing steadily and softly.

'You got brains,' Bradley said. 'Getting rid of the girl.'

Blythe made no answer.

'You just get my hands free,' Bradley said, 'and I'll forget you was even here.'

He half-turned, and Blythe said, 'Wait. I want you to look at me.'

Bradley wriggled round to face him, and Blythe put the safety catch back on to the Browning. His hands were slow and careful: the hands of a man completing an unfamiliar task, but they were quite steady.

'Knew you'd got brains,' said Bradley. 'We don't want no accidents.'

Blythe said, 'I've got brains enough to know that I daren't risk a shot – and I won't. But if you try to shout or call me poof once more – I'll knock you unconscious again.' He hefted the Browning. 'With this.'

'You bleeding ponce–'

'As a matter of fact,' said Blythe, 'I think it would be better if you didn't speak at all. Otherwise I might hit you anyway. I'd rather enjoy hitting you. That's something you taught me, you know. Hitting people can be quite fun...'

She had found the man by the boulder, but of Callan there was no sign. Then suddenly he was there, incredibly close to the crouching man. She could not believe that he could have remained invisible to her for so long as she watched, but he had done it, and crouched, in the shadow, only his head moving, questing, seeking. Three men, Bradley had said, and strained her eyes to see, but there was nothing. Suddenly Callan moved, and it was like a cat leaping on a bird: a long, silent leap, and the gunhand coming down before the leap ended, the gun-barrel slamming behind the watcher's ear, the other hand grabbing, easing down the unconscious body. Then the same wary watchfulness, and again the sudden explosion of movement to haul the unconscious man into a pool of shadow, then wriggle back to pick up his machine-pistol, take his place beside the boul-

266

der... Helena saw more movement, in the shadows by the boat. You had to watch the way an animal watches, she thought, with total concentration, and even then she could see nothing but a shadow moving among shadows, feeling its way to where Callan crouched, peering in the other direction, apparently so unaware. She wanted desperately to yell a warning, but Bradley had said three men, and of the third one she could see no sign. To watch was terrifying: to look away would have been impossible...

Keep coming, Callan thought. I want you nearer, mate. A whole lot nearer... Just so long as I can hear you. And I've got to strain for that. You're good, mate. Only you let that uniform of yours rub on the ground, and sound travels at night, especially when you're listening for it as hard as I am. He shifted position slightly, turning his head. The sound took him right to the geezer, a shadow moving among shadows. Suddenly the man called out in an urgent, hissing whisper.

'Andreas! Andreas!'

Callan continued to look ahead, and the other man crawled on. In a right two and eight he'd be, thought Callan. Blinding and swearing because one of his minions was so busy watching he couldn't hear any more. Just a little bit closer before you try again, thought Callan. Just to the end of the shadows.

Again the voice called, 'Andreas! Andreas!' But louder this time: angry. Callan stayed still.

I'll bet you're worried, old son, Callan thought. If Andreas isn't answering it isn't on account of something you've said. He's either dead or unconscious, isn't he, old son? And there's only one geezer who can find out, and that's you, and to do that you have to keep on coming. He saw the shadow move to the edge of the moonlight, and hesitate. Getting his nerve up, thought Callan. Now or never. What's it to be, old son? Keep on crawling? It's the safest way... I wonder if you've got the nerve for it. He willed his body to immobility, and waited. Suddenly the copper yelled 'Andreas' again, and came on with a rush. From the corner of his eye Callan detected a flicker of movement from the boat, but he had no time to cope with ordinary rozzers now. His business was with the boss.

Callan swung to meet him, and as he did so the other man braced himself to a skidding halt and loosed off the pistol. Bullets splattered off the boulder, and Callan loosed off a quick burst from the crouch position. The police captain was so close that he could see the bullets thudding into the man's chest, slewing him round towards the Polybios boat before he fell. The captain was dead, but in death his hands had contracted round what they held: his machine-pistol continued firing into the boat, and the poor bloody copper aboard rose to a crouch and returned the fire, spraying bullets in an arc from the boulder to the still-spouting pistol. Courageous but confused, Callan thought, and rolled over from the boulder, settled himself, and loosed off another burst. The policeman went down, and did not get up again. Considering the weight of metal in him, it wasn't surprising.

Helena wanted to be sick. In all her life until ten

minutes ago she had seen nothing more violent than a cat hunting birds, and then, after Dimitri died, in a hundred and twenty seconds, she had seen one man clubbed unconscious, two men killed, and it had been done with a kind of brisk professionalism, almost a sense of detachedness, that made it more appalling still. Callan had clubbed and killed with the same careful skill that a surgeon might have brought to the task of healing. She retched, and somehow managed not to vomit. Bradley should not see her humiliated, nor Callan... He had moved to the captain, turned him over, then progressed in a kind of controlled rush to the boat, dropped lightly aboard. There were no more shots: Helena knew there would not be.

She turned, and called down to Blythe: 'It's all right. You can come up.'

Bradley came like a lamb, with Blythe stumping along behind him holding the Browning like a hammer. They looked down at the scene below: the dead captain, the dead policeman Callan was hefting from the Polybios boat.

'There were supposed to be three,' said Blythe.

'He knocked the other one unconscious,' Helena said, and pointed. 'He's over there.'

'Jesus,' said Bradley. Blythe smiled.

'You can start yelling now if you like,' he said. 'Yell as much as you want.'

They went down to the beach.

Flying in an airplane wasn't the same without Mr Callan, Lonely thought. It was true there was booze and that, and the same kind of grub on little plastic trays, but he had no one to talk to:

269

wasn't allowed to talk come to that, and even if he had been the geezer beside him spent all his time with his nose in a book. All in foreign, it was. Not even any pictures. Five words, that's all he'd got out of him. 'Good evening,' when he sat down, and when Lonely had pointed to his throat instead of replying he'd said, 'I'm frightfully sorry,' and gone straight back to his book. Mind you it had been nice when the air-hostess came up to ask what he wanted to drink, and he'd had to point it out on the tariff card and she'd had to bend over him to see it. Little darling she was. Smelled lovely. But that looked like being all the excitement he'd get the whole bleeding flight.

Lonely smiled. He wondered what she would say if she knew the kind of man she'd been bending over. Lonely the wanted man, Lonely the rescuer of millionaires' relatives... He wondered how Mr Callan was getting on. He'd be all right. Bound to be. Hard all through, Mr Callan was. Take a job like that in his stride. All the same Lonely wished he didn't have to have that Bradley with him. Right tearaway... Better not to think about that or he might start niffing, and really give the bookworm beside him something to talk about. Better to think about the five thousand quid he had coming. Five thousand quid for one job. Lonely. Mr Big.

The air hostess said, 'Would you like a newspaper, sir?'

Lonely started to say, 'Ta,' then remembered, and nodded and smiled instead, and turned to the sports pages. Racing at Manchester tomorrow. Something to pass the time, he thought. Trust Mr

Callan to think of everything. In Birmingham there wasn't even dog races.

Callan waited for them on the beach, the machine-pistol in his hand, the Colt Python in his waist-band. The girl caught the reek of cordite that clung to him, and thought: I must think only of one thing. That I am getting away. Otherwise I shall be sick, and he will see me.

Callan looked at Blythe. 'Any trouble?'

Blythe swung the Browning by the muzzle. 'Not recently,' he said.

'Good,' said Callan. 'You and Miss Kollonaki stay here – and keep an eye on that one.' He nodded to the policeman in the shadows. 'If he starts to come round give him another tap.' He looked at the Browning. 'But not like you're hammering six-inch nails.'

He set the machine-pistol on the ground, then grabbed Bradley, shoved him towards the boat. This was the tricky part. If it worked, it was another advantage gained. And it could work. Bradley was almost stupid enough to fall for it at the best of times, and a belt over the head with a medicine bottle wouldn't have made him any brighter.

'You and me's got work to do,' he said. They moved off to the boat. 'You know anything about boats?' Callan asked.

'I've done a bit,' Bradley said.

'You can do a bit on this one then,' said Callan. He unbuckled the belt, freed Bradley's wrists. 'Get aboard.'

Bradley massaged his wrists, wincing as life returned to them.

271

'You tied it tight enough,' he said, and went aboard the cruiser. Callan followed. As Callan watched, Bradley's eyes darted about the deck: looking for the copper's machine-pistol. This was droll.

'I threw it overboard,' said Callan.

Bradley's eyes shifted to the Colt Python: he never gave up, thought Callan. At least he seems in the right mood.

Aloud he said, 'Well we've done what we set out to do.'

Bradley said, 'I don't get you.'

'Only you've done a bit more, sonny,' Callan said. 'You were going to leave me behind.'

'I do daft things sometimes,' Bradley said. 'You know how it is. I'm sorry.'

He doesn't mean a word of it, thought Callan.

'Don't try it again, that's all.'

'Rely on me,' Bradley said. 'What did you mean we'd done it?'

Callan opened the door to the wheelhouse: ignition key ready and waiting. 'What the Big Man told us,' he said. 'We've been through the motions. We killed Dimitri...'

'I killed Dimitri,' Bradley said.

'And I let you.' The words should not have been said: he couldn't utter them without disgust. But Bradley was too thick to notice.

'You saying we scarper now? Just you and me?'

'That's right,' said Callan.

'And leave that poof behind to do the explaining?'

'Right again.'

Bradley didn't just like the idea: he loved it.

272

'Start her up,' said Callan. 'I'll cast off.'

Suddenly Bradley was loving it even more; loving it so much he couldn't believe it. 'You want me to take the wheel?'

'If you can manage it,' Callan said.

'Oh I can manage,' said Bradley. 'I can manage fine.'

He went into the wheelhouse, and the engine caught and fired. Not quite as smooth as the *Galatea*, not quite so much power, but enough. Callan cast off aft, then moved forward, while Bradley watched. The boat had swung, and there was too much rope for him to reach from the boat. He leaped ashore and unwound the rope, and bang on cue Bradley let in the power, swung the boat away from Callan.

'So long, mug,' Bradley yelled. 'Give my regards to the poof.'

The boat swung away, churning white water, and Callan gave a yell of rage and fired two shots after it. He took damn good care to miss, but Bradley didn't know that: the Polybios boat went even faster.

Callan waited as Blythe and Helena came running, and looked at him, appalled. There was something rather touching in the horror they showed that he should be beaten so easily.

'My God,' said Blythe. 'What will we do?'

'Move,' said Callan, 'and quick.'

He led the way along the shore to where the outboard was moored, held it while Helena and Blythe scrambled in, and shoved off, then fired the engine, stood out towards the *Galatea*. Once, half-way there, he looked back at the village. Still

273

not a light showed. They were all still busy working hard at not hearing anything.

'Nicky died,' said Hunter.

'Do you want me to get rid of him, sir?' Meres asked.

Hunter thought: I realise that an expression of regret would be hypocritical, but surely you could find a better valediction than that?

Aloud he said, 'No. That's being attended to. I'm wondering why he killed himself.'

'Fear?' said Meres.

'Of us? I hardly think so. I had no more plans for him, and he knew it.'

'You'd have let him go?'

'Certainly,' said Hunter. 'He'd fulfilled his function. We had no further use for him. It could have been arranged.'

'But the others,' said Meres. 'The Kollonaki woman: Dimitri's friends...'

'All he had to do was avoid them. No, Toby. It wasn't fear that drove him. It was disgust.'

'Shame that he'd talked, do you mean?' said Meres. 'But he knew he was bound to talk. It's absurd.'

'Human beings very often are,' said Hunter. 'Did you see Vardakis today?'

'Yes, sir, he seemed – a little restless.'

'As well he might,' Hunter said. 'Did he want any little jobs done?'

'No, sir,' said Meres. 'It wasn't that. I thought I'd go and have a word with Bradley. As you say, sir, he's the type one should keep an eye on.'

'Indeed. And what had Bradley to say?'

274

'Nothing, sir. He seems to have disappeared. That's why I went to see Vardakis. He said he hadn't even seen the fool, but I'm quite sure he's lying.'

'Did you check with the driver fellow?'

'Jackson? Yes, sir. I questioned him very thoroughly. All he knows is that Bradley has disappeared, and I'm sure he's not lying. Vardakis is.'

Hunter sat, and thought.

'Nicky told us that Sophie was sending an observer to Crete,' he said at last.

'That dentist creature,' said Meres. 'I don't think he'd be very effectual, sir.'

'Not in the least,' said Hunter. 'Callan could cope with him... I wonder if Vardakis sent an observer too? Oh dear, oh dear. Poor old Callan.'

'Do you think Callan will muff it because of those two, sir?'

'My dear Toby,' said Hunter, 'given a sufficient incentive man can achieve anything.' He looked at the row of red files awaiting attention on his desk. 'The incentive I gave Callan was more than adequate.'

19

When last he'd seen him, Bradley had been headed at a dead run for the Turkish coast, across to the Kasos Straits: but then young men were always in a hurry; they never gave themselves time to enjoy life. Callan headed northeasterly, towards the Dodecanese: a far more relaxing voyage, and they'd get to Turkey just the same. He looked out on deck: the girl sat on a mattress, and Blythe fussed with the sandwiches and drinks he'd made below, and brought up on deck. Callan set the steering to automatic, then went out to them.

'Come and join us, old chap,' said Blythe. 'These sandwiches are jolly good if I say so myself.'

They were, too: ham and tomato, tinned chicken, sardines. Callan took one, and found that he was ravenous. The girl didn't touch a thing.

'Drink?' said Blythe. 'Whisky and water, isn't it?'

'Thanks,' said Callan, and Blythe mixed it. He might have started being a hero, but his pouring was as generous as ever.

'You know you're too much, my love,' Blythe said. 'You really are. To think you had another boat laid on like that.' Callan swallowed whisky and water. 'But weren't you being just a teeny bit elaborate? I mean, we could have left that dreadful Nutter person ashore and taken the Polybios boat.'

'We could,' said Callan. 'The trouble was an awful lot of people knew about the Polybios boat – and I wouldn't be at all surprised if that included the Greek navy.'

Blythe pondered the beauty of it, then burst out laughing.

'Oh that's absolutely perfect,' he said. 'It really is.'

'Glad you approve,' said Callan.

Blythe gulped at his ouzo.

'It's all been fantastic,' he said. 'Quite fantastic.

276

And to think I was involved in it too. Little me.'

'How's your stomach?' Callan asked.

'Never better, dear boy. I'm quite a good sailor... Oh do you mean this rubbish?' Blythe pulled the medicine bottle from his pocket and slung it overboard. 'I don't need that any more.'

'You don't need a gun, either. No more do I. Over the side, Randy.'

Blythe pulled out the Browning, looked at it, and sighed.

'Given time I think I could have got the hang of it,' he said, and threw.

'I think so too,' said Callan, and lobbed the Python after the Browning. The girl turned her back to them both.

'How are you on boats?' Callan asked.

'Oh I can aim them,' said Blythe.

'How about aiming this one for a bit?' Callan nodded at Helena, and Blythe stood up.

'Well, of course,' he said. 'Delighted. No objection to my taking my little drink along?' He picked up his glass, and the ouzo bottle: 'It should have been rum, shouldn't it? But I really do not like rum. It reminds me of my lost youth... All those hairy sailors.'

He went to the wheelhouse and took the wheel. The sailors must have taught him something: the cruiser stayed steady.

Callan said: 'Aren't you being a little hard on him? He took a lot of risks for you tonight: risks he isn't used to. He did all right.'

She turned then and faced him.

'Not him,' she said. 'You.' He waited. 'I watched you, Callan,' she said. 'I saw the way you killed.'

'You saw – all of it?'

'Yes,' she said.

'Then you know I had to do it. They would have killed me – and probably Randy there as well.' He nodded to the wheelhouse.

'I don't blame you for them,' she said.

'What then?'

'Dimitri.'

Callan looked down at his hands: they were beginning to shake. He poured more whisky. 'I didn't kill Dimitri,' he said.

'You let him die.'

The words were an accusation.

'Bradley came in with a gun out,' said Callan. 'You were there: you saw him. It wasn't in the script but he did it. I only had a hand on mine.'

'You could still have stopped him,' she said.

'Would it be too much to ask how?'

She looked at him: eyes wide and clear: intelligent eyes, trusting eyes: eyes that would soon show hurt if she went on with this.

'I don't know how,' she said. 'That's your business. But you could have done it.'

'I took his gun off him before tonight,' Callan said. 'I took the shells out of it. How was I to know he'd got more?'

'You kill better than you lie,' she said.

'All right,' said Callan. 'All right,' and drank. 'Bradley's a killer who likes his work, and we've had two run-ins before this. Once there's a gun in his hand he likes to make it go off, and if it was pointing at me when it went bang he'd have been delighted. And he'd still have killed Dimitri. Maybe I could have got my gun out and killed

278

him. I don't know. There are ways – and I've been taught them. But I didn't like the odds, Miss Kollonaki. I was scared.'

'Were you scared when you killed those policemen?'

'Of course.' He was angry now, angry at a naïveté that could put courage and terror in separate, inaccessible compartments. 'But I had an edge that time, and in any case there was nothing else I could do.'

Her eyes stayed on him: still wide, still clear.

'If Bradley was so dangerous to you,' she said, 'why did you bring him with you?'

'I didn't bring him,' Callan said. 'He was sent to keep an eye on me.'

'But why did you bring him tonight?'

'To keep an eye on him,' said Callan. 'He was having me watched. If I hadn't brought him into it he would have blown the whole thing.'

'So you set Dr Blythe to watch him?'

'That's right.'

'From what I've seen of Dr Blythe,' she said, 'you were taking a tremendous risk.'

'It worked,' he said, and even if it hadn't worked it would have paid off. If Bradley had heard Randy come in he would have swung round to face him, and that would have given Callan all the edge he needed. If Bradley had turned on the dentist, then Bradley would have died: and maybe Randy would have died too. But he didn't tell her that.

'You have been doing this for a long time?' she asked. Callan nodded. 'I thought so. And always it frightens you – and always you go on doing it. Why?'

Because it's a fix, he thought, the only fix that gives me a high. Because without the fear there can be no excitement: without the risks nothing is achieved. And I need all four: fear, excitement, risks, achievements. Without them I'm nothing.

Aloud he said, 'Once you're in it isn't easy to get out.'

'Dimitri once said something like that,' she said.

'Dimitri would know.'

He should have left it at that; he couldn't.

'May I ask you something?' he asked.

'Very well.'

'About Dimitri. He expected to be knocked unconscious. At first he wanted me to do it, then he changed his mind and opted for Bradley. You remember?'

'Yes,' she said. 'I remember.'

'But Bradley didn't belt him – he shot him. Why do you think he did that?'

'You said yourself,' she said, 'he likes to shoot people.'

'He's a strange one all right,' Callan said. 'His mates call him Nutter. That's a slang word for crazy... But he's not that crazy. He has to have some sort of reason for pulling a trigger.'

'You're saying somebody told him to kill Dimitri?'

'That's right.'

'But you can only mean my mother. She was the one who arranged it.'

Suddenly Helena began to cry. She's had the most terrible day of her life, Callan thought: seen a psychopath cut down a man she knew and liked, seen a pro killer cut loose with a machine-pistol. No wonder she needs to cry. But even so, her sobs were heart-rending. There were no words to say, or if there were he didn't know them, but at last he put his arm round her and soothed her as he would have soothed a hurt child. But the sobs continued.

Lonely didn't mind the landing: it was smooth and uneventful, and anyway he was sick of sitting in the plane. Once he'd picked out the day's winners there was nothing else to do... It was getting off that bothered him. Passports was bad enough: a geezer taking it off you and staring right into your face before he handed it back, but Customs was worse. Dozens of them there were, standing around and looking at you and sizing you up. Go through the green, Mr Callan had said, but there was as many hanging around the green as there was on the red. Mr Callan hadn't told him about that. Still, he couldn't just stand about like a tin of milk. That really would be asking for trouble.

He picked up his suitcase and moved forward with all the nonchalance he could muster at that hour of the morning. It wasn't much. After all, Customs was just like rozzers: nosey, asking questions. If they started asking what he was doing in a plane full of professors he'd be knackered... Then he saw other people go through unquestioned, felt a little better, and trudged on. Three of them were standing right near the doorway, rabbiting away. As Lonely came abreast of them, one of them looked up, and the old, familiar terror came over Lonely, but the Customs Officer simply moved him on. Lonely's scuttle accelerated. The whole world's losing its marbles, he thought. Fellers with uniforms and they don't stop you and ask questions... But it showed you Mr Callan knew his stuff, he thought. Go through the green and you can't go wrong. And here he was. Outside. A free man. After all he'd done. He couldn't have felt better if he'd busted out of prison... Lonely followed the sign that said 'Airport Bus', queued for the coach and got a double seat to himself when it came, which was just as well. Even so the feller in the seat behind him wound down the window.

Yes mate, thought Lonely, and I wonder how bad you'd niff if you'd been through what I have.

Helena's grief eased at last, and she found that she was in Callan's arms. Gently, without embarrassment, she freed herself.

'It seems that I am always providing you with reasons for holding me,' she said.

'Last time you tried to bite me,' said Callan. 'This time it was more like drown me.'

She smiled, and sought for a handkerchief. He gave her his.

'Thank you. It's all over now, I promise. I will not be such a nuisance again.'

'You've had a rough day,' said Callan. 'You should get some sleep.'

'And you?'

'Randy and I will take alternate watches,' he said. 'You get below and kip.'

She sat up.

'What a strange man you are,' she said. She kissed his cheek. 'Goodnight.'

Callan watched her go below, then went to the wheelhouse. By the look of the ouzo bottle he hadn't had much more, Callan thought. I've drunk more than him.

'Dramas?' Blythe asked.

'A bit,' said Callan. 'She's had a rough night. We all have.'

'My God yes,' said Blythe, and yawned. 'There were times when I could have done with a good cry myself.'

They agreed on watches then: four on, four off, and Blythe yawned his way back on deck, gathered up glasses, bottles, plates, and went below. Callan looked at the sea, a gleaming, shadowed silver, gently heaving. They were doing ten knots, and he would keep it at that; no need to advertise, and if nothing went wrong they'd be in Turkey in time for a hot lunch... If nothing went wrong. The whole bloody caper had been disaster-prone. A beating from Fitzmaurice, gun-shots warning him to lay off, three different bosses: Hunter, Sophie Kollonaki, Vardakis, and each one with a different set of instructions... He found that he was yawning, and that *Galatea* had gone a point off course. That wouldn't do at all. Think it through, Callan, and stay awake.

Three bosses: but only one that counted. Hunter. Busy little queen bee Hunter, gathering honey wherever he could find it. Something on Sophie; something on cousin Michael, and all stored away for the future, when one or the other of them took power in Greece. And something on both of them. The girl. Sophie seemed hardly to like her, never mind love her, but she accepted

283

Helena as her responsibility: accepted too that in the wrong hands Helena could be a weapon aimed against her. So bring her back to mummy, Callan. Michael Vardakis had other ideas: he liked the girl, no question; and he spent money on her, and influence. It cost money to house and keep her as she had been housed and kept, and it took influence to get the money used in the first place. But he didn't want her freed. As far as he was concerned, Helena was safe in Crete, so in Crete she would stay: church, and meals with the Polybioses, and a boat ride round the harbour when she was a good girl. Drive her mad that would, but at least she would be safe... *Vardakis had wanted Dimitri killed.* A threat to Helena? He doubted it. Dimitri had been with her a long time. There was no question of his harming the girl. She'd liked him, wept for him. And for what it was worth he'd seemed to like her. A threat to Vardakis? It sounded barmy. How could an insignificant peasant be a threat to a man worth millions? And yet he had to be. Vardakis had hired him to commit murder. Hired Bradley too, come to that. And Bradley had done it. Cash on delivery.

The dawn came up more quickly than he was used to in London, but beautiful still; the only pale colours of the day. The palest of pinks streaked the sky, the sunlight emerged lemon-colour, the sea changed imperceptibly from silver to blue. And Callan still worried about his problem. Bradley had come to see Dimitri die, and had extemporised as well. Leaving Callan behind to take the knock would hardly be Vardakis's idea. If Callan had been picked up, sooner or later he would have grassed, with the kind of persuasion Greek intelligence used. But surely that would have applied to Bradley too? Except it was unlikely Bradley even knew of Vardakis's existence. Or did he? The Big Man, Bradley had called him: the boss. But never a name. Vardakis had been in the business a long, long time. And he'd wanted Dimitri dead... He heard a footfall behind him, and looked up. Blythe was looking at the dawn. As Callan watched, he turned, and came into the wheelhouse.

'There is nowhere in the world, and no time, as beautiful as this,' he said, then looked at Callan's face. 'My God, you look dead on your feet.'

He took the wheel, and Callan yawned and stretched.

'Have yourself a proper sleep,' said Blythe.

'It's all right,' said Callan. 'Four hours will do me.'

He started to leave, and Blythe said: 'What happens if we're intercepted?'

'Just keep going,' Callan said. 'No more than ten knots. Heave to if they make you. I don't think they will... How good's your Greek?' Blythe hesitated. 'Come on, Randy, I need to know.'

'I've been told it's perfect.'

'Speak it then,' said Callan. 'Tell them you're the skipper – been hired by a honeymoon couple for a trip round the islands.'

'And if they come aboard?'

Callan said, 'Then we're sunk.'

Snooks Jackson sighed. It was a sound meant to convey the long-suffering of a man much irritated, much put upon. It came out like fear.

'Mr. Meres,' he said, 'we been over all this.'

Meres said, 'Then we'll go over it again.'

'He kipped here,' said Jackson. 'I done the cooking and he done the washing up. When he remembered. Sometimes we watched the telly, but mostly it was me stayed in and he went off after the birds.'

'Did you never go out together?'

'Now and again,' said Jackson. 'Just to the boozer. I don't like drinking much when there's a job on.'

'Very commendable. Which boozer?'

The Bunches of Grapes,' said Snooks. 'I told you. Round the corner in Lancaster Street.'

Meres stood up, and Snooks Jackson said, 'He's not in any trouble, is he?'

'Probably,' said Meres.

'I swear to God I know nothing about it.'

Meres came up to him, and Jackson found that he was sweating. Hard eyes, unblinking, bored into his.

'Honest,' he said. 'I mean it.'

'I think you do,' said Meres. 'If I didn't, you'd be in trouble too.'

He went to the door, and Jackson's every instinct said: Scarper, son. Get out of it. The lolly's good but that geezer's poison.

Meres turned. 'By the way,' he said. 'You weren't thinking of leaving, were you?'

'No, Mr Meres.'

'Don't lie,' said Meres. 'And don't try to leave either. If you do – you'll be in as much trouble as Bradley.'

The Bunch of Grapes was really rather a decent

sort of pub, Meres thought, considering the neighbourhood it was in. Nicely carpeted, pleasant bar and an even more pleasant absence of vinyl and formica. The barmaid too seemed pleasant: a little buxom perhaps, a little mature: but not unwholesome. Boyish charm first, thought Meres, and if that doesn't work a nice, new ten-pound note.

'Pink gin, please,' he said, and she mixed it efficiently. 'A lot of water.'

The woman added it, and Meres sipped.

'Delightful,' he said, and looked round the empty bar. 'Everybody given up drinking?' he asked.

'Bit early yet,' the barmaid said. 'We've just opened.'

'Oh of course,' Meres said. 'Stupid of me. One forgets, you know. I've been away.'

'Abroad, sir?'

'Switzerland,' he said. 'I work there you know.'

'Must be nice,' said the barmaid.

'It's pleasant enough,' said Meres. 'As a matter of fact I – but how impolite of me. Would you care for a drink?'

'My guv'nor isn't keen on me drinking with the customers.'

'Not even when trade's as bad as this?' said Meres. 'Besides, your guv'nor isn't here.'

'That's true,' she said. 'Vodka and tonic, please.'

'I was wondering,' said Meres, 'if an acquaintance of mine came in here. I know he lives round here somewhere, but I'm not sure precisely where. Oh – make yours a double, please.'

The barmaid added another measure of vodka.

'Thank you very much,' she said, as Meres

paid. 'We don't get many of your sort in here, sir.'

Meres said firmly: 'This man is not my sort. Twenty-four, tall, fair-hair, blue eyes, good teeth. His name is Bradley.'

'Oh him,' the barmaid said.

'You've seen him then?'

'Look,' said the barmaid. 'I'm sorry if he's a mate of yours, but–'

'He's not,' said Meres. 'Far from it.'

'I thought it sounded funny,' she said.

'You don't like him then?'

'Foul-mouthed,' she said. 'Very foul-mouthed. I mean you get used to language in this trade but this isn't a public. There are limits.' She sipped at her vodka. 'He's got a nasty habit of grabbing you as well. Very nasty.'

Meres said, 'Oh dear. I knew he was unpleasant, but I'd no idea it was as bad as that.'

The barmaid looked interested. 'Trouble?' she said.

Meres sighed. 'The worst. It's my sister I'm afraid. Eighteen. Little more than a child, really.'

'And that nasty Bradley–'

'If I could get my hands on him he wouldn't go near my sister again,' said Meres, and the barmaid loved it. 'As a matter of fact that's what I came back from Switzerland for.'

He broke off as two men came in and ordered lager: the barmaid served them, then waited in frigid silence till they sat down at a table.

'He hasn't been in for three or four nights,' she said when they'd gone. 'Before that he was pretty regular.'

'Come in by himself?'

288

'Mostly,' she said. 'Sometimes he was with a baldy feller. Bradley's a bacardi and coke; his mate's a half of bitter. No class, his mate. You know, common.'

'I don't think I know him,' said Meres.

'I shouldn't think you would,' said the barmaid.

'Didn't he ever appear with anybody else?'

'Not that I can think of,' the barmaid said, then: 'No. I tell a lie. Last week he was in with a foreigner. Glass of white wine, he was.'

'What sort of a foreigner?'

'Oh, you know,' she said.

Meres thought, but I don't know, you stupid cow, and smiled boyishly.

'He had an accent,' she said.

'And what did he look like?'

'Stocky built: getting on a bit. You know – a bit thin on top. All the same he looked a hard one to me. Bradley called him Theo. Had their heads down over there' – she nodded to a remote table, 'jabbering away. Then the foreign feller left.'

'With Bradley?'

'Bradley leave after one drink? You must be joking. He came back over to me. Full of himself he was. Wanted to take me out. Not that I would,' she said, and looked hopefully at Meres. 'I do have certain standards I told him.'

'Was he rude?'

'No,' she said, and seemed surprised. 'He wasn't. Said a funny thing though. At least he seemed to think it was funny. Laughed fit to bust his self– Laughed very hearty I should say.'

'What was the funny thing?' Meres asked.

'He said, "You shouldn't turn me down tonight, darling. Tomorrow I could be thousands of miles away." Any help to you dear?'

Meres hated to be called dear. 'No,' he said. 'I'm afraid not.' But he gave her another of his boyish smiles. After all, they came cheaper than ten quid.

20

He woke, showered, dressed, and went topsides. The *Galatea* was threading its way through a pattern of islets, and Helena had the wheel. Blythe, it seemed, was busy in the galley. Callan looked at the clear, blue water, dazzling now the sun had real bite in it. He took over, and she stayed beside him. To port he could see some caiques fishing, to starboard another powerboat loitered along. Nobody bothered.

'You look rested,' she said. 'I bet I don't.'

He looked at her. The strain was still there, but she was beautiful.

'It's something else you learn in this lark,' he said. 'How to relax.'

'I'm not going into this lark,' she said. 'Did my mother say I was?'

'No,' said Callan. 'All she said is she wanted you with her.'

'Politics and plotting and killing,' she said. 'I've never liked them. I never will. Would you tell her that?'

'Wouldn't it be better if you told her yourself?' he asked.

'She wouldn't listen. She never has listened to me – she's always been too busy.' Helena looked away to the gleaming, heaving water. 'I used to be happy in Crete.'

'But not lately?'

'No... Not lately. But before they put me with Euphrosyne – when I had the farm. And going on digs. That was good too.'

'You like the past more than the present?'

'The farm was very much the present,' she said. 'Making things grow – that's a battle too, in a climate like ours. But it isn't destructive. Do you despise me for that?'

'No,' said Callan, astonished. 'Why should I?'

'Because you're with my mother on this.' She turned back to him. 'Aren't you?'

'No,' said Callan.

'Then why–?'

'I get paid for what I do,' he said.

The revulsion in her face was unmistakable.

'Like killing policemen?' she said.

'Like killing policemen,' said Callan. 'They get paid for what they do, too. And that kind of copper does some pretty weird things.'

'How much?' she said. 'How much do you get? Is it a lump sum or so much per head?'

Callan said, 'Would you kindly just belt up?' But already she had gone, out on to the deck, as far away from Callan as she could get. A likeable, honest, intelligent girl, a girl of great beauty, and she found him revolting.

Randy had prepared eggs and bacon, coffee, toast and marmalade, and he brought it up on deck. It wasn't as good as Lonely's but it had pos-

291

sibilities. The islets were behind them, and there was only blue water ahead. Callan put the boat on automatic, and joined them. The girl refused: she wasn't hungry. Affably Blythe shared her portion with Callan.

'Lovers' quarrel?' he asked.

'She's just found out I get paid for what I do. She doesn't like it,' said Callan.

'I didn't like it either,' said Blythe. 'I still don't.'

'It's nice to have it unanimous,' Callan said.

'But I still don't see how we could have done this without you.' He swallowed coffee, then added, 'However unpleasant you are, you're essential. And that being so, I see no reason to dwell on your unpleasantness.'

To him I'm just like Lonely, thought Callan. Lonely stinks, but if you want the locks opened you've got to have him. And I'm unpleasant, but if you want a few coppers knocked off – he looked up from his plate. Blythe's eyes were on him.

'I didn't mean that you're unpleasant in yourself,' said Blythe.

'That's nice.' Callan's voice was bitter.

'My dear fellow, how could I possibly – after what you've done... No, no. My point is this. We act for superlative reasons, but our acts are rarely effectual. Your only motivation is greed, but you act superlatively. It is that which we find unpleasant, and can you blame us? Professionally we're mostly talkers, you know. When it comes to action, we're amateurs.'

'Dimitri wasn't.'

'Nor was Sophie – once. But Dimitri and Sophie are both of a rare kind.'

292

'Which one do you think was the better of the two?'

Blythe replied without hesitation. 'Dimitri. Undoubtedly. From all I hear he had real ability. If he'd lived he would have–' he hesitated then.

'Taken Sophie's place?'

Blythe said, 'Dimitri was what I think you call a sleeper. He went underground years ago. Left the party: became a good boy – or so everybody believed. That made him very useful to us in Crete.'

But sleepers have to wake sometimes, thought Callan, and when they do they're apt to feel the need for wider horizons.

'He'll be a hard one to replace,' Callan said.

'Sophie will take care of it.' He didn't sound all that convinced. Callan waited. 'I suppose you're wondering how I got into all this?' he said at last.

No need to wonder, thought Callan. I've seen your file.

'It had crossed my mind,' he said.

'My mother was Greek,' said Blythe. 'I loved my mother. We lived in Piraeus; my father was a shipping agent there. In 1939 he came back to England, to serve in the Navy. My mother refused to leave Greece – but he took me away anyway.' In the same matter-of-fact tones he added: 'I hate my father. Sometimes I think I must have turned gay just to spite him.'

'What happened to your mother?' he asked.

'She belonged to Sophie's party,' said Blythe. 'She was very active during the war. But she was caught. I suppose most of us will be caught eventually. The Germans killed her.'

'I'm sorry,' said Callan, and Blythe looked up at him.

'I honestly believe you are,' he said. 'It doesn't make a ha-porth of difference really, but I thank you for it.'

He gathered up the dishes then, and Callan went back to the wheel. The girl still refused to look at him.

The doctor told Kyle that he'd have to take it easy for a while, and warned him off sex and violence with all the vehemence of somebody trying to clean up T.V.: but he did it objectively, and without embarrassment. In a sense he was saying that Kyle was lucky, and in a sense Kyle knew he was. Take it easy and in a month, two months, he'd have a love-life again. If that kick had deviated by an inch he'd have been a eunuch, so the doctor said: he might even be dead. Kyle thanked him and went home and was cossetted by his mum. The lads at the station had sent him a crate of Scotch ale. Well that was one thing he could still enjoy: he opened a bottle and switched on the telly, and of course inside five minutes his mum came in to see he was all right.

'I'm fine, mum,' he said. 'Honest.' His eyes already wandered back to the screen.

'It's – not hurting?'

Sex had always been an embarrassment between them: his injury made it worse.

'I told you,' he said. 'It's all right.'

Mrs Kyle looked at the two black men on the screen, punching each other. Speed, power, incredible strength.

'Violence,' she said. 'That's all you ever see nowadays. Why should two grown men want to hurt each other like that?'

'Money,' said Kyle.

'It wasn't money made them kick you,' said his mother. 'I'm blessed if I know what it was.'

'I told you, mum. A couple of nut-cases. It was just my bad luck they picked me.'

'Well there's one thing,' his mother said. 'At least it's stopped you worrying about that other business – that smelly feller.'

'Not much I can do now,' said Kyle.

'Just as well,' his mother said. 'Oh I admit I encouraged you in the beginning, but not when you started saying this house was a police-station.'

'It's over, mum,' said Kyle.

'Did the doctor say you could drink that stuff?' she asked.

Please, mum, he thought, I've done enough for you. Believe me.

'He didn't say I couldn't,' he said.

And that should have been the start of an argument, but the doorbell rang, and she was off to answer it like a flash. His mum responded to bells more quickly than Pavlov's dogs. He took another drink of beer before she came back, and looked at the fight. Last round. Real grandstand finish. And one of them was even bigger than the black man in the car. Bloody fool, he told himself, taking on a pair like that. Ah well, all that was finished. He'd know better next time. Then his mum came back in.

'It's Detective Sergeant Walters,' she said, and he stood in the doorway behind her.

Walters said, 'Not any more, Mrs Kyle. It's Mr Walters now.'

The referee announced his decision, and the crowd yelled, half cheering, half derisive.

'Just come to see how you're doing,' said Walters.

'I'll live,' said Kyle. 'Eventually.'

Behind Mrs Kyle's back, Walters grinned, point taken, but she heard only the bitterness in his voice.

'It gets him down,' she said. 'Well it's bound to, isn't it? Hooligans like that. It was nice of you to come and see him, Mr Walters. I'll leave you to have a chat.'

She left them, and Kyle told Walters where to find another glass: poured out beer. 'Cheers,' he said.

'All the very best,' said Walters. 'From all of us,' then drank. 'Nice drop, that. Very nice.' He drank again. 'You told your mum?'

'Told her what?'

'That she's in danger?'

'She's not,' said Kyle. 'Not if I keep quiet – and the way things are I can't do anything else.' On the box an old bird started telling the world about how cereal did wonders for her constipation. 'Do you mind turning that thing off? I'm not supposed to move very much.'

'If you don't mind,' said Walters. 'I'll leave it on.'

Kyle waited warily. This could be trouble.

'I've been thinking about that last chat we had,' Walters said.

'Oh yes?'

'You were right in what you did, son.'

'And look where it got me,' said Kyle.

'That doesn't make you any less right. I've been putting out a few feelers–'

'I thought you'd retired?'

'Doesn't stop me going to the police club,' Walters said. 'Doesn't stop me hearing things either. Your inspector's hopping mad. Chewed my ear off last night about you.'

'You didn't tell him anything?'

'No, son,' said Walters. 'That's just between you and me. He still thinks it was a couple of loonies. He's mad about that as well.'

'As well?'

'What narks him most is your being warned off by Special Branch.'

'Is that who it was?'

'That's who. But I think it goes beyond that,' Walters said. 'I think they're acting for one of those cloak and dagger outfits.'

'What? Protecting that Lonely? What would they do that for?'

Walters shrugged. They do all sorts of things for all sorts of reasons,' he said. 'And a lot of those reasons are criminal. They maybe had a use for Lonely – or his heavy friend for that matter. So they warn us off.'

'Just like that?' said Kyle.

'It worked, didn't it?'

'Yes,' said Kyle. 'After I got kicked it did.'

'So there you are then,' said Walters. 'They do what they like, and the law can go to hell, and take the coppers there too.'

'Well they've done it,' said Kyle. 'My inspector may be narked, but he'll do what he's told.'

'And my detective inspector,' said Walters, 'and the station super. They have to. A copper has no choice.'

'I've learned that now,' said Kyle. 'What's the good of talking?'

Walters said: 'I'm not a copper any more. I've retired.'

Kyle looked at him: his face suddenly older, more responsible. 'Let's have it, Mr Walters,' he said.

'Whoever had you duffed is a villain,' Walters said. 'They can dress it up with all the fancy names they like: Patriotism, Queen and Country, Land of Hope and Glory... They still committed a crime. They're villains.'

'Go on.'

'I don't like villains to get away with it.'

'No more do I, Mr Walters,' said Kyle. 'I don't like being kicked in the crutch either.'

'You're out of it now,' said Walters. 'You have to be.'

'My mum,' said Kyle. 'They said they'd—'

'You're out of it,' Walters said again. 'For now.'

'And you're in?' Walters nodded. 'Why?'

'I don't like villains getting away with it,' said Walters, 'and I've got nothing else to do. They can't warn me off now either. I've retired.'

'They can do other things.'

'I'll chance it.'

Kyle said, 'What do you want from me, Mr Walters?'

'A report on how far you got.'

'Suppose they get on to you?' Kyle said. 'Suppose they find out it was me that told you?'

'Suppose we let them get away with it?' said Walters. 'Suppose they kick a whole lot of other fellers? Threaten their mothers?'

Kyle told him at last, and Walters listened, then made him tell the whole thing again. To Kyle's relief he wrote nothing down.

When he'd finished, Kyle asked, 'If you don't mind my asking, Mr Walters, are you married?'

'I'm a widower,' Walters said.

'Any family?'

'One son,' said Walters. 'In Australia.'

'I reckon that's just as well,' said Kyle.

Soon, he knew, he would be tired again. There were blokes he knew who took pills for that, but he didn't fancy it. When you led the life he did, it was too easy to get hooked. Better just to be tired, and drink Scotch when you weren't working... All the same it was a relief to hand over the wheel to Randy, yawn and stretch and look at the sea. A tiny island behind them now, and a big one coming up: golden stone crowded with olive trees. Randy gestured an enquiry.

'Chios,' said Callan, and the dentist sighed his relief. Once past Chios they were in Turkish territorial waters. Callan went on deck and dragged a mattress into the shade. Just a little lie down, he thought, a few minutes' shuteye. Sleep came to him on the run.

He was back at home, and he had left the electric blanket on so that his bed was too hot, and Lonely was playing a concerto on the vacuum-cleaner and Miss Brewis was at the door yelling. 'Mr Callan! Mr Callan!' And Christ he was tired, but the noise and heat were too much for him. He opened his eyes, and the electric blanket was the sun, the vacuum-cleaner the beat of engines: and Miss Brewis had changed into Helena Kollonaki – and that wasn't a bad trick if you knew how to work it.

'Mr Callan,' she said.

'We speaking again?'

'Randy asked me to tell you – there's another boat coming.'

He looked round: from the tiny island of Psara a gun-boat was coming up fast.

'Randy says shall we accelerate?'

Callan looked forward. Chios was still a long way away.

'No,' he said. 'Tell him to take it easy – then come back here.'

She went into the wheelhouse and came back to him: the steady pulsing of the *Galatea's* engines stayed unchanged.

'It's a pity you threw your gun overboard,' she said.

'We'll fight this one hand to hand,' said Callan. 'Sit down.' She sat on the deck. 'By me.' He patted the mattress: reluctantly she sat. Callan took his shirt off.

'You're over-dressed,' he said.

'For being arrested?'

'For what we're going to do.'

He took hold of her waist, and pulled the shirt from out of her slacks. She flinched away from his hands.

'I know how you feel about me,' said Callan, 'but do you want to visit Randy in prison?' She shook her head. 'Then be still.'

She sat, her body rigid, as he loosed the button at her throat, then all the others except the one that held the shirt fastened across her breasts, then tied the tails of her shirt just below them, eased the slacks low on her hips.

'Hand to hand fighting,' he said, and took her in his arms, pushing her back on to the mattress. She stayed rigid in his arms as he kissed her.

'You'll have to do better than that, Miss Kollonaki,' he said. 'We've got an audience.'

Slowly, unwillingly, her arms came round him, and at last she responded to his kiss; the tensions and fears of what had happened, of what was still to come, were forgotten as her body yielded to his. To be dominated was her only escape, and she accepted it at last.

Callan shifted position slightly, turning her head as her lips opened to his. Through half-closed eyes he could see the gun-boat fifty feet from them, throttled back, matching *Galatea's* speed. An officer on deck held binoculars in his hands, was raising them to his eyes... This had better look good. Callan's hands tightened on the girl's smooth flesh, and he moved once more, until he could see nothing but the black gleam of her hair, the lashes fluttering over eyes tight closed. Her mouth was an unbelievable sweetness...

'Lovebirds, lovebirds,' Randy Blythe said.

Callan sat up, one arm still round Helena. She made no move to avoid it. 'They've gone then?' he asked.

'Ages ago,' Blythe, and gestured. 'Welcome to Turkey.'

301

Callan's eyes followed the gesturing hand. Behind them Chios recorded: golden stone clouded with olive trees. One of the most beautiful islands of all and he'd missed it. It didn't bother him. Helena's skin was an even richer gold. He looked ahead: the Turkish coastline was already in sight.

'We're on automatic?' he asked. Blythe nodded. 'Tell me what happened.'

'They stayed with us for a couple of minutes,' Blythe said. 'First the skipper had a look at you, then he gave the glasses to his lieutenant and he had a look, then the midshipman I suppose he'd be. Really there was quite a queue. You were awfully good.'

Helena blushed.

'Then what?' said Callan.

'The skipper had a look at me.'

'And what did you do?'

'Grinned,' said Blythe, 'and made libidinous gestures, I regret to say, except that it was rather in character as a brutal and licentious sailor. Then they made gestures equally libidinous, and sheered off. Then I went below and found this,' he said, and showed them a bottle of champagne. 'I thought – under the circumstances–'

'Of course,' said Callan.

'Shall I be mother?'

Callan nodded, and Blythe's strong fingers popped the cork, the champagne foamed into the glasses. Blythe lifted his and looked at Callan.

'To you,' he said. 'The essential Callan. No unpleasantness at all.'

Helena said, 'I don't understand. Are you being nice to him?'

'As nice as I know how,' said Blythe.

'Then I'll join you.' She lifted her glass. 'To you, Callan.'

'I think,' said Callan, 'that under the circumstances you can call me David.'

Helena choked, then sat up, and said severely, 'We must be practical.'

Callan and Blythe grinned.

'I mean it,' she said. 'We must consider what to do... Dimitri said there would be a contact in Izmir.'

'There is a contact,' said Callan... 'But not Dimitri's.'

'Also the question of where I am to go.'

'The contact will arrange all that.'

'And where Randy is to go.'

'I think,' said Blythe, 'that I shall decide that for myself.' He swirled the champagne in his glass. 'First a holiday. I deserve a little holiday. Then we'll see.'

Callan looked at him: Randy had finished for ever scaling upper class teeth.

'Dimitri is dead,' he said. 'Long live Dimitri.'

'What a perceptive boy you are,' said Blythe.

'Will you take some advice?'

'We'll see,' Blythe said.

'Get yourself some lessons first.'

Helena said, 'I think I understand what you are talking about.' She reached out to Blythe, covered his hand with hers. 'Haven't you done enough for my mother?'

Blythe said, 'Not for your mother, nor for you either, my dear. This is for Greece. And for Greece even a drunken dentist can do more than I've

303

done. Now – are we finished being practical?'

'There is also the question of my passport,' she said. 'I am terribly sorry, David, but in all the excitement I forgot. I don't have one. The police took it from me.'

'Yes, you do,' said Callan. 'I brought you a lovely passport.'

'Of course,' she said. 'How very foolish of me. It is your business to arrange such things. Who am I?'

'Mrs Robertson.'

'And who is Mr Robertson?'

'Me,' said Callan.

'You arrange such things rather well,' she said.

Lonely sat in his room and watched the telly, waiting for the race to start. Nice room. Comfortable. Bath and shower handy. What was it Mr Callan called it? En suite. This was the life all right. Five thousand nicker in a Swiss bank, and all the ready cash he needed, thanks to Mr Callan. Nags running well too. Three straight wins and an each way crossed double. Coining it he was. No hardship being on his own, neither. Better on your own, after you've done a job. You start going with mates and they end up grassing on you. Anyway he didn't need mates. He'd got Mr Callan... If he got out all right. That was the only worry. If Mr Callan had got nicked, Lonely was right back where he started. Larceny money and goods fifteen pounds, and arson of a restaurant taken into consideration. Some hopes. You do an arson and they send you down for years and years, and there was only Mr Callan could help him with that one. Promised he'd help him: said it would be all right. *If he got back.*

Now, Lonely, he told himself. No good fretting yourself. You start worrying and you'll need another bath. Mr Callan said it might be a few days. You just relax and enjoy yourself. The horses moved up to the start, and he looked out for the one he fancied: but he wasn't relaxed. He wasn't enjoying himself very much either.

21

Izmir was hot, and colourful, and all around it were the relics of Greek, Roman and Islamic culture, just as the guide books said. They didn't see much of it. Customs, Port Health Authority, Passport Control, and that was about it. After that they went out for a late lunch of swordfish kebabs and Turkish wine, and Blythe deplored its lack of resin. Over coffee he said: 'When do you see your contact?'

'Tonight,' said Callan.

'Need me at all?' Callan shook his head. 'I think I'll be off then.'

'But where on earth will you go?' Helena asked.

'Holiday,' said Blythe. 'I told you.' He switched to Greek, and Helena looked away; then he turned to Callan. 'About your advice,' he said.

'Yes?' said Callan.

'I'll take it.' He shook Callan's hand. 'Thank you, my dear.' Then he was gone.

'What do we do?' Helena asked.

'Find a hotel,' said Callan. 'Sleep. Make our contact.'

'Couldn't we sleep on the boat?'

Callan shook his head. Hunter had other plans for the boat. In a few days two people called Robertson, with passports to prove it, would come back from their trip ashore, and sail away on her. They'd bring a skipper with them too; once Callan had made his contact. According to his passport his name would be Blythe.

'The boat's not ours any more,' said Callan. She looked a question. 'Orders,' he said, and for her, that was enough. He took her to buy a suitcase, and a change of clothes.

Their hotel was old and cool, the room high enough to diminish the street noises. He expected reluctance, but there was none. They made love, and it was pleasant, and more than pleasant: both of them, he thought, achieved content, perhaps even happiness: but there was none of the oblivious joy of the kisses aboard *Galatea*.

She said, 'I haven't had much experience of this sort of thing. I expect it shows.'

'Some questions are impossible to answer,' Callan said.

'That wasn't a question.' She raised herself to look at him. 'I'm grateful to you, Callan. If I start to think about it I shall find that I love you. But I don't want to get involved with you. Besides – you don't love me, do you?' He started to speak, and she covered his mouth with her hand. 'No. Forgive me. It's impossible to answer that question too...'

The contact was waiting in the café just as

Hunter had said he would be: red shirt, white straw hat, most of his body festooned with cameras and light meters. Callan sat down beside him, laid the *Guide to Izmir* alongside the *Guide to Izmir* the contact carried.

'Snap,' the contact said.

Callan said carefully: 'Jolly interesting guide book that.'

'Absolutely enthralling,' the contact said, equally carefully, and that was it. They could get down to business.

'Why the hell did Hunter have to send you?' said Callan.

'Look about you,' Spencer Percival Fitzmaurice said. 'The coloured people are everywhere.'

Callan looked; there were enough negroes in the café to make Fitzmaurice part of the landscape.

'Some of our brothers and sisters from Wolverhampton,' Fitzmaurice said. 'Waiting for the coach to take them to their holiday dream-home.' He looked lazily at Callan. 'You still mad at me?'

'No,' said Callan. 'What would be the point?'

'No point,' said Fitzmaurice. 'I do what Charlie says. Let's hope you do too.'

'She's here,' said Callan, and made his report.

'Charlie will be pleased,' Fitzmaurice said. 'You're to take her to the country place.'

'When?'

'All in the guide book, my friend,' said Fitzmaurice.

He finished his beer, picked up Callan's guide book, and rose.

'Nice talking to you,' he said. 'Glad there's no hard feelings.'

307

'Me too,' said Callan. 'Next time bring a gun.' Fitzmaurice left.

Inside his guide book there were two airline tickets: Mr and Mrs Robertson. Izmir–Istanbul–London. Tomorrow she'd be at the country place. Callan began to wonder what plans Hunter had for her, and told himself it was none of his business. It didn't stop him wondering...

She ate an enormous dinner, then asked to go back to the hotel. This time their love-making was more intense, more passionate, fired by remembered kisses, leading at last to a weary, satisfied release.

She said, 'I wasn't very nice to you this afternoon. And this morning I was awful.'

'You've made up for it,' he said.

'I'm worried, you see. Worried about going back my mother. I'm not like you – or Randy Blythe. I won't be. I can't be. Please don't let her make me.'

That was one promise Hunter would keep.

'I won't let her make you,' he said, and she slept like a child.

Hunter said, 'Decent of you to come along at such short notice, Michael. I've been rather looking forward to another chat.'

Vardakis unfolded his napkin: laid it on his lap. 'Do I know you?' he asked.

'Dear Michael,' said Hunter. 'Always so blunt – even then. Crete,' he added helpfully. 'Sonda Bay. Thirty years ago. I brought you some rifles.'

Vardakis looked round the club dining-room. It had a kind of dingy elegance that was very

British, and that he was beginning to like.

'I remember,' he said. 'They were good rifles.'

Hunter said, 'I'm sure you made excellent use of them.'

Vardakis waited as soup was put in front of him, then said: 'I could hardly keep away you know. Even if I had never seen you before. Your secretary's message was most intriguing.'

'Indeed?'

'You are to lunch with Mr Hunter at his club, she said, to discuss the implications of arson and kidnapping.'

'Dear dear,' said Hunter. 'A little brusque, I'm afraid.'

'So is arson,' said Vardakis. 'So is kidnapping.'

'Quite so.'

'I accepted your invitation because I wondered what such criminal acts could possibly have to do with me.'

'You commit them,' said Hunter.

'I did,' said Vardakis, 'but then so did you.' Hunter made no answer. 'Thirty years ago,' Vardakis continued. 'I set fire to some aircraft hangars and helped to kidnap a general.'

'And last week you set fire to a restaurant, and this week you kidnapped a girl. I must say, Michael, you haven't lost your touch.'

'It would be kindest to assume that you are drunk,' said Vardakis.

'Helena Kollonaki,' said Hunter. 'Living in Kronis. Your cousin's daughter, I understand. There is a strong family resemblance.'

'Are you saying I kidnapped her?'

'Caused her to be kidnapped, my dear fellow.

Just as you caused the Parnassos Restaurant to be burned to the ground.'

'Not drunk,' said Vardakis. 'Raving.'

'We can of course, prove this,' Hunter said.

'We?'

'A little group I have the honour to lead.'

'And naturally you will report your suspicions to the police?'

'Er – no,' said Hunter. 'You've been a good friend to us in the past, my dear fellow. I think you'll be an even better one in the future.'

'I don't,' Vardakis said.

'That is because you haven't thought,' said Hunter, 'and that's very unlike you, Michael, if you don't mind my saying so.'

'I cannot think without facts,' Vardakis said, and spooned up soup.

'Nutter Bradley, Snooks Jackson,' Hunter said. Vardakis's hand remained quite steady.

'What are they? Pop singers?' he asked.

Hunter said, 'I really do advise you to think, Michael.'

Vardakis thought through steak and kidney pudding, cheese and biscuits, and a bottle of Beaune, but still he admitted nothing. Hunter finished his wine.

'Does the name Callan mean anything to you?' he asked.

'No.'

'He visited your cousin – in London and in Paris. Both the houses were yours. You were in your London house at the time of his visits there.'

'My cousin sees a great many fools. I do not.'

'From what I gather,' Hunter said, 'Callan is all

310

sorts of things, but he's not a fool. He's a killer, Michael, and a very successful one. He prefers his money to be paid into a Swiss bank. A lot of mercenaries do, I believe.' Vardakis said nothing, and Hunter rose. 'I've ordered coffee and brandy in the small committee room,' he said. 'We won't be disturbed there, and there's someone I'd rather like you to meet.'

As soon as he saw Meres, Vardakis knew that he had lost, but it was not in him simply to accept defeat: somehow, in some way, he would go on fighting. Again he denied that he had ever met Bradley or Jackson. Meres played the tape-recordings: himself talking to Meres, instructing him to hire two men to bomb the Parnassos: Meres doing just that: Jackson saying he'd done it.

'Such things can be faked,' Vardakis said.

'Oh undoubtedly.' Hunter poured brandy and offered it to Vardakis, who shook his head. 'A cigar?'

'No,' said Vardakis.

'Sure? We do rather a good cigar here I think.' Hunter pushed the box to Meres. 'Where were we? Oh yes... Faking tapes. We do it all the time. Our good luck, really, that you were willing to oblige. But fake or not it would do you no good if I sent it to the right people with your dossier.'

'Dossier?'

'Our yellow file on you. It's been active for thirty years. Almost a record.'

'That also could he faked.'

'I have the testimony of a young man called Nicky,' said Hunter. 'He agrees that you strayed from the fold. He even agrees that he tried to kill

311

you with a bomb.'

'Well then,' Vardakis said.

'But he does make it absolutely clear how far you were in, in the past. No right wing government would ever trust you again.'

'I'll risk it,' said Vardakis.

'Then there is the raid to rescue your daughter–'

Vardakis knew he had lost.

'I have no daughter,' he said.

'–known as Helena Kollonaki.'

'She is the daughter of my cousin Sophie and her late husband. You have no right to smear such a good man.'

'Right?' Hunter tasted the word as if he found it unfamiliar. 'You had bad luck, you know. Before the war very few Greeks had their blood tested. But Kollonaki was a doctor – and he did. Took a bit of searching, but we found his records. His blood group was "O".'

'More lies.'

'No, no,' said Hunter. 'It would be foolish to lie about what can actually be checked... You were much easier. You have regular checkups at the Lebègue clinic in Paris. So does Sophie. So did your daughter before she was confined in Crete. All three of you have an AB blood group. Dr Kollonaki could not possibly be Helena's father.'

'If what you say is true,' said Vardakis, 'I accept that. But all you have proved is that Helena's father has the same blood group as me.'

'Bit hard on Sophie, aren't you, old chap?' said Hunter. 'Besides, I saw you together in the mountains. Quite a lot of people saw you.' He

312

waited, but Vardakis was silent. 'Let's talk about this rescue. You wanted it to fail, and you wanted Dimitri killed. Do I have that correctly?'

'I have no idea what you're talking about.'

Hunter turned to Meres. 'Is that correct, Toby?'

'Yes, sir.'

'I think that you are assuming that your orders were carried out. They were, in part. Dimitri was killed.'

Vardakis's face was impassive, but this time he had to speak.

'And Helena?'

'Callan exceeded his instructions,' Hunter said. 'He got her out.' He watched, but Vardakis's face still told him nothing. 'Callan really is a mercenary, you know,' Hunter continued. 'I offered rather more than you did. He's giving her to me.'

Vardakis's fists clenched, and Meres was on his feet at once.

Hunter said, 'Do I really have to tell you how violent Toby can be? Even here in my club? You hired him for it, after all. Don't be foolish, Michael.'

Vardakis willed himself to relax.

'What will you do with her?' he asked.

'Good God,' said Hunter, 'you don't suppose I'd ill-treat her, do you? She'll stay at our place in the country for a little while – fresh air and good food, and a little chat with me. And afterwards–'

'Well?'

'I always think,' said Hunter, 'that a daughter's place is with her mother. Don't you?'

Vardakis said: 'Tell me what it is you want.'

Mr and Mrs Robertson had seats on a light aircraft to Istanbul, and transferred to a Trident Two. No time to look at Topaki, the Blue Mosque, the Golden Horn. Charlie wanted to see them urgently. Callan bought her cigarettes and perfume at the duty-free shop, and whisky for himself: then he remembered Lonely, and added cigarettes and aftershave. She held his hand during take-off.

'I hate flying,' she said.

'You have too much imagination,' said Callan.

'I used to think you had none at all,' she said. 'I was wrong.'

When lunch was served, he ordered champagne.

'My farewell party?' she said. 'Thank you, David.'

He raised his glass to her, touched hers, and sipped.

'It's true what I told you,' she said. 'I couldn't stay with you for long, and anyway you never asked me, but thank you.'

'I did a job,' he said. 'A job I got paid for. It turned out to be a lot nicer than I expected.'

She pecked at the food on the plastic tray.

'Must I go to my mother?' she asked.

Callan said, 'That was the whole idea. Anyway, where would you like to go?'

'Out of all that,' she said. 'Anywhere away from what she does: what she wants. Maybe I could go to university; study archaeology.'

'Like Randy Blythe?'

'No,' she said. 'Not like Randy. I think Randy will be caught. Maybe killed.'

'It's possible.'

'And you don't care?'

Callan shrugged. 'How could I stop him? It's what he wants to do. And anyway do you care?'

'If I hear about it I'll weep for him,' she said. 'But I won't join him.'

Callan said, 'Universities cost money. Have you got any?'

'No,' she said. 'But Michael has.'

'Michael?'

'Michael Vardakis... My mother's cousin. He would help me... He's not like my mother.'

Callan remembered: Bradley's bullet slamming home: Dimitri's fall, the chair cracking under his weight.

'You're sure?' he asked.

She looked at him, surprised.

'Of course,' she said.

'But if he doesn't get on with your mother–'

'He gets on with me,' she said. 'He's my father,' and waited. 'You don't seem surprised.'

Callan thought: it could be true. He certainly wanted you back badly enough.

'Oh ... yeah,' he said. 'I'm surprised right enough. But how do you know?'

'He told me,' she said, 'when he came to see me in Crete. He told me because he wanted me to stay there. I'd be safe if I stayed in Crete, he said. He thought he would be, too.'

'Then why didn't you ask to stay?'

'Would you have listened?' she asked. 'Would Bradley?'

She might not like her mother, he thought, but she'd learned her lessons.

'Will you take me to Michael?' she asked again. 'He'll pay you well.'

315

'Let's take it easy for a while,' said Callan. 'Then we'll see.'

She finished the champagne, and slept. When the *Trident* made its run in to land, he had to shake her awake, and she smiled at him sleepily.

'Michael will be surprised when he sees us,' she said.

Passport control had no problems for Mr and Mrs Robertson, and Customs weren't interested either. Callan led her to the exit doors, and the limousine was awaiting: the elderly Bentley and the deferential chauffeur bustling up, happy to help with suitcases, happy just to see them.

'Welcome back to England, Mr Callan,' Fitzmaurice said.

'Ah, Fitzmaurice,' Callan said. 'You're looking well. This is Miss Helena Kollonaki.'

Fitzmaurice saluted, and held open the door. She hesitated.

'My mother—' she said.

'I told you,' said Callan. 'We're going to the country. Your mother doesn't even know you're here.'

And with that she got in, because Callan wouldn't lie to her. He turned to Fitzmaurice instead.

'Come along, my man,' he said. 'Look sharp. We haven't got all day you know. You're not in Barbados now.'

Fitzmaurice took it: he had to...

Hunter was delighted to see them: he said so, and offered them tea of his own Darjeeling blend. At first, she thought he was a wealthy friend of Callan's, and treated him with a deferential prettiness he would have loved to watch, if things had been different. It was Hunter who disillusioned her, in a single sentence. He spoke in Greek, but Callan heard his own name, and had no doubt what had been said.

'You – you lied to me?' she said.

'Sometimes,' said Callan.

'But why?'

How can I tell her I had no choice, he wondered. She thinks I'm Superman.

'You should have told me the truth,' she said. 'It would have made no difference. I'd still have come... No. No, I wouldn't. And you knew that. How very clever you are.'

Hunter rang a bell and a housekeeper appeared: plump, motherly and, Callan knew, as tough as old boots.

'Show Miss Kollonaki to her room,' said Hunter. 'I'll ring when I'm ready for her.'

She took Helena's arm, and led the girl away. There was no fight in her...

'You did well,' said Hunter.

'Well enough to get out of a red file?'

'Certainly. You're back in your yellow one, where you belong.'

Surveillance only, Callan thought. He couldn't expect more than that.

'Why did you kill Dimitri?' Hunter asked.

'I didn't,' said Callan. 'Bradley did that.'

Hunter sighed. 'Why did you allow Dimitri to be killed?'

'Bradley had the drop on me,' said Callan. Hunter's eyes on him were shrewd, unwavering.

'Getting old, Callan?'

317

'Sometimes,' Callan said. 'It comes and goes.'

'It went eventually...You got rid of Bradley.'

'That's right,' said Callan. 'On the Polybios boat. How did he do, have you heard?'

'Later,' said Hunter. 'Why didn't you kill Bradley?'

'No point,' said Callan.

'You killed two policemen.'

'There wasn't any other way.'

'According to your report to Fitzmaurice, you had a perfectly good gun, a favourite of yours, and you didn't use it on Bradley, whom you detest. Why?'

'I didn't use it at all,' said Callan. 'I don't think I do like using them any more – till I'm actually doing it. All right, I don't like Bradley. Who could? But add a few more brains and he's a lot like I used to be. And anyway, he was more use as a decoy.'

'Was he?' said Hunter. 'You imperilled the whole operation. If he'd been picked up–'

'Wasn't he?'

'Later, I said. If he'd been picked up he'd have talked.'

'But he knew nothing about you,' said Callan.

'He knew about Meres.'

'But how could he?'

'I allowed him to. Vardakis was looking for a reliable man. The matter came to my notice, and I allowed him to recruit Meres.'

'So it was Meres who set up Bradley for the Parnassos job?'

'It was... I've made sure that Lonely's no longer suspected of that by the way.'

318

'I'm obliged to you,' said Callan. 'So's he.'

'I don't think so. One gathers he did a good job of opening up the Polybios house... No doubt you're wondering why I set Meres on to Vardakis?'

'I'm not allowed to ask why,' said Callan.

'All the same I think you're entitled to know. Vardakis has enormous power and very valuable sources of information. Highly sensitive information. He may even become a member of the Greek government. That would make him very useful to me.'

'If you can get him,' said Callan.

'I've got him.'

Callan looked at the door through which Helena had left. 'Is that why you wanted his daughter?' he asked.

For once Hunter's calm was shattered. 'How the devil did you know that?'

'She told me,' said Callan.

'What a lovable chap you must be,' said Hunter. 'To get that information I had to set up two burglaries and bribe five people. And you do it all by charm. Is she fond of Vardakis?'

'Yes.'

'Excellent,' said Hunter.

'All she wants is peace and quiet, Hunter,' Callan said. 'Can't she have it?'

'It's what we all want,' said Hunter. 'Her chances are better than most.'

'What'll you do to her?'

'Chat,' said Hunter. 'Then let her go.'

'To Vardakis?'

'Well perhaps not quite that,' said Hunter, 'but they'll meet from time to time – if he behaves.'

'What about her mother?'

'Sophie? Really she has very little to offer. She was due for retirement, until you let her successor die.'

'Dimitri?'

'Her friends are really getting rather tired of her, you know. Far too many speeches, and not nearly enough action, as well as that unfortunate relationship with Vardakis. It was time for Dimitri to take over.'

'After he'd let Helena escape,' said Callan. 'The Greek coppers would never have let him go.'

'On the contrary,' said Hunter, 'the Greek coppers trusted him. After that bang on the head they'd have trusted him even more. He could go wherever he liked.'

Callan said, 'Then will you kindly tell me why Sophie's lot agreed to have her daughter lifted? Blythe even *helped* with it.'

'Sentiment,' said Hunter. 'A retirement present if you like. Instead of a gold watch they gave her daughter.'

'Is that why I went? Sentiment?'

'No,' said Hunter. 'You went for me. By the by, what happened to Blythe?'

Callan told him.

'Will he still need watching, do you think?' Hunter asked.

'It's possible.'

'Then we'll watch him.'

Callan said, 'Is it late enough now to ask about Bradley?'

'Bradley escaped too,' said Hunter. 'Somehow or other he got to Cyprus. He has friends there.

Quite an Odyssey. The Greeks can be really extra-ordinarily inept – which is just as well. I didn't want him in their hands – not alive.'

'Where is he now?' said Callan.

'On his way to London, I should think,' said Hunter. 'He may be here by now. Tomorrow he'll probably try to kill you.'

'What the hell will he do that for?'

'Money,' said Hunter. 'Quite a lot I should imagine.'

'But – but who from?'

'Vardakis,' Hunter said. 'He knows you brought his daughter here. He hates you for it.'

'But didn't you tell him I was working for you?'

'You're not,' said Hunter. 'Not officially.'

'I'm in a lovely spot, aren't I?' said Callan. 'Vardakis won't pay me and if I don't hand over her daughter Sophie Kollonaki won't pay me either – and now I'm going to be shot.'

'Suppose I paid you instead,' said Hunter, 'what would you do?'

'Take it and run,' said Callan.

'Then I'll pay you the day after tomorrow.'

'You want me to kill Bradley for you?'

'That,' said Hunter, 'or give him to me. He might have something useful – though I doubt it. But he knows far too much to be left running around unchecked. Oh by the by – I did discover who fired at you with that rifle.'

'Anybody I know?' Callan asked.

'I doubt it,' said Hunter. 'His name was Nicky.'

'Was?'

'He killed himself. Would you care to wash before dinner?'

22

Lonely was out, but he left a message. Tell him, he said, that Mr Callan was back and he'd call again later. They said they would... Callan washed, then poured himself a whisky. Hunter must be pleased with him; it was Chivas Regal. All the same the future was bleak, particularly that bit about Nutter Bradley. Take the kid with his hands any time: with his hands, that was easy. But with a gun. Nutter was as fast as he was accurate, and he had all the boundless optimism of youth. With a gun Nutter was more than a problem, he was a nightmare. And if he came looking for Callan he'd bring a gun. Then there was the money – if he lived to enjoy it. Nice to have money: no denying that. But money from Hunter tended to be earned three times over. All the same it did mean ten thousand for himself and five thousand for Lonely, and whatever else happened, the little man was entitled to his five grand.

Vardakis said: 'I think we have to talk.'

Sophie Kollonaki shrugged.

'Is there anything left for us to discuss?' she asked.

'Only one thing,' he said. 'Our daughter.'

The woman very carefully stubbed out her cigarette in an ash-tray. It was a long, and apparently totally-absorbing business.

'She is not coming back to you,' said Vardakis.

'Of course not,' she said, and she spoke without a tremor. 'You are keeping her away from me in Crete.'

'You sent a man called Callan to bring her to you,' Vardakis said.

In the same even tone she said, 'Nicky was right, then. You spied on me.' Vardakis stayed silent. 'I let Nicky give Callan a warning – with a rifle. It was one of yours, Michael. One of those you use to go killing deer in Scotland. Does that amuse you?'

'No,' said Vardakis. 'Nicky is dead.'

'I do not believe you.'

'British Security picked him up. After interrogation he hanged himself.'

She believed that all right: the fierce eyes grew fiercer still.

'Don't be foolish, Sophie,' Vardakis said. 'They also have our daughter.'

'I paid Callan to bring her to me.'

Vardakis chuckled. 'And I paid him to leave her in Crete. Hunter offered even more.'

'Hunter?'

'A Section head in British Security.'

'What will he do to her?'

'Nothing.'

'Tell me the truth, Michael.'

'It is the truth. If I do what I'm told, Helena will be safe. She may even come to see me – or you, if she wishes it.'

'Well then – surely, once she is with us, we can take her away.'

'Sophie, Sophie, how naïve you are,' Vardakis

323

said. 'Do you suppose Hunter hasn't thought of that? He has made perfectly sure I will do as he says.'

'But how can he?'

'Guarantees,' said Vardakis. 'Guarantees I can never redeem.'

'I gave no guarantees,' she said.

'You will, my dear. Before Nicky died, he told enough to destroy you. Hunter has it all. And anyway–' He hesitated.

'Go on,' she said. 'It seems we do have things to discuss after all.'

It had not been his intention to break the news gently. The urge had been to denounce, even to gloat. He found he couldn't do it.

'I am sorry, my dear,' he said, 'but you are finished. Your party no longer needs you as its leader.'

'This time I know you are lying,' she said.

'Your successor was decided on months ago.'

'You seem to be very well informed,' she said.

'I am ... I was always good at gathering information.'

'That at least is true. And who is to succeed me?'

'They chose Dimitri.'

'Dimitri? That's a cruel thing to say.'

'I agree. It is also the truth. Think, Sophie. The sleeper awakes, and comes to freedom, bringing with him information, and the adventure of a secret escape. The – what is the word the young people use? – charisma. Of course Dimitri.'

This time her voice was only just controlled. 'I might believe it,' she said, 'if I knew who told you.'

'Helena told me,' he said, 'the last time I saw her in Crete.'

'Helena spied? But she cares nothing for what I do.'

'She is your daughter.'

'She dislikes me.'

'Yes,' said Vardakis. 'She does. She also loves you.'

Her head bent then, but she did not weep.

'If she visits you,' she said at last, 'won't you be blamed by the Colonels for rescuing her?'

'No,' said Vardakis. 'You will.'

She looked up then. 'I suppose I will,' she said. 'It was my idea after all... But she had better visit me sometimes – if things are to look right.'

'I'll do what I can,' Vardakis said, then added: 'what will you do?'

'Write my memoirs,' she said, 'and knit.'

'I must tell you,' he said, 'that Dimitri is dead. Will that make any difference?'

'No,' she said. 'The committee chose him. They must have done. They will choose another.' She reached for another cigarette. 'How did Dimitri die?'

It had been his intention to lie: to blame it on the rescue operation. But her honesty was total, could be matched only by honesty of his own.

'He was shot,' he said. 'I arranged it.'

'You hate our party so much?'

'No,' he said. 'Not the party. Not even him. But there was a chance – a good chance I thought, that if he got out you and he might quarrel, and if that happened there might be violence.'

'And violence is bad for Vardakis Enterprises?'

325

'Of course it is,' said Vardakis. 'And your death would be bad for me.'

'Are you saying you still love me?'

'I always have,' Vardakis said. 'And like my daughter I also dislike you.'

She got up and walked to him, put one hand to his cheek.

'Poor Michael,' she said. He tried to cover her hand with his, but she withdrew it at once. 'No,' she said, 'my memoirs and my knitting, and that is all. I shall write and tell the Colonels so. I hope they'll be pleased.'

'I hope so too.'

'Of course,' she said, 'Vardakis Enterprises will be rid of its only embarrassment.'

Not quite that, he thought. Hunter would be a far bigger embarrassment than she had ever been, if the truth ever came out.

'So Callan betrayed us?'

'Yes,' said Vardakis.

'Strange,' she said. 'The computer told us that he had finished with British Intelligence. I did not think the K.G.B. had lied – not that time.'

'They didn't,' Vardakis said. 'Hunter offered more than we did, that's all.'

'I think it is bad that he should get away with this unpunished.'

Vardakis was a business man: he never forecast certainties.

'I think it is quite possible that he won't,' he said.

Lonely had been out for fish and chips. The posh grub where he was staying was all very well, but sometimes you fancied a hit of a change. Nice drop of bitter they did you up North an' all: went down a treat after all that salt and vinegar. He took the message up to his room, and read it through twice. Mr Callan had telephoned from London in his absence and would call again later. Nice that was: real class. Pity he'd been out though, he'd have liked to have talked to Mr Callan again. Truth was he really had been worried, with that git Bradley on the loose and Mr Callan having to look out for the bird and the poof as well as himself. Dead worried he'd been... But you could always rely on Mr Callan.

All in all it had been quite a day. Three more winners, and one of them a seven to one shot. He began to count the notes, and it was a real pleasure. Even after he'd paid the bill here he'd still have over a hundred nicker. Go on, Lonely, he thought. You're dying to see Mr Callan anyway, so do it in style. You're big time now. He picked up the house telephone and dialled the hall porter's number.

'Yes, sir?'

'I wonder if you could get me a sleeper on to-night's train to London?' Lonely said, then added, his voice choking with pride: 'First class of course.'

Dinner was a strained affair. Hunter, it was true, maintained a flow of conversation that was both innocuous and uninformative, but Helena was able to supply very little but 'Yes' and 'No', and Callan was busy with his own thoughts... They had an armoury in the country place: his best bet was to spend time there as soon as this interminable

327

meal was finished, choose a .357 magnum, and practise till he really knew the gun. An hour, hour and a half, then take it up to his room, clean it and practise again: drawing, aiming, reloading. Then maybe, *maybe*, he'd be ready for Nutter. Of course he could always run, but even then Nutter might find him, and even if he didn't, Hunter would. And running never worked anyway. Your back to the enemy was the best target they could get. He sipped at his coffee, and waited for Hunter to belt up. Practise.

'A little brandy?' said Hunter.

'Not tonight,' said Callan. 'Maybe tomorrow.'

'You're very wise, I'm sure,' Hunter turned to Helena. 'For you, Miss Kollonaki?'

'No thank you,' she said.

'Ah... A little tired after your journey?'

'A little.' She hesitated. 'Please may I talk with Mr Callan?'

'Of course,' said Hunter. 'I have things to do anyway.'

'So have I,' said Callan, and turned to her. 'Can it keep for a while?'

Hunter said, 'I would ask you to remember, Miss Kollonaki, that between the boor and the realist there is a great deal of difference.' He left.

'I do have to talk,' she said.

'Give me a couple of hours.'

The armoury was a kind of peace, once he found his rhythm, and that didn't come easy, not this time. The gun he chose was another Colt Python Magnum: .357 ammo, two-and-a-half-inch barrel... The way Bradley fought his wars, there wouldn't be any long-range shooting. After

328

that came the practice, and he practised so bloody hard he nearly wore out the gun. The trouble was his rhythm had left him: that inevitable flow of upsweeping hand coming up, the eye telling the brain what to do and the finger obeying: the two sharp cracks of sound so fast that one seemed to be the echo of the other, the way the instructors said... He knew it all, he'd done it all, but it just wouldn't come... And when at last it did, what was the use? If it took him that long facing Bradley he'd be dead anyway...

He showered and changed, and went to look for Helena. No sign of her downstairs, and maybe that was as well. There was nothing else he could say to her, nothing she could say to him... Time to sleep, and hope to God he could sleep. He went back to his room. She was in his bed.

'Look, love,' he said, 'you're making a big mistake.'

'I don't think so.'

'You don't know this place,' said Callan. 'I do.'

'You mean this room is bugged?'

'I mean all the rooms are bugged.'

'That doesn't worry me,' she said. 'I have no more secrets.'

'Maybe I have.'

'How coy you are,' she said. 'It's a good word, coy. Evocative. Isn't that what you say?'

'All the time,' said Callan. He looked at the Chivas Regal bottle: she hadn't shown it much mercy.

'Come,' she said, and patted the bedspread beside her. 'We must talk.'

'Talk then.'

'Not unless you hold me,' she said. 'If you don't hold me I never tell you a bloody thing.'

He went to her, put his arms about her. The phone rang. Callan picked it up.

'Charlie here,' Hunter said. 'I thought you might like to know your room isn't bugged for the moment.'

'Why not?'

'You'll tell me anyway,' said Hunter, 'and being overheard might cramp your style. Goodnight.'

Hunter wouldn't lie; not about that, and Callan knew it: knew too that he'd tell him everything she said, and Hunter knew that.

'Your boss?' she asked.

'Yeah,' said Callan. 'He was reminding me I've got a job to do tomorrow.'

'I've been drinking,' she said. 'I wish you'd been drinking.'

'Not when I'm working.'

She began to unbutton his shirt.

'Can't you have any fun when you're working?' she asked.

'I thought you had something to tell me.'

'I've thought about it,' she said, 'and I am in love with you. It isn't easy for a well brought up young lady to say that to a killer, but it's true.' Her fingers went on working on his clothes. 'I'm going to miss you for a long, long time.'

Callan said, 'I'll miss you too.'

'I'm sure that's true,' she said. 'Maybe for a whole week. But I don't want you to die, Callan.'

'I don't want me to die either.'

'You have a nice, witty way of humouring petulant children,' she said, and pulled at his belt. 'But

330

my mother and father will want you to die.'

'Why on earth–?'

'You cheated them,' she said. Her fingers went on working. 'Come into bed,' she said at last. 'You'll catch cold.' Her arms came round him. 'Now I'm cheating them too.'

Later she said, 'You reek of that stuff.'

'What stuff?'

'From the gun.'

'Cordite,' he said. 'I'm sorry. I took a shower, but–'

'Never mind,' she said. 'I'm sure it's symbolic.'

She moved into him again, and afterwards: 'Oh my God,' she said, 'I've just realised something... You've been practising.'

She got out of bed and poured another drink.

'I didn't tell you anything you didn't know, did I?'

'I heard your father might try something,' Callan said.

'You're going to kill him?' Callan shook his head. 'Why not? If he's going to kill you?'

'He won't come himself,' said Callan, 'and even if he did – Hunter wouldn't let me.'

She gulped at her whisky.

'I'm very unhappy,' she said.

'You're very beautiful.'

'That is for you,' she said. 'The unhappiness is mine.' She finished her whisky, put down the glass. 'If I cry, will you hold me again?'

It was late before she slept, and after that he still lay awake: unaware of the warmth and softness beside him; his mind concerned only with Bradley, seeing his stance, seeing him squeeze the trigger,

331

seeing the tight arc of the Browning as he covered them. Why should an idiot have so much talent? Why couldn't Hunter send Meres to deal with him come to that? Or Fitzmaurice? But that one was easy. Callan wasn't the Section's concern any more. If Bradley beat him, Hunter had one less problem to bother him, and he'd still get Bradley... Get some kip. Callan. You've got a big day tomorrow.

He woke at six, woke with such a total awareness he might never have been to sleep. Something was wrong. Beside him Helena groaned and stirred, but showed no signs of waking. Nothing to do with her. He sat and listened: a minute went by, two minutes, and he was sure the room was empty. But something was wrong. Think, he told himself, think. He sat up in the bed, switched the light on, and saw the telephone. Helena turned away from the light, and he thought, Lonely. I said I'd phone him back. Helena's body pressed against his. I never did phone him back. Callan reached out and dialled. Left, the night-porter said. Ordered a first-class sleeper to London. Talk about delusions of grandeur... Callan thanked him and hung up, and reached for a telephone directory. British Rail... But what station did the Manchester trains go to? Euston, was it? He dialled, and learned that the train had been cleared an hour before.

'Thanks,' he said. 'Thanks anyway.'

Helena said, 'You make so much noise.' She was still half-asleep.

'I'm sorry,' he said. 'I've got things to do.'

'But you said you wouldn't harm my father?'

'I won't,' he said.

332

'Kiss me, Callan,' she said, and as he bent to do so she was already asleep. Her mouth tasted of lipstick and whisky.

He took his clothes to the bathroom, washed, shaved, dressed in silence, in silence left her, but he couldn't leave the country place without saying goodbye to Hunter – that would upset him – and besides he needed a car. He walked to Hunter's bedroom down the middle of the corridor, staying well in the light. There was a man on duty outside Hunter's door: there always was. As Callan approached he stood up, his right hand disappeared inside his coat.

Callan said, 'Let me speak to Charlie, please.'

The man said, 'He's asleep.'

'Then if I'm going to speak to him you'll have to wake him up,' said Callan. 'That way he'll hear what I'm saying.'

'Wait here,' the man said, and went inside. When he came back be said, 'You can go in.' He sounded surprised.

Hunter wore pyjamas, dressing gown and a peeved expression. At ten past six in the morning, thought Callan, he was entitled to all three.

'What the devil is it?' he asked.

'I want to go home,' said Callan.

'At six in the morning?'

'Six eleven,' said Callan. 'It's urgent, Hunter.'

He talked about Lonely and the forgotten phone call, and Hunter poured coffee from a vacuum flask and listened.

'The girl distracted you,' he said at last.

'She'd distract anybody,' Callan said, 'particularly after she's been at the whisky.'

'You think she'll turn into a drunkard?'

'It's possible,' said Callan. 'There's an awful lot she needs to forget.'

Hunter made no notes: he didn't have to. 'What did she tell you?' he asked.

'That her father will have me killed.'

'Anything else?'

'Nothing relevant.' Hunter considered for a moment, then let it go.

'Very well,' he said. 'You'd better be off. I'll phone the garage. They'll have a car for you.'

He waited for him to leave, but Callan hesitated.

'Well?' said Hunter.

'Those two coppers I killed.'

'What about them?'

'There will be a warrant out for them.'

'Indeed there will,' said Hunter. 'For a man called Bradley and a man called Blythe. Neither you nor your odoriferous little friend are involved.'

Callan sighed.

'Poor old Randy,' he said.

Hunter said, 'I don't think he'll be an easy man to catch. He has very useful friends.'

'Funny there should be three coppers,' said Callan.

'Not at all. Vardakis tipped them off to be there.'

'Vardakis? And he's after me for treachery?'

'Callan, Callan,' said Hunter. 'The last thing you should expect of human beings is consistency.'

23

Beside the station they had this like hotel, and if you had the gelt it was smashing. They did you a bath and everything. Lonely made it a long one. No sense in waking Mr Callan at that hour of the morning... After that they did you breakfast: eggs, bacon, sausages, fried tomatoes, toast and marmalade: the lot. And even after that you could sit on a big fat chair in the lounge and get a bit more kip and a read of the paper till it was time to go and see Mr Callan and a doorman fell over himself to get you a taxi...

Callan waited in the car by his block of flats. He'd rung Lonely's gaff, and his own, and there'd been no answer. Maybe he was at Cousin Alfred's, maybe – no sense in wondering where Lonely was. Probably feeding his face somewhere if he had any money left. Callan looked around the street. No hurry. He still had twenty minutes on the meter, and he didn't want to go inside before Lonely was safely out of the way. O.K. up to now, he thought. Street's practically deserted at this hour of the morning. Four empty cars and a lot of wage-slaves hurrying for the tube and that was about it. No sign of Bradley. Not yet. But he'd be coming.

A taxi clattered round the corner, and a vision got out: pale blue lightweight suit, snap-brimmed hat, dark blue shirt and tie. It carried a brand new suitcase and paid off the driver to the manner born.

'Oi,' said Callan. 'Lord Rothschild.'

Lonely spun round and scuttled over to the car.

'Mr Callan,' he said, 'I knew you'd be all right. I knew it.' He looked at the car: an almost new Aston-Martin. 'You're doing all right an' all.'

'I'm not the only one,' said Callan, and opened the passenger door. 'Get in.'

Lonely settled himself on the seat, and lounged at ease.

'Smashing car,' he said. 'You nick it?'

'It belongs to my rich friend,' said Callan.

'You get your bird away all right?' Lonely asked.

'Yeah,' said Callan.

'So we cop from her rich uncle,' said Lonely, and sprawled out more luxuriously than ever.

No point in explanations, Callan thought, and anyway the Aston-Martin smelled nice the way it was. 'Yeah,' he said. 'We cop.'

'So all I've got to worry about now is this arson lark.'

'That's taken care of too,' said Callan... 'Or it will be soon.'

Lonely looked awed: 'You mean you been bribing the rozzers?'

'Something like that.'

'Bleeding waste of money if you ask me,' said Lonely. 'Still it'll be nice not to be a wanted man. You got another job lined up, Mr Callan?'

'Now now,' said Callan. 'We mustn't be greedy.'

'I must say I could do with a rest,' Lonely said.

Callan didn't answer. His eyes were watching the street.

336

'Anything wrong, Mr Callan? I mean I know you said you'd phone back, but I thought I'd come down anyway and surprise you like.' Callan kept on watching. 'It wasn't your money, Mr Callan. I had a few wins on the nags and–'

'Nothing's wrong, old son,' said Callan, and reached for the ignition.

Lonely said, 'We're being watched.'

Callan looked out again: the last of the bread-winners racing for the salt mines, two blokes pushing a barrow-load of fruit, a traffic warden at the end of the street looking at parking meters. Everything the way it should be at this hour of the morning, but you didn't argue with Lonely if he said you were being watched. Lonely knew.

For a moment he considered the possibility of just driving away, but if he did Bradley might shoot up the car and kill the pair of them. It wasn't on: they'd be safer indoors.

Carefully Callan said, 'I thought we might be. Nothing to worry about, old son. Let's go in-doors and I'll tell you all about it.'

He waited till Lonely got his suitcase out, humped it into the block of flats, then got out himself, crouched to lock the car-door, keeping the car between himself and whatever danger threatened, and took one last look around. The barrow-boys were turning a corner, the traffic warden was still looking at meters as if they were masterpieces: he could see nothing wrong. Nothing at all. All the same, when it came to getting into the hallway, he moved.

Lonely had the lift all ready and waiting. Nothing like terror, thought Callan, to make a man reliable in a crisis – and thank God he hasn't started to niff yet: not in a lift. He put his hand in his pocket: handed something to Lonely.

'Present for you,' he said.

Lonely unzipped the little bag and looked at its contents. Suddenly it was Christmas again. 'Mr Callan,' he said, 'you mean I get to keep it this time?'

'That's right,' said Callan. 'But mind you only use it when I tell you – or else there's trouble.'

'Cross my heart, Mr Callan,' said Lonely, and rummaged happily among pick-locks and twirls. Careful that the little man shouldn't see him, Callan loosed his coat, felt for the butt of the Colt Python as the lift crawled to a halt, the gates creaked open. Callan went out fast, but the tiny hallway was empty. As Lonely dragged out his suitcase, Callan looked down the angle of the stairs. That was empty too. He reached for his keys, then turned to Lonely.

'Tell you what,' he said, 'why don't you open up that drum?'

He nodded to the door that faced his.

'What for, Mr Callan?'

'Oh I don't know,' said Callan. 'Be a bit of practice for you.'

'Suppose there's somebody in?'

'There isn't,' said Callan. 'There's only an old bird called Miss Brewis lives there, and she's at work.'

'You sure?'

'Saw her go myself,' said Callan. It was true enough.

Lonely didn't hesitate. Half the time the things

Mr Callan told you to do sounded barmy, but all the same you wound up with five thousand nicker. And anyway Mr Callan didn't like back talk.

'Anything you say, Mr Callan,' said Lonely, and got to work. He'd have been slower if he'd used the key.

'In you go, old son,' said Callan.

'What d'you want me to nick?'

'Nothing,' said Callan. 'You just go in there and have a nice sit down. Watch the telly. Put it on nice and loud.'

'Where you going then, Mr Callan?'

'My place,' said Callan. 'The fact is old son, I'm expecting a visitor… He might get a bit naughty.'

'Physical?'

'That's it,' said Callan.

'To tell you the truth. I wouldn't mind watching the telly,' Lonely said. 'They have some good programmes on in the mornings nowadays.'

'You do that,' Callan said gently. 'I'll come and collect you when it's over.' He hesitated, sought soothing words, but no words would soothe what he still had to say.

'You may hear a bit of a noise,' Callan said. 'If you do, and another geezer comes out and I don't – let him get away – then scarper.'

'What sort of a noise?'

'Gun shots.'

'Oh my Gawd,' said Lonely.

Walters put down his field-glasses. The flat across the street was too high up for him to see into, but he'd seen enough. The heavy was back all right, and so was his smelly mate. Must have pulled a

339

hell of a good job, to judge by the clothes he was wearing... And the heavy driving an Aston-Martin. It didn't pay to be honest. Never had. But the bad boys didn't have it all their own way: not if Walters could help it. Still watching the street, he reached for the telephone and dialled.

'Hello?' said Kyle.

'You alone?' Walters asked.

'Mum's out shopping.'

'I'm at the flat I told you about,' Walters said. No answer. Still not keen, Walters thought, and I used to think you had guts.

'Your smelly friend's just turned up,' said Walters. 'And his minder.'

'Look, Mr Walters, I–'

'Smelly's got a suitcase,' said Walters. 'You ask me the heavy's just come back to pack a few things. He's got an Aston-Martin waiting. You better get over here.'

'I'm still on the sick,' said Kyle.

'Don't worry,' Walters said. 'I'll take care of the rough work.' He looked out of the window: the traffic warden had stopped by Callan's car.

'Better hurry,' Walters said.

'My mum–' said Kyle.

'We've been through all this before,' said Walters. 'What's the matter with you? You want to be a police constable all your life? This is the only chance you've got, son.' Silence. 'Look,' said Walters, 'don't you go worrying about your mum. You nick this villain and nobody'll dare touch her.'

'All right, Mr Walters,' said Kyle. 'I'll come over right away.'

Walters hung up and looked out of the window.

The street was deserted: even the traffic warden had gone. Couldn't be better, he thought. He didn't think there'd be any trouble – not when the heavy wasn't involved – but if there should be, it would be better without an audience.

Callan packed: it didn't take long. His soldiers, his books on military history, his one good suit, shirts and pyjamas. The rest of the flat was just equipment for existence: a living machine. No character, no charm, no memories. He'd leave it without regrets, and go to another just like it without anticipation. If he left it at all... He looked at the drinks table. One good belt left in the whisky bottle... Afterwards, he told himself. No good giving yourself any more handicaps, Callan. From across the hall there came the sound of gunfire, and the Python seemed to leap into his hand: then very slowly he relaxed. Lonely always did what he told him: Lonely was watching the telly...

Barmy, that's what it was, sitting there in front of the box and Mr Callan in trouble... Mr Callan was his mate. But he was the boss an' all. And anyway, thought Lonely, what good would I be if things get physical? He looked at the telly. Cowboys at ten o'clock in the morning. What was the world coming to? Baddy in the red shirt driving off all the cattle, and the goody in the white shirt too busy with his bird to know he'd bleeding well lost them. Stupid git... But somebody had been watching him and Mr Callan. No question. He went to the window, eased back Miss Brewis's crisp, clean curtains, and looked out. Nobody. Just the traffic warden coming into the flats.

341

Some poor sod going to get a ticket, thought Lonely. Or else he's got a bird here. He looked back at the telly. Posh-voiced berk telling you you could make soup just like your old mum's. All you had to do was add water... Bleeding liar.

'Rich,' the berk said, 'nourishing, delicious golden soup.'

Suddenly Lonely remembered. That traffic warden had a sun-tan.

Oh my Gawd, he thought. What'll I do? No power on earth would send him out of the flat, not even for Mr Callan. Telephone, that was it, but where was the bleeding phone? He dashed into the bedroom and there it was, under a doll with a crinoline: stupid cow. He threw it away and dialled Callan's number...

Nice tickle, thought Bradley. Dead easy. That Greek Theo knew his stuff all right. Given him the bomb, and the Browning automatic... Even supplied the uniform. It was nice to work with geezers that knew their stuff. Ten thousand quid for it too. Barmy that was. If that Greek but knew he'd have done it for nothing. Not that it would stop him taking the money... The lift groaned to a halt: grudgingly the gates jerked open and Bradley came out, slow and easy. Nobody there. Lovely. From the flat opposite there came telly-cowboy music: the sound of telly gun-fire. They'd have more than that to listen to in a minute. Carefully he wiped his hands on his tunic, opened his warden's bag and took out the Browning. The bomb lay beside it: a flat packet addressed to Callan, stamped and post-marked. All he had to do was set it the way the Greek had shown him, ring the bell and scarper... And hope Callan didn't send his mate to collect the parcel... No, Bradley thought. It's the Browning for you, old man. I want to watch you die.

He went up to the door, and sighed in relief. This was his day all right. Not even properly locked. He took a probe from his bag, inserted it between the door and the frame, and the tongue of the lock snapped back, the tiny sound it made drowned in another burst of telly gunfire. Lovely. He stood by the door-frame, and eased the door open with the barrel of his pistol. Not a sound, not a whisper. Cautiously, heart thudding, he risked a quick look. Nothing but an empty hall. Bradley made no sound at all as he eased himself inside. Kill them both, he thought, then leave the bomb anyway. Wreck his pad, too. Killing was too good for old man Callan.

To his right he could hear the sound of a shower running. Let this one be Callan, he thought. Let him be naked, degraded, when he sees me pull the trigger. He moved to the bathroom door, opened it soundlessly, and raised the Browning. The shower was going full blast, and it was empty. Behind him Callan said, 'Nice try,' and Bradley dropped into a crouch; swirling as he fell. His shot loosed off at the same time as Callan's, and the last thought he had was of himself at twelve years old, playing pontoon with the big boys for ha'pennies: You rotten bastard. You cheated me... The impact of the magnum bullet slammed him into the bathroom, and he fell, supine into the shower-stall. The water flowing into the waste pipe ran pink.

Callan looked over his left shoulder. Two inches above him Bradley's bullet was embedded in the wall; he was that good. If it hadn't been for Lonely– He went into the bathroom and switched off the shower, then looked at Bradley's body. Right through the heart... Nothing to get cocky about though. He'd had all the advantages. But even so Bradley had the faster reflexes. If he hadn't been so thick, thought Callan, I'd be dead. He crouched by the body and looked into the unzipped bag. Well well, he thought, you weren't going to leave much to chance, were you mate? Or Mr Vardakis either. He went back to the living room, dialled the long, familiar number. Better make it quick, he thought. Lonely's nerves won't stand much more of this. Her voice came on at once.

'Yes?' she said.

'Let me speak to Charlie please,' he said.

'Who's calling?'

'The Queen's Own Royal Loser,' he said. 'Callan.'

'One moment.'

And that was about all it was, then Hunter said, 'Charlie speaking.'

'There's a traffic warden in my shower,' said Callan.

'Please, Callan,' said Hunter. 'Don't be amusing. It's too early.'

'His name's Bradley,' said Callan, 'and he's dead.'

'Excellent,' said Hunter. 'Tell me about it.'

Callan gave him the lot, including the bomb.

'Really Greeks can be very difficult,' said

344

Hunter. 'It's their over-exuberance, I suppose.' He thought for a moment. 'I think I shall make Vardakis pay you after all.'

'Vardakis offered fifty thousand,' said Callan.

'You'll get fifteen,' Hunter said. 'Ten for you; five for your deplorable henchman. We don't want you to become too independent, Callan.'

Callan let it go. Fifty thousand had been offered for a murder he wouldn't commit: money he hadn't earned, didn't want to earn. But even handing over fifteen thousand would be one more punishment for Vardakis.

'Well?' said Hunter.

'I'll take it.'

'Sensible chap.'

'You'll send the cleaners?' Callan asked.

'At once. You'd better move, I think.'

'I think so too.'

'But keep in touch, there's a good chap – and if you should be offered any more little jobs – do let Charlie know first.'

So that was that. Callan picked up his suitcase and his bottle of Scotch, and left the flat. No point in a last look round: everything he valued he was carrying. For the first and last time he used the snap lock only, and didn't turn the keys of the complicated locks on his door. The cleaners would have enough to do without organising a break-in. He knocked at Miss Brewis's door. The sound of gun-fire in there was like World War II: he knocked again.

From behind the door a voice said, 'I'm warning you. I'm armed.'

'Berk,' said Callan. 'It's me. Open up.'

Furniture moved, bolts slid back, a chain came off, and the door opened at last. Lonely looked ashen. 'I thought I heard shooting,' he said.

'You know you did,' said Callan. Lonely shuddered.

'Now don't start,' Callan said. 'It's all over.'

'Bradley?'

'There isn't any Bradley,' said Callan. 'Not any more.'

Instantly, Lonely was himself again.

'In that case, Mr Callan,' he said, 'do you mind if I see the end of the picture?'

The banging on his door was even louder than the cowboys' guns. Callan sighed, and put down his Scotch. Idiot, he thought. We should have scarpered while we had the chance. He went to Miss Brewis's door, and looked through the spyhole to the one that had been his own. A young feller and a middle-aged one, both in civvies. He'd never seen them before in his life, but he had no doubt that they were rozzers. He went back to Miss Brewis's living-room. The goody had just shot the baddy and right had triumphed for another week; he switched off the set.

'Go and take a look,' he said.

Lonely scuttled to the door and Callan followed.

'Oh my Gawd,' Lonely said. 'It's the rozzer what nicked me. He's brought a mate.'

'I told you,' said Callan. 'Don't start.'

'What are we going to do, Mr Callan? They'll be there all day. You know what rozzers is like.'

'Better get rid of them,' said Callan. Before Lonely could protest, he opened Miss Brewis's door. 'Anything wrong?' he said.

They swivelled round as if he'd rammed needles into them, and when they saw him there he got an even bigger reaction.

'You're in the wrong flat,' said Kyle, then flushed at the inanity of it.

'Know me, do you?'

'I've seen your picture,' said Kyle.

Callan reached out an arm, and dragged Lonely, squirming, into the doorway. 'Know him?'

Kyle hesitated.

'Wanted for questioning,' Walters said, 'in connection with a charge of arson.'

'Wrong,' said Callan. 'We're a couple of business men. Men of substance. Arson's low.' He let Lonely go.

'Get the cases,' he said, and Lonely scuttled off. 'We're leaving,' Callan said.

Walters said again, 'Wanted for questioning,' and took a cosh from his pocket. From under his raincoat, Kyle produced a truncheon.

And all I've got to defend myself with is a .357 magnum revolver, thought Callan. But I'm damned if I'll shoot any more coppers.

He said to Kyle, 'I hear you've been unwell, son.'

Walters slapped the cosh into the palm of his hand. It made a sound like bone breaking. 'Just belt up and hand over the smelly feller,' he said.

It'll have to be you first, mate, thought Callan, and gathered himself for the kick that would end it, as the lift arrived.

At once Walters and Kyle turned to face it, which showed how little they knew. Never take your eyes off your enemy, no matter what. But

347

they did, and the lift door opened and Callan could have clobbered the pair of them, but he didn't. Two men in donkey jackets got out of the lift, and hauled a packing case out after them. Even in a donkey jacket one of them managed to look elegant: the other would never look anything else but black.

'Well well,' said Meres. 'How's your mother these days?'

Spencer Percival Fitzmaurice said nothing: just kept his hands free.

'I think you'd better go,' said Callan.

Walters made no move, but Kyle put his truncheon back in his raincoat. 'I made a mistake, Mr Walters,' he said. 'We'd better go.'

'There's no mistake,' Walters said.

'There is.' Kyle's voice was frantic with the need to get away. 'That isn't the bloke I saw. Honestly it isn't.'

He went to the lift. Slowly, reluctantly, Walters followed. Fitzmaurice shut the door for him.

'Nice meeting you, Mr Walters,' he said. The lift disappeared.

'If you only know how much I enjoy doing your dirty work,' Meres said.

Callan said equably, 'It makes a change from doing your own.'

He opened the door for them, and they took the packing case inside.

'In the bathroom,' he said, and took out the Colt Python. Meres and Fitzmaurice froze, looking into the barrel's unblinking eye. Callan dropped it into the packing-case.

'Give it back to Charlie for me, will you?' he

348

said. 'And tell him I'll let him know where to pick up the car.'

'Where we going, Mr Callan?' Lonely asked, once more sprawled at ease.

'Where d'you fancy?' said Callan.

'Well, I've been thinking,' Lonely said. 'We never did have that holiday, did we? Not what you'd call a proper holiday.'

'We'll take a holiday then,' said Callan. 'Where would you like to go?'

Lonely pulled out the dashboard lighter: lit his king-size filter.

'Anywhere,' he said. 'Anywhere you say, Mr Callan. Except Crete.'

The publishers hope that this book has given you enjoyable reading. Large Print Books are especially designed to be as easy to see and hold as possible. If you wish a complete list of our books please ask at your local library or write directly to:

Magna Large Print Books
Magna House, Long Preston,
Skipton, North Yorkshire.
BD23 4ND

This Large Print Book for the partially sighted, who cannot read normal print, is published under the auspices of

THE ULVERSCROFT FOUNDATION

THE ULVERSCROFT FOUNDATION

... we hope that you have enjoyed this Large Print Book. Please think for a moment about those people who have worse eyesight problems than you ... and are unable to even read or enjoy Large Print, without great difficulty.

You can help them by sending a donation, large or small to:

**The Ulverscroft Foundation,
1, The Green, Bradgate Road,
Anstey, Leicestershire, LE7 7FU,
England.**
or request a copy of our brochure for more details.

The Foundation will use all your help to assist those people who are handicapped by various sight problems and need special attention.

Thank you very much for your help.